TALES FROM BLACKTHORN BRIAR

SEBASTIAN NOTHWELL

CONTENTS

Cover art by Thistle Arts Studio

Cover design by Sleepy Fox Studio

ACKNOWLEDGMENTS

Thanks to Amanda, Chris, Felix, Janet, J Denise, Kyanite, María, Sierra, Succulent Scribbles, and the beta team for their assistance and encouragement in making this book a reality.
And particular thanks to Ari, without whom Wren would have never survived *The Holly King's Peril*.

MABON

Blackthorn Briar, Court of Oak and Holly
The Fae Realms
September, 1845

At first, nothing seemed amiss about the flocks of Blackthorn. The goats and the hens alike had wandered out of their shared coop that morning to feast on the grain Wren scattered before them. They continued to mingle as the hens moved on to gobbling up every manner of beetle and worm they could find, and the goats set about their acrobatics and attempts to eat their way through the thorn-vined fence surrounding the garden.

Wren turned to rejoin Shrike to break his fast within the cottage. Then staggered and spun on his heel to confirm what he'd glimpsed out of the corner of his eye.

There, amongst those who bore feathers and those who bore horns, hopped a creature who bore both.

"Butcher," Wren called out.

Shrike quickly appeared from around the corner of the cottage. "What's amiss?"

Wren pointed at the feathered and horned creature. "Wulpertinger."

For, while it did not wear the same snow-white coat as it had when last Wren saw it, it still held the shape of a rabbit with a quail's wings and a stag's antlers—now in mottled brown and grey.

"Hail, friend," Shrike said to the wulpertinger. "We almost didn't recognize you in your summer coat."

The wulpertinger sat up on its hind legs to regard Shrike as he spoke. When he'd finished, it hopped forward to meet him. Wren noticed a leather cord crossed over its back between its wings and knotted 'round a rolled scrap of birch bark.

The wulpertinger halted in front of Shrike and waited patiently while he bent to slip the bark out of the leather cord. Shrike unrolled the bark. Wren had a glimpse of the letters scrawled across it like scattered twigs before Shrike, in a voice which began slow and hesitant and finished stronger, read aloud.

An auspicious night approaches.
We invite you to remember your promise.

THE REFERENCE to a promise did not confuse Wren. The form of the messenger explained the message; the wulpertinger hailed from the Court of Hidden Folk, where Wren and Shrike had vowed to return and enjoy the company of huldrekall to ransom back Felix Knoll. Wren didn't suppose the death of Felix in the months since then had absolved them of this debt.

The reference to an auspicious night, however, Wren couldn't puzzle out. And so he turned to Shrike.

"Mabon," said Shrike.

Wren raised his brows in expectation.

"Autumnal Equinox," Shrike added. "A harvest festival."

The wulpertinger combed one of its long ears with its fore-paw.

"We did vow to return," Wren admitted. "Do you think it's safe?"

"I think," Shrike replied, "I prefer it to the harvest festival in the Court of the Silver Wheel."

Wren gave a snort of laughter.

The wulpertinger twitched its little black nose.

Wren wrote out their affirmative reply on paper—or wasp-work, as Shrike called it. He added a few illustrative flourishes as he felt might appear appropriate on a missive from two kings. Shrike rolled it up in the leather cord and tucked it into the wulpertinger's harness. The wulpertinger accepted the further gift of a sloe berry plucked fresh from the thorned vines.

With the fur around its mouth now stained purple, it hopped away down the path from Blackthorn. Then, to Wren's astonishment, it leapt up and unfurled its pheasant wings to veer off into the sky.

"I suppose I ought to have expected that," Wren said.

Shrike chuckled and slung an arm around Wren's waist. There it rested as if it'd always belonged, its warmth suffusing Wren's heart.

* * *

THE TWENTY-FIRST OF SEPTEMBER—OR rather, Mabon, Wren reminded himself—dawned with ethereal mist. He and Shrike began their journey to the Grove of Gates before the fog dissipated. Shrike carried a basket of fresh-picked sloe berries from the blackthorn vines, which made Wren feel rather empty-handed, though Shrike assured him he needn't worry on that head. Concern of any kind only seemed to strike Shrike when they reached the Grove of Gates and halted before a particular crumbling stone arch.

"Give me any sign that you cannot continue, and I shall bring us home again," he said.

It took Wren a moment to catch what he meant. He'd seen how the Hidden Folk drew their strength from draining others in revels. However, "Surely it would break the bounds of hospitality for them to harm us?"

"I doubt they would intend to harm us," Shrike reassured him. "But if they should harm you by mistake..."

Wren had no intention of falling to Felix Knoll's fate. Still, he had to admit Shrike's protective nature warmed his heart. "You shall be first to hear of it."

Shrike appeared much relieved. He offered Wren his free arm. Wren entwined it with his own. Together, they strode through the gate.

Wren braced himself for waist-high snow drifts and biting wind.

He stepped into something else altogether.

Greenery erupted all around him. Belatedly he recognized the valley limned with pine forests from his prior visit. He'd never realised it could appear so verdant.

All the fae who'd crowded into the feast-hall in winter now wandered through the lush valley amidst profusions of purple wild-flowers and bowers of bent branches overlaid with just enough deer-skin to shade those who dallied within from the brilliant sunshine. Fiddlers, drummers, and pipers dotted the landscape to send sweet music through the breeze, each with a ring of dancers around them.

One such ring stood rather near to where Shrike and Wren had appeared. The fiddler—or so Wren called them, for their instrument bore strings played on by a bow despite being a box clasped between the seated musician's knees—cut off their song with a confused, discordant half-note. The dancers all spun to see what had halted the music. Their mixed expressions of bewilderment, disappointment, and irritation turned to wondrous delight as they clapped eyes on the Kings of Oak and Holly. Scattered applause, cheers, and whoops resounded. A few enterprising fae took off through the revel to bring word of the kings' arrival to their fellows.

Shrike, looking no more comfortable with this attention than Wren felt, bowed, and Wren followed suit. Looking back from whence they'd come, Wren saw they'd just stepped through an arch of purple-flow-ering vine. He hadn't seen anything of the kind when last he'd visited. Belatedly he realised it likely withered to nothing in the winter months. He gave silent thanks that his Shrike proved cleverer than him by half and had known how to find it under the snow.

The fae who'd gone to play the role of town crier left a trail of jubilation behind them as they went. Shrike led on in their wake, and Wren followed him up the winding thread of commotion to the centre of the throng.

Here a raised wooden dais stood with a familiar black walnut throne upon it. The Mistress of Revels appeared much the same as when last Wren saw her. Her strong chin held high, her broad shoulders thrown back, a crown of thistle and harebells nestled amidst her mighty antlers. The only difference Wren could see was that her gown of patchwork leathers had let down to become a mere skirt, leaving her bronzed chest bare. Wren glimpsed her breasts for but an instant before he forced his gaze literally anywhere else.

Dozens of beautiful fae flocked around the dais. Some to promenade before their mistress. Others to pick from the horseshoe-shaped banquet table laid out in front of it. Wood-carved like the throne, with its curving crossed legs carved into serpents and wolves, it held a feast fit for two kings. A flock of pheasants laid out on a wreath of their own iridescent wing-feathers surrounded the centrepiece of a roast stag decorated with its own antlered skull bleached white by the sun. Horns-of-plenty disgorged apples, pears, elderberries and lingonberries—the latter alongside pots of honey and their own jam interspersed with cheese both in wheels and crumbling piles. Links of black pudding (of all things, Wren marvelled to himself) surrounded the bright scarlet pots of lingonberry jam. Those who chose apples, Wren noted, cut them width-wise rather than length-wise to reveal pips in the pattern of a five-pointed star. And those who didn't prefer fresh pears might partake of some preserved in lingonberry juice. For drink, he beheld fae pouring the same mead he'd seen them drink in the feast-hall in winter but also elderberry wine and lingonberry water.

Against all this, Wren began to fear the offerings of Blackthorn Briar would prove paltry—perhaps offensively so.

Yet as Shrike presented their basket of sloe berries to the Mistress of Revels, a gleam lit her eyes, and her smile grew into a grin.

Perhaps, Wren supposed, it was enough to know the meagre gift came from the mysterious court which held no subjects save its two kings.

"Kings of Oak and Holly," the Mistress of Revels declared when they'd finished bowing. "We bid you welcome to our realm. Eat, drink, and be merry."

Shrike thanked her for the privilege.

"Will you participate in our rite?" the Mistress of Revels enquired.

Shrike turned to Wren.

Wren cleared his throat. "Forgive me, Mistress. I know not what the rite entails."

"We feast upon each other," she explained.

Wren's eyes flew wide despite himself.

"Symbolically," she added almost as an afterthought. "We rejoice in the strength the summer has brought to our bodies and share them with one another. It honours the harvest to devour each other thus. It would prove a still greater honour if we might devour kings."

Wren, who'd symbolically devoured Shrike more oft than not in the months since Midsummer, had to admit the idea held a certain thrill for him. He glanced to Shrike again.

Shrike inclined his head.

Wren swallowed hard and turned back to the Mistress of Revels. "We would be honoured to participate."

"Then these," the Mistress of Revels continued, gesturing to the loose row of fae at her left with a broad sweep of her arm, "are those who have volunteered to show you our hospitality first-hand. Pick those as would suit your tastes," she added. "None will take offence."

Wren, somewhat overwhelmed at the sheer number of beautiful fae looking over both him and Shrike with hungry eyes, felt more relieved than otherwise at this addition. He glanced to Shrike to see what he thought of it.

Shrike gazed down at him with a smile that said as well as words that the choice was rather up to Wren.

Wren would make a liar of himself if he claimed no particular fae had caught his eye. Pointing felt rather rude, so instead he screwed his courage to the sticking-place and strode up to one in particular.

"Your pardon," Wren said to a fellow who looked as if someone had given him a Payne's grey watercolour wash; a pale slate blue all over mottled with dappled silver, with blue-black close-cropped curls and beard and tufted tail, and ridged corkscrew horns spiralling up from the sides of his head. "Would you care to join us?"

The Payne's grey fae, who stood as tall as Shrike if one ignored the horns, split his beard in a smile. "Aye, m'lord."

Wren bid him go with Shrike and went on to make the same enquiry of two other fae; an antlered and fox-tailed ginger as short as Wren himself, though more slender, and an enormous burly brute who stood a full head taller than Shrike before one accounted for his horns and whose deep russet coat darkened to black over his hands and hooves.

Three seemed like a nice round number. Not so few as to give offence to those not chosen and not so many as to appear greedy.

The Mistress of Revels clapped her hands to dismiss her gathered subjects. To Wren's relief, few appeared disappointed for more than a moment before all formed into clusters of two or three or more and wandered off to enjoy their own feasts.

Wren cleared his throat as he turned to Shrike and their three companions. "Is there somewhere a little out of the way where we might...?"

The Payne's grey fae smiled and bid them all follow him. A short way off, just past the banquet table and down the hill, there lay an unclaimed pile of furs, with branches bent over them to form a domed roof laid with deerskin.

"Perfect," said Wren, which seemed to please the three fae greatly.

It occurred to Wren, as he regarded the fae he'd chosen for their companions, that he hadn't the first idea what they were, exactly. The one with the Payne's grey coat he thought was probably huldrekall, but as for the fox-tailed fae and the hulking blood-bay brute, he couldn't say. He cleared his throat. "Forgive me—I'm a stranger to your realm and unfamiliar with your custom. Are you all... huldrekall?"

After all, the last time he and Shrike had ventured into the Realm of the Hidden Folk, Shrike had told him the most polite thing to do was to ask.

The Payne's grey and the fox-tailed fae exchanged a smiling glance before telling Wren they were both huldrekall, to Wren's surprise. The blood-bay brute, in a deep and rumbling voice, identified himself as an incubus.

"And what may we call you?" Wren asked, glancing between the three fellows.

"Hull," said the Payne's grey huldrekall.

"Rikke," chirped the fox-tailed ginger.

"Drude," rumbled the blood-bay brute.

"Butcher," said Shrike, to Wren's surprise.

"And Lofthouse for myself, I suppose," Wren added.

"Before we begin," said Hull. "Is there anything you would prefer we not do?"

Wren hesitated, uncertain how best to delicately phrase his desires. "I would prefer if no one ventured into my fundament."

It wasn't that he objected to the practise altogether. Indeed, the notion more excited him than otherwise. But as he'd never done it before—or rather, had it done to him—he would prefer to have it done first with his Shrike alone, instead of amongst strangers.

Against all odds, the fae seemed to understand him, exchanging sage nods.

"And you, m'lord?" Hull asked Shrike.

Shrike shrugged his left shoulder. "I'm game for anything, so long as we may return to our own realm under our own power afterward."

Wren, who hadn't thought to specify, gave thanks his beloved proved far more clever than himself.

"We've no intention of bringing any harm to the Kings of Oak and Holly," Hull reassured them with a slight bow.

The handsome half-smile Wren loved so well curled up one side of Shrike's perfect mouth. "Then shall we begin?"

And, under the hungry gaze of the Hidden Folk, he turned to Wren, cupped his cheek in his palm, and drew him in for a kiss. Deep and languid, just as Wren liked best. A claiming kiss, he realised. One which marked him out as Shrike's forevermore—and marked Shrike as his—no matter what occurred on this eve. The thought of it thrilled him to his core.

As they broke apart, Hull stepped forward.

"May I?" he asked Wren.

Wren, his pulse unaccountably fluttering, nodded.

Hull cradled Wren's jaw in his fingertips and bent to kiss him. Wren, who'd kissed no one but Shrike since they'd met, and had kissed precious few gentlemen before him, hadn't the first idea what to expect. Hull proved gentler than one might suppose, his touch carrying a tentative curiosity. He waited to open his mouth until Wren opened his, and only then did their tongues meet, still with that same tender exploration, as if the experience were as novel for him as it was for Wren.

Then they parted, and Wren opened his eyes to find Hull halfway into pulling his shirt over his head. It was a shirt in the style which had been fashionable in the age of Wren's father or grandfather, with flowing sleeves and a loose open collar. Wren supposed Hull favoured it because it went easily over his horns.

A quick glance around showed all the other fae doing likewise. Rikke had the least to do in throwing off his tattered shawl. Drude had worn the same flowing shirt and knee-breeches as Hull; the thin white of the shirt had done little to disguise his broad crimson chest and stout middle, and the removal of his black woollen breeches revealed a prick in proportion to the rest of his enormous body.

Shrike likewise disrobed. The speed and ease with which he did so— out in the open, under the sun, in front of a horde of fae—astonished Wren at first, until he stifled his shock by reminding himself that Shrike was fae, after all, and the fae had no mortal moral qualms against the nude form. They'd done the very same at Midsummer. And after all, Wren enjoyed the sight of him. His sun-kissed skin, his well-earned muscles, his scars like a weathered map of forgotten lands which Wren delighted in navigating.

Wren felt less delighted at the prospect of baring his own body. He knew his reluctance was ridiculous. He had, after all, shown everything in the Midsummer duel—though he still blushed to recall it, much to Shrike's amusement.

Even then, however, his body had merely been observed from afar. Whereas the three strange fae gathered before him now would experience it first-hand. He knew himself not half so beautiful as any huldrekall or incubus. No matter what Shrike might say to the contrary.

Shrike watched him now. The gleam of eager anticipation in his dark eyes turned to concern which knit his brow. A single stride closed what distance remained between them. He bent his head, and Wren upraised his face to meet his kiss. A brief one, nonetheless sweet, and one which Shrike followed by turning his lips to Wren's ear as he enfolded Wren in his arms.

"We don't have to do this, if you don't wish it," he murmured. "We may merely dance or feast. Or go at once. You need but give me a sign."

"I want to," Wren insisted low into his collar, knowing those keenly pointed ears would still hear him. "I just..." He trailed off, uncertain what he needed, until inspiration struck. "Will you help me?"

Shrike gave him a curious look but questioned him no farther. He kissed him again, this time slipping his hands beneath the lapels of his frock coat and sliding them up the sleeves until the whole thing shrugged off Wren's shoulders and fell to the ground. Cravat, waistcoat, boots, trousers, shirt, and smalls followed suit. Under the watchful gaze of the three strangers, Wren realised more keenly than ever before what a ridiculous amount of clothes he wore by fae standards.

Then Shrike's palms, deliciously warm against Wren's bare skin, slid beneath his under-shirt and drew it up over his head. When his vision cleared of white cotton, he beheld all of the fae—Shrike included—staring at his body. Not with derision, as he'd feared, but with appreciation. Despite the countless freckles spattered across his skin, and despite the soft swell of his stomach, all three strange fae looked on him with no less interest than before.

As Shrike withdrew, Hull stepped forward.

"I'd be honoured to devour a king," he said to Wren, his voice husky and low.

Wren glanced to Shrike again, saw his sly half-smile, and returned to Hull. He nodded.

Hull dropt to his knees. Wren beheld his corkscrew horns, the blue-black close-cropped curls tousled over his head, and his Payne's grey shoulders dappled in silver. Likewise, he beheld a hollow in his back, from where his shoulder-blades ought to have begun, tapering down to just above the root of his tufted tail. The Payne's grey deepened into darkness within the hollow. Dappled skin smoothed over the ragged edge, with occasional tufts of fur giving the illusion of a mossy crevice within a fallen tree.

Then Hull raised his arm to take Wren in hand, paused, and lifted his face to meet Wren's gaze.

"May I?" he murmured.

Wren, his prick twitching at the barest brush of his fingertips, nodded again.

Hull wrapped it in his hand. It pulsed in his palm, stiffening even before he began to stroke it. He leant forward and kissed its tip. His lips opened. The head slipped inside.

Wren came undone.

Hull's tongue, velvety-soft beneath the head of his prick, drew teasing, coaxing knots around him, slipping beneath the fore-skin to encircle the ridge, tracing the vein underneath from its root all the way up to the slit at its tip. His cheeks hollowed as he swallowed Wren down in earnest.

A familiar weight settled against his shoulder-blades. Wren glanced over his shoulder to find Shrike braced against him, back-to-back, whilst Drude and Rikke both knelt before him. Shrike turned his head likewise, smiled to see Wren, and shifted his position enough for their mouths to meet in a kiss. All the while Hull plied his mouth to Wren below, drawing unseemly sounds from his throat to echo within Shrike's mouth.

An enthusiastic moan from Hull resonated through Wren's prick, just as Wren broke off his kiss for breath. He turned to regard the huldrekall, who had dropt a hand to his own cock and abused it furiously. As delightful as Wren found the sight of Hull kneeling before him, he regretted that his posture blocked his beautiful dappled-grey prick from view. His fingertips traced the ridges of Hull's horn before he thought better of it.

"May I...?" he asked, his voice coming ragged.

Hull raised his gaze to meet Wren's with a mischievous gleam and withdrew his mouth from his prick just long enough to reply, "Please do."

The words alone almost sent Wren over the edge. Then Hull bent forward and took him between his lips again.

Wren wrapped his hands around his horns and held tight just to keep himself together. The relentless ministrations of Hull's tongue and hollow cheeks, matched by the low moans of pleasure from Hull at both his own self-abuse and Wren's grip on his horns vibrating up through Wren's prick, sufficed to send him to the brink again.

Then Shrike turned his head and caught Wren in a kiss again and flung him over the precipice. With an obscene groan into Shrike's mouth, Wren poured torrents down Hull's throat. Hull followed him but a moment after, his hips and arm stuttering with a final moan to wring the last of Wren's seed from him.

Wren's knees buckled. Shrike held him upright but barely. Then a rough groan announced Shrike's own spend—the familiar sound sending a thrill through Wren's heart and his prick twitching to life again—and together they descended to the pile of furs beneath.

No sooner had they settled than Shrike seized him in his embrace for another all-devouring kiss. Wren felt more than content to sit back and become a feast for him. Yet he didn't want to leave the other fae out. Hull certainly deserved more for his service. As the kiss ceased, Wren looked 'round, expecting to see him still kneeling before him. But Hull had vanished, and after another bewildered whirl, Wren found him standing before Shrike and holding out his hands to him to draw him up and lead him elsewhere.

Shrike shot Wren an enquiring glance.

Wren granted him an encouraging nod.

Shrike returned to Hull with a grin and clasped his forearms to haul himself upright. They didn't go a great distance away; just far enough for Shrike to have room to lie back against the furs whilst Hull slipped his arms beneath his knees in preparation for something which Shrike seemed to find a very exciting prospect. Rikke soon joined them.

In their absence, Drude approached Wren.

"Shall we?" he enquired, his deep rumbling voice nonetheless gentle.

The voice alone would've sufficed to send Wren spilling into his hand. He nodded.

The soft furs beneath them both provided welcome relief as Drude's not-inconsiderable weight settled astride him. Thighs thick as another man's waist slid over Wren's own and pinned his hips between them. The embrace of Drude's enormous arms kept him upright, the corded muscles like tree-branches coaxed into the shape of a king's throne, as Drude bent his head to meet Wren's lips in a kiss. Hair like curtains of black rain tinged red with blood fell on either side of Wren's face. The very hair which had drawn Wren's notice in the first place, as long and dark as Shrike's, though lacking his bolts of quicksilver. The kiss itself, from lips unexpectedly soft and with a tenderness that belied the fanged mouth, deepening into a slow hunger as his tongue drew out Wren's own, sufficed to stiffen Wren's prick again, much to his own astonishment.

It was Drude who broke away to breathe; Wren felt as if he'd forgotten how. He glimpsed Drude's face, his strong jaw off-set by his soft smile, and dropped his gaze between them both to see Drude's interest had grown as much or more than his own.

All other gentlemen of Wren's intimate acquaintance fell into one of two categories; those who showed their true length whilst flaccid and those who grew into their full length when aroused. He had assumed Drude, already enormous at rest, fell into the former category. To his astonishment, however, he now beheld a rod which had grown full inches as it drew itself upright.

Something no less astonishing lay beneath the proud pole. Where most other gentlemen—Wren himself included—had a sack, Drude instead had nestling petals, two within two, like a delicate scarlet rose.

Whilst Wren stared, Drude's hand slipped down beneath the pole to the petals. His fingers gently parted them to reveal a hollow, as crimson as the rest of him, and gleaming wet. Something which Wren had oft heard his fellow university students declaim the virtues of, but which he'd never encountered first-hand.

"Is this all right?" Drude asked, his voice a low rumbling murmur.

Wren, bewildered but no less intrigued, nodded.

Drude kissed him again. A roll of his hips crossed his blade against Wren's. The petals followed in its wake, gliding up the length from hilt to point. With a final forward shift, Wren's cock slipped inside the— well, the cunt, Wren supposed, for he didn't know a better word for it. It felt both like and unlike what he'd experienced before. Not so unyielding an entrance, perhaps, but just as blazing hot and slick and tight. Drude sat back with a groan, sheathing Wren within him to the hilt in a single smooth thrust.

A gasp escaped Wren. His hands clenched against Drude's broad back, his nails digging furrows into the skin. As before, he felt the core of his very being consumed by the narrow strait, and while Drude moved, rolling his hips in wave after ceaseless wave, Wren sliding in and out of him again and again, ever-returning to that steadfast hold, it was all Wren could do to hold back his spend before Drude could satisfy himself. His hips moved of their own accord, thrusting up into him, delving deeper and deeper.

Drude's own cock slid between their bellies. Its tip stood well past Wren's navel and left a trail of seed in its wake. Wren dropped a hand to it, his curiosity still insatiable. He wrapped his palm around it; his fingertips met around its girth, but barely. He gave it an upward stroke, exploring its considerable length—the velvet-soft skin, the vein pulsing beneath, the flesh rigid as iron. A low groan rolled up from deep within Drude's chest and resounded through Wren's own ribs. Wren clenched his fist around the blade and was rewarded with the sight of doubled fangs biting Drude's lower lip. Then Drude darted forward—far faster than Wren would've expected a man of his size to move—and seized Wren's mouth in a kiss.

Long dark hair, like and unlike Shrike's, enfolded, hid, and shielded him as Drude's cunt consumed him and the enormous brawn of the incubus's massive frame encircled him in the iron hold of mighty arms as they embraced and Drude's ravenous mouth devoured him. Drude's hips ground down, his thighs clenching around Wren's waist. The monster prick trapped between them throbbed. A hollow groan resounded through Wren's throat from Drude's lips, and with a few quick thrusts, the crimson cock erupted in a geyser of hot seed, splashing against Wren's chest like molten silver. In the same instant muscles deep within Drude clamped down on Wren's cock as if to wring his spend from him. So utterly consumed within and claimed without, Wren could do no more than succumb to ecstasy. He collapsed in Drude's embrace.

The sheer brawn of Drude's frame supported him with ease, even as the incubus shifted his weight and Wren's soft prick slipped out of him as he settled down beside rather than atop him. Wren, whose vision had spun away to darkness in a sea of stars, knew only the soft touch of lips against his own; then they trailed down, gently marking his throat and collar until he felt the hot wet tongue licking Drude's seed from his chest. The mouth returned to meet his afterword in a kiss of salt and something more.

Wren had felt so wrecked from his own spend he could hardly move. To taste the seed on Drude's tongue, however, revived him. And as Drude continued kissing him—long, slow, languorous kisses, almost heartbreaking in their tenderness, each one breathing renewed life into Wren—something else revived as well, much to Wren's continued astonishment. He'd thought himself done for in that last spend, and yet, under Drude's influence, his cock stirred again.

A familiar hand caressed his cheek. Wren lolled his head towards it and forced his eyes to open.

Shrike sat beside him; his silver-shot raven locks tumbling over his shoulders and across his brow in dozens of fairy-knots, beads of sweat sparkling against his dashing scars, bruises borne of kisses beginning to bloom along his collar, gloriously naked and softly smiling. He ran his hand through Wren's hair and trailed his fingertips along the curve of his ear.

"Enjoying yourself?" Shrike murmured.

Words could hardly suffice. Wren nodded.

Shrike chuckled. "One more, d'you think?"

"Yes." The sound burst from Wren with all his remaining strength. "Please."

Hull returned—Wren hadn't even realized he'd gone—bearing a wicker tray laden with apples, honey, and berries. Shrike retrieved his dagger to slice a sliver of apple and dipped it in honey before bringing it to Wren's lips. The taste of it, cool and crisp and sweet, proved sweeter still once he'd swallowed and Shrike followed it up with a kiss. The whole of his world seemed to centre upon it, and only when Shrike withdrew did he recall they weren't alone.

In the interim, Rikke had approached and now stood before them with his fox-tail feverishly lashing.

"My turn," he said with a flash of a feral grin.

Wren had chosen Rikke mostly for his resemblance to himself; the small frame and freckles he thought might appeal to Shrike. He looked the most like a mortal, to Wren's eyes at least, if one ignored the antlers and tail. Yet rather than fixate on Shrike, Rikke's golden gaze flitted between them both.

"How would you have me, my lords?" he asked.

Wren couldn't even begin to imagine. "How would you like us?"

A gleam flashed through Rikke's eyes. "Both at once?"

Wren blinked. Him in one end and Shrike in the other, he supposed, and he had to admit the notion appealed to him. "Certainly."

All the fae—Shrike included—began to rearrange themselves. If Wren didn't know better, he would've assumed they'd rehearsed it. As matters stood, he sat in place, bewildered, until they settled into their final configuration; Shrike facing Wren, with their thighs entangled; Hull behind Shrike; and Drude behind Wren, with the root of his enormous rod nestled between the globes of Wren's arse and its tip rubbing against the small of his back.

Rikke stood where he had before, still glancing hungrily between Shrike and Wren. There didn't seem to be enough room for him to fit between them on his hands and knees as Wren had supposed.

Just as Wren wondered if he ought to raise his voice and point this out, Rikke leapt between them and sat down astride Wren's lap, facing him. Wren, stunned, could but blink as Rikke twined his slender arms around his shoulders.

"Will you fuck me, my lord?" Rikke purred.

16

Wren, still bewildered, nodded nonetheless. If he were to fill Rikke from the bottom, positioned as they were, he knew not how Shrike would find his way into Rikke's mouth.

Rikke seemed in no way confused by their configuration. With a slight shift of his hips, he aligned Wren's prick with his hole. Wren, still slick from his previous encounters, slowly sank inside the tight heat, a broken moan escaping his throat as he did so.

Rikke appeared still more satisfied than Wren felt, catching his lower lip between fierce fangs and making a sound almost like a purr of pleasure. Then he turned over his shoulder to address Shrike. "And you, my lord?"

Shrike's hands descended to Rikke's waist. He lifted him just halfway off of Wren's length.

And set his own prick against the same hole.

If Wren had seen it, he would've doubted his eyes. As matters stood, he almost doubted his body, though his shaft knew well the sensation of Shrike's own and recognized it as it slowly forced its way past him to enter Rikke.

Rikke's eyes fluttered shut and his head fell back with a long, low sigh.

Wren had oft delighted in taking himself and Shrike in the same hand, sliding them together in his fist to bring them both to the brink.

And now he found the sensation both familiar and strange, as inch by inch Shrike slipped in beside him, a fit so tight it hardly seemed as if it were possible, Wren cleaved so close to him it seemed they would become one flesh within Rikke, until Shrike had sheathed himself to the hilt.

Wren thought he might die.

He hardly had a moment to grow accustomed to the unfathomable sensation before Rikke arose on his knees. Shrike and Wren slid halfway out of him before he slammed down again. Wren seized Shrike's shoulders to keep steady. He clung on through plunge after plunge, until he found himself thrusting up to meet Rikke, and then his clenched grip became one of convulsive pleasure.

Shrike shuddered in his embrace as Hull entered him—and how

incredible to see it, the sensation playing out across Shrike's handsome features, how his perfect mouth fell open in a silent gasp, how those long lashes descended over dark eyes, the heavy brows knitting and coming undone over and over as Hull thrust into him, sending Shrike thrusting into Rikke against Wren in turn. Shrike slipped a hand down between Rikke and Wren—no small feat, given how their chests lay flush against each other—to take hold of Rikke's cock; the resulting strokes drawing yips of ecstasy from Rikke's lips. And all the while Drude clutched Wren tight and frotted against his backside. Wren knew not how long he might hold out against the overwhelming sensations.

On impulse, Wren reached out and seized Shrike's jaw in his hands to pull him in for a kiss over Rikke's shoulder. Shrike gasped into his mouth, then slipped his own free hand behind Wren's head to draw him in deeper. The familiar taste of vanilla and woodsmoke from those beloved lips sufficed to send Wren tumbling over the precipice of his own spend. His seed spilled deep within Rikke and over Shrike still thrusting alongside him. Shrike likewise shuddered, his groan resonating through Wren's own throat as his seed joined Wren's, mingling with their crossed swords.

In that same instant, Rikke cried out, and further drops of mistletoe spattered against Wren's chest. Hull stuttered to a halt within Shrike with a satisfied sigh. Seed splashed against Wren's back as Drude shuddered beneath him.

And still Wren kissed Shrike, until he could support himself no longer.

He fell back limp against Drude's brawny chest. It rose and descended underneath him in rhythm with his own shuddering gasps. He remained dimly aware of Rikke's slender weight across his hips and an unfamiliar tongue eagerly licking Rikke's spend from his chest. Drude's tongue he recognized on his back; moreso for the tender kiss Drude left on the nape of his neck when he'd finished. Then Drude slipped away, as gently as he'd come, leaving Wren sprawled on the furs. Rikke's weight lifted, and Wren slid out of him, almost painful for his over-sensitive prick to endure. He bit his lip against a discomfited moan.

"Steady."

The sound of Shrike's low burr above him proved ample balm to any exhaustion or pain Wren might feel. He forced his eyes open and beheld Shrike kneeling over him, taking a damp clout from Hull and using it to wipe his prick clean. Then another clout, and he began to do the same service for Wren. The sensation of pain gave way to pleasure soon enough. He'd grown again to half-mast by the time Shrike finished cleaning him off, and groaned in disappointment when he withdrew his hand.

"More," Wren moaned.

Shrike pressed a finger to his lips to quiet him. Wren licked it. But as he opened his mouth to try and suck it—to draw Shrike in, to show him what he intended for the rest of him, what he hungered for more than anything—Shrike withdrew his hand altogether.

An unseemly sound of protest escaped Wren's throat at this unjust deprivation. Any further argument halted as Shrike brought the rim of a drinking horn to Wren's mouth. The taste of lingonberry water wasn't quite what Wren had wanted, but a thirst he hadn't realised he'd possessed struck him as it touched his tongue, and he drank down the horn in earnest.

No sooner had Shrike set the empty horn aside than Wren pounced on him.

"Please," he gasped against Shrike's lips when need for breath forced him to break off the kiss. "Please, please, please..."

Shrike kissed him again. A delight, as ever, yet Wren feared he meant to shut him up with it and would still leave him wanting.

But even as the fear crossed Wren's mind, he felt a well-accustomed weight settle across his thighs. Beloved hands cradled his jaw as Shrike straddled him. A slight cant of his hips sufficed for Wren to slip inside the familiar and perfect sheath.

Already slick with what the others had given him, yet still he felt tight as a vise around Wren's prick. He rolled his hips, and Wren moaned into his mouth, overcome. To have Shrike's strong arms around him; to fill his every breath with his vanilla-woodsmoke musk; to plunge again and again into that tight wet heat; to take his sword in hand in turn and stroke its satisfying heft in his fist; to have his Shrike again, even after all this—it took all Wren had left in him to hold off until he wrung sweet bursts of mistletoe from Shrike's cock before he, too, spent, deep within his Shrike. He collapsed in his embrace, satisfied at last.

Wren awoke, he knew not how long after, still gently yet firmly held in Shrike's arms. Someone had thrown the rabbit-fur cloak over their bare legs. He heard Shrike's low burr overhead, conversing with someone he couldn't quite perceive with his cheek laid against Shrike's chest. With an effort, he raised his head and craned his neck to see to whom Shrike spoke.

Hull sat beside him in all his Payne's grey glory. Neither he nor Shrike seemed to have noticed Wren's stirring. They remained in earnest discussion. Wren caught snatches of it here and there, his mind still muddled by the afterglow.

"...skeps," he heard Shrike say, amongst other things, and Hull echoed it in his response.

Wren licked his lips. Both they and his tongue felt rather dry. He thought he might listen better if he had something to whet his whistle. He attempted to slide upright.

The moment he moved, the conversation ceased as both Shrike and Hull snapped their attention to him.

"Good morrow, our Holly King," said Hull.

Shrike, meanwhile, slipped his hand through Wren's hair and murmured into it. "How d'you feel?"

"Good," Wren said with more honesty than he might have done otherwise, adding, "Thirsty."

Hull reached out of Wren's sight and returned with a drinking horn of lingonberry water. He handed it to Shrike, who held it to Wren's lips as before. Wren drank deeply.

An ecstatic yelp came from behind him. Wren turned to find Rikke some ways off, his arse propped up on his knees and his head buried in his folded arms to muffle the unseemly sounds that burst from his throat as Drude claimed him from behind.

"Rikke is insatiable," Hull confided in an apologetic tone.

Wren could hardly blame him.

"If I may be so bold as to ask, m'lord," Hull continued. "Would you consider granting me the gift of letters? I know our runes already," he added as Wren blinked in bewilderment, "but I should like to learn yours. I can repay you with honey. Or mead. Or assistance in beekeeping. Or something else, if you prefer. You need but name it."

"Certainly," Wren replied. Then, "Why?"

Hull gave him a wry and wistful smile. "Acquiring skill keeps boredom at bay. I've spent the last century beekeeping, and whilst I enjoy it, I require something more."

Wren still didn't quite understand. Yet further enquiry felt rude. He turned to Shrike.

"Fae perish when they lose the will to live," Shrike murmured.

Something Wren had heard already. How it applied here, however, baffled him. Still, he worked at it, until at last he realised, "D'you mean fae can literally die of *ennui?*"

Shrike and Hull gave him identical confused looks.

"Of boredom," Wren elaborated.

"Oh, yes," Hull said as Shrike nodded solemnly.

"Well," said Wren, still digesting this discovery. "I certainly wouldn't want you to die for want of literacy."

Hull grinned. "Many thanks, my lord."

Shrike, meanwhile, raised a hand to trace Wren's jaw with his fingertips and draw him in for another kiss.

"Are you satisfied?" he murmured against his lips as they parted.

Wren twined his arms around his shoulders and replied, "Kiss me once more; then I'll be content."

And to his delight, Shrike indulged him.

MR GRIGSBY'S CLERK

Staple Inn, London
Autumn 1845

No one blamed Ephraim Grigsby for what had happened.
Possibly, Ephraim thought, because no one remained to blame him.

His ward, Felix Knoll, had vanished first. More than a month passed without any hint of where he'd gone.

Then, all in one day, Ephraim's other ward, Miss Flora Fairfield, had disappeared from her academy. Ephraim's clerk, Wren Lofthouse, had gone in pursuit of her and likewise had never been heard from again. Felix's uncle, Mr John Tolhurst, had also attempted to find Miss Fairfield.

And been found that very night in his own rooms.

Dead.

With his throat cut.

Perhaps Ephraim ought to have feared for his own safety. His friend,

Dr Hitchingham, certainly thought so and had no compunctions against saying it aloud.

But Ephraim didn't feel afraid. No more so than usual, at any rate.

What he felt most of all was guilt.

He should have known Felix was frittering his fortune away. The boy had asked for an advance on his trust fund often enough. Any daft fool would've seen what it meant, but Ephraim had assumed the charitable opinion that Felix merely wanted things. He didn't assume Felix would find a means to get them by throwing himself into such debts as would weigh down an earldom.

He should have seen Miss Flora was unhappy. As her guardian, he ought to have realised her misery and either shielded her from it or removed her to somewhere she might find joy again, before she took it upon herself to run away.

He hadn't the faintest idea what he ought to have done about Tolhurst, but good Lord, a man must do something against cold-blooded murder.

And he knew not what he could have done to rescue Lofthouse from meeting the same fate.

One thing alone prevented Ephraim from sinking into total despair. A month after Miss Flora vanished from Mrs Bailiwick's Academy, he received a letter in her hand—from Canada, of all places—assuring him of her good health and happiness and begging him not to worry. While he could not follow this last instruction, it still did his heart good to think her safe and sound. Likewise it renewed his hopes that he might yet hear from Felix again once the young gentleman had improved his prospects.

There remained no such hope for Tolhurst—dead, throat cut, in his own rooms in the quiet streets of Rochester—but while Ephraim mourned the loss of any good man, he could not with honesty say he missed Tolhurst, having never known him well enough in life to feel the absence of him afterward.

Wren Lofthouse, however, he missed very much.

Particularly as the violent beginnings of summer faded into a quieter season towards autumn. Which would, in due time, draw ever nearer to Christmas.

Some gentlemen might not consider Lofthouse good company for holiday cheer or otherwise. Ephraim found comfort in the presence of a sharp-minded young man with a marked talent for figures and fanciful notions alike and little patience for dilly-dallying. In certain moments now and again, Ephraim caught glimpses of his own younger self in his clerk. As a confirmed bachelor, Ephraim had no children. Lofthouse, a second-cousin once-removed on his mother's side, had come to embody something of a son he'd never had.

And now Lofthouse had vanished.

On the same night Tolhurst had been murdered.

Given both had sought Miss Flora, Ephraim couldn't help but assume a connexion between the two events. He hoped Lofthouse had escaped whatever assassin had come after Tolhurst. He hadn't the foggiest notion why anyone would seek to take the life of those who sought Miss Flora; he'd asked Miss Flora herself this in his reply to her letter—in the most delicate possible language, of course—but he'd yet to receive a reply.

And so he waited alone in his office day after day for some word from his wards or clerk.

His solitude had some comforts. He had his friend Dr Hitchingham to dine with most evenings. And occasionally during the day, a queer little cloud-grey bird with a fearsome black mask like a highwayman would perch on his windowsill and cock its head when he noticed it.

Ephraim Grigsby had many faults, but he flattered himself that impatience was not among them. He could wait as long as necessary for word from Felix or Lofthouse.

Even if the thought of Lofthouse's fate gnawed at him.

On one particular October morning, when the first delivery of penny post had failed to bring word from Lofthouse or Felix, Ephraim settled into another lonely day at the office. He brewed a kettle of tea—which Lofthouse had always done, and which Lofthouse had helped him drink, but now he brewed and drank alone—and sat down at his desk to glance over the *Times* and watch the sparrows flit through the fog. It'd taken him a few weeks to get over the habit of reading aloud certain particularly amusing tidbits, now that he no longer had his clerk to hear them. Today, however, he successfully kept his thoughts in his head rather than letting them slip past his lips to echo throughout the silent office with no one to listen.

Then the ringing of the door-bell shattered the silence.

Ephraim leapt up from his chair. He regretted it quickly, his knees reminding him post-haste they no longer appreciated such rapid motion. Still, he put them through their paces as he scrambled to open the door and peer down the stair-well to the landing below.

A gentleman stood at the bottom of the stair.

Not, Ephraim realised with a sinking heart, Lofthouse or Felix. The gentleman stood far too tall to pass for either—more in line with Tolhurst or Butcher. As he turned his face upward to meet Ephraim's stare, he revealed a face which couldn't have seen many days beyond thirty years. And a handsome face, at that. One that bore a sun-kissed brow, dark yet twinkling eyes, a long nose with a noble arch, a jaw strong enough to attract notice even beneath the close-trimmed black beard, and full lips beneath the moustache that wore a smile like sunshine breaking through storm-clouds.

Ephraim's pulse gave an uncomfortable flutter, as it sometimes did when he arose too quickly from his desk.

"Good morrow, sir!" said the gentleman in a hearty tone. Ephraim couldn't quite place his accent—a very slight one, with a touch of a burr and a hint of a lilt which defied all efforts to pin it down. The deep bass of his voice thrummed through Ephraim's own ribs in a manner which made his knees feel weak for reasons beyond rheumatism.

Ephraim put these feelings away into a little locked drawer in his mind, as he always did, and cleared his throat. "Good morning! How may I assist you today, sir?"

"It's my hope I may rather prove of some assistance to you," the gentleman replied, mounting the stair two steps at a time and doffing his hat as he did. His cropped black hair tumbled in loose waves from beneath it. "Mr Sven Hull, at your service."

"Mr Ephraim Grigsby at yours," Ephraim replied despite his continued bewilderment.

Mr Hull beamed. He looked still more handsome up close than at a distance. "I heard through a friend that your office required the services of a clerk, sir. I should like to volunteer for the post."

"Oh!" Ephraim hadn't expected anything at all this morning, but certainly not anything like this. Mr Hull's strapping frame appeared better suited to sailing a ship or swinging a scythe than clerking. The moment the thoughts occurred to him, Ephraim tried very hard to stop thinking about Mr Hull doing either—for more reasons than he cared to acknowledge—and resolved to think of him as a clerk and nothing more from that moment on.

Mr Hull gazed down at him with more patience than Ephraim deserved. "You do require a clerk, do you not, sir?"

"I do," Ephraim admitted with some small reluctance. Lofthouse had, after all, given his notice before he vanished. While Ephraim still hoped to hear from him again, he knew he would not return to fulfill the same role. This knowledge did nothing to quash the twinge of disappointment in Ephraim's heart.

Mr Hull, meanwhile, continued beaming handsomely as he withdrew something from his waistcoat pocket. "I've a letter of recommendation, sir—if you care to read it?"

Ephraim accepted the folded letter from Mr Hull's strong and well-formed hand, which made the note it held appear miniature. The wax seal on the back of the letter bore a crest of oak and holly leaves intertwined across a pair of antlers. This, however, did not strike Ephraim's nerves quite so hard as the sight of his own name and address on the reverse.

Written in a hand Ephraim had never thought he'd have the good fortune to see again in all his days.

Without a word—without a thought—Ephraim broke the wax seal and unfolded the letter close before his face to read.

MR GRIGSBY —

Allow me to apologize for my hasty departure from your employment. Matters progressed in the discovery of Miss Fairfield's whereabouts in a manner which made it impossible for me to remain in London. I did, however, ask her to write to inform you of her good health and happiness, which I hope she has done by this time. I write now to perform the same courtesy. I am steward to the estate of an eccentric but very kind gentleman and quite content in my position.

I realise I also left you without clerical assistance in the office. This letter will then serve a dual purpose; to whit, to recommend the services of one Mr Sven Hull, its bearer. You will recognize him as rather a tall fellow with a black beard and something of the Scandinavian in his blood. I assure you he is both capable and qualified to perform any duties which you entrusted to my care and keeping whilst in your employ.

Your obedient servant,

Mr Wren Lofthouse

EPHRAIM LOOKED up from the long-awaited letter to find its bearer wearing a patient smile.

"You've met with Lofthouse?" Ephraim blurted. "You've seen him?"

"I have," said Mr Hull.

"How does he get on? Is he happy in his new place?"

"He gets on very well," replied Mr Hull. "And enjoys great happiness."

"And does he..." Ephraim hesitated, uncertain if it was his place to ask. "Does he find time to practice his art?"

Mr Hull brightened further still. "He does, indeed. He showed me several very promising sketches."

"Oh!" The delighted syllable burst from Ephraim. Not just delighted to hear that Lofthouse had made good use of his considerable talents—talents which Ephraim himself could only admire and never aspire to—but to learn that Mr Hull had earned Lofthouse's trust to an extent which allowed Lofthouse to reveal his art to him. Ephraim himself had only glimpsed it here and there in the margins of Lofthouse's work. "How wonderful!"

Mr Hull looked as though he quite agreed.

"Well then, sir," Ephraim continued, glancing at the letter again. "Lofthouse declares you seek employment and recommends you for the post he left behind. Do you wish to clerk?"

"I do, sir."

"I'm afraid you may find it rather dull," Ephraim added apologetically.

"I've no fear of feeling dull, sir," said Mr Hull.

Ephraim couldn't quite work out what exactly he meant by that, but it seemed to carry an air of enthusiasm regardless. "Very well. If you've no lodgings of your own, there's a room upstairs. Shall I show you?"

* * *

THE HOLLY KING had described Mr Ephraim Grigsby, Esq., as an awkward but well-meaning elderly fellow.

He'd made no mention of "charming" or "handsome," which Hullvardr considered unjust omissions.

The road which had led Hullvardr from the Realm of Hidden Folk to Staple Inn was a long and winding one, but one which he nonetheless considered worth wandering. It had begun at Mabon, when the Oak and Holly Kings had returned to repay the debt they'd incurred that winter. The Mistress of Revels had offered them their pick of her willing folk, and they'd selected Hullvardr, amongst others, to enact their rite.

Delightful enough to be chosen to join the Oak and Holly Kings for the ritual. More delightful still to discover he had more in common with the kings than he'd supposed—namely, the Oak King's beekeeping. Languid conversation followed frantic lovemaking, and through that a peculiar notion grew in Hullvardr's mind. He'd asked the Holly King if he might earn the gift of letters from him.

And the Holly King agreed.

Hullvardr had already learnt runes centuries ago. The lessons of the Holly King merely added new runes to their number. The trouble came when new runes resembled old runes but represented different sounds.

This, however, Hullvardr had sorted through quick enough to earn the Holly King's favour.

"I have heard," the Holly King had remarked one morning in Blackthorn Briar as he looked over Hullvardr's handiwork, "that the Hidden Folk find the mortal realm easier to navigate than other fae. Does iron not sap your strength?"

"It does," said Hullvardr. "But we may draw equal strength from the presence of mortals."

The Holly King nodded sagely. "Do you visit the mortal realm often?"

"Not of late," Hullvardr admitted. "But I have before oft enough."

"Would you care to return to it?"

"Of course," Hullvardr replied with a smile. "A good reason for me to learn your letters."

"You've learnt well, and quickly, too," said the Holly King. Before Hullvardr could thank him for his praise, he added, "Would you be interested in putting it to use in the mortal realm for some time?"

This sounded rather like a quest. "For how long?"

"Six months, at least, if all goes well." The Holly King hesitated. "Possibly as long as thirty years. You might return to the fae realms often, but the bulk of your work would remain amongst mortals."

"What sort of work?" Hullvardr asked, equal parts bemused and intrigued.

"Clerking," said the Holly King.

Hullvardr cocked his head to one side.

The Holly King continued. "There is a mortal in London who requires the services of a good and honest clerk. He looked after me for more than a decade. Arguably, he saved my life. I left him rather suddenly, and since then he has remained bereft of aid."

"Is this how you would have me repay you for teaching me your letters?" Hullvardr asked.

"In part," said the Holly King. "I should think I'd be somewhat in your debt afterward, depending on how long you remain with him. And should you agree to clerk for him, he would pay you in mortal coin besides."

Hullvardr had little use for mortal coin. If it would repay the Holly King for his lessons, however, and grant him a boon besides, it seemed a worthy quest to undertake. "I'd be honoured."

The Holly King's smiles came but rarely. The one Hullvardr glimpsed after accepting his offer glimmered bright as sunlight glinting off a rushing stream.

The lessons of letters changed afterward. A whole new set of symbols emerged, representing the numbering of things. Tomes ruled with lines—ledgers, the Holly King called them—filled with numbers as Hullvardr took instruction on how to move them from one column to another, and when they might change, and when they must remain the same, and why.

"It's mostly copying," the Holly King explained. "Taking down figures and scribing out multiples of leases and wills and contracts and what-have-you. The rest of it is valeting, which is easy enough, though it may bruise your dignity."

Hullvardr assured the Holly King he didn't consider such work beneath him. The Holly King appeared relieved. He told Hullvardr how the mortal preferred matters; most of it was what Hullvardr already did for himself, and he hardly minded doing it for another.

After this came lessons in how to blend into mortal society. A great deal had changed in the mortal realm since Hullvardr last visited. More intricate rituals of greeting and conversation had emerged. And a great many alterations in costume had occurred. Hullvardr had some experience with this, having seen how the Holly King garbed himself and having the honour of watching the Oak King divest him of his garb at Mabon. He had never yet worn it on his own frame, however, until one morning he arrived in Blackthorn Briar for his tutoring and found the Holly King awaiting him with an armful of vestments.

"I took the liberty of a quick dip into Rag Fair," the Holly King explained, hanging the garments on willing blackthorn vines that grew out of the briar wall for his purpose. "Butcher is of a like height to yourself, I believe, and what fits him may fit you. Would you care to try them?"

Hullvardr needed no further urging to strip out of his shirt and breeches.

The Holly King's eyes went rather wide. He cleared his throat and turned his head to take down a shirt rather like the one Hullvardr had just thrown off.

With the Holly King's assistance, Hullvardr slipped into his new wardrobe. The sheer number of layers felt a little overmuch, but fairly comfortable overall, and from what he could glimpse of himself in the hand-mirror the Holly King held up for him, he thought he cut a rather dashing figure. The Holly King likewise declared it suited him. Yet he did not seem quite satisfied.

"Butcher told me that the Hidden Folk have ways of disguising their more... distinctive characteristics," the Holly King began.

"Glamour, you mean," Hullvardr replied with a smile.

"Indeed." The Holly King hesitated as if he feared giving offence. "May I see it?"

Hullvardr, eager to show off his power to the Holly King, called upon the strength within him to spin a gossamer guise around himself. His horns and tail vanished from view. His legs seemed to straighten; from his trouser-cuffs, stockings and boots appeared instead of hooves. He abandoned his dappled blue coat for something like the Holly King's own skin, though less freckled pale.

"Will this do?" Hullvardr asked, taking secret pleasure in the Holly King's evident wide-eyed astonishment.

"Quite well, I think," the Holly King replied, still staring.

Hullvardr beamed.

"You will require a pseudonym," said the Holly King. At Hullvardr's confused glance, he added, "A name other than your true one. One which might pass without notice amongst mortals. 'Hull' will do well as a surname. Have you any idea as to what given name you might prefer?"

"Sven," Hullvardr replied. Many mortals he'd delighted had borne that name.

The Holly King appeared likewise pleased. "Very well, then—Mr Sven Hull."

Hullvardr bowed in the mortal fashion and followed it up with a hand-clasp, to the Holly King's continued approval.

"There is one point more, however," said the Holly King.

"Name it," Hullvardr replied.

Still, the Holly King hesitated. "While I know it's possible for you to feed without doing any harm to mortals…"

"Preferable, even," Hullvardr added.

The Holly King nodded and went on. "What becomes of you if perchance you find no willing mortals to feed upon?"

"Nothing," Hullvardr explained. "While it's always better to share a feast with friends, one may cook and eat alone and feel satisfied."

The Holly King looked very much relieved.

Hullvardr had spoken true and believed in what he'd said. Now, however, faced with Mr Grigsby standing before him, he wondered if he might not find it a more difficult promise to keep.

Mr Ephraim Grigsby, Esq., had attained an age which few mortals survived to see. One which Hullvardr himself had not oft witnessed close-hand. Time leant a fragility to his frame, with nevertheless an undercurrent of queer confidence borne of inner wisdom. He moved like one with bones of spun glass. Blue veins stood out beneath his diaphanous skin like streams of molten silver. Lines of lacework beset his noble brow, and the proud chin jutted forth to hint at the strong jawline now half-hidden by jowls, as if too demure to peer out from behind a curtain. His keen and clever eyes gleamed the bright blue of rivers fed by glacial ice. The whole of him appeared as delicate and ethereal as a spider's web, or the pale wax of the honeycomb brimming with molten gold, and, to Hullvardr's eye, as precious as enchanted filigree. Most fae never acquired marks of age like these, no matter how many centuries they endured. What a rare joy it would prove to hold this gossamer grace in his arms.

Mr Grigsby, oblivious to Hullvardr's ever-increasing fascination, took him into the office and led him up the stair to the garret. All looked as the Holly King had described. Perhaps a little better, Hullvardr thought; the Holly King's unease in his ill-suited role tainting his memories of what Hullvardr found a bright and cheerful haven in the

TALES FROM BLACKTHORN BRIAR

midst of London. Or perhaps the presence of Mr Grigsby merely brightened it in Hullvardr's eyes.

"Here you are!" Mr Grigsby declared, opening the door at the very top of the stair. "It isn't much, but it's quite convenient to the office."

Hullvardr hadn't encountered many homes with multiple floors before, but the sloping roof and exposed beams reminded him of mortal houses he'd visited long ago. A bed lay beneath the window streaming what pale grey sunlight could trickle through the fog, just enough to illuminate the desk, chair, and wash-stand with a small round mirror. Cobwebs hung in many corners. It felt odd to imagine the Holly King living here for more than a decade; the equivalent of Hullvardr spending a century.

"Will it suit?" Mr Grigsby asked, a touch of worry in his tone.

"Very well," Hullvardr assured him with a smile.

It sparked something in Hullvardr's heart to see that smile reflected tenfold in Mr Grigsby's face.

"I'll let you settle in, then," Mr Grigsby continued. "Take your time— I'll meet you downstairs when you're ready."

And with that, he vanished down the stair, leaving Hullvardr bereft without him.

It didn't take Hullvardr long to unpack his carpet-bag. He spent far more time surveying the room itself; all its nooks and crannies, including the hollow board beneath the bed which the Holly King had warned him about.

The Holly King had also described the wash-stand to him, which made it a less bewildering object than it might have proved otherwise. He examined himself in its mirror, wondering idly if his glamour held enough of his own innate beauty to attract Mr Grigsby's notice. He took it off, just for a moment, to compare. His own dappled grey-blue face stared back at him, his horns spiraling up on either side of his head from amidst his blue-black curls, his long bell-shaped ears hanging down almost to his shoulders, and his doubled eye-teeth showing in his smile. The glamour looked rather dull by comparison, he thought as he put it on again, but it would do well enough for now.

Then he turned to the desk. The Holly King's own papers, pens, and ink still filled it. Hullvardr took them out and began writing to inform the Holly King of his arrival and reception. While he waited for the ink to dry, he went to the window, cracked it open, and whistled.

By the time the letter was dry enough to fold over and seal with beeswax, the wulpertinger had arrived.

It perched on the windowsill and wiggled its little black nose, blinking all about it at the strange room. Hullvardr gave it a dried elderberry. When it had disposed of this, he handed over the letter, which it took in its now purple-stained teeth. Then its wings unfurled and it swooped off into the fog, where no one besides the sparrows would take any notice of it.

Hullvardr had made no mention in his letter of his intentions towards Mr Grigsby. In truth he'd not yet decided on what they were. He wouldn't feed on him, of course—wouldn't dare chance even a taste, lest he destroy something truly beautiful—but to stay away altogether would drive him distracted. The Holly King had sent him to protect as well as serve.

"Not that Mr Grigsby is likely to make enemies," the Holly King had explained. "But he ought to be looked after all the same."

And now, having met the gentleman, Hullvardr found he heartily agreed.

* * *

EPHRAIM HAD to admit there wasn't much to occupy any clerk in his office. Still, Mr Hull seemed to settle in comfortably and performed what few small tasks Ephraim set him to with alacrity.

When the afternoon turned to evening and the hour arrived to shut the office up, Ephraim turned to Mr Hull and invited him to dine at the Red Lion with himself and Dr Hitchingham. He'd made the same offer to Lofthouse every evening for over a decade.

Unlike Lofthouse, however, Mr Hull replied in the enthusiastic affirmative.

"Oh!" said Ephraim, equal parts astonished and pleased. "Very good.

It's only a short walk, and I think you and Dr Hitchingham will get on well together."

Mr Hull smiled. He had a very kind smile, with a warmth that shone in his eyes and which drew Ephraim's notice perhaps a little more than it ought.

As they strolled together to the Red Lion, Ephraim likewise noticed how Mr Hull walked with his hands clasped behind his back and his face upturned, taking in his foggy surroundings with a contented smile and with his boot-heels clicking against the cobblestones. And, though he bore far longer and younger legs than Ephraim himself, he still restrained his stride to match Ephraim's shorter and more doddering steps.

Dr Hitchingham arched his brows rather high when Ephraim appeared in the Red Lion's back parlour with a stranger in tow.

"Allow me to introduce my clerk, Mr Hull," Ephraim said, unable to disguise his proud smile. "Mr Hull, this is my dear friend, Dr Hitchingham."

Mr Hull met Dr Hitchingham's proffered hand-clasp with a hearty shake. The slight upward tilt at the corner of Dr Hitchingham's lips bespoke his approval despite the thin line of his mouth.

No sooner had they all sat down to dinner together than Dr Hitchingham began his interrogation.

"And where are you from, Mr Hull?" asked Dr Hitchingham.

"Norway," Mr Hull replied candidly. "I hail from a clan of beekeepers."

Ephraim blinked.

Dr Hitchingham raised his brows. "If I may be so bold as to ask, what brings a beekeeper to clerking in London?"

"I had the good fortune to attend school," said Mr Hull, nothing daunted. "And having something of a wanderlust in my blood, I wished to put my education to good use in far-off lands. An acquaintance—Mr Lofthouse—mentioned there might be such a position available in Staple Inn, and so I came, and here I am."

Ephraim wished he'd had even half Mr Hull's courage in his youth.

Dr Hitchingham made a noncommittal sound. "And how do you find London?"

"Delightful," said Mr Hull. "Vibrant and lively. Full of fascinating people."

Ephraim caught a glance from Mr Hull at this last comment. For a moment he thought he saw a peculiar gleam in Mr Hull's eye, but he told himself he must have imagined it.

After dinner, Dr Hitchingham shook hands with both Ephraim and Mr Hull and went on his way up the street to his lodgings over his practice. Ephraim and Mr Hull walked in the opposite direction back to their office. Dinners with his friend always proved a balm to Ephraim's soul, but somehow tonight he felt still more fulfilled than usual. He supposed it was pride in his clerk, who had performed well in the face of Dr Hitchingham's questions.

They'd gone halfway back to Staple Inn when a passerby stopped them beneath a street-lamp on the corner.

"Please, sir," the man croaked. His left arm balanced him on a crutch; his right he held out palm-up. By the dim gaslight, Ephraim saw his gloves had worn away at the fingertips. "Alms for a poor sailor what's lost his leg in the rigging?"

Ephraim hesitated. This wasn't the first time such a person had approached him. He always gave them coin, of course—one could do little else, when there but for the grace of God went he—but Dr Hitchingham had chastised him for his weakness in this regard on many occasions. Ephraim resigned himself to appearing a weak fool in front of his handsome clerk.

But before he could reach for his purse, Mr Hull had already delved into his own pockets and withdrawn a coin to press into the beggar's hand. It didn't look like a ha'penny or any other piece Ephraim recognized. He assumed it came from Mr Hull's native soil. It glinted gold in the light of the gas-lamp regardless, and the beggar thanked him warmly before scurrying on his way.

"Dashed good of you," Ephraim said when the beggar had gone.

Mr Hull shrugged his left shoulder. "If they're bold enough to ask, their need must be dire."

"Indeed!" said Ephraim, equal parts astonished and delighted to hear his own feelings echoed by his handsome clerk.

* * *

LOFTHOUSE HAD TAKEN on valeting duties one by one over the course of months spent in Ephraim's employ. Whether he did so to while away the tedious hours in a rather slow office or out of frustration with the admittedly doddering way Ephraim himself performed the same duties, Ephraim couldn't say.

Mr Hull, in contrast, began his second morning as Ephraim's clerk by bringing the hearth-fire back to life; making tea, sausage, and toast for breakfast; and laying out the morning post and paper on Ephraim's desk—all without hesitation and without Ephraim asking. Ephraim only knew he'd arisen by the gentle tap-tap-tapping of his boot-heels on the staircase as he passed by his bedchamber door on his way down to the office proper.

"Mr Lofthouse told me how you prefer things done," Mr Hull offered by way of explanation when Ephraim himself arrived down-stairs to find all this done.

Ephraim, his brows still raised in surprise, conceded that was exactly the sort of thing Lofthouse would do.

Throughout the next few weeks, Ephraim and Mr Hull fell into a routine. Mr Hull performed his valeting duties each morning, sat at the desk across from Ephraim all day, went to dinner with him of an evening, and parted ways afterward. Sometimes Mr Hull went out again after dinner; Ephraim assumed to consort with his fellow clerks.

"Have you made friends in London?" Ephraim asked his clerk on a quiet afternoon a fortnight into his employment.

Lofthouse would have withdrawn from the question. Mr Hull, however, brightened.

Then he was off, telling Ephraim all about how he'd gone down to the Green Man and met almost every other clerk in Staple Inn. How they'd taught him all the popular songs, and how he'd taught them a few from his own country in turn, and how they'd met up for strolls in Hyde

Park on their half-days, and how they planned to attend theatricals together when next they all had a night off.

Ephraim, astonished, listened intently and with great appreciation. Where Lofthouse had remained reticent and secretive regarding how he spent his hours outside of the office, Mr Hull proved open and candid.

Which wasn't to say Mr Hull didn't have his own peculiarities.

For one, he said, "Good morrow!" rather than, "Good morning." Ephraim didn't mind this in the least. After all, Mr Hull was not a native speaker and had likely adopted the archaism as the nearest thing to the phrase in his own language. Ephraim found he rather liked the ring of it. To say nothing of his clerk's enthusiasm in greeting him each day.

For another, he had the odd habit of ducking under every doorway he walked through. While Ephraim admitted Mr Hull stood rather taller than most gentlemen, he still had a few inches to go before he risked even brushing his dark locks against the upper part of the door-frame. Yet he stooped beneath them all to give himself at least another foot of leeway. He did so rather gracefully, Ephraim had noticed. A delicate bend of his waist and a smooth sweep of his shoulders, as a dancer might do to reel from one step to another over the threshold. Though Ephraim rather liked to watch him do it, he carefully kept his gaze averted, lest Mr Hull think he mocked him for his eccentricity.

On occasion, Mr Hull would remove his frock coat and hang it on the back of his chair whilst he worked. Ephraim's blood ran too thin in his veins to go without his own coat in the autumnal chill of the office, but he supposed a much younger gentleman like Mr Hull might find the crackling fire made the air a touch over-warm. Whenever Mr Hull divested himself of his coat, however, and went about the office in his shirt-sleeves, Ephraim found it rather difficult to concentrate on his own work. The pale thin cotton shirt clung to Mr Hull's broad shoulders and allowed an indecorous glimpse at the corded muscles of his arms beneath. Even the waistcoat, though made of thicker stuff, only served to draw attention to Mr Hull's svelte waist and heighten the contrast against his burly upper half. And when, for example, Mr Hull stood up from his desk and turned his back to take down a volume from the shelves, Ephraim couldn't help but observe how tight his trousers fit around his behind.

All this, Ephraim thought, was rather more than a gentleman ought to notice about his clerk. And so he set his mind to ignoring it. Whether or not he succeeded in this task he preferred not to reflect upon.

Still more difficult to ignore than Mr Hull's youthful vigour was the attention he paid to Ephraim in turn.

On the first morning in Staple Inn, Mr Hull had asked how Ephraim liked his tea. Ephraim replied he preferred a dash of cream without sugar. Every morning afterwards, Ephraim had arisen and gone downstairs to find a steaming cup prepared likewise at his desk. Never once did Mr Hull require a reminder or ask again. Nor did Ephraim ever have to ask to have his cup refilled. The moment he reached the dregs, it seemed, Mr Hull had the teapot and creamer in hand, and, gently taking the cup from Ephraim, would dispense without spilling a drop. When he handed the cup back, however, his fingertips had a tendency to brush against Ephraim's, and the warmth of his touch sent a shiver over Ephraim's frame, the cause and implications of which he chose to ignore. Instead, Ephraim noted Mr Hull took his own tea black and resolved to prepare it for him as such, if he ever made it into the office before Mr Hull.

In addition to general sweeping and dusting of the office, Mr Hull also took it upon himself to add some decoration. The first to draw Ephraim's notice were the delicate fern fronds in a little glass case beside the window.

"They don't mind the shade," Mr Hull said as Ephraim puzzled over the addition. "And I thought perhaps you might like a spot of greenery amongst your work."

Ephraim hadn't known he'd wanted such a thing, but now that he had it, he realised it was exactly what he'd needed for some time now.

"Woodbridge recommended mignonette as well," Mr Hull continued. "I could bring that in tomorrow—with your permission, sir."

"Woodbridge?" Ephraim echoed.

"A friend of mine," Mr Hull explained. "Works as a gardener."

Ephraim supposed gentlemen of all professions might be found at the Green Man or in Hyde Park—and either of these places, he mused, seemed poetically perfect for a gardener to wander.

And accordingly, the mignonette appeared in the windowsill the next morning, sweetly fragrant despite its lack of bloom. Though, Ephraim noted, not quite fragrant enough to disguise the queer honey-suckle and elderflower scent of Mr Hull himself, seated just across from him.

One might say, as doubtless Dr Hitchingham would, that this was all just as much as any clerk ought to do for their employer. Ephraim might have agreed with this, were it not for how, whenever they dined at the Red Lion, Mr Hull made a point to reach the table in the back room first and draw out Ephraim's chair for him and wait for him to settle before he seated himself. This behaviour drew even Dr Hitchingham's notice. Ephraim didn't mind, and supposed this must be how all clerks conducted themselves in distant lands. The thrill he felt at having an admittedly extraordinarily handsome young man perform such atten-tive services on his behalf, he shut away in the little lock-box in his heart and did not dwell upon.

And every morning, as Ephraim arose to shave and dress, he heard the gentle tap-tap-tapping of Mr Hull's boot-heels on the stair—a sound which became somehow sweeter than birdsong.

* * *

EVEN WITH THE ache of iron hanging in the air, London held many opportunities for one of the Hidden Folk to feed.

Hullvardr had heard other fae speak on the virtues of The Globe for a few centuries. It had burnt down, rebuilt, shuttered, and vanished since then, but upon his arrival he found London held many other theatres with no less enticing entertainments. Some even still performed Shakespeare's works, including a staging of *A Midsummer Night's Dream*. The play proved a delight, combining dance and puppetry and live animals with mortal mimicry of fae magic which baffled Hullvardr. The exhilaration of the audience around him well satisfied his hunger. His curiosity, however, he satisfied by lingering at the stage door and catching one of the fellows who'd worked behind the curtain. By offering to share a drink, he gleaned a great deal regarding limelight and gaslight and how to make glistening glass and shivering metal move together to mimic a waterfall. He satisfied his hunger again on his knees in the alley behind the tavern, to the enjoyment of the theatre worker as much as himself.

He found it more satisfying still the next morning, when Mr Grigsby enquired where he'd gone the previous evening. Hullvardr regaled him with the recounting of the theatrical thrills and beheld the brilliant twinkle in Mr Grigsby's eyes as he heard it.

"Perhaps," Hullvardr ventured, "you might accompany me to another performance, sir?"

Mr Grigsby demurred; the theatre ran rather too late. He feared he'd fall asleep in his seat and embarrass Hullvardr with his snores.

Hullvardr didn't find the prospect embarrassing in the least. However, as Mr Grigsby would not be moved on that point, he contented himself with offering the invitation each night he went, and when Mr Grigsby inevitably refused, relaying the theatrical experience to Mr Grigsby on the morning after, which seemed to please Mr Grigsby almost as much as Mr Grigsby's evident delight pleased Hullvardr.

Dancing, to Hullvardr's bewilderment, proved more difficult. On prior adventures in the mortal realms he'd cavorted with them by bonfires under moonlight in shadowy hills. Not so in London. He spent a fortnight wandering and wondering where dancing might occur, until, finding nothing, he asked his fellow clerks outright one evening at The Green Man. The other clerks commiserated with his bad luck—had he arrived in summer, he might have joined them at Algar's Crown and Anchor or another traveling outdoor dance hall. In the colder months, however, there remained a few avenues; though not, they added confidentially, in this side of town. His new acquaintances led him to rowdier taverns in other neighbourhoods. There, if the crowd could collect enough coin to persuade the fiddler, the tables and chairs would be swept aside, and cavorting could begin. So many mortals dashing together in each other's arms, their sensations heightened by the music and rippling with the tension of attraction, provided a veritable feast for Hullvardr.

Hullvardr had sense enough not to mention these particular adventures to his employer. He could not, however, restrain himself from wondering how it might feel to dance with Mr Grigsby. Slower than with the youths in taverns, yes, more halting and perhaps more awkward—but all the more charming for it, and what a joy it would feel to prove his own strength and lend his own grace by carrying him through the steps.

Finally, one morning when he could contain himself no farther, Hullvardr ventured, "Do you dance at all, sir?"

Mr Grigsby blinked. "Heavens, no—though I will confess I once cut a dashing figure at certain county balls, but those days are far behind me."

Hullvardr didn't see at all why that should be so. However, when he pressed the issue, Mr Grigsby only shook his head and declared even if a lady would deign to dance with him, he would not humiliate her by asking.

He did not say what he would do if his clerk asked him to dance. Hullvardr spent many merry minutes imagining the possible result of that particular enquiry.

When neither theatre nor dancing would satisfy, Hullvardr wandered through Hyde Park. The sight of trees, however youthful, and greenery, however artificial, did something towards soothing whatever homesickness he might feel. As much or more soothing than the setting were the like-minded gentlemen he met beneath the shadow of Achilles and followed to still more shadowy corners of the park. Under the cover of darkness and the eternal fog, Hullvardr feasted with soldiers, sailors, servants, and sundry others. He left his gentlemen better off than he found them—more contented, certainly, if a touch winded—and would have felt the same, if he could banish the thought of Mr Grigsby from his mind. For while he grasped one fellow's prick in his palm and slipped another's between his lips and slid his own between the thighs of still another, as he heard their gasps and moans and groans and felt their shivers and shudders in his arms, all he could think on was what

Mr Grigsby might sound like, feel like, taste like. He could well imagine his stiff and awkward frame coming undone in his embrace, the delicate lacework of his flesh, the soft sounds that would escape him as Hull-vardr devoured him.

Still, Hullvardr spent his evenings with strangers in Hyde Park and found his hunger satisfied.

Though not quite so much, he mused as he meandered back down the foggy streets towards Staple Inn, as a night with Mr Grigsby might.

* * *

"Do you have any plans for Christmas, Mr Hull?" Ephraim asked on a snow-muffled afternoon halfway through December.

"None at all, sir," Mr Hull replied, much to Ephraim's surprise. "Do you?"

"Oh, nothing very interesting, I don't think," Ephraim admitted. "The landlady at the Red Lion roasts a goose for the occasion, and I partake of that, and then I read a little Dickens in keeping with the season. Rather too quiet for most, I'd imagine, but more than enough for an old goat like myself." He hesitated. "Would you care to join me?"

Mr Hull's already-ebullient countenance brightened further still. "I'd be delighted, sir."

"Splendid," Ephraim blurted, equal parts pleased and astonished. While Lofthouse had spent every Christmas in the office, Ephraim suspected he didn't enjoy it overmuch. What a wonder to have Mr Hull's enthusiastic acquiescence to join him for the holiday.

"I'm intrigued by local tradition," Mr Hull went on, to Ephraim's continued delight. "Perhaps we might forge some new traditions together."

To this, Ephraim heartily agreed.

* * *

THE ANNOUNCEMENT that the Kings of Oak and Holly would perform their Winter Solstice ritual in solitude came as a shock to many in the fae realms. Rumours flitted from court to court that certain fae had received secret invitations to participate in the ceremony. Hullvardr knew otherwise, being more privy to the wishes of the Oak and Holly Kings than most. And he felt more glad of it than most, for with the rite held behind the writhing walls of Blackthorn Briar, it left him free to make his own plans to celebrate the solstice.

Hullvardr had heard, from certain gentlemen he'd encountered in Hyde Park who worked in the households of other gentlemen, that a delightful mortal tradition had sprung up regarding mistletoe on their wintry holy days. Finding mistletoe in London proved a touch more difficult than finding it in the fae realms, but a Saturday afternoon stroll through the woodier paths of the park sufficed to show Hullvardr an oak beset with vines bearing milky white berries. Climbing said oak to retrieve the mistletoe caught more than a few eyes. Still more took note as he ascended another tree—this time an evergreen—and plucked some sprigs. A smile and a wave from the upper branches sufficed to send most passersby on their way, and no one had arrived to stop him by the time he plucked his prizes and descended back down to stand amongst the roots.

Then, he need only bundle it all together beneath his coat and smuggle it back into the garret.

If Mr Grigsby noticed Hullvardr looking thicker around the middle than usual upon his return to the office, he made no mention of it. Hullvardr continued on upstairs and spread the boughs and vines out all across the floorboards. The next evening, and the one after, he did not venture out after dinner but instead went upstairs to work on his plans.

And each night before he went to sleep, he satiated himself in his own hand with the thought of what fruits his plans might bear.

* * *

ON SUNDAY EVENING—THE twenty-first of December—Ephraim invited his clerk to join him and Dr Hitchingham for dinner.

Unlike every other evening since Mr Hull had entered his service, Mr Hull declined.

Ephraim knew his disappointment at this was disproportionate to the event itself. Still, he felt it keenly, even as he smiled and wished Mr Hull a good evening.

Mr Hull, for his part, returned a warm smile of his own and added a cheerful wave as Ephraim departed the office.

Far from offering his sympathies, Dr Hitchingham made no secret of his refusal to share in Ephraim's disappointment.

"If I may be frank with you, old boy, I'm rather glad of it," said Dr Hitchingham. "I've been meaning to speak candidly with you for some time regarding his service."

Ephraim, who'd only just sat down and not yet taken a bite of dinner, found his appetite vanished. "What could you possibly have to say to me that you couldn't say in front of him?"

"Only this," Dr Hitchingham replied, looking at his plate rather than at Ephraim as he carved up his roast. "He never gave you any history of employment or recommendations from past employers."

"He had the best recommendation," Ephraim countered. "From Lofthouse himself."

Dr Hitchingham made a noncommittal sound. "I've my opinions on Lofthouse's service as well. But we were speaking of Mr Hull. You say he carried a letter from Lofthouse."

"He did."

"And have you heard from Lofthouse since then?"

"Oh, yes!" said Ephraim, happy to be the bearer of glad tidings. "We correspond regularly. Hardly a week goes by that I do not hear from Lofthouse."

"And do you put your letters to him into the post yourself?"

"Goodness, no." Ephraim chuckled. "That is rather the point of having a clerk, is it not?"

Dr Hitchingham made a noise which might have been a muffled snort. "And do you receive his letters direct into your hand from the post-boy?"

"No," Ephraim said again. "Mr Hull brings my letters every morning. Do you fear him so deficient in his duties?"

"On the contrary. I fear he may prove all too attentive."

"If there is such a thing," said Ephraim, "I've yet to encounter it."

Dr Hitchingham set both knife and fork aside to meet Ephraim's bewildered gaze. "You take on this young man because he carries a letter from your former clerk. Your former clerk who has never contacted you before this moment since he left your service. Then you strike up a correspondence with your former clerk—a correspondence which always passes through the hand of your fresh hire."

"Again," said Ephraim, "that is rather the point of having a clerk."

"I wonder," said Dr Hitchingham, "if Mr Hull is not merely the conveyor of your former clerk's correspondence, but also its source."

Ephraim furrowed his brow. "I don't follow you."

"Every letter you receive from Lofthouse comes from Mr Hull," Dr Hitchingham said in the tone he used whenever he thought Ephraim particularly dull. "Perhaps Lofthouse is not writing the letters."

A silence grew between them.

"Balderdash," Ephraim declared.

Dr Hitchingham gave his own *harumph* in reply but said no more on it.

Conversation turned to Dickens and when Dr Hitchingham would join his son's family for the holiday season. Ephraim's mind wandered far off, even as he spoke, to think on his clerk. Not to entertain any of Dr Hitchingham's ludicrous suspicions, but to wonder how Mr Hull fared alone in the office and where he would find his dinner. Ephraim hoped he wasn't too hungry and that he might eat at least as well as Ephraim himself.

Dinner concluded. Ephraim braced himself for Dr Hitchingham to voice his suspicions again as they bid their good-nights, but either Dr Hitchingham proved wiser and more tactful than Ephraim anticipated, or he knew Ephraim would refuse to hear it, for he breathed not a word of it. They shook hands and parted ways, each gentleman continuing on alone into the evening.

While the streets remained cold and dark, the windows of the office in Staple Inn shone bright and gold through the fog, and Ephraim opened the inner door to find it transformed with holiday cheer. Intricately-woven garlands of evergreen boughs and mistletoe sprigs adorned the window-frame, the mantle, the ceiling beams, and the doorway leading to the second-storey stairwell. A glance upward showed the final garland over Ephraim's head on the arch of the door-frame he'd just stepped through.

Mr Hull knelt before the hearth, stirring the embers with a poker to coax them back to life beneath the copper tea-kettle. He turned as the door creaked open and had dropt the poker and leapt to his feet with a smile as Ephraim entered.

"Happy Christmas, sir," said Mr Hull.

"Did you make all these yourself?" Ephraim asked, his voice soft with wonder.

Mr Hull beamed. "I did."

"They're splendid," Ephraim declared, though the word hardly felt adequate. "Just the thing for the season. What a marvelous surprise!"

"It was nothing," Mr Hull said with a grin.

"Whatever made you think of it?"

"Mistletoe is a sacred herb in my homeland," Mr Hull explained. "When I discovered it grew here, as well, and had become a symbol of the season, I couldn't resist bringing some in."

"I'm very glad you did," Ephraim declared.

Mr Hull looked more pleased than ever. Though he didn't so much as glance at the garlands. His warm gaze remained fixed on Ephraim himself.

"I've also heard," Mr Hull said, "that a curious tradition has developed in London."

He stepped nearer as he spoke. Presumably to gesture upward to the garland, as he did. But Ephraim didn't follow his hand to note the decoration. Instead he found himself distracted by his clerk within arm's reach; the way his brawny frame towered over him, and how the heat of his body filled what little space remained between them, and the sight of his noble profile turned upwards with a smile towards his own handi-work. Every breath brought the scent of his masculine musk—with curious notes of honey and elderberries—to Ephraim's notice. He ceased to breathe.

Then Mr Hull turned that smile toward Ephraim again. Not an ebullient grin, as he oft wore, but a soft crescent of his perfect plump lips, paired with lashes lowered over dark eyes. Eyes which seemed to flick down to Ephraim's own mouth before they met his gaze.

"They say," Mr Hull continued in a lower tone, "that those who meet beneath the mistletoe must kiss to bring good fortune."

Ephraim cleared his throat. "Yes—well—servants often indulge in such superstitions for their own merriment."

"Only servants?" enquired Mr Hull. His dark gaze never broke from Ephraim's own.

"And young persons," Ephraim conceded.

"Might gentlemen take part in the tradition, as well?" asked Mr Hull.

Ephraim hesitated. Thoughts he didn't wish to entertain clouded his mind. Impossible notions. Dangerous ideas. Mr Hull didn't mean to imply anything of the sort. He merely meant to ascertain, as one newly arrived to English shores and unfamiliar with their custom, whether or not he might, as a gentleman, kiss a lady beneath the mistletoe. Ephraim told himself this even as Mr Hull's gaze flitted to his lips again.

"They might," Ephraim conceded. After all, Mr Hull was a handsome young gentleman, and young ladies liked to be kissed by handsome young gentlemen. Or so Ephraim had been told all his life.

Mr Hull bit his lip.

Before Ephraim could remind himself not to take any notice of it— before he could do anything more than gawk at the expression which threatened to knock his legs out from under him and send his pulse into palpitations—Mr Hull shut his eyes and leaned down.

And those perfect lips met Ephraim's own in a kiss.

They were as soft as they appeared. And warm, as well. Astonishment opened Ephraim's own lips in a gasp, and Mr Hull took them between his own. His tongue slipped into Ephraim's mouth. The beard scraped against Ephraim's chin and sent a thrill down to parts which hadn't stirred in longer than he cared to remember. The scent of elderberries and honey filled his lungs. Strong arms encircled him in a warm and gentle embrace. Ephraim melted into it.

For an instant.

Then Ephraim summoned all his strength—more strength than he'd ever dared hope to possess—and shoved Mr Hull off of him.

Mr Hull struck the door-frame with a thud that shook the wall. He staggered, caught himself against it, and stood staring at Ephraim.

Ephraim's breath came ragged. His arms trembled at his sides. He told himself it was his anger.

"Sir?" said Mr Hull.

As if he hadn't just taken unspeakable liberties. As if he hadn't just committed an outrageous obscenity. As if he hadn't just awoken and broken Ephraim's heart in the same instant.

Ephraim forced his fists to unclench and his speech to steady. "Sir."

Mr Hull appeared, if anything, confused. "If I've offended you, sir, then I—"

"If!?"

Mr Hull's eyes flew wide.

Ephraim felt rather startled himself at the height and ferocity of his own voice. He tried again. "What the deuce do you think you're doing? What did you mean by all—" He waved desperately at the damned garlands. "All this?"

Mr Hull did not appear any less confused. "I wished to celebrate the season by acting on my feelings. I had thought them reciprocated."

"Reciprocated?" Ephraim echoed with a hollow laugh.

"Are they not?" Mr Hull asked.

Ephraim chose not to answer that particular enquiry. "I may be an old fool, but I am not so foolish as to believe myself an irresistible object of attraction to—well, to anyone, really, but particularly not to a young gentleman of good countenance and sound mind."

Despite all, Mr Hull smiled. "A good countenance, you say?"

Ephraim wished he could find the strength of will to hate that smile. "I know you are not sincere, sir. Therefore I must ask myself what you hope to gain from this. Advancement in the field, one may suppose, though you might have that at a far cheaper price merely by going on as you've already begun. You've proved yourself a fine clerk with the makings of something still better; you might secure an articleship within the year. You needn't take such measures as these to gain my approval or my assistance in such matters—you might have both simply by asking—so I must assume your motives lie elsewhere. And, though it pains me to think on it, I fear the simplest solution may prove true. You desire money."

Mr Hull's smile had vanished. Bewilderment reigned in its wake. "Sir?"

"You are an intelligent young man, as I've already said." Ephraim checked his tone, which had grown a touch too sharp for his liking; his wounded pride stretched his patience to its breaking point. "Do not pretend you cannot understand me. It insults us both."

Still, Mr Hull appeared bewildered. "You pay me handsomely, sir."

"I do," Ephraim admitted. "But recent events have reminded me that certain young gentlemen believe they require far more funds than they may typically attain—unless through criminal means."

"Criminal?" Mr Hull echoed.

Ephraim forced himself to meet Mr Hull's gaze. "Blackmail, sir."

Mr Hull's beautiful dark eyes flew wide. His perfect lips fell open for speech.

"You intend blackmail," Ephraim reiterated, cutting him off. He knew better than to give his silver-tongued clerk the opportunity to sway him. "And I shall not let you speak it, for your own sake as much as mine. Let this remain a mere suspicion on my part, and let this suspicion drive me to release you from my employ without making a black mark upon your record of service. I wish you better fortune and better sense in your next position. Good day, sir."

Mr Hull continued staring at him. "Sir—"

"I said good day."

* * *

Mr Grigsby may as well have struck Hullvardr a mortal blow.

He'd felt his feelings reciprocated. He'd known it. With every kind enquiry after Hullvardr's own well-being, with every appreciative look Mr Grigsby had flicked up and down his frame whenever he'd entered a room, with every wistful glance Mr Grigsby had cast towards him

50

whenever he departed his company, with every lingering touch as Hull-vardr handed over his tea and his letters and their fingertips brushed together with incidental elation, with every word of greeting and good-bye brimming with something Mr Grigsby never dared speak but Hull-vardr could hear nonetheless.

And particularly just now, when their lips had finally met after months of dancing around the question. How a breathless gasp carrying all he couldn't say had escaped Mr Grigsby's throat. How that delicate mouth had opened beneath Hullvardr's own, welcoming the caress of his tongue. How Mr Grigsby's stiff frame had melted into his embrace. Hullvardr had felt the shackles of what seemed like centuries of self-restraint shattering in his arms, if only for a moment.

Yet Mr Grigsby denied them. Denied both Hullvardr's advances and his own desires, despite all evidence to the contrary.

And Hullvardr's conscience demanded he take his employer at his word.

"You may pack your things," Mr Grigsby said, regardless of Hull-vardr's inner turmoil. "Then you must go. Tonight."

Hullvardr nodded his assent, unable to speak around the unaccount-able lump in his throat. He'd almost held something gossamer and precious in his hands—only to dash it against the floorboards in his clumsy efforts to capture it. And any effort to regather the broken shards would only hurt them both.

Against his every instinct, Hullvardr turned away from Mr Grigsby and went upstairs.

Packing his things didn't take much time or much thought. Which made matters worse, as it left his mind free to wander over what went wrong. The Holly King had warned him how men who lay with men were viewed in the mortal realm and what dangers awaited them—but Hullvardr had thought, surely, in the quiet solitude of their little office, blanketed by fog and secreted behind closed doors, Mr Grigsby could indulge himself in just a taste of what they might have together, if he wished. The gentlemen in Hyde Park certainly didn't seem to mind any risk, and they had only the cover of darkness in the woodier depths.

Four thick walls, stout doors, and shuttered windows seemed safe enough to Hullvardr's mind.

Hullvardr dreaded the prospect of explaining his failure to the Holly King. Yet even with that before him, he found it less daunting than the thought of leaving Mr Grigsby behind. It felt wrong beyond words to abandon him alone in the empty office, knowing full well his only friend in all of London wouldn't return to him until after the New Year.

Self-denial was not a trait oft found amongst the Hidden Folk when a willing partner awaited them. Hullvardr couldn't understand Mr Grigsby's refusal—but he would honour that refusal nonetheless.

* * *

EPHRAIM HAD NEVER BREATHED a word of his secret to anybody.

He'd had infatuations and indiscretions at school, of course— everyone had. Yet somehow, while all his fellows seemed to grow out of it, he never did.

He didn't harbour any particular dislike for the fairer sex. But when he compared his own feelings to, for example, how his friend Dr Hitchingham had pined for his wife throughout their courtship, cherished her in their marriage, and mourned her after her passing, the nearest thing Ephraim had ever known to it was his own infatuations with Thomas, Harry, or Richards. All of whom, like Dr Hitchingham, had gone on to settle down with respectable young ladies in matrimony.

Like Ephraim, Lofthouse had remained a bachelor far longer than most fellows and never seemed to take an interest in the fairer sex beyond the book-keeping aspects of assisting Ephraim in tending Miss Flora's fortune. Ephraim sometimes wondered if Lofthouse was more like himself than like other young gentlemen. If so, he hoped Lofthouse might lead a less lonely existence. Ephraim took comfort in recalling how Lofthouse had found at least a friend in Butcher. And perhaps, Ephraim thought but didn't dare to hope, Lofthouse had meant something more than friendship when he mentioned finding his place in the household of a "kindly eccentric."

Ephraim, however, had contented himself with Dr Hitchingham's friendship these past forty-odd years—nearer to fifty, now.

And he might have died content with it, if not for Mr Hull.

Ephraim caught himself looking to the doorway where Mr Hull had gone. He forced his gaze upward in search of a distraction but saw only the mistletoe garland adorning the frame overhead.

He ought to tear them all down, he thought. Then he thought of how much taller than himself Mr Hull had stood, and how he'd have to get out a step-stool and drag it all over the office, all the while forced to think on the kiss he'd rather forget as he tore down all evidence of the foolish tradition that'd caused it. His shoulders and knees ached with a weariness that went beyond his brittle bones.

He'd do it in the morning, he decided, and went up to bed.

It took far more minutes than he cared to count of lying on his back and staring up into the darkness to fall asleep. Dreams he didn't wish to reflect on sent his body tossing and turning amidst the bedclothes, and he awoke in a tangle at sunrise. He felt wretched and couldn't remember why.

Then, as he descended the stair to the office, he caught sight of the mistletoe garland strung up over the door-frame.

Shame, regret, and a wistful longing he didn't care to acknowledge washed over him in wave after wave and left him drowning. He couldn't bear to look at the mistletoe, much less touch it. He'd take the garlands down tomorrow.

Perhaps he would feel better then.

Ephraim brewed his own tea, toasted his own bread, and fetched his own post and paper. Then he sat at his desk and kept his gaze firmly down upon it, lest he catch an errant glance at the mistletoe garlands which loomed over him all around, wilting beneath the weight of the memories they carried. No one called. No birds flitted past the window, the chill of the season driving them to roost in the eaves and not venture out. Dr Hitchingham had already gone to his son's household, so Ephraim dined alone at the Red Lion and returned to his empty office with the wilting mistletoe garlands shuddering in the draught like so many ghosts.

They looked no better the next day. Ephraim resolved not to acknowledge them. Perhaps, as they wilted, they might transform beyond recognition, and then he could bear to see them long enough to toss them into the fire. Still no one called, and no birds braved the cold. Ephraim dined alone.

Christmas Eve dawned. The garlands had withered into something unrecognizable. Yet Ephraim still knew them for what they were. He could not take them down. Perhaps in another few days they might wilt off their nails altogether and drop to the floor, where he could sweep them up like so much ash.

Ephraim had spent the last ten Christmases with Lofthouse. He'd hoped spending it with Mr Hull might spare him the pang of missing his former clerk. He'd intended to read Dickens aloud to Mr Hull, who he thought might enjoy it more than Lofthouse had. Now, however, as he brewed and drank his tea alone in his empty office, he supposed he might as well read it silently to himself.

Even as his eyes ran over the words on the page, he found his thoughts wandering. The words of Dr Hitchingham, which he'd tried to banish ever since he heard them, rang in his ears. He dreaded the dinner they would have when Dr Hitchingham returned from his son's household. To be betrayed by his clerk was one thing. To admit to his closest friend how wrong he'd been regarding his clerk's character felt like the very definition of adding insult to injury.

Yet Ephraim didn't spend the holiday altogether alone. A bird deigned to visit his windowsill. Not one of the roosting sparrows, but the queer little grey puff with its black highwayman's mask. It lingered for some time, hopping about the windowsill and peering keenly through the glass. Ephraim wondered if he ought to let it inside to enjoy a little warmth from his fire before it went on its way. But as he reached for the window-latch, it veered off and vanished into the fog, leaving him alone once more.

Christmas Day dawned as cold and grey as Christmas Eve. Ephraim wished he could dismiss the holiday with a "Bah! Humbug!" as Scrooge did. Though he didn't want to bring the wrath of four ghosts down upon his head. If spirits did visit him, at least one must be Tolhurst, and

TALES FROM BLACKTHORN BRIAR

while he bore the living man no ill will, he'd no wish to see his pallid corpse standing before him with blood pouring from his throat.

Yet what form the other spirits would take proved still more trying to Ephraim's nerves. If one should be Felix and another Lofthouse...

The downstairs bell rang.

Ephraim dropt his book and jumped up from his seat in a fright. His hips creaked in protest and his back twinged. *A Christmas Carol* bounced off the desk and tumbled to the floor in a heap.

The bell rang again.

Ephraim coughed to dislodge his heart from his throat and made his way to the door.

When he opened it and peered down into the stairwell, what he beheld didn't make him any less wary of ghosts. Two gentlemen had begun climbing the stair. One tall, the other short, both garbed in black, though the tall one wore a heavy hooded cloak. At the creak of the door opening, they raised their heads, and Ephraim saw two faces he never expected to glimpse again.

"Lofthouse!" Ephraim cried.

Lofthouse grinned—which quite astonished Ephraim, his smiles having always appeared few and far between in years past—and doffed his hat. "Happy Christmas, sir."

Beside him, Butcher likewise smiled and turned down his hood to take off his feathered cap, but Ephraim hardly noticed. Instead his gaze fixed itself on Lofthouse's countenance, more freckled than ever before and all the brighter for it, cheeks rosy and eyes bright with cheer, no longer the wan ghost of a youth who'd laboured in Ephraim's office for so long.

So great was Ephraim's excitement to see his prodigal clerk returned to him that he welcomed both Lofthouse and Butcher into the office without recalling what state he'd left it in not moments before. It came back to him in an instant, like breaking through the ice of the wash-basin on a winter morning, as he watched Lofthouse's glance flit between the wilted garlands still hanging over window, mantle, ceiling beams, and both door-frames, then to the book crumpled pages-down on the floor beside Ephraim's desk.

Ephraim pretended very hard that the garlands didn't exist. He approached his desk in a manner desperately designed to appear casual and picked up the book. A few brisk brushes of his hand smoothed out the pages. He set it down again and looked up to find Lofthouse still looking at the withered mistletoe. Butcher, at least, didn't seem to notice anything amiss.

"Is Mr Hull about?" asked Lofthouse.

Ephraim's heart dropped into the pit of his stomach like a stone plunging down a fathomless well. "He's no longer in my employ."

"Oh?" said Lofthouse, meeting Ephraim's gaze again with a concerned look.

Ephraim hesitated. "I don't mean to speak ill of your friend, but I discovered certain defects in his character which made him ill-suited to this office."

Lofthouse raised his brows. "I'm sorry to hear of it, sir."

Not half so sorry as Ephraim felt to speak it, but he managed a sympathetic smile nonetheless. "Make yourselves comfortable—there's a third chair upstairs, won't take me a moment to fetch it."

"In the garret?" Lofthouse asked.

"The very one," said Ephraim.

But before Ephraim could take a single step towards the second-storey staircase, Lofthouse shot a speaking glance at Butcher, who gave him a brisk nod in return and strode off upstairs.

Ephraim swallowed his instinctive utterances of you-mustn't-trouble-yourself and thank-you-kindly, as Butcher had gone from the room. He turned to the fireplace to put on tea but found Lofthouse had already got the tea-caddy off the shelf and pulled out the poker to stir the embers into life beneath the copper kettle.

"Do sit down, sir," Lofthouse said without looking up from his work.

Ephraim supposed he may as well sit down. As he watched his former clerk make tea as he'd done more than a hundred times before, he noted how the freckles had spread from Lofthouse's face down to the backs of his hands, as if they tumbled out of his sleeve-cuffs.

The thud of boot-heels on the stair announced Butcher's return from the garret with the third chair. The kettle sang out soon after, and then all three gentlemen sat close around the two desks with teacups and saucers in hand.

Ephraim cleared his throat. "Allow me to offer my congratulations on your new position, Lofthouse."

A rosy tint flourished beneath the freckles. "Thank you, sir."

"And are you likewise employed by this gentleman, Mr Butcher?" Ephraim asked.

Butcher furrowed his brow and looked to Lofthouse.

Lofthouse cleared his throat. "He *is* the gentleman, sir."

"Oh!" Ephraim said before he could think better on it. Most gentlemen didn't fetch chairs or garb themselves in medieval trappings. Then again, Lofthouse had described his employer as an eccentric. "In that case, Mr Butcher, I thank you for making Lofthouse so happy in his new position."

A small yet warm smile graced Butcher's lips. It brought to mind another smile which Ephraim had grown accustomed to glimpsing in the office these past few months. One which had brought him great joy until just a few short days ago.

"We've brought you something," Lofthouse said, jolting Ephraim out of his miserable musings. "Just a small thing, in the spirit of the season."

Butcher, meanwhile, reached beneath the manifold depths of his cloak and withdrew a beautifully blown bottle with a cheerful green ribbon tied 'round its neck. Liquid of a promising dark plum shade sloshed within.

"Sloe gin," Lofthouse explained as Butcher handed the bottle over. "Made with berries from Mr Butcher's property."

"Goodness!" said Ephraim. "How magnificent. Thank you both very much. I only wished I'd known you were coming—I haven't anything in return."

"Your hospitality is a still greater gift," said Butcher in a low burr.

Ephraim blinked, astonished as much by Butcher speaking at all as by the words themselves. "Very kind of you to say so, sir."

Another smile twitched at the corner of Butcher's mouth.

Ephraim set the bottle aside on the desk next to Dickens. It would make a delightful tonic to share with his guests after dinner. He tried very hard not to wonder what Mr Hull might think of it, if he had remained. "Will you stay for dinner?"

"I'm afraid we cannot," Lofthouse replied—and for once, appeared genuinely pained to have to give his refusal.

"Oh." Ephraim couldn't quite keep the disappointed syllable in his head where it belonged.

"But," Lofthouse continued, "we thought we might just pop in and see how you've got on since we went away so suddenly."

Very suddenly, indeed. And so very much had happened since. Ephraim hardly knew where to begin telling it. With gentle hesitation, he asked, "Have you heard what became of Tolhurst?"

A grimace flickered across Lofthouse's face. "I have."

Ephraim clucked his tongue. "Dreadful. The poor man."

Lofthouse said nothing, though both Ephraim and Butcher looked at him keenly.

Ephraim tried to change the subject. "Have you heard anything of Mr Knoll?"

"I have not. Though I hope, by this time, you've heard something from Miss Fairfield?" Lofthouse pronounced her name as though it felt unfamiliar on his tongue.

"I have!" Ephraim took delight in replying. "She gets on quite well in Canada. She's staying with a friend of good standing and has every hope of making a better match than she could ever have found in England."

"Oh?" said Lofthouse, evidently startled.

"Indeed!" Ephraim hoped he didn't disappoint him by saying so. Perhaps Lofthouse had entertained his own romantic notions regarding Miss Flora. Nevertheless, Ephraim refused to speak on the matter with anything short of honesty. "Mr Daniel Durst—a shipping clerk, and one well on his way to promotion in his firm."

"Oh!" Lofthouse appeared not in the least bit disappointed. Rather relieved, in fact. "I'm glad of it."

Ephraim declared himself likewise.

Lofthouse sipped his tea. Butcher followed suit. A silence fell; not altogether uncomfortable, but one which Ephraim hadn't the least notion how to break.

Then Lofthouse cast another speaking glance at Butcher.

Butcher caught the glance. Very casually, he raised a hand to his raven hair. A lock had escaped the leather cord at the nape of his neck, and he brushed it out of his face.

And tucked it behind his ear.

Ephraim had never seen Butcher's ears before. Butcher wore his hair long—longer than fashionable gentlemen had worn theirs even in the distant years of Ephraim's youth. This long hair quite hid his ears from view. As a consequence, Ephraim had never thought twice about Butcher's ears. Out of sight, out of mind, as the old saying went.

Now that he saw one, however, he couldn't help noticing how it had not the rounded top of his or most gentlemen's ears, but rather came to a long knife's-point.

The instant he noticed it, Ephraim looked away. His gaze fell on Lofthouse.

Who caught his eye, then glanced significantly at Butcher's ear, before meeting Ephraim's gaze again. As if he expected Ephraim to say something.

Ephraim hadn't the least notion what his former clerk was on about. For himself, he'd never stoop to allow his gaze to linger on any peculiarity of appearance—much less comment upon it.

The silence stretched on as Lofthouse continued to watch him with anticipation. Gradually, however, the anticipation ebbed, and Lofthouse set down his empty teacup with a sigh.

"I'm afraid we must be off," he said, rising from his chair.

Butcher said nothing, but drew his hair forward to hide his peculiarity once more, before rising alongside Lofthouse.

Ephraim, meanwhile, fought the unaccountable panic building in his breast as he showed them out and wished them both a happy Christmas.

"Happy Christmas, sir," Lofthouse echoed. Then, after a moment's hesitation, he added, "Whatever offer Mr Hull made to you, sir—for what it's worth, I believe his intentions were sincere."

The mention of Mr Hull gave Ephraim a pang. He covered it up with a smile and bid cheerful good-bye to Lofthouse and Butcher.

Only after they had gone did Ephraim recall he never told Lofthouse why he'd sacked Mr Hull.

* * *

EPHRAIM EXPECTED nothing on Boxing Day.

This day, at least, he felt accustomed to spending alone, as he'd always allowed Lofthouse the full freedom to do as he willed with it— which usually meant either Lofthouse left the office altogether and wandered off through London, or, as the years went on, shut himself up in the garret from dawn to dusk.

Which made it all the more surprising to hear, shortly after breakfast, the ring of the downstairs door-bell.

Ephraim, confused, nevertheless went to answer it. Perhaps, he thought, Butcher and Lofthouse had come again. Or perhaps Felix would finally return after his mysterious disappearance.

Yet when Ephraim opened the door into the stairwell, he found not Felix nor Lofthouse nor Butcher, but Mr Hull standing in the hall below.

Mr Hull looked just as Ephraim remembered—despite his efforts to forget. All that had changed was the expression on his face. Where once had shone a quiet delight, there now fell a shadow of solemn concern. When those dark eyes met his own, Ephraim found he couldn't speak.

Mr Hull removed his hat. "May I come in?"

Dr Hitchingham would advise him to say no. Ephraim didn't have his friend's strength of character. "Of course."

A gleam of something like hope came into Mr Hull's dark eyes.

Ephraim turned his back on it and left the door open behind him.

He put the kettle on, partly because that was what one did when one had a visitor, and mostly because if he busied himself with the tea-caddy and fire and water and kettle, he didn't have to look at Mr Hull or listen to the peculiar tapping of his boot-heels on the floorboards as he ascended the stair and sat at his desk. Yet his awareness of Mr Hull remained.

The kettle whistled. Ephraim transferred its contents to the pot and assembled the tray. With equal parts reluctance and anticipation, he turned from the fire towards the desks.

Where Mr Hull still sat, watching him with those dark, compelling, enormous, beautiful eyes.

Ephraim steadied himself to bring the tray across the room and set it down on his desk. He poured a cup for Mr Hull and handed it over. As Mr Hull took the teacup from him, their fingertips brushed together. A spark seemed to pass between them at the touch—one which threatened to take hold in Ephraim's heart and burn it all to cinders. He shivered, then cleared his throat to disguise it and sat down.

A heavy silence descended upon the office, as thick as the fog swirling past the window-panes outside, broken only by the sipping of tea as each gentleman in turn avoided the other's gaze.

"I've made a promise to Mr Lofthouse," said Mr Hull suddenly.

"Oh?" said Ephraim, trying and failing to feign indifference. It might have gone better if he hadn't dropped his teacup into its saucer in astonishment when Mr Hull spoke.

A hard swallow traveled down the length of Mr Hull's slender and beautiful throat. "I may return and make an offer once more. If I am refused, then I must depart forever and never bother you again."

Ephraim's heart leapt into his throat. In a voice of forced calm, he asked, "Lofthouse knows?"

"He has known for some time, sir."

Ephraim hardly knew what to make of that. "Lofthouse said he thought your offer a sincere one."

"It is."

Ephraim knew still less what to make of that. He beheld his clerk sitting before him—his broad and tall frame hunched in on itself over his tea; his black hair tumbling in all directions in the wake of his hat, tousled as if by sleep or something more; biting his perfect lip beneath his beard as his enormous dark eyes fixed Ephraim with curious uncertainty. If all this was offered up to him in all sincerity, then…

But that was absurd.

Ephraim cleared his throat and stirred his tea. "I've no wish to take advantage of a young gentleman and ruin all his prospects."

"If I may be so bold as to ask, sir," said Mr Hull. "How old do you think I am?"

Ephraim would have very much preferred to demur. However, he couldn't escape the piercing gaze of those dark eyes. "Nearer to thirty than forty, surely."

Mr Hull smiled knowingly.

Ephraim furrowed his brow. "You will shock me very much if you claim anything above five-and-thirty."

Mr Hull smiled still. "Then I shall make no claims."

Ephraim didn't know what to make of that.

"Mr Lofthouse told me you would appreciate honesty," said Mr Hull. He hesitated, then added, "I would like to show you how I truly look."

Ephraim had known that beard was too good to be true. He waited for Mr Hull to peel it off his jaw and reveal it as a mere fur and wax contrivance.

Yet Mr Hull did not reach for his beard. Instead he closed his eyes and breathed deep.

His form shivered—as if he were the mere reflection of himself in water and a stone had dropped into the stillness, sending ripples across the surface.

And in the wake of these ripples emerged something unlike Ephraim had ever seen.

The beard remained. Several other additional details, however, appeared.

For one, the shade of his skin had transformed from a pale peach to a slate blue dappled with silvery-white. His ears had turned into those of a goat, hanging down in the shape of bells or lilies, and covered in blue velvet. His black hair acquired a blue sheen, and amidst his curls emerged a pair of spiraling ridged horns.

Something flickered in the corner of Ephraim's vision, and he tore his gaze away from those self-same warm dark eyes that had captivated him the very moment they first met his own, to find a blue tail tufted with blue-black fur waving idly back and forth like a cat's. It drew his notice further down, where he saw not the customary boots poking out beneath the hems of Mr Hull's trouser legs, but a pair of blue-black cloven hooves.

Ephraim's heart leapt into his throat. His breath came shallow around it. Before he could speak even a syllable of all he felt, the room spun, and he fell sideways into darkness.

* * *

EPHRAIM DID NOT NECESSARILY EXPECT to open his eyes again.

When he did, he found himself staring upward at the ceiling beams of his own office. His back and shoulders, however, didn't have unyielding wooden floorboards beneath them. Instead, the soft yet strong grasp of two mighty arms held him. He rolled his head to the side and beheld Mr Hull gazing down at him—appearing as he always had, with rounded ears, sun-kissed skin that held not the slightest hint of blue, and neither horns nor hooves nor tail to speak of; though his black curls stood up at odd angles, his dark eyes had gone wide, his perfect lips pressed together in a thin line, and his brows knit with worry.

"Are you all right, sir?" asked Mr Hull.

Ephraim didn't quite know how to answer him. In an abstracted sort of way, he quite liked to be held so gently in the brawny arms of his very handsome clerk. On the other hand, he was not quite so old yet as to feel totally bereft of dignity, and dignity demanded he put a stop to this sort of nonsense.

"Shall I fetch Dr Hitchingham?" asked Mr Hull.

"No," said Ephraim, the singular syllable coming out sharp.

Mr Hull flinched. Still, he said no more on the subject. And when Ephraim struggled to sit up, he didn't attempt to prevent him but rather assisted him in rising and kept a supportive hand on his elbow to guide him to his desk chair.

"Show yourself," said Ephraim the very instant his weight had settled. "Your true self."

Mr Hull hesitated. "Perhaps we ought to wait until you feel more yourself again. You went down rather hard the last time."

"I'm altogether myself, thank you very much," said Ephraim. "I wish to know for certain I've not run mad. You may show yourself, or you may leave me well enough alone."

Mr Hull searched Ephraim's face for a moment. Then long lashes fluttered down over dark eyes as he turned his head a little to one side. He drew in a deep breath. It left him in a low sigh, and as it did, his form shimmered, and where once had stood an ordinary-though-handsome clerk, there now stood a creature with corkscrew horns, cloven hooves, and a tufted tail, dappled slate blue all over—somehow even more beautiful for how strange he appeared.

Again, Ephraim's pulse stuttered out of place. But he kept his breath steady, and soon enough his heart settled down into its regular rhythm.

Mr Hull opened his eyes. He held Ephraim's gaze for a moment. Then he knelt before him. A dappled blue hand took one of Ephraim's own, its grasp as gentle as moth's wings.

Ephraim let him take the liberty. The warmth of his clerk's fingertips suffused his hand, his soft touch sending a thrill of illicit pleasure through Ephraim's whole frame, unlike anything he'd felt in more years than he cared to count.

Slowly and gently, and watching Ephraim's face all the while, Mr Hull brought Ephraim's gnarled knuckles to his perfect lips. The sheer tenderness of the kiss threatened to overwhelm Ephraim. He felt rather like a fairytale prince. He wondered what he'd done to deserve this, and many other things besides.

"What are you?" Ephraim asked, realising how rude the question sounded only after it left his lips and regretting it much. He tried again. "Are you a faun, perhaps? Or satyr, or—an incubus?"

Mr Hull didn't appear in any way offended. "Huldrekall. One of the Hidden Folk. Fauns, satyrs, and concubi are my cousins."

Ephraim would never have believed him if the proof weren't kneeling before his very eyes. Yet his mind wandered to yesterday and what he'd glimpsed when a certain visitor had tucked his hair behind his ears. "Are you at all acquainted with Mr Butcher?"

"I am," said Mr Hull.

"Does he have horns, hooves, and a tail as well?" Ephraim realised these were not polite enquiries, but he couldn't leave them unanswered, lest they drive him distracted.

"No," said Mr Hull. "He's a different sort of fae than myself." A thoughtful pause ensued. "Though he does have antlers of his own, in season."

Ephraim wondered what season that might be. And how he himself had ever become so lucky as to have kneeling at his feet his handsome clerk—nonetheless handsome for all his horns and hooves and tail—who had confided a desire to kiss him. His hand reached for those marvelous corkscrew horns before he checked himself halfway. "Forgive me—may I…?"

Mr Hull smiled and inclined his head.

Slow and gentle, Ephraim brought his fingertip to the point of the horn. Like Sleeping Beauty pricking her finger on the spindle, he thought, though he himself neither collapsed into insensibility nor awakened from a dream. Instead, he found bone, smoothed over and more blunt than he'd expected.

"Is this why you duck under doorways?" Ephraim asked.

Mr Hull chuckled. "Aye."

Ephraim ran his hand gingerly down the ridged spiral, halting when he felt Mr Hull shiver beneath his touch. He glanced down to find Mr Hull's eyes half-shut and his lower lip caught between his teeth. Impulse bid Ephraim continue his exploration down to the base of the horn—whereupon a satisfied rumble emerged from Mr Hull's throat—then trail down through them lamb-soft curls to the bell-shaped ear. He traced its velveteen edge and beheld Mr Hull biting his lip again.

"You still wish to kiss me?" Ephraim asked, hardly able to believe it.

Mr Hull met his gaze again with a smoulder of desire. "I do."

That look, combined with those words, left Ephraim almost too breathless to say what he must. "Then, Mr Hull, you had better lock the door."

A gleam lit those dark eyes. Mr Hull leapt up and dashed for the door. His hooves tapped against the floorboards as he went, as rapid as raindrops on the roof. Belatedly, Ephraim recognized the sound which had greeted him every morning since Mr Hull's arrival.

The deadbolt fell into place with a click and a thud. Mr Hull turned from the door and regarded Ephraim with a look of one who beheld something precious beyond words and could scarce believe his fortune.

Ephraim, for his part, had not yet quite determined this wasn't all a dream.

Mr Hull's return proceeded more slowly and with more caution than his mad dash for the door. As if he were a medieval maiden approaching a unicorn in the wood and feared to frighten it away.

Nothing could frighten Ephraim away now.

Mr Hull reached him at last. He knelt before him again and brought his hands up to cradle Ephraim's jaw in his fingertips. He closed his eyes, tilted his head, and, finally, lowered his lips to meet Ephraim's once more.

The second kiss proved still more potent than the first. Again astonishment opened Ephraim's lips; again Mr Hull slipped his tongue within, inspiring sensations Ephraim couldn't have begun to imagine but for which he knew he would hunger forever after. Yet despite his ravenous state, starved as he'd been these past forty years and more, he still required breath, and this forced him to break off the kiss long before he felt sated.

A low moan escaped Mr Hull's lips. "Mr Grigsby..."

"Ephraim." His own name fell from his mouth without thought.

Mr Hull cocked his head to one side, a velvet ear trailing down to his shoulder.

"Call me Ephraim." Words which Ephraim had wished to say so many times before but only now found the courage to pronounce.

A wondrous smile revealed Mr Hull's eye-teeth as rather more numerous and pointed than most fellows.

"Ephraim," he echoed in a low murmur. It reverberated with a reverence that thrummed through Ephraim's own rheumatic ribcage and sparked a flame in his heart.

"And... may I call you Sven?" Ephraim ventured, though he hardly dared to ask.

"If you like," said his clerk, easy enough. "Though Hull is nearer to my true name."

"Hull, then," said Ephraim, the name feeling both familiar and strange without its title.

Hull bent to grant him another kiss.

"If I may be so bold as to suggest, sir," he murmured against Ephraim's lips when they broke apart to breathe, "shall we retire to your chamber?"

Ephraim hadn't expected matters to progress so quickly. Then again, he'd never expected them to occur at all. And far be it from him to deny Hull now, when everything he'd spoken and shown had so far outstripped all Ephraim's hopes. He managed a brisk nod.

Hull, grinning, took Ephraim's hands in his own to draw him up out of his chair. He kept his hold on one hand and laced their fingers together—to Ephraim's delight—and led him away upstairs.

Ephraim had never given a great deal of thought to his bedchamber beyond practical necessity. Certainly he'd never imagined inviting anyone else into it. He gave thanks he kept it tidy and had nothing within to shame him; though, as he glanced over the desk, chair, wash-stand, trunk, and clothes-horse, he wished for a touch more in the way of decoration. The walls, at least, had a few of Lofthouse's early water-colour landscapes, before he'd hidden his art away altogether from Ephraim's eye.

Hull, by contrast, had eyes for Ephraim alone.

No sooner had Ephraim bolted the door and shut the curtains than he found himself entangled in Hull's embrace once again. On instinct he seized Hull by his lapels, their crisp edges crumpling in his fists. Before he could even think to apologize, however, Hull had shrugged his frock coat off altogether and let it fall in a heap to the floor. A gentle blue hand took Ephraim's wrist and guided his fingertips to waistcoat buttons. Ephraim hadn't undone another man's waistcoat since university. His fingers trembled with more than age as he fumbled his way through the button-holes until the waistcoat joined the frock coat at their feet. He felt more conscious than ever before of how the heat of his own blood failed to reach his fingertips as he stripped away the warm wool to reveal the shirt beneath. Hull seemed like a bonfire under his touch, his inner blaze burning through the thin linen to warm

Ephraim's hands, the diaphanous fabric doing nothing to disguise the muscular dappled-blue flesh behind it.

Hull slipped out of Ephraim's grasp to untuck the hem of his shirt from the high waist of his trousers and strip it off over his head with all the carefree ease of a youth about to dive into a mountain stream. Ephraim steadied himself with one hand on the bed-post and gazed in awe at a figure few clerks could claim. The rippling brawn of an honest tradesman unveiled before him—arms and shoulders accustomed to hauling far more than ledgers, their broad expanse narrowing to a taut waist, the navel just visible above the fall-front of the trousers, with a trail of dark blue hair over it leading down beyond.

Then the fall-front tore open beneath clever blue hands, and the trousers likewise fell away. What they revealed appeared rather like other gentlemen's, save the colour, and more than Ephraim had ever hoped to see again in all his days. A sapling grew from amidst the dark blue moss, standing at half-mast with a delicate upward curve to the tapered tip just peeking out from beneath its foreskin. Perfect, to Ephraim's eyes.

And yet, despite all his evident beauty, Hull hesitated.

"There is one more thing I must show you," he said.

Ephraim, hardly able to speak for all his want, nodded.

Under Ephraim's enraptured gaze, Hull turned—every movement slow and measured—until he faced away from Ephraim altogether, so that nothing should obscure the truth.

And the truth, Ephraim had to admit, was rather extraordinary.

Where one might expect to behold a wall of solid muscle, there instead appeared a hollow in Hull's back. It looked rather like a hole in a fallen tree, broad where it crossed the shoulders and tapering down to a rough point just above where the tail began, with its ragged edges smoothed over by skin and occasional tufts of fur like moss. Within, there appeared only a deeper blue cavern, as though Hull were hollow all the way through—though Ephraim heard him breathe and had felt his heart beat and beheld him move about in a way which required the support of bones he couldn't see.

Hull turned his head and peered over his own shoulder at Ephraim, so shy he seemed almost coy, to see what he thought of it.

Ephraim had to admit the sight dizzied him somewhat. But in no way did it dissuade him.

"Does it hurt?" Ephraim asked.

"No." A wry smile curled up one side of Hull's perfect mouth. "Quite the reverse."

An intriguing declaration. Ephraim raised a tentative hand. "May I...?"

Hull's smile broadened. He granted Ephraim a nod.

Ephraim reached into the hollow, careful not to touch anything within, though Hull didn't seem to fear he'd do any harm. The interior felt cold, like frost seeping in through a window-pane. Rather at odds with the warmth of the rest of Hull, Ephraim thought.

As he withdrew, the back of his hand grazed the rim. A groan of pleasure escaped Hull. The whole hollow seemed to echo with the sound.

Ephraim hardly had time to wonder at it before Hull whirled 'round and recaptured him in a kiss.

He felt content enough to let Hull steer him backwards towards the bed and to fall on his back as they reached it and allow Hull to loom over him. Discontent arose in his mind, however, as Hull began to work though the knot of his cravat. He knew he didn't look half so well as Hull. Even as a young man he couldn't have compared. He'd never had such brawny shoulders, or so slender a waist, or such supple thighs. And time had not improved matters. Ephraim thought of his own body as rather like a candle stub; a fat puddle of tallow drippings with a wilted wick.

Hull, however, didn't look as though he saw a candle stub. He untied, unbuttoned, unlaced, and peeled back the myriad garments hiding Ephraim's shame from the world with all the tenderness and wonder of Nature's own gentle hand unfurling the petals of a rosebud into full bloom. And his desire for Ephraim, given the blown pupils of his dark eyes, the biting of his lip, and the ever-strengthening sapling against and between Ephraim's thighs, only increased with all he uncovered. When at last he had Ephraim bare before him, his hungry gaze swept over his whole frame for one glorious and ravenous instant—then he swooped down to devour Ephraim with another kiss.

And yet, while Ephraim's own withered branch stirred more than it ever had in many years, and even managed to overturn a few leaves, it did not grow quite as stout and strong as perhaps it ought.

Ephraim broke off their kiss. To breathe, or so he told himself. Yet his sigh emerged with a frustration he couldn't disguise.

Hull withdrew at once.

"What's amiss?" Hull asked, his voice low and tender. The very sound of it strummed Ephraim's heart-strings.

Still, Ephraim hesitated. "I'm afraid I may rather disappoint you—in performance, if not appearance."

Yet Hull only smiled. He leaned in close to press a kiss to Ephraim's throat, which became a trail of kisses up past his jaw, each one more delicious and precious than the last.

"Don't think on it," Hull murmured, his warm breath ghosting over Ephraim's ear and making him shiver. "Just know that whatever may or may not occur, I am content."

Ephraim wanted so badly to believe him.

Hull kissed him again, their lips meeting in what felt to Ephraim like perfect bliss. Then he dipped lower to his throat, his collar, just above his fluttering heart, down over the swell of his stomach, to the wilted wick beneath.

This he took into his mouth.

Ephraim fell back against the bed-clothes with a shuddering gasp. Warmth had suffused all of Hull's kisses, but this was another thing altogether—hot and soft and wet and surrounding the very core of him, swallowed down to the hilt. The lips felt as if he were enfolded in silk. The velvet tongue gently lapped at first; then it slid down the shaft to trace the vein on the underside all the way back up until it slipped beneath the foreskin to encircle his cock-head and dwell on the slit at the base of the tip, then back down, washing over him again and again, ceaseless as the sea, relentless as the rippling tides. His hands fisted in the counterpane as, slowly yet surely, and incredibly, Hull raised him to half-mast.

Hull himself had already achieved a full stand. Ephraim recalled how it'd felt against his thigh—hard as adamant and throbbing hot—even if he couldn't feel it now that their positions had altered. He could, however, see how Hull's hand fell below his own waist, and how his arm moved as he stroked himself, slow and steady; then faster, more frantic as his mouth drew upon Ephraim; until a moan of unrestrained pleasure rumbled up from his throat to resonate through Ephraim's cock, and he thrust against the bedclothes as he began to suck Ephraim in earnest, and Ephraim found his own rheumatic hips thrusting into Hull in turn.

And even if Ephraim couldn't spend—even if all that would come from him was grave-dust and lost hopes—then by Jove, that would be enough.

This resolution had just occurred to him when Hull's hips stuttered against the mattress, his arm jerked, and a long, low groan reverberated through Ephraim's cock as Hull finished himself off.

And in the same instant, though Ephraim could hardly believe it, his own prick pulsed to a full stand in Hull's mouth—then a roaring wave of ecstasy overcame him as he, too, spent; pouring seed in throbbing torrents down his throat, more than he ever knew he had within him, stars appearing in the night sky of his eyes forced shut by the sheer power of it, until he collapsed wrung-out and wrecked into his own bed.

With what little consciousness remained in him, he felt Hull crawl up over him again, and a kiss descended to meet his mouth, the familiar scrape of beard and the soft balm of perfect lips. He tasted himself on Hull's tongue—and something more, something sweet as honey with the faint hint of elderberry wine. His strength returned.

Ephraim opened his eyes to find his handsome blue clerk in bed beside him, in the midst of twining his arms around his shoulders and pulling him closer until they lay chest-to-chest and the burning embers of Hull's heart warmed his own. His strong pulse resounded through Ephraim's own ribs; Ephraim could no longer tell which heartbeat belonged to whom. It hardly seemed to matter.

They lay together for some time; Ephraim knew not how long, and for once he didn't care. He could spend eternity in this embrace. Yet still one question nagged at him, until he could no longer keep it at bay.

"May I ask you something?" he ventured at last.

Hull furrowed his brow in bemusement but nodded all the same.

"How old are you, really?" Ephraim asked.

Hull shrugged. "Roughly seven centuries."

"Seven *centuries?!*" Ephraim choked.

Hull looked abashed. "Roughly."

Ephraim didn't intend to shame the man for his age—throwing stones from glass houses and all that. "You look very well for seven centuries."

Hull laughed and kissed him for it.

JACK IN THE GREEN

October 31st, 1845
London, England

*J*ack Barrowcliffe rather enjoyed Hyde Park by night.

The crisp autumnal evening invigorated him as he strode from Knightsbridge Barracks into the depths of the park toward the statue of Achilles. His fellow Horse Guards had relieved him from his post not a moment too soon, in his opinion. Now he could set out to find good company and good coin in the same bargain.

He took up his usual post against the plinth and settled in to watch the shadowy figures passing by. One, at least, must prove amiable to his advances. The blue coat, white trousers, and gleaming black riding boots of his uniform oft did the trick. Even without them, he knew his chiselled jaw attracted notice, as did the corded muscles his trade had given him. On a typical night he would encounter many strangers interested in what he had to offer. He'd even found a regular partner of late

—a fellow who told Jack to call him Hull, paid well, and had a talented tongue besides.

But neither Hull nor anyone else approached him beneath the shadow of Achilles on this eve.

As the minutes drew on into hours and the chill seeped through Jack's uniform, he thought, at length, he had better go and satisfy himself in the barracks. He pushed off from the plinth and stretched his stiff frame with a final glance 'round to see if anyone noticed. No one did. Perhaps he might try again on the morrow.

Jack knew the path from Achilles to Knightsbridge by heart. He didn't need moonlight, starlight, or lamplight to navigate through Hyde Park at night, even with the lingering fog.

Which made matters all the more puzzling when, as he stepped through the trees, he found himself in a part of the park he didn't recognize.

The trees towered over him moreso than before. Yet he could see further, for the fog had dissipated into a mere mist rolling along the moss beneath his boots, and the moon shone overhead, framed by a ring of the uppermost branches surrounding the clearing. No hint of a path remained underfoot. Instead, stone ruins loomed all around him. Staircases to nothing fell off long before they reached even the lowest tree-limbs. Arches stood half-tumbled in every direction—though the Wellington Arch, Jack noted, didn't number amongst them. And directly beneath him lay the stone rim of a well, filled in with rot and overlaid with moss.

Nothing appeared dangerous, and all remained very quiet, yet Jack found himself unnerved. Glancing behind him showed no hint of the Hyde Park he remembered. Which left onward as the only way to tread. While he might not have his steed beneath him at this very moment, he remained a Horse Guard. So he threw back his shoulders and marched on.

He did not, however, pass beneath any of the arches. That seemed rather a touch too far. Perhaps it made him a superstitious fellow to think so. He dared any of the other guards to do otherwise in his place. As none were present, none answered his challenge, and so he pressed on, down the mossy way between the trees deeper into the wood.

While the trees and fog of the park tended to muffle the eternal noise of the city, Jack had never encountered a silence so complete as this. Only his own footsteps seemed to make any sound as his boot-heels crunched against dried leaves and fallen twigs. He did not flinch at the hooting of an owl. Hyde Park had owls, too, after all.

Then something flickered in the corner of his eye.

Jack whipped his head toward it. At first he couldn't find it amidst the undergrowth's gloom. Then it moved again, hopping along a thorned vine, and Jack beheld a little grey songbird with a queer black mask cocking its head at him.

Jack cocked his head back at it.

The bird took flight, vanishing into the shadows.

Only after it had gone did Jack realise how unusual it seemed to see a songbird in the night.

Still, he forced the bizarre notion to the back of his mind and marched on. The woods grew deeper and darker as he went. It had just occurred to him that perhaps he ought to turn back and attempt to retrace his steps to Achilles when the trees opened into a clearing.

And in that clearing stood a man.

A short man—shorter than Jack himself by a good head, at least. One with chestnut hair beneath his hat. He wore a dark frock coat and trousers like an ordinary clerk, with a long grey scarf winding around his throat.

Jack felt rather more relief than he'd have liked to admit at the sight of an ordinary-looking fellow amidst their strange surroundings. And this particular fellow looked more than ordinary. He looked, to Jack's eye, rather familiar. A dim and distant memory from a year or so ago bubbled up in his mind, of a timid gentleman and a tall brute caught out in the barracks stables, and of a night walk which ensued between the timid gentlemen and Jack himself, for which Jack had been well paid.

All of which combined to make Jack grin and emboldened him to call out, "Good evening."

The familiar ordinary fellow flinched. His head whipped 'round to face Jack with wide-eyed astonishment. Still, with a hard swallow, he replied in an almost even tone. "Good evening. What brings you here?"

"Looking for amiable company," Jack replied, as he oft did. Then he paused. "I know you, don't I?"

The fellow's small, sharp features turned a shade paler beneath his freckles. "Perhaps."

"Don't take a fright—I'm discreet enough," Jack reassured him. "But we did meet in Hyde Park, so I recollect. Gawain, isn't it? Bit o' Welsh on your mother's side?"

The fellow relaxed. "Yes. And, if I recall correctly, I may call you Jack?"

Jack grinned. "That you may."

A shy smile appeared at last, more brilliant for its rarity.

"I remember likewise," Jack went on, "that you paid in advance for a service I never yet rendered."

Gawain blinked. "Well, yes."

"Seems like I owe you one, then."

A hard swallow travelled down Gawain's slender throat as his dark eyes swept over Jack's frame from head to foot. "One might say so."

Jack wondered what it might take to get this fellow to ask for what he so very obviously wanted. "Queer place, this. Never found it afore. Easy to get turned 'round in."

"Difficult to discover," Gawain admitted.

"Not likely for any prying eyes to stumble across it," Jack continued.

"No, not very likely."

Jack ceased glancing over their admittedly beautiful surroundings and fixed his gaze on Gawain. "Shall we settle our accounts here, then?"

Gawain licked his lips, which seemed promising for Jack's purposes. "We could. Only—my friend should be along shortly. May we wait for him?"

Jack again recalled the taller fellow with long dark hair, queer garb, and a handsome chiselled face. "The more the merrier."

Gawain looked much relieved.

Jack cast another glance around them. The moon shone brilliant overhead. Almost too bright. Whatever wind had dispelled the fog from this queer spot, Jack hadn't felt more than a breeze. He dropped his gaze from the moon to Gawain. No less puzzling, that one. A gentleman; clerk, most likely, judging by the ink-stains on his fingertips and shirt-cuffs. He fidgeted with those cuffs now whilst he glanced about. Turning his head as he did displayed his slender throat to full advantage. His freckled lower lip slipped between his teeth.

"While we wait," Jack began.

Gawain jumped as if Jack had shouted and not merely spoken.

Jack withheld a smile. He didn't mean to tease the fellow. But he did mean to have a bit of fun with him. "Might I steal a kiss?"

Gawain licked his speckled lips with the barest hint of his tongue. Jack wondered if he even knew he did it, and if so, if he realised how irresistible he looked when he did.

"You might," Gawain said at last.

Jack approached him.

Gawain held his ground and his breath alike.

Jack halted before him—near enough to feel the heat of his breath arising, near enough to count the freckles on his splendid lips, near enough to stare down into those dark eyes gazing up at him with ravenous wonder—and bent his head for a kiss.

While Jack loved a fellow who knew what he wanted and how to go about it, there was something to be said for those just beginning to realise their own desires. The tentative touches turning to insatiable hunger, as Gawain showed him now, proved a powerful aphrodisiac. When Jack broke off for breath, Gawain followed him for a moment before he drew back. His dark eyes opened with a sigh which sounded equal parts mournful and satisfied. His bashful gaze met Jack's.

Then he caught sight of something over Jack's shoulder.

Jack turned to find another gentleman emerging from the trees. Despite the abundant undergrowth, he'd approached in total silence. Even now, watching him stride to meet them, Jack hardly heard his boot-heels on the forest floor. And what boots they were—tall black leather, like a highwayman, with the tops folded down over the knees. They well matched the rest of him clad in a black tunic, hose, and long cloak billowing behind him. Another fellow might feel taken aback at the approach of so striking a figure. For Jack, however, something of familiarity hung about the gentleman. He looked precisely as Jack remembered, which was comfort of a sort.

"Butcher," said Gawain. "You remember our friend Jack."

A sly and handsome smile crept up one side of the tall fellow's face as he replied, in a deep and rumbling burr, "I do."

"Jack," Gawain continued, "this is my associate, Butcher."

Butcher proffered his hand. Jack clasped and shook it heartily. The fellow had a strong grasp which Jack well appreciated.

"Jack has just reminded me," Gawain went on, "that we rather owe him a debt."

The sly smile grew into a grin. "We do, indeed." And, turning to Jack, Butcher added, "May I?"

Jack didn't oft encounter gentlemen as tall as himself—outside of his fellow guards, at least. For Butcher, he had to tip his face skyward rather than bending down to meet his kiss. His lips felt warm as summer sunshine on Jack's own, and the kiss burned hotter as it deepened, his mouth opening beneath Butcher's to welcome him and Butcher obliging with a languid embrace. This, then, was the one who knew what he wanted and how to go about it.

All told, Jack thought as they parted, he could see what Gawain liked in the man.

Jack glanced between the handsome pair. "Bit nippy, don't you think?"

Gawain, to Jack's delighted surprise, took the hint at once. "We might know somewhere warmer."

He shot an enquiring look at Butcher as he spoke. Butcher gave him a nod.

"Lead on," said Jack.

And so, with another searching glance at Butcher, Gawain took the lead, going back up into the forest the way Butcher had come.

The path narrowed and the woods thickened as they went. Soon the branches grew together overhead tight enough to block moon and starlight both. Jack caught the barest glimpses of thorned vines knitting the tree-trunks together on either side. He could hardly see his own hand in front of his face, much less perceive anything in the deep shadows ahead of Gawain. Now and again, he thought he saw a flicker of movement ahead, as though the vines slithered away from the path. More likely last night's gin had come back to haunt him.

Then, all of a sudden, the path ahead yawned wide and revealed a meadow amidst the thorns. Silvery moonlight illuminated a waterfall through the trees that fed a stream cutting the meadow in twain. In the centre of the meadow stood a round stone cottage with a thatched roof. A game-keeper or grounds-keeper's cottage, Jack supposed, which might explain Butcher's profession if not his garb.

The cottage within proved somewhat more of an oddity. Upon crossing the threshold, behind Gawain and ahead of Butcher, Jack found it lit by moonlight streaming in through porthole windows and the faint glow of embers in the hearth. This appeared ordinary enough to Jack.

But when Butcher stoked the embers to light a pair of beeswax candles, he illuminated what in shadow Jack had taken for a rough-hewn wooden table in the centre of the round cottage but turned out instead to be an enormous tree-stump hollowed out and fitted up with copper taps. He'd never entered a game-keeper's cottage before, but he felt fairly certain such things weren't standard issue. Still, while it might be odd, it was hardly concerning.

The bed tucked in by the hearth likewise didn't resemble any bed Jack had beheld before. Frankly, with its round withy-woven frame and piles of quilts and furs, it seemed rather more like a nest. Still, it looked cosy enough for Jack's intended purpose.

"Make yourself at home," said Gawain, so softly Jack almost didn't hear him.

Jack took him at his word and joined Butcher in hanging up his outermost layers at a series of hooks hammered into the wall between the bed and a workbench. As good as Butcher looked in his striking cloak and boots, he looked still better out of them. Jack had an eagerness to get his hands on those broad shoulders or inside the woollen hose to feel the supple thighs beneath.

Gawain likewise hung up his coat, scarf, and hat, and tucked his ankle-boots against the wall. Then he looked between Jack and Butcher, evidently at a loss for what might come next. Jack looked to Butcher as well with an eyebrow cocked in invitation. Butcher met Jack's gaze with a sly smile before turning it on Gawain.

"What shall we do with him?" Butcher asked.

Gawain appeared at a total loss for words.

Jack had seen this sort of arrangement before. Soft-spoken Gawain had the money, while rough Butcher had seduced him and now led him down the path of fleshly delights, with Jack along for the ride.

"I'm game for anything," Jack said with a ready smile. "So long as you've got something to ease the way."

Gawain looked more relieved than otherwise. Still, he didn't speak up until he received another encouraging glance from Butcher, at which point he turned again to Jack.

"May I fuck you?" Gawain blurted.

Not something Jack had expected to hear from one of Gawain's small frame and timid temperament, but surprises kept things interesting. He smiled. "If I can taste you first."

Gawain's dark eyes went quite wide. He glanced to Butcher—who smiled—then returned to Jack with a nod.

Jack sank to his knees before him. While he might in a moment require aid in puzzling out how to relieve Butcher of his woollen hose, he knew how to get around a gentleman's pair of trousers well enough. Buttons and ties fell away beneath his fingertips. By the time he delved inside to draw Gawain out, he found him already hard as iron in his hand.

"You're well ready, aren't you?" Jack said, glancing up with a grin.

A handsome blush arose beneath Gawain's freckles.

Jack gave him a few quick strokes in his fist—the hitch in Gawain's breath going straight to his own cock yet trapped in his trousers—then brought his lips to the head and let it slip into his mouth.

A bitten-off moan escaped Gawain. Jack glanced up to see his head turned aside and his freckled lower lip caught between his teeth.

Just the taste of him would've satisfied Jack. To find him so sensitive, so responsive, so alive to every flick of Jack's tongue or bob of his head —well, that was assuredly a delight. Experimentally, he slid his tongue beneath the foreskin to encircle the ridge of the head. A shudder ran over Gawain's whole frame.

Then, swift and silent as a shadow, Butcher slipped behind Gawain. His strong arms wrapped around the slender torso—as much to hold him up as to caress him, it seemed. His mouth fell to Gawain's collar, torn open by his own hand. Another shiver passed through Gawain. He might have collapsed altogether, Jack thought, if it weren't for Butcher's embrace.

Gawain's hands, meanwhile, fell upon Jack's shoulders. As Jack redoubled his efforts to wring another quiver from him, his grip tightened—but released with haste. This occurred again when Jack's own hand fell to his trouser ties to unfetter and stroke his prick, now fully hard from the sight, sound, and taste of Gawain writhing in the throes of newfound pleasures. This was what Jack loved about sucking cock. To hold another man inside him, to draw him out until he could bear it no further and all pretence of self-command fell away, to watch him come undone at the mercy of his mouth. And Gawain, the sweet lad, fulfilled every part of this fantasy. The sight of Butcher behind him— holding Gawain captive in his mighty arms whilst biting bruising kisses onto his throat—wasn't half-bad, either.

But the third time Gawain caught and released him, Jack let his cock slip out of his mouth altogether.

"You can be a bit rougher," Jack pointed out. "If you'd like."

Gawain's eyes flew wide. He swallowed hard. "How d'you mean?"

Jack gave a half-shrug. "Pull my hair?"

Gawain took a sharp breath as his fingers clenched hard around Jack's shoulders.

Jack grinned. "Or that."

Before Gawain could say anything more, Jack descended. Any words Gawain might have spoken were lost in the choked-off gasp that escaped him as Jack took him into his mouth again.

Jack's renewed efforts were rewarded as Gawain, at last, seized him 'round the back of the head and tangled his knuckles in his hair. The sharp burn and lingering ache enhanced every sensation Jack felt. A wonderful contrast that made the familiar grip of his own fist on his cock and the taste of Gawain on his tongue all the sweeter.

And better still as Gawain surrendered his restraint and began thrusting into Jack's mouth in earnest. Jack opened his throat and swallowed him down, hollowing his cheeks. Murmured reassurances in a low burr resounded above him and intermingled with wanton moans. Then they cut off with a gasp as Gawain's hips stuttered.

"Forgive me, I—"

Jack appreciated the warning. Still, he didn't leave off, and instead redoubled his efforts, until at last the cock pulsed against his tongue and Gawain rewarded him with wave after wave of salty tide. Jack swallowed all but a few drops which slipped out between his lips as he let Gawain fall from his mouth.

Gawain himself collapsed in Butcher's arms. Yet Butcher held him upright. Jack sat back on his heels with more than a little satisfaction as he admired the result of his hard work, his fist still idly stroking his own prick.

A kiss from Butcher revived Gawain, who, with his aid, staggered to the nest. Butcher laid him down with a glance equal parts sly and, to Jack's surprise, fond. Then those dark eyes shot up to meet Jack's gaze, and the brows raised in unmistakable invitation.

Jack joined them.

No sooner had his knee graced the withy frame of the bed than Butcher's hand shot up and seized Jack by the collar to drag him down for a kiss. Jack appreciated his boldness and showed him so by returning his embrace with enthusiasm. Presumably Butcher wished to taste his lover on Jack's tongue. Jack felt more than willing to oblige him. His hands wandered in the meanwhile, descending to Butcher's waist and further down to feel the supple thighs beneath the woollen hose. There likewise he felt a hard staff equal to his own.

"You as well?" Jack enquired as they broke away for breath.

Butcher's gaze swept him up and down in a long look of evident appreciation. With a handsome half-smile, he replied, "Not just yet."

Which was disappointing, but as he followed it up with another kiss, Jack didn't entirely mind.

* * *

WHEN SHRIKE HAD RETURNED from an evening's flight to tell how he'd espied the Horse Guard in the Grove of Gates, Wren knew not what to think.

"The very same?" Wren demanded. "You're certain?"

Shrike avowed he was, in fact, certain.

"Do you think he seeks recompense for the stolen horse?" Wren asked.

Shrike doubted it, as the horse had returned of its own accord the morning after its theft.

"For what, then, has he come here?" Wren wondered.

"I don't think he came on purpose," said Shrike. "I think he wandered through Hyde Park, as I suppose is his wont, and stumbled through the ring."

"Oh," said Wren. Then, "Does that happen often?"

"Now and again," Shrike admitted. "Particularly when the veil between realms thins on Samhain."

Wren took a moment to absorb this information. Then he cleared his head with a shake and returned to the matter at hand. "What ought we to do about him?"

Shrike gave a half-shouldered shrug which rather left it up to Wren.

Wren considered the problem. "If he's lost, we ought to help him, at the very least."

Shrike raised his brows as much as to say, "And what more?"

"And," Wren added, warmth rising in his face, "we might owe him something of a debt in the vein of the Court of Hidden Folk."

Shrike's low laugh went straight to Wren's heart—and parts further south, as well.

They ventured forth together into the dark forest toward the Grove of Gates to find the lost guard. When they drew near, however, and heard the crunch of a stranger's boot-heels over twigs and fallen leaves, Wren held back.

"Perhaps," he said, "we ought to approach him one at a time, so as not to overwhelm him and give alarm."

Shrike blinked down at him in bemusement. Then, with a shrug, he assumed his form of a little grey bird with a black mask. He alighted on Wren's shoulder and nestled his beak against Wren's jaw. Then he flitted off amidst the trees. Wren lost him in the shadows.

And so Wren went forth, alone, to confront his old fantasy. His heart filled with dread. If Jack should prove angry with them for stealing the horse. If Jack didn't remember them at all. If Jack wasn't even Jack, but another horse guard unknown to them both, and how to explain the fae realm to a total stranger?

These thoughts brought Wren to a part of the wood he didn't recognise. Only then did he realise he could no longer hear footsteps beyond his home. And Shrike remained entirely unseen.

So Wren thought it prudent to halt and rest a spell in a convenient clearing, rather than wander on and get himself further lost.

It was then that Jack stumbled upon him.

Jack, who smiled to see him. Jack, who very much remembered their queer meeting. Jack, who declared himself ready, willing, and able to fulfill the promise made so many months ago.

And when he had his smiling Shrike again beside him, what else could Wren do but invite the horse guard back to Blackthorn?

Having the matter settled and his Shrike at his side ought to have put Wren's nerves to rest. Instead, they increased with every step towards the cottage. He gave thanks Jack followed behind him, so he needn't witness the convulsions his countenance endured as waves of hot and cold chased each other across his skin.

Fucking the fae was one thing. Fucking another mortal man, however... that, Wren had not yet done. He'd never supposed he ever would. The prospect felt equal parts exhilarating and daunting.

Still, there was something to be said for the fulfillment of a fantasy some twenty years in the making.

By the time he'd led Jack across the cottage threshold, Wren thought the anticipation might kill him. Then, to have both Jack and Shrike turn to him, and for Shrike to ask him to give voice to his wildest dreams.

And to reply with the most idiotic question Jack had likely ever heard.

May I fuck you? Wren could've strangled himself.

Yet neither Shrike nor Jack had looked askance at this. And Jack had countered with his own audacious offer.

If I can taste you first.

The fae realms had given Wren more than his fair share of experience in having his cock sucked, true enough, but he'd never yet received anything of the sort from the mouth of another mortal man.

The resulting act exceeded Wren's imaginings. The thrill of Jack sinking to his knees before him. His teasing words and coy glances as he took Wren in hand. Then to slip between those wry lips and sink into the hot, wet, soft abyss of Jack's mouth. To hear him ask for rough handling and to feel him moan through Wren's own prick as Wren obliged him with fists clenched in his hair. All this flew far beyond what Wren had envisioned alone in his garret as he abused himself with thoughts of a fumbling anonymous encounter in Hyde Park.

Likewise, his fantasies had never accounted for his Shrike.

He'd never dared to dream of one he might call his very own. Nor ever even begun to imagine how it might feel to have his stalwart presence at his back, his strong embrace holding him whilst bruising kisses fell on his collar and a thrilling tongue paid tribute to his cock below.

To have two men lavish him with affection—one beloved and familiar, the other wild and unknown—it was all Wren could do to not shame himself and spend at once. Yet spend he did. And to not just imagine, but to see and feel another mortal man swallow his seed, would have sufficed to make him spend again.

All sense fled him as he lost himself in his ecstasy. Even as he fell, Shrike's strong embrace caught him and bore him hence to their nest. There he lay in his delightful stupor, half-convinced he'd dreamt the last hour of his life, save that Jack didn't fade away alongside the mist of his mind but instead remained to kiss and fondle his Shrike. The sight of Jack's rough affections devoured by his own ferocious lover proved more than enough to entice Wren's cock to life again. Thus revived, he drew himself up on his elbows. This, at last, attracted his companions' notice.

Jack cast his eyes down to give Wren's stirring prick an appreciative glance. He met Wren's gaze again with a raised brow. "You did promise me a good fucking, as I recall."

"So I did," Wren admitted, though he felt hardly equal to the task. The spirit was willing, of course—more than willing—but given Jack's vast experience, he couldn't imagine how his own paltry efforts could possibly measure up. Instinct led his gaze to Shrike, his lighthouse and anchor both on these unknown and untamed seas. Shrike, who'd fucked scores of men before Wren ever came along, and had fucked several alongside him afterward, for that matter. Surely he would know what to do whilst Wren flailed and drowned in his own overwhelming desires.

And indeed, as their eyes met, it seemed Shrike understood his difficulty at once.

Shrike bent to kiss him. His gentle and reassuring caress invigorated Wren, reawakening him like a fairy-tale prince. Then he fell to nipping along Wren's jaw, trailing quite naturally up to his earlobe, where, after a few kisses more, his lips came to rest.

"How do you want him?" Shrike murmured into his ear.

Wren forced himself to reply with honesty, though he couldn't even whisper it without hesitation. "I want to see his face."

A gleam shot through Shrike's dark gaze. He kissed Wren again, then withdrew. His lips returned to Jack's ear and said something too low for Wren to catch. Whatever it was, Jack replied with an enthusiastic grin.

Shrike began to strip. Jack followed suit. Both men seemed in a race to bare themselves, each pausing between garments just long enough to catch Wren's eye with lascivious looks. Soon they were both gloriously naked, and if the events of the evening hadn't already brought Wren to a full stand again, the sight of two handsome men—one mortal, one fae—nude before him and well ready to do as he wished would've done the trick. Shrike's muscles rippled beneath a sea of scars; scars which Wren had traced with his tongue more times than he could count, and yet never enough. Jack himself proved just as brawny, years of equestrian training rendering him almost as strong as the horses under his rein, with a virile pelt of dark hair covering his chest and trailing down over his navel to meet the nest surrounding his magnificent prick. Together, Jack and Shrike looked like two warriors come to do battle over Wren's body. The intoxicating scent of their mingling masculine musks over-powered Wren's senses.

Then both men fell upon him.

Jack below and Shrike above at first, Shrike seizing his mouth in his own whilst Jack's tongue lavished his cock again, each kissing his way up or down his body until their positions reversed, and Wren tasted himself on Jack's tongue as Shrike left off sucking him just long enough to retrieve the bottle of oil from the chest at the foot of their bed.

Shrike anointed Wren's prick with a firm yet tender hand. Jack broke off kissing him to straddle his hips, rather like Wren himself had done to Shrike just last Samhain. It felt auspicious to Wren that the fae holy day should once again entail an erotic rite. Unlike last Samhain, however, Jack reached back to align Wren's cock with his hole and sat back upon it.

Wren seized Jack's waist in a convulsive grip. Truly, he thought, Jack's experience had granted him ample wisdom, for if he hadn't sucked Wren off before now, and this instead had proved his first spend of the evening, it would've overcome him before he'd even breached his entrance.

Jack, heedless of Wren's struggle, bore down. The cock-head slipped inside. The tight ring of muscle clenched around his sensitive ridge sent a shudder of pleasure through Wren's whole body. Then he sank further, inch by torturous inch, sliding into that slick soft heat until, at last, with a sigh, Jack sat back altogether, and sheathed Wren in him to the hilt.

Shrike, meanwhile, had slipped behind Jack. Wren couldn't see precisely what he did, but he could gather from how he braced his muscular thighs against the outside of Jack's own strapping legs and drew himself up until his chest lay flush against Jack's back that he had nestled his own cock between the globes of Jack's arse—much as Drude had done to Wren on Mabon. And, as Shrike began to frot against Jack's backside, he thrust Jack bodily forward, and drew him back with arms wrapped 'round his chest and waist, so that with every roll of Shrike's hips, Wren's cock slipped out and delved back into Jack, as if he fucked both men at once.

Wren knew well, and loved well, how Shrike looked in the throes of fucking. Even now, as Wren glimpsed him over Jack's shoulder, Shrike caught his lip between his teeth—an expression no less enticing for its familiarity. So too the way his eyes fluttered shut as his breath caught. When they opened again, their dark gaze fixed unerringly on Wren; hungry, possessive, devouring Wren's pleasure in their stare. Wren knew not what contortions his own features underwent, but whatever they were, they met with Shrike's evident approval.

Jack's face, meanwhile, which had begun so cock-sure and composed, now came undone in wild abandon—though no less joyous for it. He had satisfaction writ in every knot of his brow and flash of his grin between gasps. His handsome jaw appeared all the sharper as he clenched it to drive Wren deep within him. His beard-shadowed throat looked still more enticing as he flung his head back over Shrike's shoulder in ecstasy, and Shrike bent to kiss bruises on it to match those adorning Wren's own collar.

To see another mortal man take pleasure from riding his cock—something Wren thought he'd never know—struck something to the very core of him. The sensations within Jack, the tight heat clenching 'round him, left him deliciously overwhelmed. His ecstasy brought him to the brink of shameful tears. He couldn't withhold himself, and so he dared to thrust up into him, bringing him down on his cock again and again with the grip he kept on the jutting crest of his hipbones.

"That's the ticket," Jack hissed. "Just like that—just there—harder—yes—bugger—fuck—!"

This last came as Wren wrapped his fist around Jack's cock. The satisfying heft of it filled his palm. A few swift strokes sufficed to send him spilling over Wren's fingers. Jack's whole body went taut as a plucked bowstring, his back arching, his head thrown back, mouth agape as a strangled cry burst from his throat. He clenched 'round Wren, and this, with a final thrust, drove Wren over the precipice of his own pleasure. He lost himself deep within Jack. Shrike's low moan resounded somewhere above him. Then both men collapsed atop him, their reassuring weight pinning Wren to the nest.

They didn't linger long. Shrike rolled off to his left; Jack to his right.

Each curled around either side of Wren, all three men gasping to regain their breath, but nothing daunted in sharing their prize. Jack caught Wren's lips in his own with rough kisses. Shrike caught Wren by the wrist and took his fingers into his mouth to suck Jack's seed from them.

Wren, altogether wrung out by the culmination of his fantasy, could do no more than he wished, and surrendered to their affections. His heart filled to bursting. He didn't say so aloud, but with every caress, every kiss, every lingering look, his soul spoke the words on the tip of his tongue.

Thank you.

* * *

SHRIKE never tired of watching Wren experience new things.

From the Wild Hunt to the Moon Market, to Ostara and Mabon, it remained a delight to witness his mortal companion's newfound wonder at everything Shrike had taken for granted over the centuries. The way his dark eyes flew wide, how his bespeckled lips would part, the soft gasp escaping his throat, and the quickening of breath and pulse alike—all filled Shrike's heart 'til it brimmed over with affection for his gallant Wren. The unexpected arrival of a mortal acquaintance to join them on Samhain intrigued Shrike with the chance to give his Wren something else he'd never yet had.

But this Samhain in particular was new to Shrike as well.

He'd never seen Wren quite like this. Wren who, unlike Shrike, had never lain with another mortal man before. Hands trembling, hardly able to speak for nerves, brimming with not just want but *need*. And looking to Shrike to guide him through the dark forest of his own desires.

A charge which Shrike happily accepted.

To slide his hands up Wren's shirtfront and feel his heart pounding against his palm beneath the shuddering ribs, every gasp and choked-off moan echoing in Shrike's ears. To have Wren's pulse fluttering like moth's wings under Shrike's lips as he kissed bruises onto his throat and collar. To hold him as a most willing captive in his embrace. To carry his slender weight through the storm-tossed waves of his own passions. To feel him come undone in his arms and Jack's mouth alike.

And again, to see him shudder with illicit pleasure as he slipped inside Jack. To watch him fall apart in the throes of ecstasy. And to lavish him with well-deserved affection afterward.

Jack hadn't shirked his duty, either. Shrike had thought him handsome at their first meeting so many months ago beneath the shadow of Achilles. He found him no less comely now at his unexpected return. Yet he watched him tonight not just for the pleasure of gazing upon a well-formed face and body, but to make sure he gave Wren all the courtesy he deserved. Even if Jack couldn't possibly know how much this moment meant to Wren.

And Jack had risen to the challenge admirably.

The three men lay entangled in bliss for some time after their fuck. Shrike felt content to remain so all night, if the other two were willing.

Wren, however, began to shift uneasily. He slipped out of Shrike's grasp and crept out of the bed.

Shrike raised his head to watch him as he went. A touch of concern clouded his mind. Perhaps Wren hadn't enjoyed himself quite so well as he'd thought. Perhaps some lingering regrets as to how the evening had gone had forced Wren to withdraw. Perhaps this long-awaited moment hadn't been all Wren wished. Shrike readied himself for the chance he might need to leave the bed likewise to comfort him.

But, as Wren crossed the cottage, his face came into the candlelight, and Shrike beheld the same serenity as before on his bespeckled features. He halted at the hollow stump, picked up the linen hanging over its rim, and turned on the copper tap. Shrike belatedly realised he was, after all, merely washing himself off.

Shrike lay back again, satisfied. He let his head loll across the furs to see how Jack got on.

Jack hadn't roused at Wren's slipping away. His contented sprawl displayed his body to advantage. Sinewy arms, broad shoulders tapering to narrow waist, and well-turned legs all dusted with dark hair. At the sound of the running tap, however, his blue eyes opened and fell upon Shrike's face. His gaze swept across the length of

Shrike's frame. When he met Shrike's gaze again, he cocked an eyebrow.

Shrike no less admired Jack's body. Still, there was more than the two of them to consider, and so he looked again to Wren at the hollow stump. Wren hadn't minded sharing Shrike with their partners at Mabon. However, they had all been fae. Jack was mortal, and perhaps this would cross some mortal boundary Shrike hadn't yet discovered.

Wren didn't seem to dislike the idea. On the contrary, as he glanced between Shrike and Jack, his dark eyes shone with intrigue. The grip of his hand around his freshly cleansed prick subtly altered. His bespeckled lip caught between his teeth as he granted Shrike an almost imperceptible nod.

And so Shrike reached out to twine his arm around Jack's shoulders and drag him into an embrace. Jack kissed with a well-practised ease, cocksure and bold. His moustache scraped against Shrike's face in an intriguing contrast to his slick tongue betwixt Shrike's own lips.

Shrike had fucked a few mortal men before Wren. None since, save Wren himself.

And now, to have Wren watch him as he claimed their shared bounty made the claiming all the sweeter.

A few words dropt in Jack's ear sufficed to entice him to turn himself over. He braced up on his knees whilst burying his face in his arms amidst the furs. Shrike knelt behind him. A splash of oil went over his cock. Then he lined it up with Jack's hole, already slick with Wren's seed, and slowly sank inside.

The low groan of deep satisfaction that rumbled up from Jack was echoed in Shrike's own throat. The hot, tight, wet sheath surrounded Shrike's sword in pleasure which only increased as he drew himself out almost to the tip and, with a snap of his hips, slammed into the hilt again. Jack moaned and rocked back against him. Shrike indulged him with another snap, and another, building into a frantic rhythm that brought both men to the brink. He let his hand slip from Jack's waist to stroke his cock—much to Jack's evident delight, as further muffled moans resounded from the nest of furs he'd made for his head. He spilled over Shrike's hand. Shrike lifted his gaze to meet Wren's. The sight of him losing himself in ecstasy whilst he watched sufficed for Shrike to sow his seed into the furrows Wren had already ploughed.

Shrike collapsed atop Jack. With his lips flush against his skin, it felt only natural to kiss bruises onto his shoulders and the nape of his neck to match the ones adorning Jack's front. Low murmurs of appreciation resonated beneath him.

Yet move he must. And so he slipped out of Jack to join Wren at the hollow stump. Washing up quickly turned into an embrace between them; then Wren led him by the wrist back to the nest, where Wren settled in between Jack and Shrike as if their embrace were moulded for him alone. Shrike stroked Wren's chestnut locks in one hand and Jack's walnut strands in the other, both leaving fairy-knots in their wake.

It seemed to Shrike that Jack had granted not just Wren but both of them a splendid evening. He deserved something more than coin for his troubles.

And Shrike had an intriguing idea of what form that reward might take.

* * *

ALL TOLD, Jack felt he'd had a very satisfactory evening.

The double-fucking had filled every wanting crevice within him, and the two gentlemen had done it with far more affection than he typically received. Their attentive efforts left him wrung out and well-spent. If it weren't for dereliction of duty, he thought he could have happily spent another night here in this mysterious cottage which no one else had spoken of in Hyde Park.

As matters stood, he gave thanks tomorrow was Sunday, and he likely wouldn't be missed until noon. Then he slipped beneath the waves of sleep that had arisen in the wake of ecstasy's torrential tide.

He opened his eyes to sunrise, birdsong, and the sight of Gawain's freckled arse slipping off the bed and meandering across the cottage.

Gawain went first to his shirt hanging on the wall-hook, which he slipped over his head. It was an old shirt, Jack realised, not because it was discoloured or worn, but because it was cut and sewn in the style of some fifty years past. Then Gawain retrieved the copper kettle hanging from the ceiling beam. His back arched as he stood on his toes and stretched to reach it. A nagging thought in the back of Jack's mind scolded him for not getting up to help the smaller man, but more of him simply enjoyed the sight of masculine muscle going taut beneath bespeckled skin.

When Gawain turned to fill the kettle at the copper tap, however, he caught Jack's stare.

"Oh!" Gawain said, his voice soft despite his evident surprise. "Good morning."

Jack returned him the same greeting.

Gawain raised the kettle. "Tea?"

Jack agreed with a nod. He watched as Gawain hung the kettle over the hearth, stoked the embers into flames, and retrieved a wooden tea-caddy. By daylight, Jack noted, both the cottage and Gawain appeared still more handsome and welcoming.

Then the cottage door opened.

Jack bolted upright.

The figure who stepped over the threshold, however, was not his superior officer or any stranger, but Butcher.

Only then did Jack realise Butcher's absence from the bed. He must have arisen before Jack and Gawain both; likely to gather the basket of eggs and wooden bucket of milk he now carried into the cottage. Jack relaxed and offered his host an apologetic grin.

Butcher returned him a small handsome smile and joined Gawain at the hearth. Jack set about dressing himself in the meanwhile. Soon the crackle of frying eggs joined the whistling of the tea-kettle and, with the addition of cheese and toasted bread, a hearty breakfast ensued.

Jack, satiated in all possible ways, could've happily spent the whole day with his newfound companions. But as the sun crept ever closer to its zenith, he knew his fellow officers would soon wonder where he'd gone.

"Do you know the way back to Knightsbridge?" he asked his hosts. "I'm not sure I recall the path from last night."

"Could you find your way from Hyde Park?" Gawain replied. "We may guide you so far as that, at least."

Jack wagered he could and thanked his hosts for their trouble.

"Before you go," Butcher began.

Jack hesitated. It sounded very much as though Butcher wanted another fuck. And while Jack's spirit felt quite willing, his flesh—more specifically, his satisfactorily sore arse—would likely prove weak.

But rather than bend Jack over the workbench or the bed, Butcher instead sank to his knees before him.

A grin crept across Jack's face. This, he could enthusiastically assent to. He settled his palms onto broad shoulders as Butcher's clever hands undid the fall-front of his trousers.

Gawain watched with a wide-eyed but by no means disapproving or disinterested stare. Moreover, he echoed Jack's own gasp as Butcher took him in his fist and gave a few swift, strong strokes.

But when Butcher bent to take Jack in his mouth, Gawain belayed him with a hand laid on his shoulder.

"May I...?" Gawain asked, his gaze flicking between Jack and Butcher's bewildered glances.

Butcher looked to Jack.

Jack shrugged, a half-smile tugging at the corner of his mouth. "By all means."

Butcher arose. Gawain went below. Jack leaned back to brace his arse against the polished edge of the hollow tree stump, not wanting to overwhelm Gawain with his grip.

Gawain took him in hand, a lighter and softer touch than Butcher had, yet no less eager. His tentative grasp sent a delicious shiver up Jack's spine. It only increased as Gawain parted those beautiful bespeckled lips and brought them to his cock-head. He sucked cock like he kissed, with a hunger that hardly dared to show itself until desire overcame restraint, beginning in timid caresses of the tongue and resolving into lavishing licks as he discovered he enjoyed the taste. He fit half of Jack's shaft in his mouth, his fist handling the rest as he hollowed his cheeks. Jack resisted the urge to thrust, not wanting to overwhelm the man. His knuckles clenched on the wooden rim as

Gawain moaned around him and ravenously sucked as if he wished to devour Jack altogether.

Then, in an over-eager effort to swallow him down, Gawain fell into coughing and had to spit him out. Butcher had him by the shoulders at once, steadying him as he knelt and drawing him up when he made the effort to stand.

"Pardon," Gawain croaked, blinking back tears from the corners of his eyes as he looked up to Jack.

Jack knew full well he'd done nothing to require a pardon and murmured as much as he bent to reward his stalwart efforts with a kiss. Gawain melted into it and gave a sigh as Jack withdrew.

Butcher, after first seeing to it that Gawain was truly all right, took up his post on his knees before Jack. He had none of Gawain's bashful hesitance. He took the cock into his mouth with a confidence even Jack himself couldn't claim. His already-sharp cheeks honed their edge as they hollowed around Jack's prick. His tongue delved beneath the fore-skin to encircle his cock-head in a snare of sensation, paying particular tribute to the slit, before sliding along the vein to lavish the shaft with ravenous fury. It was all Jack could to do to keep his hold on the rim behind him. If his knuckles clenched any tighter he felt sure the wood would crack.

Gawain kept kissing him all the while with a needful hunger Jack eagerly indulged. The gentle affections of Gawain above and the furious devouring of Butcher below threatened to tear Jack in twain; a fate he would hap'ly succumb to.

Then Butcher let Jack slip out of him just long enough to say in his low rumbling burr, "You can be a bit rougher, if you'd like."

Jack laughed to hear his own words echoed back to him. He took Butcher up on his offer and drew his hair into his fist. Butcher groaned around him—a sensation which threatened to bring Jack to his knees as well. He thrust into his throat. Butcher greedily swallowed him down. It wouldn't take much more to bring Jack to the brink.

But as he wrapped what felt like a yard of raven locks around his fist, it revealed something he'd not yet noticed in all their intimate acquaintance.

Jack had seen many things over the years.

Knife-pointed ears, however, didn't number among them.

The shock tightened Jack's grip. Another long low moan reverberated through Butcher's throat, and this, combined with the thrill of the unknown, sent Jack over the edge of exhilarating ecstasy.

He returned to himself—still upright by some miracle—to behold Gawain drawing Butcher up to seize his mouth in a kiss. Gawain's ears, Jack noted, had the same rounded crests as his own.

Jack braced his palms against the rim of the hollow stump behind to keep himself upright. Gawain and Butcher seemed in no hurry to end their embrace.

Which gave Jack a moment to consider all he'd seen.

A sane man would take the sum of the facts—an unknown path through an unfamiliar wood, with vines that seemed to slither away from a fellow as he walked along, ending at a cottage filled with earthly delights, and at least one host bearing ears like arrowheads—and conclude he'd either run mad or fallen into some trap. Distant echoes of a ballad about a man taken by the fae for a sacrificial All Hallows Eve tithe floated through Jack's mind.

But Jack hadn't entered the Horse Guards because he preferred a life without the spice of danger. And besides, his hosts had proved beyond polite thus far, and promised to see him safely back to familiar territory.

Gawain and Butcher broke off their kiss and turned to Jack.

"Shall we?" asked Gawain, glancing at the door.

Jack nodded, and Butcher led them all out.

By the light of day, Jack beheld the meadow he remembered from last night. Now, however, he could clearly see the wall of thorns surrounding it.

He could likewise clearly see how, when Butcher went down the overgrown path, the thorned vines withdrew into an arched tunnel.

Jack's heart did an acrobatic flip which left him somewhat light-headed. Still, he steeled his nerve and gave no hint he thought any of this out of the ordinary, even as he followed a knife-eared man through a most unnatural forest.

Within a quarter-hour the thorns withdrew altogether. Jack found himself beneath a canopy of more familiar-looking trees, though still far more ancient than anything in Hyde Park. The autumn leaves flickered like flames in the breeze some hundred feet above his head. The trunks which bore them stood far too broad for any man, let alone Jack, to span their width with his arms.

The path led on until the forest opened into a mossy clearing filled with stone ruins. Half-tumbled walls with arrow-slits and peaked windows missing their leaded glass, staircases and towers crumbling before they reached their full height and thus climbing upward into nothing, gateways and arches bereft of their walls and leading nowhere. And yet, it all held a nagging familiarity in the back of Jack's mind.

Butcher and Gawain walked past the ruined monuments toward a ring of stones on the ground; the remains of an ancient well, now filled up with dirt and spilling ferns rather than water. There they halted and turned to regard Jack.

"This portal will take you home," Butcher declared.

Jack glanced to the ruined well and back up to his hosts. He could read nothing in Butcher's stoic face. Gawain appeared a touch apologetic, like one who knew his companion had said something odd yet couldn't contradict it. Jack supposed he might as well trust them this one step further.

"Good morning, then," said Jack. "I'm game for another round, if you ever find yourselves a-wanderin' in search of good company."

"Likewise," Gawain blurted. He coloured soon after, seeming to judge his own speech as rather over-eager, though Jack found his agreement as charming as his flush.

"You'll know where to find us," said Butcher.

Jack cocked his head at that. But Butcher seemed confident in what he'd said, so with a shrug, Jack bid them farewell and stepped into the ring.

He half-expected nothing at all to happen.

Instead, he felt as though the world spun with him as its axis.

When his vision cleared and his head ceased swimming, he found himself in a grove. Saplings had replaced the ancient trees. Fog clouded the sunlight overhead. The distant and familiar cacophony of Hyde Park filled his ears with the echoes of hoof-beats, rattling carriage-wheels, and frivolous conversation of passers-by. He stood alone in a ring of toadstools. Neither Butcher nor Gawain nor any hint of the ruins remained.

Jack stepped out of the ring. He had arrived whole and hale, so it seemed, and as he strode off, he found a familiar path soon enough which led him back to Knightsbridge, just as his hosts had promised. Apart from the delicious ache in his arse, nothing remained of his evening encounter.

Or so he thought, until he arrived in his barracks and, in removing his coat, found it rather heavier than he recalled. He delved into his pockets. There he found three shillings and a grey feather.

"'When shall we three meet again,'" he murmured to himself, twirling the feather in his fingertips and not bothering to suppress his grin.

WINTER SOLSTICE

Blackthorn Briar, Court of Oak and Holly
The Fae Realms
Winter Solstice

"You don't have to do this," said Shrike. "A word of surrender would do."

"No," Wren replied with shocking rapidity. "It's all right, I—" A nervous laugh escaped him. He bit it back. "I've rather looked forward to it."

They lounged together upon Shrike's wool-and-rabbit-fur cloak laid out on the roof of the old warren watchtower. Shrike had built a fire to chase away the nearest tendrils of frost on the well-worn stones. Still, his breath left him in a cloud which mingled with the mist that poured from between Wren's bespeckled lips. Holly and mistletoe bloomed along the crenelations surrounding the rooftop, having grown along the walls as Shrike and Wren ascended the tower to perform the Solstice ritual.

No raucous throng surrounded them. They sat alone together in their own realm, beheld only by thorns and ice and what round song-birds hadn't yet sought shelter in warmer climes.

"As a king once advised his princely son," Wren had said when he broached the idea of a private ritual rather than a public ceremony, "by being seldom seen, we may be ne'er seen but wondered at."

Shrike didn't quite follow. Still, he felt satisfied to trust Wren's judgment in this matter. From what rumours he'd heard in the Wild Hunt, the Queen of the Court of the Silver Wheel still intended to hold her own hollow rite of blood.

The true magic, however, would be done here and now.

Wren had shucked his boots and frock coat when Shrike had spread his cloak over the stones. No sooner had Wren admitted his eager anticipation of the act than his hands fell to Shrike's tunic ties. Shrike never tired of watching Wren strip away the layers to reveal the body Shrike knew almost as well as his own. Still better than watching was joining in, and so Shrike gladly untied Wren's cravat in turn. All told, their vestments fell away with far more tenderness and far less violence than they'd done in the Midsummer ritual. But Shrike felt no less passion as his lips chased his fingertips across Wren's exposed skin, and Wren shivered with more than cold beneath his bruising kisses.

Corded muscled rippled beneath Wren's freckled skin. The last six months had seen him unchained from his desk in the dim chambers of Staple Inn and sent him hunting, harvesting, and hewing. His slender arms had thickened to meet the challenge and his narrow shoulders had broadened beneath the yoke of honest labour. There still remained some tender softness beneath the trail of dark hair running down from his navel. Everywhere else, however, had hardened.

Much like Shrike did as Wren straddled him.

Wren himself already stood at half-mast. He stiffened further as Shrike took them both in hand, their cocks sliding together in his fist, twin blades in a single sheath. Wren's clenching fingers buried themselves in the rabbit-fur lining of the cloak. Then he recovered himself and began fumbling through the folds. From a hidden pocket he retrieved a glass vial of oil.

And almost dropped it again when Shrike traced his cock-head on an upward stroke.

A huff of laughter escaped Shrike at Wren's shudder and bitten-back moan. Wren repaid him by nudging his hand out of the way to take command of their twin staves and slather both in glistening spermaceti.

Then he rose up on his knees, slid himself forward, and reached back to align Shrike's cock-head with his hole.

Shrike ran his rough hands over Wren's rigid and trembling thighs. Wren had seen more sunshine in the last six months than had graced him in over a decade in London, or so he said. It had brought out his freckles more than ever before. Even now, on the cusp of winter, on the darkest night of the year, they trickled down over the tops of his thighs. Shrike idly traced a pattern between the disparate speckles. Wren shivered anew.

And impaled himself on Shrike.

Breaching the tight muscle felt like an arrow-shaft piercing a silver ring suspended on spider-silk at the far end of the field—pride in claiming a prize few others could ever hope to achieve, and disbelief at one's own luck in attaining such a victory. An honour indeed, one which Shrike well appreciated the gravity of. For as Wren had never before penetrated another's body in the way he'd done to Shrike on Midsummer, nor had his own body ever been penetrated by another.

Until Shrike.

The soft, hot, silken sheath clenched around him. The sight of his shaft sinking into Wren by fractions of an inch proved almost as intoxicating as the sensation of slipping in ever-so-slowly toward the hilt.

Wren's own prick had softened in Shrike's palm at the first breach. It stiffened anew as the tip of Shrike's cock grazed the acorn within him. A gasp escaped his bespeckled lips. Shrike braced a steadying hand against his quivering thigh, his eyes searching Wren's face for any sign of pain. But even as Wren bit his lip, he smiled. When his lashes left off fluttering, he met Shrike's look at last with blown pupils and hungry gaze.

And, with a sigh, sheathed Shrike's blade to the hilt.

It felt as if it were made for him, like leather moulded to fit the particular curve of a scimitar. Wren's prick fit into Shrike's fist likewise.

SEBASTIAN NOTHWELL

The heft of it pulsed in his hand. Milk-white beads of mistletoe bloomed from the tip. Shrike smeared them over the cock-head with the pad of his thumb. A muffled keen escaped Wren's throat.

Shrike couldn't quite keep a sly smile of satisfaction from his lips. "Will you not call out for your king, Wren?"

Wren's exasperated laugh broke off with a gasp as Shrike tugged his prick.

How well and how fondly Shrike remembered how Wren had wrestled him down into the green grass of the tourney field on Midsummer, how he'd thrust his rigid blade into Shrike's sheath, how he'd bent him double and fucked him and whispered his true name and commanded him to come, and how his spend had thrilled through his whole frame.

Now, upon the Winter Solstice, it was Shrike's turn to lie still and withhold his spend. Despite Wren biting the freckles that adorned his lower lip. Despite the tight heat encompassing his cock. Despite Wren daring at last, in minute increments, to move.

Fucking himself on Shrike's prick.

He hardly moved his hips at first, looking almost as overwhelmed by the sensation as Shrike felt. Then the corded muscles in his trembling thigh tightened beneath Shrike's palm. He raised himself 'til Shrike's cock slid halfway out of him—then slammed down again, drawing twin groans of pleasure from them both. Again and again, each swifter and harder than the last.

All the while Shrike forced his own hips into still submission. He would move only as his Wren commanded, even as Wren yielded to him.

And even as his own hand wrought ever more pearls of seed from Wren's blade.

"Shrike," Wren murmured; his thighs trembling, beads of sweat sparkling on his brow, his breath coming in gasps. "Fuck me, fuck me, fuck—"

Shrike rolled his hips to meet his thrusts.

A broken moan escaped Wren. "More—harder—please, I'm nearly—"

Shrike wanted nothing more than to grant him everything he begged for. Still, there remained a ritual to enact. "Do you yield?"

102

"Yes," Wren hissed. "I yield, I yield, please, fuck—"

Shrike let his hand slide up from Wren's thigh to brace against his jutting hip-bone as he thrust up into his Wren. His other fist gave his cock the swift, sharp strokes he knew Wren liked, until Wren shuddered within and without, clenching around Shrike as seed like snowdrops began spilling over Shrike's knuckles.

"Shrike," Wren whispered in a broken rasp. "Come now, come quick—"

Shrike did not need to be told a third time. The delicious shiver of his true name upon Wren's soft lips thrust him over the brink of ecstasy. The ferocity of his lust broke through all restraint, and he poured forth torrents into Wren's willing vessel. He beheld Wren's head thrown back, his mouth agape in a silent cry, his whole frame trembling with delight as Shrike filled him with the potent seed of the Oak King.

In the same instant, he felt the heart-stopping force of the rite fulfilled, another wave of pleasure cresting over them both as Wren collapsed atop him in his embrace.

Some moments passed before either caught breath enough for speech. Shrike spent them staring up at the wintry stars, which matched those sparking at the edge of his vision as his pulse returned to its customary rhythm. He cradled his fallen king in his arms, combing his fingers through his chestnut locks, untangling and weaving knots as he went. Wren's shaking breaths shuddered through Shrike's own ribcage, then gradually grew steadier.

"All right?" Shrike whispered.

Wren nodded against Shrike's chest with a dreamy sigh.

"Nothing hurt?" Shrike continued.

Wren tilted his chin up to shake his head.

"Are you certain?" Shrike pressed.

Without opening his eyes, Wren reached out and traced Shrike's lips to shush him, mumbling as he did so, "I'm fine. Better than fine. Now shut up and kiss me."

Shrike obeyed his fallen king.

THE HOLLY KING'S PERIL

Blackthorn Briar, Court of Oak and Holly
The Fae Realms
January 1st, 1846

*W*ren still didn't understand what, exactly, they were hunting.

"It's an ethereal beast," Shrike explained—not for the first time—as he strapped on his leathers. "The rite of its capture ensures the strength of the Wild Hunt."

Wren, who wore just the same woollen suit he'd worn through all his years as a clerk, leaned against the hollow stump in the centre of the cottage as he patiently waited for Shrike to ready himself. All had sprung into motion rather suddenly from his perspective; a starling had arrived shortly after dawn bearing a missive from Nell, who had scrawled the words WHITE HART onto a scrap of birch-bark, and this was enough to send Shrike into a frenzy to join the Wild Hunt. "And it appears but once a year?"

Shrike grunted as he tightened a belt. "Sometimes once a year.

Sometimes twice. Sometimes but once in a decade. Three years have passed since last we sighted it. It appears according to its wont."

Wren stared at him. "It *wants* to be hunted?"

"Aye."

"Why?"

Shrike shrugged. "It presents a challenge."

Wren had some familiarity with the figure of a white hart as the symbol of Richard II—and as the name of at least one public house in every village in England, so it seemed. It'd come up in *The Merry Wives of Windsor* as well, though Wren had never thought much of the bard's comedies, much preferring the histories and tragedies in that order. He'd made an exception for *The Merry Wives* due to its tangential connection to the *Henriad*.

All this he relayed to Shrike, who listened with more interest than any of the Restive Quills had ever suffered to show Wren. Shrike had heard of Shakespeare before he'd met Wren—*A Midsummer Night's Dream* being a vague shadowy reflection of certain historical events of the Fae Realms. He'd even humoured Wren in his reading of favourite passages aloud for amusement as they huddled together in the nest before the fire through the long cold winter nights of Blackthorn.

"But I never thought it real," Wren concluded. "Beyond the random chance of a fawn being born white and growing up into a hart, I mean. Will you catch it?"

Shrike served him a knowing smile. "I shall certainly try."

Wren himself had no chance of catching the white hart. Or any prey, for that matter. Still, it sounded like a most singular sight, one which he wished to witness for himself. And he never tired of watching Shrike hunt. The glint in his keen eyes, and how the sheer strength of his lithe form sprang into swift strikes, stirred within Wren a hunger which Shrike felt only too happy to satisfy afterward, with the heady musk of blood and sweat mingling with his familiar vanilla-woodsmoke scent.

All the same, Wren did carry a pen-knife in his waistcoat pocket as he went forth with Shrike into the chill January morning out of Blackthorn Briar and toward the Grove of Gates.

Unlike the fox-hunts of Wren's youth, the Wild Hunt had no permanent meeting-place. It met wherever its prey would be found. The first time Wren had attended, when Shrike had surprised him with a stag in Hyde Park, they'd arrived late in the midst of the hunt.

This morning, however, stepping through a peculiarly perfectly-round arch of tight-packed slates held in place by their own collective weight—the moon gate, Shrike called it—brought them to the hunting grounds whilst the fae still gathered.

Or so Shrike had claimed it would. When they passed through the moon gate, however, Wren beheld a pale field of snow-drifts scattered across crystal blue ice. Pines limned the shores beside and behind them. To the north, however, the crystal blue seemed to go on forever, forming the whole of the horizon. February wasn't particularly balmy in Blackthorn Briar, but this was an even deeper cold than he'd awoken to in the cottage garden.

Wren shivered beneath his heavy wool cloak with its rabbit-fur lining. For once, it wasn't Shrike's cloak. Rather, it was the one Shrike had created for him in the original's image. Made from the same black wool and silver rabbit-fur, and running much shorter to match Wren's smaller frame, it appeared a slightly shrunken version, though no less well-crafted. Wren had watched in fascination as Shrike sewed it in idle hours through the summer and autumn, finishing just as wintry breezes began to blow through Blackthorn Briar. Wren's own eagerness to join the hunt stemmed at least in part from the opportunity to show off the cloak—to display his beloved's talents to their deserved audience. Still, he found he missed the familiar vanilla-woodsmoke musk that enveloped him whenever he borrowed Shrike's cloak.

"Where are we?" Wren asked.

"The Lake of Eternal Ice," Shrike replied.

Wren stared at their surroundings in disbelief. "This is a lake?"

"Aye," Shrike answered with more patience than Wren deserved.

"Where's the opposite shore?"

"Yonder."

Wren shot him an exasperated look.

Shrike only shrugged. "It's a broad lake."

Wren supposed that answer would have to satisfy.

The icy wind that swirled through the air carried with it the distant murmur of merriment from somewhere amidst the pines. Shrike held out his arm for Wren to take and led him towards the sound. The trees provided some shelter from the wind's bite as they went and soon they came upon a clearing where fae had begun to convene.

Aside from the far greater variety of folk, it reminded Wren very much of the gathering before a mortal fox-hunt. Rather than the distinctive red riding coats, or "hunting pinks," as society called them, the fae wore costumes in every cut and colour. Wren glanced over the throng in search of familiar faces—Nell, the ambassador, Tatterdemalion, or perhaps even some of the hidden folk he and Shrike had met at Mabon. He did espy Lady Aethelthryth; difficult not to, given her perch atop her steed standing some seventeen hands high. As Wren peered through the crowd, however, he found many in the crowd staring back, some halting in their tracks or silencing their own murmuring conversations to do so. He supposed he ought to expect such a reception. After all, the Oak and Holly Kings hadn't been seen outside their realm since the Winter Solstice.

A nymph with damselfly wings dared to approach. Wren wondered how she didn't freeze mid-flight, clad only in a diaphanous chiton which seemed to flow in breezes beyond those felt across the icy lake.

"Good morrow, my lords," she said, alighting barefoot on the snow before them. "May I offer my congratulations on the success of your Midwinter rite?"

Heat flooded Wren's face. His tongue, leaden in his mouth, couldn't have moved for speech even if he'd known how the deuce to reply to her. No mortal maiden had ever spoken to him so brazenly.

Shrike thanked her with a bow. The nymph beamed and continued on her way.

"Well," Wren mumbled as she went out of earshot. "At least part of me is warm."

Shrike cast a fond smile down at his burning cheeks. "It becomes you."

Wren took a little satisfaction in that despite himself. "How did she know...?"

Shrike blinked. "The days grow ever longer."

"Oh." Wren supposed that provided proof enough for fae purposes.

The howling of the hunting horn spared Wren any further embarrassment. The broad-chested, moss-bearded, antlered leader of the hunt —whom Wren could not think of by any appellation other than Herne, particularly given their prey on this occasion—sat astride his enormous wolf in the midst of the motley throng, head and shoulders above all. He brought the yard-long curled hunting horn down from his lips just as Wren glanced over to regard him. Herne gestured to those fae who fluttered above the hunt, Tatterdemalion and the damselfly nymph amongst their number, and with a decisive thrust of his arm, sent them scattering in all directions.

Wren looked to Shrike for an explanation.

Shrike bent to murmur into Wren's ear. "He sends them to sight the white hart."

"Why not send the wolves and hounds to track it?" Wren asked Shrike in a low tone. "Would they make too much noise?"

Shrike shook his head. "It has no scent."

"Oh," said Wren. "Right. Ethereal and all that."

Shrike smiled and smoothed an errant lock of hair out of Wren's face. Even in this icy realm, his gentle touch spread warmth.

Not many more moments passed before a particular fluttering fae flitted back to whisper in Herne's ear. Herne raised his horn to his lips again and blew a rousing note. The body of the hunt, already on pins and needles for the chase to begin, shivered into readiness. Herne's wolf howled along with the horn. A kick of his heels saw it bounding away over the snow, and the hunt followed with thunderous tread.

Shrike, however, hung back, and therefore so did Wren. Only after the hunt had abandoned the hollow did Shrike go forth, and then in a slightly sideways direction, and on foot besides. He made no move to summon a stag for them to mount, as they'd done in past hunts. Wren supposed it'd seem a touch odd for them to ride a deer and force it to watch them stalk and kill another deer. And Shrike appeared confident in his abilities to catch the white hart up on his own two legs.

Though, as they went along carving their own path through the forest, Wren wondered if Shrike had accounted for his mortal companion.

In the months following the Summer Solstice, Shrike had taught Wren many things—the tending of a garden, the rearing of goats and hens, the keeping of bees, and the butchering of game. Amongst and amidst all this, he had likewise attempted to instil in Wren some knowledge of the hunt. How to track and shoot, yes, but more importantly how to move unperceived through the wilderness. According to Shrike, Wren had made great progress.

However, as they moved through the pines surrounding the Lake of Eternal Ice, even Wren's mortal ears picked up the echo of his own footsteps as a patch of snow-turned-ice or a dead twig crunched under his heel. Shrike, meanwhile, travelled in total silence. And at a far quicker pace, too, having to halt and turn several times in their journey to wait whilst Wren picked his noisy way through the trees. Though Shrike gave not a word nor a gesture nor even a hint of complaint—indeed, he appeared more pleased than otherwise whenever he turned over his shoulder to espy Wren behind him—Wren couldn't help but feel his presence held Shrike back. Doubtless Shrike would've caught the damned white hart by now if he didn't have Wren dragging him down.

In the midst of Wren's bitter self-reproach, Shrike halted again. But rather than turn to Wren, he instead crouched over something in the snow.

Wren caught him up and stood beside him, bending over his shoulder to try and see what he perceived. At first Wren saw nothing and thought perhaps whatever sign the white hart had left could be caught by fae eyes alone. Then, as he tilted his head and squinted, a shaft of sunlight coming through the pine-needles glanced off the snow just so, and he beheld the faint and delicate impression of a cloven hoof-print. The indented snow seemed to shimmer with iridescence. He caught his gasp before it left his throat.

Shrike continued kneeling for some moments longer. Only the infrequent whistling of the wind through the pines broke the silence.

"Would it be cheating to use the acorn spell?" Wren whispered. It sounded as loud as a shout to him in the snow-muffled wood.

Shrike shot him a startled glance which quickly transformed into a bemused smile. He replied in his soft burr, "Not cheating. Merely fruitless."

Wren supposed he ought to have guessed than an ethereal creature with no scent might have other tricks to prevent its discovery through magical means.

Shrike arose and slung his longbow off his back to string it. Then, turning to Wren, he whispered, "Wait here."

Wren felt more relieved than otherwise to hear the command. No longer need he worry about dragging Shrike down or holding him back. He nodded.

A slight smile graced Shrike's lips. He strode off in utter silence. Soon he vanished amongst the trees, leaving Wren quite alone.

Too late, Wren wondered how Shrike intended to find him again. He glanced around. None of the surrounding trees or stones or sticks or snow appeared particularly notable to his mortal eyes. Perhaps Shrike's keen fae sight found something more remarkable in this quarter of the wood. Or perhaps he would use the acorn trick again, as he'd done when he'd first sought Wren out more than a year ago.

The wind had persisted throughout the course of the hunt. Sometimes it howled across the lake. Other times it whistled through the trees.

Now, however, as Wren crouched alone in an unremarkable spot, the wind whimpered.

Wren cocked his head at the sound. For a moment he thought he'd imagined it. Then it came again; a distinct cry of pain carried along in the biting wind.

Shrike had told him in no uncertain terms to remain where he was. Still, as Wren sat and shivered and listened, the sound of another creature in agony wrenched even his hardened heart. He arose to follow where the cry might lead. Perhaps it was nothing. Or perhaps he might do something useful in the hunt after all.

The whimpering wind wound through the trees on an unfamiliar path. Wren winced at the sound of his own boots crunching through the dead sticks and snow. The pained cries—not true screams, but rather the bitten-off involuntary sounds of one who didn't wish to reveal their wounds to the world yet felt their agonies all the same—grew louder as he went. Soon enough he stumbled on their source.

In a queer hollow where the snow swept against the enormous roots of ancient pines lay a faun. Sprawled, rather, with one leg caught aloft in a snare tied to a tree-branch. The particularly fine wire had encircled their hoofed foot between hock and pastern, drawing tight and slicing deeper and deeper into the furred flesh as the faun struggled. They had an unstrung bow slung across their back and a quiver belted around their waist. Their arrows had spilled across the snow in their fall. Now they struggled to retrieve them, their whole body stretched taut to bring their fingertips a fraction of an inch away from the arrowheads which might serve to cut them free from the snare which, if they continued struggling, looked well on its way to slicing through a tendon and crippling them.

"Are you all right?" Wren called out, more to announce his presence than to receive the obvious answer.

The faun glanced up, startled, and choked off another yelp of pain as even this slight yet sudden movement drew against the ever-tightening snare.

"Let me help," Wren added in haste.

The faun stared at him.

Wren held out his hands, palms upraised, to show he meant no harm.

Hazel eyes with horizontal pupils flicked up and down Wren's frame. The bell-shaped ears, which had pinned back against the skull amidst the dark cropped curls, flopped down to their natural restful position, and the rest of the body relaxed soon after, like a longbow unstrung.

Wren forced a polite smile and approached the faun with measured steps. He reached toward the snare, then hesitated, seeking permission with a glance. The faun granted it in a nod.

The slender snare, slick with blood, proved far too tight to untie by hand. However, it was not wire, as Wren had first supposed. Rather it was some sort of vine, dried and prepared in fae fashion to create a springy yet unyielding thread. Wren followed its path back to the tree-branch securing it in place and found the knot there as impossible as the loop around the poor faun's leg. Unable to find purchase on either knot with his fingernails, Wren dipped his hand into his waistcoat pocket and withdrew his pen-knife.

The faun's goat-eyes flew wide. In an instant their whole body tensed again, the ears pinned back, and their gaze flicked from the sharp point to Wren's face and back again.

Wren didn't see the cause for alarm. The pen-knife's blade ran hardly as long as his own thumb. Certainly not a weapon capable of any real violence. Then, as he puzzled over it, he recalled that, unlike most blades in the fae realms, his pen-knife had a cutting edge of steel—otherwise known as an alloy of iron. No wonder the faun looked nervous.

"I'll be careful," Wren promised.

The faun didn't look as though they entirely believed him, but with a hard swallow, they nodded nonetheless.

Wren slipped two fingers beneath the snare and slid the pen-knife between them, careful to keep its cutting edge pointed in the opposite direction from the faun's flesh. He gave a swift tug toward himself and away from the faun. The snare snapped in twain.

"There you go," Wren said, quickly shutting the pen-knife and tucking it back into his pocket.

No sooner had the blade vanished than the faun leapt up. Wren scarce had time for a belated flinch. He'd hardly supposed they'd prove so spry considering all they'd endured. Yet there they went, hopping around on one hoof to regather their lost arrows. They'd snatched up most of them before they turned to find Wren still staring. Wren half-expected a reproof for his rude silence. Instead, the faun smiled a most charming smile, one which revealed a very handsome dimple in their left cheek.

"Many thanks, my lord," said the faun.

Wren didn't think he would ever get used to hearing that title. Still, he forced a smile as he replied that the faun was most welcome, adding, "Have you anything for your wound?"

The faun blinked at him, looked down at their bleeding leg, then back up with a shrug.

Wren couldn't take quite so casual a view of the matter. While the snare had not cut anything vital—or so it seemed to Wren's eye, untrained in medical science—it had almost flayed the flesh, leaving a gory mess in its wake. Fae might not prove so susceptible to infection as mortals, but it couldn't be good for the faun to run amok through the wild woods with such a wound.

And so Wren dipped his hand into his waistcoat pocket a second time.

The faun took on a wary stance. Wren didn't blame them. But rather than another iron blade, Wren withdrew his handkerchief.

"May I?" he asked, gesturing to the faun's grisly leg.

The faun cocked their head to one side in consideration, then hopped nearer and extended their wounded limb.

Wren bandaged it as best he could, tying the corners of his handkerchief into a neat little bow.

The faun smiled their thanks. Yet still they shivered as they glanced around the wood.

Against his better judgment and in defiance of Shrike's warning echoing even now in his mind, Wren slipped his cloak off his shoulders and held it out to the faun.

The faun's brow furrowed in confusion. They glanced from the cloak to Wren and back again. Then, at Wren's nod, they took the cloak with a reverence Wren had thought none but himself felt for Shrike's handiwork. Their shivering ceased as they drew it over their shoulders.

"Many thanks, m'lord," they murmured again, running their fingertips through the rabbit-fur as if to marvel at its softness, as Wren himself had oft done.

Likewise again, Wren assured them it was nothing, even as he suppressed a shiver of his own. It seemed the faun's chill had passed to him in exchange for the cloak.

The faun bowed deeply. Then they bounded off into the wood, swift as a deer, startling Wren once more before they vanished altogether.

Wren wasted some moments blinking in confusion in their wake. Then he turned, intending to go back the way he'd come.

And realised he had no idea which direction he ought to go.

The same howling wind which had carried the faun's cries to his ears had swirled through the snow and obscured what few tracks he'd left behind like waves washing footprints off the sand. Shrike could have probably followed the trail of broken twigs and crushed pine-needles to trace precisely where Wren had gone. Wren, however, could not. And so he stood in the midst of the forest feeling particularly stupid. The lack of his cloak didn't improve matters; while his wool coat and scarf had proved sufficient for London winters, they left him shivering in this icy realm.

Though, Wren observed as he spun in an idiotic circle looking for his own tracks, the faun, as fae, likely knew precisely where the hunt had gone. He could do worse than follow them.

And so he stumbled off into the wood.

The faun had vanished from mortal sight. Nor could Wren's dull ears hear their hoof-beats. Yet he recalled—vaguely—what direction they had bounded off in. He went on in that way for some time, making the straightest line the winding wood would allow. A muffled silence hung over him, broken only by the occasional rustling of the wind through the branches and the crunch of his own footsteps over icy twigs.

Just as his self-doubt overcame his resolve and he cursed himself in earnest for having ever strayed from the point where Shrike bid him stay, he glanced up to find the trees thinning ahead.

A change of scenery, for once, had the very effect most quacks declared it would, in that it instantly upraised Wren's hopes that he might not be quite so lost after all.

Continuing on through the thinning trees brought Wren to the lake-shore. No sign of the faun or any other of the hunt appeared to his mortal eyes. But if nothing else, on shore he could at least see and be seen. And, being an awkward mortal, he'd left a readily apparent trail behind himself through the woods as he went. And furthermore, unlike the ethereal white hart, he had a scent. If worse came to worst, Shrike could seek the aid of the wolf pack in tracking Wren down.

Still, the wind bit far more fiercely without the cover of the trees and the comfort of his cloak. Wren drew his scarf up over the nape of his neck until it almost touched the back-brim of his hat and tucked his gloved hands into the elbows of his overcoat. Nevertheless, he shivered. Perhaps, he thought, he ought to return to the wood—just a few steps in, mind—to shelter himself whilst keeping an eye on his surroundings.

Then something glimmered in the corner of his eye.

Wren whipped his head toward the spark. Squinting against the wind and the sun glinting off the snow, he beheld a pale form out on the lake. Long slender legs ending in delicate hooves pawed at the snow, and a regal head with its crown of silvery antlers bent to drink from a dark hole in the ice.

Wren had never seen an ethereal creature in all his life. Yet in an instant, he recognized this for what it was.

The white hart.

Wren knew not how he'd stumbled upon such luck. He stood down-wind, as Shrike had told him he ought to do if he wished to catch anything. And it seemed as though the trick worked. The hart took no notice of him.

He had an urge—a very mortal urge, he supposed—to approach the wondrous creature. Not to hunt or harm it; he hardly had the skill for that, though upon reflection, he thought his steel pen-knife might more than suffice when hunting a creature of fae origin. But rather in this moment he wished to see it better and fix the image in his mind. Already he cursed himself for leaving his sketch-book at home. A memory would have to suffice if he wanted to immortalise it in his art.

Wren took a cautious step toward the lake-shore.

The hart continued to drink.

A few more sideways skulking steps brought Wren down to the lake's edge. He dared to slide his boot-heel onto the ice. It held his weight. Indeed, it felt as solid as any dance-floor at a country ball. He slipped another stride out. Then another. And another. The ice withstood his weight.

All the while, the hart ignored him.

Wren held his breath as he drew within a few yards of the beast. Almost without thinking, he raised a trembling hand toward it.

The hart's head darted up. It moved as fluidly as water tossed on the wind. For an instant, their gazes met, Wren's dark eyes flown wide in astonishment and the hart's glowing with an inner liquid light.

Later, when he had a moment to reflect on the incident, Wren would realise his error. He, a mortal man, weighed some ten or eleven stone. The white hart, being ethereal, weighed nothing unless it chose to.

And in that instant, it chose for its hooves to prove as hard as adamant as it struck the ice and bounded away.

A sound like a thunderclap resounded across the lake. The crack shot across the ice from the point the hart had struck, spreading from the drinking hole and shooting between Wren's boots. He had just time to perceive it before another noise burst the air, this one like lightning cleaving an ancient oak in twain, as the ice shattered beneath him.

Wren plunged into darkness.

Cold like a thousand knives raking his skin. Cold fit to turn his very veins to ice. Cold that burned in his bones in a way he'd never realised cold could do before. He wanted to shut his eyes against it. He couldn't.

And a very good thing that turned out to be, for he was not alone.

Shafts of sunlight pierced the water from the jagged hole in the ice overhead. By their illumination, Wren glimpsed a shadowy thing. It glided through the water beneath him; he knew not how many fathoms down, but not far enough. Its smooth undulating form, dappled like a leopard in shades of grey, ran some three yards long, if not longer, from head to tail. It had a maw like a hound on a skull the size of a horse's—as long as Wren's thigh and as broad as his shoulders. The eyes were pure black, almost human in their shape, but nothing human in the promise of cold death behind them. And as it rolled through the water, it fixed its hungry gaze on Wren.

The sight forced the breath from his lungs in an incoherent yell. He gulped freezing water in its wake. Now he had ice within him as well as without. His heart ceased to beat.

Yet he must escape.

The thought consumed him. He forced his frozen legs, weighed down with wet wool, to kick. His trembling arms clawed through the water as he sought in desperation for the shafts of sunlight still beaming down from the hole he'd fallen through. It felt as though he crawled through molten lead. The cold burned him inside and out with every thrash of his limbs.

But it drew it him nearer to the surface nonetheless.

At last, just when it seemed sheer exhaustion would drag him down to the dark depths forevermore, his flailing fingertips breached the biting wind above. Instinct forced him to recoil from the sensation, dry cold feeding on wet cold to shatter his nails, but survival demanded he try again, and this time, his hand closed on the jagged rim of the hole in the ice.

He ought to have hauled himself up all at once. As matter stood, he could only do so by degrees. His limbs convulsed with the cold, jerking him to and fro, whilst he struggled upward. He got his face above the water, spilling out what had filled his lungs, gulping down freezing air that scraped his throat on the way down and again as he coughed, droplets of ice still stuck inside him. He threw both arms across the ice. The soaked sleeves of his coat stuck fast and held him up even as his strength failed and he could draw himself out no further. He knew he had no hope of saving himself. Yet, with water still sputtering up from his throat and the biting wind burning in its wake, he couldn't even whisper, much less shout for aid. If he could but catch his breath... if he could regain his strength... if he were to close his eyes, just for a moment, to restore himself...

"No—Butcher, you daft bastard! You're too heavy, you'll fall straight through!"

The shout jolted Wren out of his waking dream. A voice he recognised. A woman's voice. He turned his head despite his stiffened joints and squinted against the sunlight reflecting off the snow to see who had spoken.

Several shadows clustered at the shoreline. One figure in particular strained against others clinging to their arms and legs to hold them back. This, Wren knew, even with the ice-water freezing his lashes together, was Shrike.

Another shadow slithered towards him across the ice. A figure crawling on their belly, smaller and more slender than Shrike, moving far faster than Wren himself could have done. Only when they drew within arm's reach and thrust out an unstrung longbow towards him did he recognize Nell.

"Oi, Lofthouse—catch hold!"

Wren forced his frozen fingers to unclench and try their grip against the bow. With an effort, he peeled his sodden garments off the ice. They stuck again elsewhere, but by then Nell had begun reeling him in. His shoulders emerged from the waters. The wind nipped the nape of his newly-exposed neck. He kicked his legs to try and propel himself further out.

Then it struck.

Dozens of dagger teeth pierced him through all along his right-hand side. The crushing bite forced a scream from him. He whipped his head 'round to see what had caught him—as if he didn't already know.

The cold, dead eyes stared back at him above the wolfish muzzle.

Wren, half-frozen and bleeding out, had no power to save himself.

Then a blade plunged into one of the eyes.

The creature released him with a shriek fit to shatter glass. It veered off, taking the blade with it. Hands seized Wren under his arms.

"Come on, Lofthouse—up, up, up…!"

Wren scrambled to get his legs under him as Nell lifted. The jagged ice scraped against his wound as his waist emerged, then his hips, then his knees. Nell drew him into an embrace, twining her arms through his and linking her hands behind his back. From someone else, in a different sort of moment, it might have felt tender.

"I've got him!" Nell barked over her shoulder. "Reel us in, now!"

With a jerk, they began to slide together across the ice. What sort of magic drew them along, he knew not. It worked in pulses; a slide of some few yards, then a rest, then another slide. Wren's sodden and swiftly-freezing clothes stuck to the ice with every halting, only to be torn free in the successive tug. Every jerk of the line sent fresh stabs of agony down his right-hand side. He took advantage of the pauses to raise his head, despite exhaustion dragging him down, and try to glimpse his Shrike.

A light appeared on the shore. Something flickering bright just where the trees began. A light-house, Wren thought at first, then realised what a stupid thought that was and how far his mind had wandered between cold and pain. It was firelight, though, that much he knew. He could not yet feel its warmth, though he dearly wished to.

He beheld, likewise, a thread linking Nell and himself with the cluster of figures on shore. Nothing of magic, but a common rope, which he now perceived tied around Nell's waist. Following the line brought his eyes to his beloved. What a dashing figure he cut, Wren thought in his foggy mind—with the firelight behind him, strands of silver-shot ink whipping in the wind, and his strong arms hard at work hauling in the rope. Those who had held Shrike back now bent along-side him to reel Nell and Wren in. Amongst them Wren recognized the ambassador, a rather familiar-looking wolf who dragged the rope with its teeth, and the faun still wearing his cloak. Yet ever and again Wren's gaze returned to his Shrike, his own northern star guiding him back home.

Then the rhythm of the line changed. No more fits and bursts but a steady and rapid slide. Wren's final glance showed Shrike hauling hand-over-hand, his breath escaping his clenched teeth in plumes of dragon-smoke. Just a few yards remained between them. Even this felt insur-mountable to Wren until the ice turned to rock beneath him and Nell tore her arms free from his frozen garments and, at long last, his Shrike descended like a thunderhead, his cloak billowing around them both as he swept over Wren and drew him up into his embrace.

On all prior occasions, Shrike's embrace had sparked a kindling warmth spreading from Wren's heart to the whole of him. But the icy plunge refused to leave Wren's bones, and all he knew of Shrike's embrace was his strong grip and his woodsmoke musk.

Shrike carried Wren as if he weighed no more than a leaf. He did not bear him far; a few strides into the wood toward the flickering light, now a crackling fire. There he laid him down with his familiar fur-lined cloak beneath him.

The fire had grown larger and brighter than Wren would've thought possible in the time it'd taken Nell to drag him to shore—though, he supposed, he had no real idea how long it'd been. Less smoke, too, than he'd assumed the snowy evergreen branches would've produced if cut fresh from the living trees. No sooner had he thought this, however, than a sharp crack caught his ear, and he glanced toward it to find the nymph in her gauzy chiton breaking a dead branch off a nearby pine. As he watched, she reached up again into the green and wrapped her fingers around another living branch. It withered in her grasp, the needles fading from blue-green to green-yellow and finally the burnt orange of desiccation. With another crack, she broke it off, and threw both branches into the hungry flames.

The fire's warmth seeped through the frozen wool of Wren's outer garments to barely touch his flesh. Rather than bring comfort, it reawakened his nerves to burn and set him shivering.

Then Shrike's hands fell to the buttons of Wren's overcoat.

Wren's jaw had clenched too tight to allow him to voice any protestations against the loss of his clothes. The cold felt bad enough with them on. Furthermore, in the increasingly wandering pathways of his mind, a sense of shame bubbled up. Nevermind how many fae had already beheld his naked body at Midsummer and Mabon both. All that left his throat, however, was a pitiful whine.

"Steady," Shrike murmured to him—gentle, sympathetic, and swift. So too were his hands as he stripped off the sodden wool and soaked cotton. In some places they stuck stiff together despite the fire's warmth; then Shrike took out his hunting knife, slicing through seams and cutting off buttons to cleave the overcoat, jacket, waistcoat and trousers from Wren's shivering body. The glint of firelight off the knife's keen edge put Wren in mind of his own pen-knife slicing through the snare entrapping the faun, though he found he had far more trust in Shrike than the faun had felt for him.

When Shrike came down to shirt and small-clothes, however, he halted. His eyes widened as they fell to Wren's waist. His jaw clenched.

Wren, trembling like a leaf in a storm, couldn't command his head to tilt down to try and see what Shrike saw. But the more Shrike peeled away his clothes, the stronger grew the burn of his wound. It felt as if the monster's maw bit him afresh with every breath. Trickling threads of something cold spilled over his side as a half-circle of knives stabbed again and again into his gut, searing as they withdrew. He'd never suffered anything like it in all his days. He hardly knew if he shuddered with pain or cold. Both, probably.

A hard swallow travelled down Shrike's throat. Then, to Wren's bewilderment, he set aside his knife and turned his clever hands to his own clothes. He cast aside his tunic and hose. His shirt pulled off over his head to reveal the body Wren loved so well, the myriad scars telling tales of valour. Yet rather than throw it down to join the rest of his wardrobe, Shrike kept his shirt in hand and took up his knife again. Swift strokes slashed the linen into strips.

Then the blade descended to slice the buttons off Wren's own shirt-front and split open his under-shirt from stem to stern. Wren still couldn't see what Shrike beheld beneath it all. He could see only Shrike's own face and the haunted look in his dark eyes as his jaw clenched and unclenched. Yet he worked quick to wrap the strips of his own shirt around Wren's waist. The cold ought to have numbed the wound, Wren thought. Instead, it burned, throbbing with new agony as Shrike pulled the makeshift bandage tight. A whimper escaped Wren's throat. Murmured apologies fell from Shrike's lips in reply.

The wind felt like a cat o' nine tails scoring Wren's bare skin. But not for long. No sooner did Wren lie bare than Shrike bundled him in his fur-lined cloak. The familiar sensation of the warm rabbit-fur paired with the scent of vanilla and woodsmoke reminded Wren of what he'd lost. He tried to explain and apologise for his own missing cloak, but his locked jaw would only unclench to chatter, and no words could escape him.

Shrike, in his own nakedness, slipped into the furred folds beside him and wrapped himself around Wren's smaller frame. His long legs twined through Wren's. His scarred chest pressed flush against Wren's shuddering ribcage, careful to avoid the fresh wound. His strong arms encircled Wren's narrow shoulders and held him fast. The warmth of him burned as bright as the bonfire. It seemed to flow from his heart into Wren's own veins. Wren wanted to hold him in turn, to wrap his own arms around those broad shoulders, but his joints had gone stiff and would move only in fitful jerks of their own accord. The familiar rise and fall of Shrike's breath filled his ears, with the fire crackling behind them.

"How did you find me?" Wren asked. He had to wrench his jaw open to do it, and his voice left him in the merest creaking whisper, yet Shrike's keen ears perceived all.

"You heard it yourself," Shrike murmured, his warm hand tenderly stroking Wren's frozen brow. "The cracking ice. It resounded for miles."

"Herne will be glad of it," Nell said, tossing another branch onto the fire. "You found the quarry. Another successful hunt, thanks to the Holly King."

"Nell," Shrike said in a foreboding tone.

Nell glanced to him, then Wren, then Shrike again, before dropping her gaze to the flames and saying nothing further.

* * *

SHRIKE WANTED MURDER.

Bad enough for his Wren to have fallen beneath the Eternal Ice. But to see him wounded set Shrike's mind aflame. Wave after wave of fear chased by rage consumed him. He'd not felt its like since he'd beheld Larkin's corpse crumpled in the midst of their cottage's burning ruin. Wretched recollections of Rochester—when Tolhurst had dared lay a hand on his beloved—renewed themselves in Shrike's mind as he gazed on Wren, once again the victim of unjust violence.

Flesh which had been marked only by the gentle dusting of beloved freckles now tore open in the ragged gashes of a monstrous bite. The blood had frozen into crystals like garnets along the edges of the wound. His nail-beds and lips alike had turned blue with cold. The icy pall of his face proved a sharp contrast against the memory of the endearing rosy hue that had bloomed not even an hour ago when the nymph had congratulated them on their successful midwinter rite. The lips disturbed Shrike most, having faded from a speckled peach to corpse-like translucence. He wished he could kiss life back into them. Yet his efforts to breath his own warmth into Wren's mouth seemed to make no difference.

Whatever fell creature had done this would rue ever drawing breath when Shrike had done with them.

Yet it had slipped away beneath the ice, and even his own towering rage couldn't force him to abandon his Wren in pursuit of vengeance.

Wren had protested the stripping of his garments, however feebly, which Shrike took as a good sign. It meant the madness had not yet seeped in to replace his lost warmth. As Shrike curled around him in the cocoon of their cloaks, Wren began at last to shiver—another good sign, for it meant his body hadn't yet given itself up to a grave of ice and would fight back to cling to heat.

They didn't fight alone. Nell, the ambassador, and the nymph all fed the bonfire's flames, keeping it fierce and bright. The faun who wore Wren's cloak—and how the sight of it on a stranger's shoulders had startled Shrike—had vanished into the wood soon after returning it to Shrike's care. The wolf, meanwhile, curled up at Shrike and Wren's feet, and leant its furred warmth to their limbs.

Yet still Wren felt frozen in Shrike's arms.

"What good is the power of the Holly King if it doesn't protect him from cold?" Shrike muttered.

"The power of the Holly King is probably the only reason he's survived this long," Nell replied. "Any other mortal would have frozen to death before we could fish him out."

Shrike gave some small thanks for that. Still, something dreadful had occurred before they could rescue Wren from beneath the ice. From the look of the bite—a sight which he knew would haunt him forevermore—he had some idea what had done the foul deed. He looked to Nell again. "Kópr?"

Nell confirmed it with a brisk nod. "Mottled skull-crusher. You'll know it if you see it again. It took my dagger in its left eye."

Shrike already owed her more than he could ever repay for dragging

Wren back from the depths. His infinite debt increased twice-over for this blow she'd struck his heart's hunter.

Glass clinked against glass as the ambassador searched within his satchel. A mumbled minced oath came from beneath his mask. Then a victorious gasp escaped him, and he withdrew something particular. He pressed a vial into Shrike's hand. It held a faintly lavender concoction with a viscosity appearing half-honey and half-vapour.

"A draught of suspended sleep," the ambassador explained. "It will keep him alive whilst we await assistance."

"For how long?" Shrike demanded.

"Until the spell is broken."

Shrike's patience wore even thinner than before. "And the spell is broken by…?"

"A kiss," the ambassador replied, nothing daunted. "Traditionally."

Something Shrike would have gladly bestowed upon Wren under any circumstance. Still, "And it's safe for mortals? Not just fae?"

"Perfectly safe!" the ambassador assured him.

Shrike wished he could believe him even half as wholeheartedly. The ambassador had never meant them any harm before, though Shrike knew well the harm that could be done with good intent.

But if he did not accept the potion, he likewise knew, though he did not dare to think, that Wren had no chance of surviving on his own. The cold would have slain any mortal. The wound made matters still more dire. He hadn't the means to halt the flow of blood from the bite, and—

Shrike uncorked the vial. He steeled his nerve and brought the draught to Wren's bespeckled lips.

"Drink," he murmured.

Wren opened his mouth without question. Without even opening his eyes. His trust in Shrike proved absolute, beyond anything Shrike could have asked or expected. The knowledge broke Shrike's heart. As if it weren't already shattered by Wren's suffering.

Shrike tilted the vial. Its contents travelled down Wren's throat in a single swallow. His breath slowed the moment Shrike withdrew the empty vial from his perfect lips. Soon it seemed as though he didn't breathe at all. Yet Shrike could still feel his heartbeat beneath his palm clasped against his chest, steadier and far slower than before. He'd seen Wren sleeping many a time since they'd met. Yet never had he seemed so still and quiet and peaceful as this. In another moment, Shrike would have kissed him simply to reward his beauty and celebrate their bond. In this moment, however, he resisted the urge he'd so oft indulged afore. He satisfied himself instead by burying his face in Wren's collar and holding him tight.

The sun had passed it zenith when the faint ringing of sleigh-bells echoed through the trees.

Shrike raised his head—he hadn't even realised he'd fallen asleep, much less knew how long he'd lain so. Wren remained in his suspended trance, as the ambassador had promised. The wolf lay curled at their feet. The ambassador, the nymph, and Nell still sat by the fire. Judging by the pile of kindling beside it, they'd spent many of the hours withering and hacking more wood to feed the flames. Whatever quiet conversation may have passed between them ended as both looked toward the sound.

No hoof-beats accompanied the bells. Only the curious swishing sound, like low-hanging branches dragging across snow-drifts, grew louder and louder as the sleigh approached. It came into view at last, emerging from the tree-line to curve along the lake-shore, its silver-blue blades gleaming like icicles, pulled by long-furred felines the size of sheep padding across the snow on their nearly-silent paws, driven by a pair of huldra.

Shrike had heard tales of the wildcats who drew the sleigh for the Mistress of Revels but had never glimpsed them before today. He wished Wren were awake to see it. What a marvel it would seem from his mortal perspective.

The sleigh slid to a stop some yards from the bonfire. The blonde huldra remained at the reins. Her companion, who appeared her twin save for the sable hue of her hair, leapt down and approached the motley group huddled 'round the flames.

"The Mistress of Revels regrets very much the misfortune that has befallen the Holly King," the sable huldra declared. "She hopes the Oak King will accept our aid in bearing him hence."

Nell, the nymph, and the ambassador all turned to Shrike.

Shrike assented with a nod. He sat up, taking care none of his movements unbundled Wren from the furred cloaks. His clothes, however, did not lie where he left them. A glance 'round the bonfire showed them hung up on branches over the flames beside Wren's own garments, the latter having gone from frozen to soaked and now on their way to dry. Shrike supposed the ambassador had hung them up; Nell wasn't a laundress, and the nymph didn't seem the sort, either. Wren had oft told Shrike he smelled of woodsmoke and how he admired that particular aspect of his masculine musk. Now, with their clothes roasted over an open pine flame, they'd both smell very smoky indeed. Wren might find that amusing if he were awake, Shrike thought, and then regretted thinking it for the pang it gave him afterward. He donned his shirt, tunic, and hose with a quickness. The ambassador, meanwhile, plucked Wren's raiments from the branches and folded them up neat.

Wren remained asleep all the while, bundled in Shrike's and his own cloak. Shrike would have fain carried him alone. Still, he felt glad for the aid of the ambassador and Nell, who took up their posts on either side of Wren's legs as Shrike lifted him beneath the shoulders. Together they all conveyed Wren to the sleigh. Shrike sat on the bench with bundled Wren laid out over his lap. The wolf curled up at their feet. The nymph had wandered off into the wood amidst the confusion, but Nell and the ambassador remained, clinging to the back of the sleigh balanced on its runners. Shrike turned to the huldra who had resumed their places at the reins.

"You have our thanks," said Shrike.

"And you have ours," the sable huldra replied. At Shrike's bewildered look, she continued, "Our Court has a vested interest in the continued good health of winter."

The blonde huldra picked up the reins and shot an enquiring glance at Shrike.

"To Blackthorn Briar," said Shrike. "An' it so please you."

With a sharp nod and a flick of her wrists, she set the sleigh in motion. Silver bells rang out through the wood as they went. Pines flew past in a blur of green.

Shrike hardly noticed them. His gaze dropped to Wren in his arms. Only his face remained visible, asleep and serene yet pale as ice. A spike of desperation pierced Shrike's heart. His hand delved beneath the furred folds, seeking, until it found Wren's cold fingertips and clasped them close.

And, though the whipping wind tore the sound from his lips ere he spoke it, he whispered, "Hold on."

BLACKTHORN BRIAR HADN'T SEEN SO many souls all together since the Summer Solstice. This gathering proved far less festive. Nell, the ambassador, the wolf, and the faun had all accompanied Shrike and Wren not just to Blackthorn but into the very cottage. Shrike felt more gratitude than he could express at their willingness to abandon the hunt for the white hart. He wished he could show them better hospitality. Yet he couldn't tear his gaze from Wren, much less offer food or drink or good company.

Nell, as she so oft did, made herself quite at home—this time much to Shrike's relief. She took the copper kettle down from where it hung in the rafters amidst dried lavender and other herbs, filled it with water from the hollow stump, and hung it over the fire Shrike had stoked to a blaze in a feeble attempt to bring warmth back to his beloved's body. Shrike didn't take much notice of her doings until she pressed a steaming mug of tea into his hand some moments later—he knew not how long, for he'd not taken his eyes off Wren all the while. Now, glancing 'round, he found her handing off another stoneware mug to the faun and setting the third on the night-stand beside Wren's sleeping head. Likewise she set out a clay bowl for the wolf. For herself, she had her tin cup from her hunting pack, and the ambassador produced a delicate porcelain cup of his own from his clanking satchel. The matter of tea seemed settled without Shrike's interference, and so he returned his focus to his Wren.

Shrike felt well-accustomed to performing chirurgy on himself. The myriad scars that bedecked his body attested to that. He'd even done it for Nell now and again in the midst of particularly bloody hunts.

Now, however, as he gazed down on the frail form of his beloved, half-curled in their bed, with shivers still passing over his skin despite the quilt and furs tucked around him and the fire roaring in the hearth of Blackthorn's cottage, Shrike knew not where to begin.

Mortals were far more delicate than fae. While, unlike fae, their flesh could withstand things their spirit could not, so too could their spirit withstand far more than their flesh might bear, and so they oft slipped away from wounds which fae could endure for years.

And as he gazed on Wren's sleeping face, his heart stayed his hand.

"Is there anything more the Court of Hidden Folk may do?"

Shrike flinched at the faun's voice, low and soft though it sounded. He turned to find them looking as startled as himself at his reaction. He supposed, now that he beheld them perching their hip against the rim of the hollow stump, that they couldn't stay long; the Mistress of Revels needed her sleigh and steeds returned.

Still, before they left, Shrike had one request. "Does any member of your court have the skill in chirurgy to save a mortal life?"

The faun worried their lower lip between their teeth. "I don't know. But I may enquire. If there is one who can, we shall send them here."

Shrike nodded. The faun bowed and departed the cottage.

"More tea, my lord?"

Shrike snapped his head 'round to regard the ambassador. The ambassador, however, was not looking at him but rather delving into his clinking satchel.

"It would do some good, I think," the ambassador continued. "Particularly if we were to add a dash or so of this."

From his satchel he produced a round bottle about the size of a crab-apple. The pale pink liquid within swirled with a streak of darker pomegranate shade.

Shrike stared at the ambassador, then the bottle, then the ambassador again.

"A tincture of heart's-ease," the ambassador explained. "For—well, the obvious purpose, I suppose. Unless you would prefer something stronger," he hastily added in response to Shrike's increasingly incredulous stare. "There's an elixir of poppy essence and distilled—"

Shrike had no intention of taking anything. He had no need of physick for his own body. Wren needed all. Yet, rather than any of this, what fell out of Shrike's mouth when he forced it open at last, in words so dull they almost defied enquiry, was, "How is it you are so bedecked with potions?"

The ambassador blinked. "My brother is an apothecary and alchemist of some renown."

"In the Court of Spindles?" Shrike couldn't keep from wondering aloud, his astonishment proving too great to restrain. Strange enough that a noble bloodline in that realm would suffer a single son to live, let alone two.

The ambassador's cat-slit eyes flew wide behind his mask. For the first time in all their brief acquaintance, Shrike heard something approaching fear in his voice as he replied, "No, no—well, he was, yes, but he escaped it some years hence. I followed in his footsteps. He dwells in Fathomseek now."

From whence the mortal half of Nell's family hailed. Disparate threads Shrike had observed throughout the years began to weave together before his mind's eye. "And there he tends mortals as well as fae?"

"Indeed," the ambassador said, sounding relieved to have moved on from the subject of his own ancestral realm.

"Would he tend...?" Shrike's voice faded as his eyes fell again to Wren's pale sleeping face. The bespeckled lips had not yet regained their rosy hue. He cleared his throat and tore his gaze away to see how the ambassador might answer.

The ambassador hesitated, leaving all Shrike's hopes upon tenterhooks. Then a resolve came into his masked gaze to match the tightening of his jaw. "He does not oft venture out of Fathomseek—or out of his laboratory, for that matter—but I will endeavour to persuade him to make an exception."

"Do," said Shrike.

The ambassador bowed deeply. Not just to Shrike but turning to do the same to Wren's sleeping form afterward. Then he tipped his tricorn hat to Nell—who gave him a bare nod in reply—and departed the cottage.

In his wake, Nell met Shrike's gaze.

"I think," she said, "you need me here."

Shrike heartily agreed, though even if he were the sort to unburden himself in speech, the pain in his throat would hardly allow him to say so.

Thankfully, Nell didn't need him to.

Nell didn't require much from anyone—or so Shrike had observed of her throughout the years. It served him well now, as she made her own supper from his stores and kindly shared it with him and the wolf, and hung her hunting hammock from the rafters of his cottage to sleep in. The wolf, once it had finished eating, curled up before the fire. Shrike himself slipped into the nest beside his Wren, gently enfolding his small frame within his own long one and willing his warmth to seep through their skin into the cold bones of his beloved.

The night stretched dark and cold and long. Shrike didn't find much sleep in it. He hardly dared to close his eyes, their gaze fixed on the slow and subtle rise and fall of Wren's chest and the barest parting of bespeckled lips which had not yet regained their rosy hue. Whilst Shrike could not kiss him, lest he break the spell, he could run his fingers through his chestnut locks, stroke his cheeks which had grown pale beneath their freckles, and chafe his hands between his own to try and bring some warmth back to the blue nail-beds. Then he laid his head beside Wren's on the pillow and murmured low into his ear. He wasn't one for chattering or long speeches. Yet he couldn't bear the thought of Wren dreaming himself alone. And so he talked himself hoarse until dawn.

* * *

EVERYONE else in Blackthorn arose with the sun. Nell made herself breakfast and shared it with Shrike and the wolf. Then, with the wolf at her side, she went out to tend the flocks. Shrike remained in the cottage. Nothing, he thought, could persuade him from Wren's side.

Then a knocking came upon the cottage door.

The noise startled Shrike out of his sombre meditative state. He whipped his head towards the door, then just as quickly back at Wren. Wren had stirred not a whit. No sound, it seemed, could wake him from his induced slumber.

With many a wary glance back at his sleeping beloved, Shrike crept toward the door. He reminded himself, as he hesitated with his hand on the latch, that none could pass through the wall of briars if they meant him or Wren harm. He drew a steadying breath and opened the door.

A page stood before him, clad in the green-gold livery of the Court of Bells and Candles. They bowed. Shrike nodded his head in return.

"Our Lady Aethelthryth slew the white hart," the page began.

"My heart leaps for her," Shrike replied dully.

The page either didn't perceive Shrike's sarcasm or chose not to acknowledge it. "She recognises the Holly King's role in her victory and is grieved to hear of his peril. Would the Court of Oak and Holly accept her aid?"

"Has she a chirurgeon experienced in saving mortal lives?" Shrike growled.

"Yes," replied the page.

Shrike blinked. "Oh."

"Shall we send them?" asked the page, nothing daunted.

"Aye," said Shrike. Then, because he knew he should, though he hardly felt it, he added, "Thank you."

The page bowed and withdrew.

Shrike shut the door. His arm remained braced against the doorframe afterward. He let his brow fall to it with a heavy sigh. How long he stayed there, he knew not. Crackling logs tumbled against each other as they collapsed in the hearth-flames behind him.

"There's a spot of luck," said Nell.

Shrike, who'd half-forgotten she was there, whirled at the sound of her voice.

"Her bone-setters break curses," she continued in response to his bewildered glance. "Surely they can handle a bite."

While little brightness could penetrate the fog of gloom that hung over Shrike's mind, he had to admit her words sparked a spot of hope. He knew well the legend of Lady Aethelthryth. How her wicked sister had coveted her throne and conspired to slay her with a curse, and how she had nearly succumbed, save for the fortuitous aid of the summoned chirurgeon, who had dwelled in the Court of Bells and Candles ever since. Lady Aethelthryth would never walk again, true enough, but she yet thrived, which was more than could be said for those who'd cursed her.

Still, Shrike's sober good sense demanded he reply, "If she will spare us a chirurgeon at all."

Nell raised an eyebrow. "She'd better. For her sake."

* * *

SHRIKE DIDN'T EXPECT to hear back from the Court of Bells and Candles before the se'en-night was out.

Which made the knock at the door the very next morning all the more confounding.

Nell, still in the midst of breaking down her hammock, shot a raised eyebrow at Shrike. The wolf likewise leapt to its feet and looked to him.

Shrike left off stroking Wren's hair and went to answer the door.

And before him stood a mortal.

She stood shorter than he or Nell, though not so short as Wren. Her hair likewise surpassed his chestnut locks to burst into the true colour of flame, though she cropped it just as close, if not closer. Her clothes appeared plainer; a hooded robe covered all but her head and hands in rough brown wool. One hand rested on the leather satchel she'd slung over her shoulder. The other braced against the thick neck-ruff of the pack-stag who followed a half-step behind her, laden with two leather cases balanced on either side with straps across its back.

"The Oak King, I presume?" she said, after the silence had stretched for a long moment.

"Aye." Shrike's voice creaked with disuse.

"My Lady Aethelthryth has sent me to tend the Holly King," the mortal continued.

Shrike blinked. "You are her chirurgeon?"

"Aye," she replied with more patience than Shrike thought his due. "And bone-setter besides. You may call me Everilda."

Shrike bowed and set about unpacking her steed.

Released of its burden, the stag looked to Everilda. At her nod it wandered off towards the back of the cottage where Shrike could just glimpse its joining the goat herd in gnawing at the briars surrounding Blackthorn. The goats didn't seem to mind their strange companion.

Shrike led the way into the cottage with a leather case under either arm—one considerably heavier than the other. Everilda took in the singular round room in a sweeping glance which came to rest on Wren. Nell, Shrike couldn't help noticing even in his distracted state, never took her eyes off Everilda. The wolf slipped out the door into the garden.

Everilda approached the nest. Shrike followed and, at her indication, set down her leather cases beside her. From the heavy one she took out a gyrdel-book. From the other she withdrew a gilded heart's-vine and glass fever-wand—tools Shrike had seen used on other wounded fae after tournaments or hunts, yet never had the privilege of himself. She slipped the fever-wand between Wren's lips. The brass bell of the heart's-vine she pressed against Wren's ribs, then lowered to the rude bandage wrapped 'round his waist. She listened intently through the prong in her ear all the while. Nothing her instruments told her seemed to surprise her. At length she turned to Shrike.

"What tonic has he taken?" Everilda asked.

"A draught of suspended sleep." Shrike strode to where his cloak hung on the wall-hook beside Wren's and dove into its pocket to retrieve the empty vial.

Everilda accepted the vial from him. She uncorked it and sniffed the residue, then nodded, much to his relief.

"It'll keep him peaceful through the chirurgy," she assured him. "Where shall we lay him out?"

Shrike glanced between her and Wren already lying peaceful in the nest.

"A hard surface would serve better," she added in answer to his unspoken question. "Something to brace against while I work. Easier to clean before and after." Her gaze flitted over the room and landed on Shrike's work-bench. "Would you object to the use of...?"

Shrike strode to the work-bench and cleared it off in three sweeping armfuls.

Everilda raised her brows. "That'll do nicely. Have you a cauldron?"

Shrike leapt to fetch it. At her bidding he filled it with scalding water from the hollow stump and hung it over the fire to grow still hotter. When it boiled, he tossed it over the work-bench. Steam hissed up from the cleansed wood.

Everilda glanced at Nell. "Can you carry him between the two of you?"

Shrike felt as if he could carry Wren on a journey through all the realms and fight off any foe who dared to cross their path. He did, however, bear a great appreciation for Nell's assistance in gently lifting Wren from their nest and conveying him to the work-bench.

As they laid him down, Shrike kept his hand against the back of Wren's head to shield it from the unyielding boards. Laid out on the bare wood, he appeared still more frail than he had when swathed in quilt and fur. At the chirurgeon's bidding, they set him on his left side, for the wound ran down his right flank. Shrike withdrew his palm from beneath Wren's skull, and the sight of him lolling across the oak in the wake, even for but a moment, plunged a knife into Shrike's ribs and sent him scrambling for something, anything, to support his helpless frame. Wren's own scarf hung on the wall hook. Shrike snatched it up and rolled it into a pillow to slip beneath Wren's head. Perhaps he imagined it, but he thought a slight sigh of relief escaped Wren's barely-moving chest.

Everilda, meanwhile, had set her kit down on the stool and opened it to reveal a set of gleaming silver tools. Then she went to wash her hands and arms up past her elbows in the scalding spray of the hollow stump. At a significant glance from her, Nell did likewise, and shot the same glance back at Shrike. With some reluctance, Shrike followed their lead. It took him but two strides from Wren's sleeping form. Those two strides felt like a thousand leagues. The warmth of the water he hardly felt at all. He hastened to return to his post by Wren's head.

With clean hands the chirurgeon took up her silver shears and began to cut through the makeshift bandages. Very little blood had seeped through, leaving the merest pinpricks of scarlet on the outermost layer. To see the wound again—the raw and ragged edge torn by serrated teeth—shot Shrike's heart into his throat. Yet the frozen garnets of blood remained to seal it shut. Whether an aspect of the Holly King's power or the remnants of a curse from the Lake of Eternal Ice, Shrike couldn't say. Still, he gave thanks Wren had not bled out.

"He's no worse off than William Wyncelowe," Everilda declared.

Shrike shot her an alarmed glance. But, whilst her words had baffled him, to her they seemed to suggest that Wren stood a far better chance than Shrike had hoped for. Or so he judged by her serene face and the soft surety of her voice.

Her soft and serene surety continued as she murmured a brief spell. Shrike could not perceive its immediate effect, though he trusted it did what she wished it to do.

Then she reached forth and gently touched the frozen garnets. They melted at her fingertips.

Blood began to flow down Wren's side.

Shrike had beheld bleeding wounds before. He'd caused most of them. Scores upon hundreds upon thousands throughout his centuries.

But to see Wren bleed staggered him.

Shrike swallowed hard and dropped his gaze to Wren's face. Though his lips retained their bluish tint beneath the freckles Shrike loved so well, and a dark bruise had crept beneath his eyes, his visage still held the same serenity Shrike had seen laid beside him every night since the summer solstice. To this Shrike clung, and upon it he pinned all his hopes, closing his ears against the clink of silver instruments and the shuddering wet sounds of the chirurgeon's work and turning them instead toward the faint whisper of Wren's slow and steady sleeping breaths.

"Vinegar," said Everilda.

Shrike glanced up. Nell handed the vinegar jug to Everilda, who uncorked it and poured it over Wren's side. Shrike's eyes followed the movements before his mind could catch them up and force them away. He glimpsed Wren's wound again—stitched up with silver threads and smeared with gore, the streams of vinegar just barely beginning to wash it away—then forced his eyes away, down to Wren's face, where Shrike kept his head cradled in his hands as if they could shield him from all this.

"Linen," said Everilda.

This time Shrike knew better than to look up. In idleness he stroked Wren's chestnut locks, tying and untying knots in his fingers' wake. There, at least, the frost had long-since melted, freeing the soft strands from icicles like blades.

Only when Everilda withdrew from the work-bench to wash her hands and instruments in the hollow stump did Shrike dare lift his gaze again.

Vinegar had washed the blood from Wren's body. Its pungent scent yet hung in the air. Pale linen bandages sewn together tight around him, the edges of their wrapping clean and crisp, hid all his wound from sight. They shifted ever-so-slightly with each of his slow breaths.

"We may put him back to bed now," Everilda announced, startling Shrike out of his reverie.

Shrike caught him up under his shoulders. Nell took command of his legs. Together they returned him to the nest. His head lolled against the pillow toward Shrike. A slight sigh escaped him, though his eyes remained closed.

"When shall I wake him?" Shrike asked, forcing himself to temper his hopes.

"In an hour or two," Everilda replied.

Shrike's heart soared to hear it.

"We've work to do in the meantime," she continued. "The beast's teeth have punctured his entrails."

Shrike's own entrails twisted at her words.

"He'll need plenty of tea and broth to sustain him," Everilda went on, heedless of Shrike's inner turmoil. "Best start brewing now."

Shrike leapt to do as she bid. Lavender and chamomile pulled down from the bundles hanging in the rafters alongside the copper kettle. The taps in the hollow stump filled kettle and cauldron alike with hot water which grew hotter as Shrike hung both over the hearth and stoked the flames. Nell went out to the garden for eggs and goat's milk. She returned to crack the eggs into the cauldron and whisk them into gossamer strands amidst the boiling water. The milk joined the pot of honey on the stone slab beside the hearth, awaiting the tea.

"Is the old warren watch-tower in use?" Nell asked.

Shrike blinked at her. "Only to keep sheaves."

"Even better," Nell declared. "Might I borrow a few to make it fit to live in for the next fortnight or so?"

The request was not even half so odd as her bothering to ask permission to do as she wished. Shrike, still bewildered, nevertheless assented with a nod.

"You've got the ambassador and his brother arriving… well, within a few days, if he can find him and coax him into leaving Fathomseek," she explained with a shrug. "Cottage is already a touch crowded. Thought it'd be better to set up camp not too far off. And if memory serves, Lofthouse prefers fewer eyes on him when he's not wearing at least three shirts. Unless he's making a rite of it."

A chortle escaped Shrike despite all. "Aye, that'd do. Thank you."

She waved him off and, with a significant glance at Everilda, gathered up her bundle and left the cottage.

What Everilda made of Nell's glance, Shrike couldn't fathom. She merely took up her fever-wand and heart's-vine again. The fever-wand slipped between Wren's pale lips. The brass bell of the heart's-vine pressed against his ribs, then moved to the ivory wrappings 'round his waist.

Shrike forced himself to cease watching her. Yet he couldn't keep his gaze from returning over and again to Wren's sleeping face whilst he sliced and chopped and crushed herbs to add flavour to the stirring stew. Goat's milk gave it body. He melted cheese into it for good measure. He wished he had marrowbone to toss in.

An hour or so passed. Shrike knew not how long precisely. It felt like an age. The stew simmered. And Everilda, at last, turned to him and said the words he'd awaited ever since Wren had swooned in his arms.

"You may wake him."

Shrike leapt up from the hearth, his heart in his throat. A single stride brought him to Wren's bedside. There he knelt and took Wren's cold hand between his own. He glanced to Everilda to find she'd turned her back and busied herself in her instrument case.

So Shrike held his breath, bent his head, and, as he'd fiercely wished to all these long hours, bestowed a kiss upon his Wren.

* * *

THE FIRST THING Wren knew was the gentle sensation of familiar lips against his own. Vanilla and woodsmoke filled his lungs, and he smiled even before he opened his eyes to find his Shrike's handsome face above him.

The second thing he knew was a sharp ache throbbing through his right-hand side. His breath hitched and he bit back a pained groan. A shiver ran through his whole frame and refused to leave him.

Shrike's soft smile fell into concern. His fingertips alighted on Wren's brow—his touch warm as sunshine—and trailed down his cheek in a tender caress. His lips parted for speech.

Wren got there first. "Gave my cloak away."

Shrike blinked in bewilderment.

"To a faun." Wren's voice came out in creaks and cracks. He would've said more, but his shivers increased and his teeth began to chatter.

Shrike's mouth set in a grim line. He turned from Wren toward the hearth—for, Wren realised now that Shrike's beloved form no longer filled his vision, he lay not in the icy forest but in their own bed in Blackthorn cottage.

A scraping sound arose from the crackling fire as Shrike worked the poker. Wren felt he could watch him in contentment forever. But he espied something over Shrike's shoulder that drew all his attention.

A woman stood in the cottage.

Not Nell, either. An altogether stranger, dressed in the dull brown robes of a monk—or a nun, Wren supposed, for while she wore her auburn hair cropped close, it lacked a tonsure. She busied herself in digging through a leather case and producing a great deal of clinking noise. And as Wren stared, he realised her close-cropped hair revealed ears shaped much like his own.

Wren supposed his icy plunge had strained his nerves to their breaking point. Now he saw shadows as spirits and imagined an entire woman standing in their cottage.

Unless she was real.

Wren forced his gaze away from the conundrum and looked back to the familiar form of his own dear, sweet Shrike. He wanted to call him back to bed, to lie beside him and curl around him and entwine himself with his beloved's warmth. Only he mustn't call him Shrike just now, in front of company. Assuming the company was real. But neither could he recall what it was he ought to call him instead. And all the while his wound throbbed.

Shrike turned to the woman. "Ought he to eat or drink?"

"Oh, thank God," Wren blurted. "You can see her, too."

Shrike whirled 'round to blink at him.

The lady laughed. "Aye—and I can see you, as well."

Shrike stood. The poker in his hand had been replaced by a flannel bundle in his arms. He brought it to the end of the nest and tucked it beneath the furs and quilts by Wren's bare feet. Only when its warmth seeped into his skin did Wren recognize it as a hot brick—or, given Blackthorn cottage's construction, a rock.

This done, he returned to kneel at Wren's side, taking his hand in his own with a soft smile. His warm palms folded their warmth over Wren's frozen knuckles. Wren wanted nothing more than to take him by the wrist and draw him into bed beside him. But the presence of the woman gave him pause. Worse still, over Shrike's shoulder, he beheld her approach the nest with her leather case.

"I'm called Everilda," she said, relieving Wren of having to ask. "You may have some broth in a moment, but first I must ask; how do you feel?"

"Well enough." The polite reply fell from his lips without thought. With a touch more honesty, he added, "Cold."

He dared another glance at Shrike, his gaze flicking from one dark eye to the other, searching for answers. He couldn't speak his myriad questions aloud, for he couldn't think of a way to phrase his enquiries which wouldn't give offence.

Shrike seemed to hear him regardless, for he murmured, "She is chirurgeon and bone-setter to Lady Aethelthryth."

Wren didn't know much of Lady Aethelthryth beyond that she had numbered amongst their allies in the midsummer duel at the Court of the Silver Wheel. He supposed that would suffice for trust.

"No pain?" Everilda cut in.

Wren caught his tongue before it let slip another polite lie. "Bit of a stitch in my side, but you don't have to…"

He trailed off as he realised, given how naked his body felt beneath the furs aside from something snug wrapped 'round his middle, that she likely already had.

Everilda went on, nothing daunted. "Is it a sharp stabbing pain or more of a dull ache?"

"Burning ache," Wren decided after he'd taken a moment to focus on it—which he'd rather not have done, frankly. He hesitated before adding, "Gets sharp if I breathe in too deep."

Shrike's grip on his hand tightened.

Everilda nodded. "All rather to be expected, I'm afraid. But," she continued, withdrawing a curiously familiar bottle from her leather case, "an elixir of poppies ought to blunt its edge."

Shrike let go of Wren's hand for just a moment to turn again to the hearth and pour a cup of tea. The scent of chamomile and lavender wafted up alongside the steam. Everilda passed him the laudanum bottle. Shrike dispensed a few drops into the tea and gave it a dollop of honey for good measure. Then he slipped his strong arm beneath Wren's shoulders and raised him up to drink.

Wren had to reach for the cup twice before his clumsy fingertips met the handle. He couldn't support its weight—couldn't even tip it on his own—but still he could do enough to signal to Shrike his readiness to drink and when to draw it away again. The hot tea slipping down his throat became a warm balm spreading through his chest. For a moment he felt almost himself again. Then the warmth faded and the shivers resumed. Intermittent ones, chasing each other across his skin like summer zephyrs rustling through oak branches, rather than the bone-shattering convulsions he recalled on the lake-shore. But shivers none-theless.

Shrike set the empty cup aside and laid Wren down as gently as an autumn leaf's descent. Wren had half a notion to coax Shrike down alongside him into a sweet embrace. Yet the presence of Everilda still unnerved him. He'd already disrobed thrice-over in front of fae ladies. That was more than enough to blush for. The prospect of doing anything of the kind before a mortal woman, however, mortified him.

Everilda didn't seem in the least bit mortified. She had, at last, got what she wanted out of her kit and now approached the bed. From the leather case she withdrew an instrument which appeared very much like a brass ear-trumpet affixed to a rubber tube, with a brass bodkin at the other end. Brass wires spiralled up the tube-like vines and, indeed, had little brass ivy leaves sprouting from them. Wren watched as Ever-ilda briskly rubbed the mouth of the ear-trumpet—which he now saw wasn't hollow, but instead solid brass—against her palm. Then, with a glance seeking his permission, she drew back the bed-clothes just far enough to expose his bare chest. She laid the ear-trumpet firm against his ribs over his heart, stuck the brass bodkin in her ear, and turned her gaze towards the rafters whilst she listened.

Wren could only imagine how fast his heart beat with the panic of having a mortal woman see his naked form. He forced his attention away from her face and towards her instrument. As his eyes traced the brass vines, he realised the ivy leaves seemed to furl and unfurl in time with his own pulse. Though he supposed that could just be delirium.

Whatever Everilda gleaned from this experiment seemed to please her. She removed the brass bell from his chest and, with another enquiring glance at him and Shrike both, pulled the bedclothes still further down to expose a wide sash of ivory linen wrapping Wren from ribs to hips.

Wren gave silent thanks she halted there—though he knew she must have already seen what he had below the water-mark of his hip-bones. It was his first time seeing what had become of his wound since he lay on the icy lake-shore. The crisp linen contrasted against his memories of Shrike cutting his own shirt to pieces. He supposed it'd been re-dressed after surgery. The strips of Shrike's shirt were likely cast away. He felt a guilty pang at that and all the other trouble his foolishness had caused.

Everilda laid the brass bell against the ivory bandage. Its weight gave Wren a twinge but nothing worse. She listened intently, moving it now and again over the breadth of his stomach, though she never ventured near even the perimeter of his wound. As before, whatever she heard she seemed to take as a good sign, and when she withdrew her instru-ment, she did so with a smile. She tucked it away into her leather case and brought out something else—a glass tube, about as long and slender as a pencil, rounded off on both ends, with a minuscule blue fish embedded in the middle.

"Hold this under your tongue," she said.

Wren shot an enquiring glance at Shrike. Seeing he seemed to find nothing about this out of the ordinary, Wren supposed this was just routine fae medicine and opened his mouth for the chirurgeon.

She tucked one end of the glass under his tongue and bid him close his mouth to hold it.

To Wren's astonishment, the fish began to move. It wriggled and swam away from him, up towards the end of the tube, and as it went it changed colour from blue to green to yellow and, finally, an orange like flame. It halted about a half-inch shy of the rounded end and began to swim figure-eights in place.

Everilda plucked the tube from Wren's mouth and peered at the fish with an approving air.

"Can you stand?" she asked him.

"What?" Wren blurted.

Everilda appeared unperturbed. "Just a quick turn 'round the cottage. Then straight back to bed."

Wren stared at her, then turned his confusion on Shrike. He felt he could hardly sit up, much less walk.

Yet the small smile that graced Shrike's lips looked so gentle, so hopeful, and so encouraging, that Wren couldn't bring himself to deny him an attempt, at least.

"All right," Wren said, his voice sounding weak even to his own ears.

Once again, Shrike's strong arm slipped beneath his shoulders and helped him sit up. His wound twinged, but already the laudanum had begun to do its work, and the pain ebbed.

He had a moment's hesitation when it came time to withdraw the bedclothes altogether and swing his legs out. But just then, Everilda held out his own night-shirt, and then turned her back to him whilst Shrike drew it over his head. Wren supposed the mortification of having a strange woman touch his intimate garments was the lesser evil compared to her seeing, again, what lay beneath them.

Then, with a great deal more work on Shrike's part than on his own, he stood.

His legs felt equal parts stiff and insubstantial. Ethereal, his mind supplied, though he moved not even half so graceful as the white hart. He leaned heavily against Shrike and made his way with slow staggering steps out from the bed. When they reached the hollow stump, he laid a hand on its rim and kept it there to guide him as he went. His other arm remained locked in Shrike's.

By the time they made it back around to the nest, Wren's legs trembled. Shrike laid him down feather-gentle. Beads of sweat trickled from Wren's brow. Shrike dipped a clout in a bowl and washed Wren's face in cool water that smelt of lavender.

Wren had never suffered any real injury in all his life. Not even a broken bone whilst climbing a tree or riding, which might have at least proved himself a man to his father. His experience with illness remained limited to a bout of pox as a child; he remembered little of it beyond his nursemaid keeping him abed when he'd much rather have been up playing with his tin soldiers. Good fortune had seen him escape the cholera outbreak at Oxford unscathed.

All of which meant the plunge beneath the ice and the ferocious bite came as something of a shock.

The alternate numbing and burning of the frigid waters had dulled the pain of the attack when he'd received it. He realised it now that he'd reawakened in the warmth of Blackthorn cottage and found the ripping agony of monstrous teeth throbbing through his side despite the laudanum's attempts to dull it.

Wren had assumed—as he supposed all gentlemen assumed—that if he ever did get caught up in the throes of dire illness or injury, he would simply buck up and press on and push through it.

Instead, he found himself weak and pathetic and rendered utterly dependent.

What must Shrike think of him? Shrike, who until Wren had come along had stitched up all his own wounds with gritted teeth and nothing more?

Everilda seemed pleased, at least. No sooner had Shrike laid Wren down than she approached the nest with her instruments again. Wren submitted to the tube beneath his tongue and her listening to his gullet. Both produced results she deemed satisfactory, adding, "I'll return by noon if you don't need me before."

She packed up her instruments as she spoke. With a nod to Wren and another to Shrike, she departed the cottage—much to Wren's relief.

Shrike, meanwhile, descended on him the moment the cottage door shut behind her and laid another kiss on his lips. Neither pain nor exhaustion could keep Wren from kissing him back. He would have kissed him forever, for the sheer joy of it, but Shrike withdrew, and Wren hadn't the strength to follow him.

"I gave her forewarning," Shrike said, turning to the fire, "that you might not feel at ease in the company of a strange woman."

"Oh," said Wren. He added a belated, "Thank you."

Shrike smiled as he ladled something fragrant from the cauldron set in the hearth into a clay bowl. The savoury scent wafted up to fill the cottage. Wren hadn't felt hungry before. Now, as Shrike brought the broth to him, he realised he'd grown ravenous.

With Shrike's continued assistance, he sat up braced against a pile of pillows. All his strength went toward remaining upright. This left him nothing with which to grasp or raise the spoon from the bowl. So it was left to Shrike to bring both to Wren's lips and dispense spoonful upon slow spoonful to his withered Wren.

Whenever Shrike happened to glance away—either down to the bowl to procure another spoonful, or, when Wren's exhaustion overcame his hunger and it became apparent he could consume no more, off to the stone slab beside the hearth to set the half-empty bowl aside—Wren searched his face. A furrow of worry appeared now and again between Shrike's brows. Nothing more as of yet. Wren dreaded the inevitable arrival of disappointment, disgust, and disdain in Shrike's eyes.

But as Shrike returned to him, he inevitably did so with the small handsome smile Wren loved so well.

As Shrike raised his hand to brush his knuckles against Wren's brow, Wren summoned all his strength to catch him by the wrist. He intended to drag him down into an embrace beside him. The most he could manage, however, was a feeble tug.

Shrike took the hint regardless.

He bent to grant Wren a kiss, all the sweeter for its brevity. Then he withdrew and busied himself with his tunic ties. Tunic, shirt, and hose all fell away, leaving his beloved form bare beneath Wren's gaze. At last, he slipped beneath the quilt and furs beside Wren. Wren had shivered again as the bedclothes shifted. But the shivers left him when Shrike curled around him, careful to avoid his wound, yet nonetheless embracing him with all the warmth Wren craved. It required very little from Wren to coax another kiss out of him.

"I'm sorry," said Wren as their lips parted.

Shrike furrowed his brow. "What for?"

"It's my fault you lost your chance at the white hart."

Shrike continued staring at him for another moment or two. Then his hand came up to brush Wren's hair off his brow and trail down his cheek in a tender caress.

"I did almost lose my heart," Shrike murmured. "But he is found again, and reawakened, and now all is well."

* * *

WREN AWOKE that very evening to find Everilda had returned to haunt the cottage.

At least, he assumed it was the same evening. He at least felt confident it was evening, given the moonlight streaming in through the eastern windows.

She sat on the edge of the hollow stump and made low conversation with Shrike, who no longer lay naked beside Wren in bed but had evidently got up in the intervening hours to don his clothes and now knelt before the hearth stirring the cauldron. Wren wondered how many hours Everilda had spent here whilst he slept. She'd promised to return at noon. The thought of her watching him in near-silence for so long unnerved him. Had she arrived whilst Shrike still lay naked abed beside him? The fae didn't look askance at such things, Wren knew, but she wasn't fae.

His own shirt hung on the wall-hook at the opposite end of the nest. He felt rather well-rested and thought he might have enough strength and cunning to retrieve it without her notice. She was mortal like him, after all. Her senses couldn't be so keen as Shrike's or other fae. He would feel far more comfortable, he knew, with a shirt between his bare flesh and her gaze.

But the moment he endeavoured to sit up—not even successfully moving his body, just tensing muscles in preparation to move—his wound reminded him of its existence with an agonizing pulse of pain which began as the sudden stabbing of a dozen-odd daggers and bled out into a burning ache that spread through his whole frame.

While he did his best to stifle his unmanful yelp, a strangled sound nevertheless escaped his throat, and both Shrike and Everilda whipped their heads toward him.

Shrike leapt up at once and flew to Wren's side. There he knelt and seized his hand in his own, whilst the other cupped Wren's cheek as his deep burr murmured, "Steady—steady."

Everilda, meanwhile, poured a mug of tea from the kettle and added a few drops of laudanum. This she handed off to Shrike, who brought it to Wren's lips and cradled the back of his head to bring him up to it.

Wren gladly drank of the potion. He felt less glad when Everilda pulled back the quilt and furs to expose him to his hip-bones.

"A sharp pain?" she asked him, her eyes on his bandage. "Like something ripped or snapped?"

"Just a twinge," Wren insisted. "Fading already."

She didn't look convinced. "The bandage ought to be changed. We'll see what lies beneath it and judge better then. After the poppies have a chance to do their work," she added, with a glance at the mug Wren had not yet emptied.

With Shrike's assistance, Wren dutifully sipped his tea. It took a quarter-hour for him to finish. As he sipped, Everilda busied herself by filling a cauldron from the hot tap in the hollow stump and setting it over the fire to boil. After another quarter-hour had passed, Everilda asked him if his pain had diminished enough to allow him to stand.

"You need only walk to the work-bench," she explained in response to his wary expression.

His wariness did not, however, arise from his feeling daunted at the prospect of further pain. He glanced to Shrike, to his shirt still hanging on the hook, and back again.

Shrike understood him in an instant and arose to retrieve the shirt.

By the time he'd returned to Wren, Everilda had turned away to tend to her boiling water—which Wren still didn't understand the purpose of, but if it kept her back to him whilst he dressed, he thought it all the better. Shrike helped him throw his shirt on over his head and tug its hem down past all he wished to disguise.

Everilda hauled her cauldron off the fire and across the cottage to Shrike's work-bench. Wren had just time enough to note how curiously barren it'd become whilst he slept before she heaved the cauldron and sluiced boiling hot water over the whole of it.

Wren glanced to Shrike to see what he thought of the steam rising off the wood of his work-bench.

Shrike, however, seemed not to notice anything out-of-the-ordinary about her actions. Instead he wound his arm through the crook of Wren's and, once Wren had swung his legs out over the edge of the bed, gently drew him upright until he stood on his own two feet.

Wren leant heavily on Shrike and hobbled towards the work-bench. As he drew near it, he noted curious dark blotches in the wood-grain. Not knots, but rather sprawling irregular stains of a red so dark it seemed almost black, as if someone had spilt port wine.

Belatedly, he recognised it as blood.

And, as he was the only one with a gaping wound in his side which had just recently been stitched up by a chirurgeon, and no bloodstains appeared anywhere else in the cottage, he was forced to conclude that the chirurgy had occurred on Shrike's work-bench, and the blood was his own.

Again he turned to Shrike. It felt natural to seek reassurance in his warm dark eyes. But Shrike didn't meet his glance. Shrike's gaze had fallen to the bloodstain, and the grim line of his mouth and the hard clench of his jaw bespoke his displeasure. A shudder overtook him—one Wren could feel with their arms so entwined—and he looked away.

A pang struck Wren. He knew not how to begin to apologise for despoiling Shrike's work-bench. Nor did he know how to scrub out blood from wood. He wondered what it would cost to replace the stained planks. Surely someone in the Moon Market knew carpentry. He made note to investigate the matter when he had strength enough to wander out of Blackthorn under his own power.

But before he could even begin to compose an apology, Shrike had turned to him with a wan smile and, as if Wren weighed no more than the ethereal hart itself, picked him up to seat him upright atop the work-bench. Wren's pulse fluttered for reasons beyond surprise or his invalid condition.

"Thank you," Wren managed, startled but no less grateful. He couldn't support his own weight. Still, with his arms arranged around Shrike's shoulders, and Shrike standing firm and strong as any oak, he kept himself from collapsing.

Everilda, meanwhile, had gone to scrub her hands and arms from fingertip to elbow in the scalding hot water of the hollow stump.

"Now, then," she said as she returned to the work-bench. "If you would be so kind as to remove your night-shirt."

Wren balked. He'd only just got it back on. And now she wanted it taken off again.

Evidently aware of his reasons for hesitance, she added, "It's nothing I've not seen before."

Which was true enough. And yet, it did not make Wren feel any more comfortable. "Yes—well—still."

Another moment of awkward silence passed whilst Everilda and Shrike waited with more patience than Wren deserved for him to say something sensible.

"Perhaps," Wren added, more out of desperation than any good idea, "you might turn your back, and I could, er, drape... something...?"

Everilda raised an eyebrow, but after exchanging a glance with Shrike, she turned around nonetheless.

With Shrike's assistance, Wren got his nightshirt off over his head. Then he carefully arranged it across his left thigh so the folds covered what he considered absolutely necessary. The resulting display was not what most mortal women would consider decent, but it would have to do.

Wren cleared his throat. "I'm ready."

Everilda turned 'round and took him in with a quick up-and-down glance. Wren thought he caught something like amusement at the corners of her mouth. Then she selected a pair of silver scissors from the myriad instruments she'd laid out. The stitches of the linen gave way beneath their blades. As she unwound the bandages from around his waist, the clean crisp outer layer gave way to another where dark spots of rust had soaked through.

Likewise, dark spots began to gather at the corners of Wren's vision. His head felt curiously light. His breath quickened.

Gentle fingertips caught him beneath his chin. Wren acquiesced to their bidding, which forced his gaze away from Everilda's work and up towards Shrike's face.

"Don't watch," he murmured. "Look at me."

Wren found this advice rather easy to follow, since he quite enjoyed looking at Shrike. At the moment, however, he couldn't help noticing how pale Shrike had turned, and how his smile, while sincere, appeared nonetheless wan.

Still, the sight of it leant Wren strength, and he found he breathed easier whilst he gazed into Shrike's eyes.

The sound of ripping thread and fabric continued. The bandages fell away altogether. Wren's stomach lurched as his gut sank free. Something cold and wet trickled down his side. His skin itched in its wake. A scraping sensation ensued along the lips of his wound and forced a hiss from betwixt his clenched teeth.

"Your pardon," said Everilda. "There is some cleaning yet to do."

Wren, having helped Shrike treat his wound after the midwinter duel, braced himself for the sharp scent and sharper sting of vinegar.

He did not expect a singular and sudden stab from an unmistakable needle pricking one of the teeth-marks. Nor the unaccountable sensation of something withdrawing a quantity of fluid from within him. A whimper escaped him alongside it.

"Your pardon," Everilda repeated, her voice low and not unkind. "Nearly done."

The needle slipped out—a sickening feeling which made Wren's stomach lurch again. The scent of vinegar filled his nostrils as cold liquid poured over his wound. Then a damp clout, likely soaked through with the same stuff, daubed away at the bite in much the same manner as he'd daubed Shrike's wound after the winter solstice duel.

Several minutes passed and several clouts dampened and discarded before Everilda ceased cleaning the wound. Wren began to tremble despite Shrike's support. Beads of sweat had broken out and trickled down his brow before Everilda daubed him dry. Then a tight belt of linen coiled 'round him, binding up what felt as if it threatened to spill out, layer upon layer, until Everilda pinned it in place and took up needle and thread to stitch it secure. Wren felt glad of it, for he found it braced him up. Though he felt gladder still when Everilda stepped away and declared him fit to return to bed.

With Shrike as his crutch, Wren hobbled back to the nest. Everilda washed up at the copper tap and refilled the cauldron to set on the hearth. Then she brought her queer glass tube to Wren's mouth again.

"Under your tongue," she said, "an' it so please you."

Wren obeyed. The fish turned crimson and swam furiously toward the far end of the glass. Everilda tsk'd as she took it back from him to examine.

"Feverish," she declared. "Not surprising, given the infection. I'm more surprised it didn't set in earlier. But we've a cure for that," she added, much to Shrike's evident relief, his brow having grown more and more furrowed and knotted as she spoke.

The cure came in the form of a mug filled with water, into which Everilda dispensed a few drops of a viscous mauve liquid from a vial in her instrument case.

"Drink this," she said as she handed the mug to Wren.

"What is it?" he asked.

"Tincture of mould."

Wren stared at her.

"It consumes the infection," she explained.

Wren didn't doubt it. He'd seen mould consume more than a few books in his day. Which made him not quite so confident as Everilda appeared to be that the mould would merely consume the infection and not go on to consume his whole body altogether.

But a glance at Shrike showed no trace of surprise or suspicion in his fine fae features. And so Wren surmised this tincture of mould was yet another vagary of the unknown magicks at work in fae medicine, something which had proved true through centuries of practice and yet made no sense to his mortal mind.

He accepted the mug from Everilda and downed it in one gulp. It had a chalky taste that clung to his tongue. He pulled a face as he passed the mug back. No sooner had it left his fingertips than Shrike held out another to take its place, this one brimming with hot tea that smelt of honey and chamomile. This Wren took with more enthusiasm. Its sweetness helped banish the miserable memory of the mould.

"You ought to take more plain water as well," Everilda noted. "As much as you can stomach. It'll help flush the infection from your veins."

Shrike arose to fill a mug at the copper taps before she even finished her explanation.

* * *

BY THE CLOSE of the first se'en-night since he'd awoken from chirurgy, Wren had his surfeit of convalescence.

The pain wearied him, true enough, but Everilda's anodynes kept the worst of it at bay. What irritated him most of all was the sheer boredom.

While the events of last winter might not have always proved pleasant, they had at least kept him occupied. This winter had begun well enough; his first Winter Solstice as the Holly King exceeded his expectations, and he'd hoped the season would continue on in that vein. The white hart hunt had seemed promising from the outset.

Now, however, he couldn't even venture out-of-doors to stroll with his Shrike through the wintry wood.

Wren missed those promenades more and more with every passing hour. Shimmering branches sheathed in ice, lacework frost creeping over the ground, the soft snow settling over the whole forest in a reverent silence, the frozen fog of his breath contrasted against the snug warmth of his fur-lined cloak wrapped 'round him, crafted by his beloved's hands and a scaled-down match for the very same one which hung about Shrike's own shoulders, and Shrike's arm entwined with his beneath.

And then he'd gone and done just about the most idiotic thing possible in the Wild Hunt, paid full price for it, and shackled himself to the nest within Blackthorn cottage for the foreseeable future.

He did walk several times a day. Technically. But to take the same circular route about the one-room cottage hour after hour and day after day had begun to try his patience and sanity alike. Each stroll passed but a quarter-hour, which seemed both too long and too short by Wren's reckoning. Switching between sunwise and widdershins helped some, though not nearly enough. To have his Shrike beside him, with their arms entangled and Wren's head against Shrike's broad shoulder, helped a great deal more.

Indeed, Shrike had become the one bright spot in Wren's cold and lonely doldrums. Wren had known him sweet and gentle before. Now, in his hour of need, Shrike had become exceeding tender. Not just in the way he held him as they slept, or how he cupped the back of Wren's head as he fed him spoonfuls of broth, or how he held his hand and stroked his hair and murmured reassurance whilst Everilda peeled back his bloodied bandages to clean the wound. But likewise in his encouraging smiles and his evident joy whenever Wren opened his eyes anew after far-too-many hours asleep.

Wren spent most of the first few days sleeping. Whenever he awoke, Everilda had her instruments upon him and then commanded him out of bed to either take another turn around the hollow stump or sit on the work-bench to redress his wound—often both—and by the time these ordeals had finished he felt so exhausted that all he could do was crawl back into the nest and slumber again.

By the middle of the week, however, he returned to bed to find he retained strength enough to remain half-upright leaning against the pile of pillows. After a quiet moment or two in which sleep didn't come to claim him, he asked Shrike if he might have his copy of *Gawain and the Green Knight* to read. Shrike dutifully brought it to him. But when Wren opened the book, he found the words blurred before him on the page, and he could not will his gaze to remain on a single line. He furrowed his brow in consternation. No doubt the laudanum was to blame.

"May I?" asked Shrike.

Wren rolled his head across the pillow to regard him. Shrike had his hand held out for the book. Wren gave it over—or rather, he gave a vague gesture with the book towards Shrike, and Shrike understood at once.

Gently accepting the book from Wren's feeble grasp, Shrike turned to the first page and began to read aloud. The mellifluous rhythm of the poem itself, uttered in the low rumbling burr of his beloved, soothed all Wren's irritation. He relaxed against his piled pillows and let his eyes rest upon Shrike's face to watch his dark gaze travel across the page and his perfect lips sound out the syllables. Thus he spent a more pleasant afternoon than he'd known since his rescue from beneath the ice.

Wren had grown accustomed to the luxury of bathing whilst in Blackthorn. His wound reduced him once again to the stand-up wash. Or rather, the sit-down or lie-down wash, for he lacked the strength to stand under his own power. Here again Shrike came to his rescue.

For the first few days whilst the infection still raged within him and his flesh blazed with fever, Shrike sat by him and continually bathed his burning face with lavender water. Even as the fever ebbed and he felt just a touch warm rather than boiling, Wren found he enjoyed the gentle ministrations. He liked less to have Everilda in the cottage watching them both in their intimacy. For the most part her gaze remained cast down in her gyrdel-book as she examined and added to her notes. Wren didn't much like the idea of her writing about him, either, though he conceded it was probably necessary to track and plan his treatment.

Then, in about the middle of the week, the fever faded altogether. Everilda still made him drink the tincture of mould—against its return, she said, and Wren supposed he ought to follow her advice whether or not it made sense to him. But she no longer remained in the cottage at all hours. Instead she limited her appearances to dawn and dusk.

Which left Wren and his beloved blissfully alone together at last.

Everilda had washed Wren's wound and its surrounding flesh whenever she refreshed the bandage. Anything further than that, however, Wren felt far more comfortable leaving in Shrike's hands.

And what capable hands they were.

Even laying on the unyielding oak of the work-bench with naught but a roll of linen to shield him somehow proved soothing with Shrike lathering and rinsing his body. The heat of the hearth-fire, which Shrike had never allowed to go out since Wren awakened, kept the whole cottage so warm that no chill or draught touched his bare skin. The warm water sluicing the grime off his flesh felt almost as indulgent as a full bath in the hollow stump. And to have Shrike's tender ministrations performing all filled Wren's heart past brimming.

Three days without a morning shave had rendered Wren's cheeks, jaw, and throat more than a touch bristled. Shrike had never plied a razor to his own face—at least, not that Wren had ever seen in the year they'd spent together. Yet Wren felt no fear with the blade at his throat held in Shrike's fingers. And with the same slow, methodical care that Shrike took to his leather-work, he shaved Wren's face as smooth as glass.

While Wren didn't mind bathing on the work-bench, however, it seemed to trouble Shrike. More specifically, the dark blotches left behind by Wren's bleeding body. Whenever Shrike looked on Wren himself, he smiled. The smile faded into a grim line whenever his eye alighted on the irregular rusty blemishes.

The third time Shrike's gaze fell on the stains only to jerk away with a shudder, Wren could no longer bear it in silence.

"Forgive me," Wren blurted.

Shrike blinked at him, bewildered. "Whatever for?"

"For ruining your work-bench."

Shrike stared at him.

Wren gestured toward the largest stain, a sickening pool of dull crimson rust that had seeped into the wood-grain to form veins of gore.

Shrike's face drained of colour. "It's no fault of yours."

"It's my blood," Wren protested.

Shrike served him an incredulous glance. "Aye. And *that* is why it troubles me."

The laudanum forced Wren to form the obvious conclusion more slowly than he otherwise would—or at least, he hoped himself cleverer than he felt in that moment. He certainly didn't sound very clever when he replied far too little and far too late, "Oh."

A wan smile graced Shrike's worried countenance. His weathered hand arose to cradle Wren's jaw. His thumb caressed his cheek. "It's my own horror to bear. I never meant to burden you with it."

Wren still didn't feel entirely exonerated. "Could we scrub it out in the spring? Or is it too far gone?"

Shrike hesitated. "Sand it out, mayhaps. If it's not soaked in..." He trailed off with a hard swallow. It seemed even thinking on it long enough to speak of it proved beyond his endurance.

Wren summoned all his strength to catch him by the hand.

The touch seemed to startle Shrike. Still, it drew his mind out of whatever horrors bloomed behind his eyes in the remembrance of how the blood-stains came to be. He brought Wren's hand to his lips and laid a gentle kiss against his knuckles.

"Let's get you back to bed," Shrike murmured, his low burr rumbling through Wren's own chest. "Lest you take another chill."

Wren felt more than satisfied to acquiesce to return to the nest and suffer to be tucked in with more tenderness than a heart could very well bear.

The following day, when Wren again felt somewhat stronger than before, he asked if Shrike would bring him his gyrdel-book and pencil. Shrike obliged him at once. Yet, much like *Gawain and the Green Knight* before it, Wren found that while his spirit yearned to draw, his flesh remained too weak to follow through, and the laudanum still muddled his head besides. He swallowed his disappointment and instead contented himself with paging through the sketches of last year's spring and summertime. The thought of the coming vernal season comforted him; at least he could go out-of-doors then, when the days grew longer. The springtime rites would prove a welcome celebration.

But as his mind turned toward Ostara, he recalled what it had wrought for Shrike just one year ago.

The cottage door creaked open, interrupting his grim realisation. Everilda entered.

"Good morrow, my lords," she said, shutting the door behind herself. "How do you fare?"

"Well enough," Wren said, truthfully.

She smiled. "Do you feel up to a task?"

Wren exchanged a glance with Shrike, who seemed just as confused as himself. Warily, he replied, "Depends on the task."

"Physical exercise," she said. "To strengthen your body and repair the damage done to your muscles."

The notion of doing something towards regaining his strength held great appeal for Wren. "Like walking, you mean?"

"Something like that," Everilda said in a tone which suggested nothing of the sort.

The exercises proved more complex than mere walking. First she had him lie on the work-bench, on his back with his knees drawn up and his feet braced flat against the wood.

"Draw your navel down toward your spine," she said as though it were a very sensible thing to say. "Don't lift your head or shoulders. Hold until the count of three."

Wren did as she bade him. It sounded easy enough. It felt much harder. His wound twinged as his muscles tugged against it. Nothing gave way, however, though she made him repeat it five times over.

Then, still on the work-bench with his knees drawn up, she told him to slip his hands beneath the hollow of his back. He tightened his stomach just as before and, at her instruction, flattened his back against his hands and canted his hips upward and inward towards his ribs. Again, he had to hold for three seconds, after which he must relent with a "gentle release." It felt more ridiculous than painful. Still, five repetitions sufficed to send beads of sweat trickling down his temples.

"I've one more, if you feel up to it," said Everilda.

Wren nodded, determined.

Again she bid him tighten his gut. Then she had him lower his knees to one side, then the other, holding each side until she said he might relax.

"Keep your shoulders flat," she warned, not for the first time.

Wren set his jaw. If so simple an exercise as this would see him fit to stand under his own power again, then he'd not let himself fail, no matter how it tired him.

By the end of it, he felt as though he were back in the old warren watch-tower running up and down the stairs with the ambassador to train for the Summer Solstice duel. Everilda's exercises, he thought, felt more gruelling and left him in a similar amount of pain, though he supposed the wound was to blame for that.

No sooner had Everilda announced he might cease than Shrike swooped in with lavender-water to bathe Wren's sweat-streaked brow. Wren dearly appreciated it. Still, a pressing concern loomed in the forefront of his mind.

"Will I be well again by Ostara?" Wren gasped out.

Silence reigned in the wake of his enquiry. He rolled his head toward Shrike and beheld his brow knit in confusion and concern alike.

"Ostara?" Everilda echoed. She, at least, appeared to give the question serious consideration. "You ought to feel well enough to attend certain festivities by then. Though I would advise against dancing. We'll see when the day draws nearer."

Festivities were the least of Wren's concerns. "But I'll be able to tend the goats by then? See to the hens? The skeps?"

Everilda blinked at him. "You may tend them within the fortnight, if you feel called to do so."

"You won't have to," Shrike added with atypical haste.

Wren shot him a startled look.

"All is in hand," Shrike explained in a tone Wren supposed he meant to sound soothing. "Whatever I cannot do, our friends are more than willing to take up."

For now, Wren thought. "And what happens when your antlers come in again?"

Shrike balked.

Wren turned to Everilda. "Have you seen anything of the like before? Fae growing antlers and the pain it causes?"

Everilda raised her brows. "Some. The hidden folk have their own methods of looking after it. Few other fae grow antlers. But those I have seen do well enough with a tonic and rest." She glanced at Shrike. "Does it pain you greatly?"

Shrike looked as though he'd rather talk about anything else. "No."

"He could hardly stand," Wren countered. "The least light blinded him. He collapsed at his work-bench. They grew more than an inch a day and hollowed him out from within. It lasted a month."

Shrike stared at him.

"Do you not remember?" Wren snapped. He regretted his sharp tone at once; Shrike didn't deserve it, after all he'd done for him. But his denial of his own agony tried Wren's patience to its limit.

Shrike seemed to take the outburst in stride. In solemn tones, he admitted, "I remember."

"And who's to look after you if it happens again this year?" Wren demanded.

"As I understand it," Everilda cut in, "if antlers are seasonal, the first year is the worst, and the pain diminishes with each recurrence. I could return to take a look at them, if you'd like. Assuming I'm not still here already."

Even in the midst of his frustration, Wren had to admit he liked the sound of that. "I'd appreciate it."

Everilda looked to Shrike. Shrike assented with a nod.

"Still," Wren couldn't help but add. "You said I'd be well by then?"

Everilda hesitated. "To a point. You may carry light burdens. But I'd advise against anything heavy or strenuous. Nor ought you to stand over-long."

"Until...?" Wren prompted.

"Three months, at least," she replied. "Two years for a full recovery."

Wren's heart sank.

* * *

FAE RECOVERED from injury far faster than mortals.

Shrike had always known this. Yet to have proof of it before him now, in the form of his beloved enduring day after day of agony, wrested his heart in twain.

The skull-crusher bite would've laid Shrike up, true enough, but he would have fully recovered within a few months, if not in a fortnight or two. It staggered him to hear from the chirurgeon's own lips that his Wren would require years to regain his strength.

And for Wren to think of Shrike's suffering when Wren himself lay overcome with pain was more than Shrike could well bear.

Everilda did not remain long in the cottage after giving her dire prophecy. Her removal didn't improve Wren's aspect. He grit his teeth and, with Shrike's aid, sat up from the work-bench. His frustration remained evident in his stormy brow as he hobbled back to the nest. Shrike could tell he had no wish to lie down again, but his body demanded it, and so he acquiesced with a grimace, sitting back against the pillows and glowering at the wall.

Shrike knew not what to do. So he filled the tea-kettle and another mug of plain water for Wren besides.

The offering seemed to startle Wren out of his bitter reverie. He accepted the water nonetheless, alongside Shrike's aid in drinking it, with a murmured thanks. Their silence resumed, though it didn't feel half so comfortable as a silence between them otherwise would.

Wren broke it first. "What you must think of me—weak and useless—"

Shrike balked. "You're neither."

Wren's rolling eyes came to rest on Shrike's face.

Shrike didn't oft feel compelled to speak. But the pain in Wren's gaze demanded he give voice to his thoughts. "You've shown yourself strong enough to survive this. And strong enough to persist in pursuit of your recovery."

Wren appeared to at least be considering the matter rather than dismissing it outright.

Shrike dared to take his hand. After a moment, Wren clasped his in turn.

"You don't need to prove your strength further," Shrike spoke on. "You deserve to rest. And to do so doesn't make you weak."

Slowly yet surely, the fury drained from Wren's face. Indignant furrows left his brow. His jaw unclenched. He looked on Shrike with eyes no longer glinting with sparks of wounded pride but rather the soft, dark, warm gaze that Shrike loved so well. He brought his hand with Shrike's clasped within it up to nestle against his hollowed cheek.

Then, with a gesture whose rapidity belied the force required to make it possible, he threw his arm around Shrike's shoulders and drew him down into an embrace so he might bury his shuddering breaths in Shrike's collar.

And Shrike, relieved just to have him alive in his arms, held him tight.

* * *

WREN NEXT AWOKE when the sun had nearly reached its zenith.

Sunlight, however, had not roused him. A brusque entrance through the cottage door had.

He turned his head towards the clattering clamour and opened his eyes to discover Nell just inside the doorway knocking snow from her boots. She had her unstrung bow in one hand and a brace of ducks in the other.

160

"What?" she said as Shrike arose from where he knelt at Wren's bedside and strode across the cottage making fervent signals for her silence. "Oh—pardon. But he's awake now, anyway," she added, peering around Shrike's shoulder to look at Wren abed.

While Wren didn't exactly enjoy her looking at him when he lay clad in his night-shirt and naught else, he didn't mind it quite so much as he did others. For one, she and Shrike were friends, and over the past year that familiarity had begun to leak into her dealings with Wren. For another, she was fae; therefore Wren could feel tolerably certain she thought far less of his bare form than most mortals. And for a third, she'd seen it all before at Midsummer and the lake-shore both.

"It's the fattiest thing in the forest," Nell went on, heedless of Shrike's efforts to quiet her. "Everilda said he needed something suety to keep him from wasting away."

So saying, she raised her feathered prize to eye-level, though it seemed to Wren she did it more for his sake than for Shrike's.

Wren glanced to Everilda, who remained seated by her instrument-case with her eyes cast down at her gyrdel-book. He supposed she saw no need to intervene between friends.

"How are you faring, Lofthouse?"

Wren, startled by the direct enquiry, jerked his head back to face Nell, who smirked on regardless.

"Well enough," he answered, which had become the common reply.

"Glad of it," she replied, and seemed to mean it sincerely.

She and Shrike both went to the work-bench—to clean the ducks, presumably, and ready them for the stew-pot. Shrike worked in his customary silence, which by no means prevented Nell from speaking on about all she'd seen in the wood on her hunt and speculating on what future hunts might hold.

Contrary to Shrike's apparent concerns, Wren didn't mind having her chatter fill the cottage. Both her arrival and the sound of her voice provided a welcome change to break up the monotony of his convalescence. Even if he had difficulty following the precise threads of her conversation after the laudanum dose Everilda gave him. His mind, as it so often did under the influence of that particular anodyne, wandered.

He found himself wondering how long Nell had been in Blackthorn since his plunge beneath the ice. Long enough to converse with Everilda about what best to feed an invalid. Not the whole duration of his convalescence, surely, for she must have other things to tend to in her own life —though, Wren realised belatedly, he hadn't the foggiest idea what those other things might be. He didn't even know where she lived. What was her trade? What responsibilities must she be shirking to hunt for Blackthorn's larder?

Regardless of his unspoken questions, she soon had her quarry plucked and cleaned and skewered on a spit over the hearth, with the drippings collecting in a pan. The crackle and hiss of roasting duckflesh filled the cottage alongside the savoury scent of cooking fat.

Wren quite enjoyed Shrike's cooking. And the myriad soups he'd consumed since his convalescence began had all been very good. But as the aroma of roast duck filled his lungs, he missed more than ever before the taste of solid food.

Everilda, meanwhile, plied him with her glass and brass tubes. Then she made him drink two more mugs of water and more tincture of mould on top of that. She continued on listening to his stomach as he drank.

"You might," she said at length, surprising him a great deal, "try a morsel of something solid, if you're feeling up to it."

Wren's heart and stomach both leapt at the notion. He glanced to Shrike tending the duck over the fire and saw a reflection of his own joy in those dark eyes.

While Blackthorn Cottage possessed knives and spoons, Wren had never yet seen a table fork in Shrike's grasp. He didn't expect one now. In the months since he began dwelling in the fae realms he'd grown accustomed to tearing apart a roast with his bare hands in the medieval fashion.

And at this particular moment, with Wren's own strength not quite up to the task, it was Shrike who peeled flesh from bone and held a morsel to Wren's lips.

The buttery meat all-but-melted on his tongue. He hardly needed to chew it, but chew he did—more for the novelty of having something to chew after a week-and-a-half of soups and stews. It slipped down his throat and settled into his stomach.

Yet Shrike's fingertips remained poised at his lips. For what reason it never occurred to Wren to question. He knew only the enticing aroma of hearty fare and the gentle slide of Shrike's thumb-pad across his lower lip. His tongue darted out before his mind could catch up to his instincts.

Only after he'd licked the grease from Shrike's fingers did it occur to him to feel modest.

He flicked his gaze over Shrike's shoulder to determine who had seen him do something so wanton and bizarre. Neither Nell nor Everilda, however, seemed to take any notice of him or Shrike. Indeed, they appeared entirely focused on each other. Nell sat close by Everilda—so close their knees touched—and bent her head for low conversation, her lips never ceasing to move, more for speech and less for eating. Everilda remained demure with downcast eyes but seemed by no means displeased with the attention, judging by the unaccountable smile Wren had never beheld before tugging at the corner of her mouth.

"Another?" Shrike murmured.

Wren, satisfied that Nell and Everilda cared not what he and Shrike got up to, nodded.

Afterward, with supper polished off and Wren's stomach feeling far more satisfied than it had in some time, Nell arose and stretched. Wren noted she did so in a way which flexed the muscles of her arms—well-honed from the drawing weight of her bowstring.

"I'll be in the watch-tower if you need me," she said, and while she looked at Shrike as she spoke, Wren nevertheless had the distinct impression she intended her remark for Everilda's ears. With that, she donned her cloak and left the cottage.

Wren waited a few moments after the door had shut before he asked Shrike, "What does Nell do for a living?"

Shrike shrugged. "She does as she pleases."

Wren was on the point of asking what the deuce that meant when the cottage door swung inward again and Nell herself stood on the threshold once more.

"Oi, Butcher," she said, as easily as if she hadn't just bid her good-byes not five minutes past. "You've two more guests on the way."

Shrike arose with furrowed brow. "Who?"

"Dunno. Just espied a pair comin' up the thorned path. They're a ways off yet. Want I should greet 'em for you?" she asked, raising her hand to the bow slung over her shoulders.

"No," Shrike said as quick as Wren thought it. "I'll go and see what they want."

* * *

SHRIKE FOLLOWED Nell out into the snow with no small amount of misgivings. He kept his hand on the pommel of his misericord beneath his cloak. Though none who intended harm could pass through the wall of thorns, he still felt wary whilst Wren lay frail and weak within the cottage.

"There they are," Nell muttered, jerking her chin towards two shadows on the path ahead.

One stood hardly as tall as Wren. The other stood as tall as Shrike himself and, unless Shrike's keen eye had failed him, had horns and a tail both.

Shrike stepped forward, his lips already parting to demand the strangers announce themselves. But before he could speak—

"Hail and well met, my lord!"

The moment the familiar trill reached his ears, Shrike relaxed his alert stance. "Hail."

For the ambassador, as promised, had returned to Blackthorn Briar.

"I've brought a companion alongside me," the ambassador continued. His form grew more distinct as he approached; Shrike could see his twirling hands.

"Your brother?" Shrike guessed—for so the ambassador had hoped. Though Shrike had supposed the two brothers would prove more alike in form, not all fae bore great resemblance to their siblings.

"Nay," a far deeper voice rumbled. But familiar nonetheless.

Shrike took another step forward. "Drude?"

By now the traveling companions were well within sight, and Shrike could behold for himself that their acquaintance from Mabon had arrived in all his crimson glory.

Nell shot Shrike an enquiring glance. When he granted her a nod that bespoke of no danger, she slung her bow back over her shoulder. "Well met, fellows. I'll be in the warren watch-tower if you need me."

And with that, she vanished off into the very shadows the ambassador and Drude had emerged from.

"I do hope we're not interrupting anything," said the ambassador. "How fares the Holly King?"

"Better than you left him." Shrike winced. His words sounded far more accusatory than he'd intended. "Glad to have you returned, I'm sure. And," he added, turning to Drude, "we are glad to meet again. What brings you here? Did you find each other in Fathomseek?"

"We met on the path," Drude offered up by way of explanation. "Word of the Holly King's peril has spread throughout the realms of hidden folk. Forgive me, I don't mean to impose, but—if there's anything I may do? Labour? Provisions?"

At first Shrike knew not how the incubus might assist their cause, but the latter suggestion struck him. "Butter."

Drude blinked. "Butter?"

"The chirurgeon said it'd be the best thing for him," Shrike explained. "Mild enough to digest and fatty enough to keep him from wasting away. We haven't any here—the goats give good milk, but it doesn't churn up the way cow's will—and I daren't go bartering at the Moon Market just now, when..." He trailed off, unable to give voice to his worst fear. If something were to happen to Wren whilst he was away, he'd follow him into the grave.

Drude seemed to understand him nonetheless. "We've an abundance of it. If I may rest the night here, I'll set out at dawn and return by dusk."

"Thank you," Shrike said, though the words hardly felt sufficient.

"And I," said the ambassador, "have brought a little something, though not quite all I promised, for which I do apologise. My brother cannot leave Fathomseek at present. But he has sent me along with several potions—" Here he gestured to his clinking satchel. "Based on

165

my description of the Holly King's plight, for the chirurgeon to dispense at their discretion—and," he added, "written receipts of all ingredients, for the chirurgeon's review."

"Thank you," Shrike said again, feeling just as inadequate as before. He hesitated. "I'm afraid we can only offer you the meanest quarters in return. Nell is camped in the warren watch-tower. It's filled with thatch, but little else."

The ambassador waved him off with a twirling wrist. "Think nothing of it. We'll make do."

And, to Shrike's surprise, Drude seemed to agree with him.

"Is the Holly King well enough for company?" the ambassador enquired. "I should like to offer my wishes for his swift recovery. And I believe my travelling companion feels much the same."

Drude appeared much abashed. "Not to presume that he should remember me, but…"

"You're remembered fondly," Shrike assured him—for he was, by Wren and by Shrike as well. "He'll be very happy to see you both."

* * *

WREN, stuck abed in his convalescence, could do little else save wait—however patiently or impatiently—for his Shrike's return.

When he did at last emerge through the cottage door again but a few minutes later by Wren's reckoning, he did so alone. Evidently Nell had gone on her own way back to her camp in the old warren watch-tower. The sight of Shrike's smile proved a balm for Wren's anxious heart.

"The ambassador has returned," Shrike announced with the air of one who'd expected it.

Wren, who'd had no idea the ambassador had come and gone in the first place, much less announced any intention to come back, felt more than a little bewildered. He had a dim recollection of seeing the ambassador on the lake-shore—so dim he'd assumed he'd imagined it.

"Drude is here as well," Shrike added, furthering Wren's astonishment. "They'd both like to see you, if you're feeling up to it."

"Drude?" Wren echoed, astonished but by no means averse to the idea. He'd no notion that the incubus even remembered their encounter at Mabon—though Wren recalled it very well himself, with a blush borne of pleasure rather than shame—much less thought well enough of him to want to visit in his convalescence.

"They won't take offence if you're not well enough for visitors," said Shrike, rousing Wren from his contemplative fugue. Evidently he'd taken a touch too long to answer him. Still, rather than any expression of impatience, Shrike wore an encouraging smile.

"I'm well enough, I think," Wren replied, drawing himself up on his arms to lean back against the pillows in an almost-upright posture.

Shrike's smile broadened. He opened the cottage door just far enough to poke his head out and say something beyond the range of Wren's hearing. When he withdrew into the cottage once more, the door opened in his wake. The diminutive ambassador skipped over the threshold with Drude's massive crimson bulk following him.

Wren had never beheld so many folk in Blackthorn cottage at once. It ought to have felt crowded. Instead, he found it rather cosy. He had but a glimpse of the ambassador—a cheerful wrist-twirling wave paired with a trilled greeting—before Everilda arose to join him in earnest conversation at the work-bench. Shrike followed.

Drude, meanwhile, after taking an admiring glance around the cottage, made a bee-line for the nest. He had to crouch to keep his horns from knocking things down off the beams as he went but appeared nonetheless cheerful as he knelt at Wren's bedside.

"Good evening, my lord," he said, his voice as deep and sonorous as Wren remembered, though under very different circumstances. "I hope the night finds you well."

"Better than I was," Wren admitted. He ought to have felt more nervous than he did, he thought distantly. Perhaps it was the laudanum. Or perhaps it was because both the ambassador and Drude were fae, and thus like Nell cared not for mortal qualms. Or perhaps it was because the ambassador had already witnessed the solstice ritual, and Drude had taken Wren inside him not half a year past. Modesty felt a touch foolish at this point. He supposed he needn't stand on ceremony with him. Though he would've rather stood before him and at least appeared strong rather than lain weak as cobwebs in his nightshirt. "And yourself likewise?"

"Very well," Drude rumbled. "Our herds gave plenty of wool this year, so there's more than enough to keep me at my loom."

"You're a weaver?" Wren said, as if that weren't obvious. He blamed the laudanum.

Drude didn't look as though he considered the question stupid. If anything, he appeared bashful. "And thread-spinner. And a shepherd in the summer months, when they need more hands."

Wren's gaze fell to Drude's garb. At Mabon he'd worn a thin white shirt, black woollen breeches, and naught else. Now, however, Wren realised he had on a black woollen waistcoat with its hems trimmed in embroidered tulips as scarlet as his own natural coat. "Did you do this yourself?"

"Aye," Drude said, sounding almost shy.

Wren wondered if unfounded modesty regarding one's own talents was a prevalent trait amongst the fae. Shrike and Drude certainly held it in common. "It's beautiful."

Drude mumbled his thanks.

"Forgive me," Wren continued. "I know nothing of the craft. How do you...?"

With some coaxing, Drude filled the better part of half an hour with almost everything Wren wished to learn of wool-working. His words came more readily as he went on, his voice growing stronger and his posture relaxing from his humble hunch into something more approaching ease. Only when a yawn escaped Wren did his hesitation return.

"Pardon," Wren begged even as another yawn threatened to overtake him.

Drude didn't seem to take it personally. "The hour grows late. I fear I've overtaxed you."

"Not at all," Wren protested. "It's wonderful to have you visit. The days run together otherwise."

He would've said more, and likely most of it ill-advised, of how it touched him to see Drude's evident concern for his well-being, but

Shrike had taken notice of the first yawn and arrived at Wren's bedside by the second.

"All right?" he asked, laying a hand on Drude's shoulder. Not a correcting hand, Wren noted, but rather a familiar one.

"I'm fine," Wren said.

Drude arose regardless.

Without thinking, Wren reached to give him a parting handclasp.

And after a stunned blink, Drude returned it warmly.

Shrike smiled and slung his arm across Drude's shoulders as he saw him out of the cottage, giving him a glance Wren had seen a hundred times before, one which said as well as words, *Just as I told you.*

Wren didn't have long to wonder at it before sleep claimed him.

The next morning he awoke well after dawn. Drude had already set off, but the ambassador remained and regaled Wren with a steady stream of polite nonsense which Wren found very difficult to navigate under the influence of laudanum. Shrike coaxed the ambassador away from Wren's bedside with the prospect of comparing notes on their progress with letters—both were literate by now, but their reading tastes differed, which gave ample points for comparison and discussion. At any rate they conversed low enough for Wren to fall asleep again.

And when he opened his eyes that evening, he found Drude returned with a hamper full of what seemed to be at least a dozen pounds of butter.

WREN FELT NO LESS restless by the end of the first fortnight.

He felt stronger, to an extent. Pacing the cottage no longer exhausted him. Everilda's exercises grew less painful and more possible. He could fill his hours not just with sleep but with sitting up in bed or at the work-bench to read or sketch—though, confined as he was, he had precious few worthwhile subjects to draw beyond his Shrike.

And while he appreciated Shrike's gentle hand taking care of him, he found himself wishing those tender caresses would turn into something more.

On one afternoon, with Everilda not due to return until evening, and Shrike cooking their repast over the hearth-fire whilst Wren sketched his beloved face illuminated by the flames, Wren thought he had his chance. When Shrike stepped away to let the cauldron boil on its own, Wren caught his eye. And as Shrike knelt by his side and took his hand with a smile, Wren reached up to catch him by the jaw and draw him down for a kiss.

Shrike had kissed him oft since his initial kiss had awoken Wren. And while Wren loved every one of them, his desire demanded something deeper. He parted his lips beneath Shrike's own and tried to draw him into his mouth. Shrike followed him. Amidst breathless gasps, something desperate stirred between Wren's thighs—and between Shrike's as well, unless he were much mistaken.

But when his fingers fell to Shrike's tunic ties and began to fumble them free, a firm yet gentle hand caught them in its warm grasp.

Wren broke off kissing him.

"Will you not lie with me?" Wren asked, hating the desperation evident in his creaking voice.

It seemed to shock Shrike as well. He blinked down at him. Then a wan smile besmirched his perfect lips. It tore Wren's heart in two directions; he loved to see Shrike smile, yet the knowledge of what this particular one meant sent all his hopes plunging into fathomless depths.

"Not just yet," Shrike murmured in the low rumbling burr that set Wren's soul aflame and yet now denied him any expression of his passions.

Wren stared at his beloved, all his fears realised. His convalescence had revealed him for the weak, frail, pathetic creature he truly was when compared against Shrike's brawny courage. And now Shrike loved him not.

Shrike bent to kiss Wren again.

Wren—heart bruised, head spinning, thwarted desire knotted up within him—cut him off. "I know I'm not much to admire now, but we might still..."

He trailed off, half in shame at his own pathetic speech and half at the bewildered look Shrike cast down at him.

Shrike studied him a moment longer, his dark gaze searching Wren's own. Then his hand arose to caress his cheek. Wren couldn't resist leaning into the gentle touch. Even as his heart burned with indignant denial.

"You've everything worth admiring," Shrike murmured. "Everything worth desiring. But your wounds are dire. If I were to hurt you…"

"You wouldn't," Wren blurted. He wished he could withdraw the words even as he spoke them—no schoolboy had ever sounded more desperate or more wretched—and yet his tongue spilled on. "I'm stronger now. I can…"

He trailed off again at the look which clouded Shrike's handsome features. Not exactly pity, but near enough to it to ignite his indignation.

"When you're well again," Shrike said in a tone which reminded Wren far too much of a nursemaid.

A disappointed sigh escaped Wren's lips.

Something hissed in the hearth. Shrike turned away to resume tending it. Wren picked up his gyrdel-book and pencil again. He attempted to continue his sketches. Instead, he tapped the pencil against the page as his mind turned its rusty cogs to try and find a solution to his problem. He found but one conclusion.

If he wished for Shrike to love him again, he must do the unthinkable.

Wren found the opportunity to put his abominable plan into action when he awoke one morning just after dawn to find Shrike gone—likely out to tend the flocks—and Everilda seated by the fire writing in her gyrdel-book. The moment Wren moved, she glanced up.

"Good morning, my lord," she said, setting aside her book and taking up her instruments in its place.

Wren submitted to the ritual of glass and brass whilst she assessed his vitals. Then, after noting whatever conclusions she drew from him into her gyrdel-book, she filled a mug with water and made him drink.

"We've not broken our fast yet," said Everilda. "The Oak King will return soon."

Just as Wren had suspected. He'd awoken at the most opportune moment. And yet he couldn't find the words to ask Everilda what he most needed to know before she returned to her seat and her book.

She was a doctor, he reminded himself sternly. She'd already seen all of him inside and out. She knew all about the peculiar living arrangements between the Oak and Holly Kings. She'd dwelled amongst the fae for—well, he knew not how long precisely, but longer than himself at any rate. And likely she'd tended mortal men and women long before that; tended mothers in childbed and counselled wives and husbands. There was nothing he could possibly say that would shock her.

Furthermore, he had perhaps mere moments before Shrike's return. If he wanted an answer, he must ask now.

"Everilda," he said. The force required to expel the name from his unwilling lips leant it a queer cadence.

She looked up from her gyrdel-book with a mild countenance. "Yes?"

"I've a question for you." He swallowed hard. "In confidence."

Mercifully, she arose and drew close to his bedside, kneeling down to hear him.

Now that he had her attention, Wren knew not how to begin. "It's… of a rather delicate nature."

Everilda blinked rather like a cat.

Wren summoned all his courage. "When would it be considered safe —medically speaking—for Butcher and I to…" He could not continue looking her in the eye if he wished to finish his enquiry; his gaze flicked toward the wall. "That is to say—when might we engage in…" He cleared his throat. "Well, in… in intimacy?"

A silence fell. Wren kept staring at the wall.

"I think," said Everilda, "I take your meaning."

Wren still couldn't look at her, but a sigh of relief escaped him none-theless.

"I wouldn't recommend anything involving your fundament," she went on.

Wren choked on nothing.

"But," she persevered regardless of his reaction, "if you were to remain supine, and the Oak King were to do most of the work, as it were, you may engage in intimacy whenever you liked. Not to excess," she added, "and if you find yourself out of breath or otherwise exhausted, cease. But within reason, I see no danger in it."

As much as it pained him to discuss such matters with a mortal woman, Wren had to admit her words carried welcome tidings. Still, he couldn't look her in the eye as he replied, "Thank you." He hesitated as a thought occurred to him. "Will you tell him so? He'll not believe it from me."

A pause ensued. Wren feared he'd overstepped and offended until she replied, "As you wish, my lord."

He thanked her again, this time making the considerable effort to force his gaze to meet hers.

She graced him with a flicker of a smile and returned to her gyrdel-book.

Not a quarter of an hour later, the cottage door creaked open. Shrike stepped through to knock the snow from his boots and set his egg-basket and milk-pail on the work-bench.

Everilda turned toward Shrike. Wren expected she would arise and bid him join her for a quick private word in the garden.

Instead, she fixed her eyes upon him and said in a perfunctory tone, "The Holly King bids me tell you that gentle lovemaking should pose no danger."

Wren's face felt as if it'd burst into flames.

Shrike raised his brows and glanced between Everilda and Wren. After a moment's pause, he said to Everilda, "I'm glad of it."

Wren wished himself dead.

Everilda departed the cottage without taking his pulse or temperature. Perhaps she knew his present metal state had altered both beyond medical explanation. Or perhaps she simply trusted he was out of danger. Regardless, even after she'd gone, Wren kept his burning face turned toward the wall.

Familiar footsteps trod the floor. A weight settled onto the bed beside him. Calloused fingertips graced his jaw and gently bid him turn his head towards their owner. Wren screwed up his courage and relented.

Shrike smiled down at him.

Even in the midst of his mortification, the sight of that masculine mouth softened in a gentle curve warmed Wren's heart.

Shrike stroked his flaming cheek. "You blush handsomely."

This did nothing to help said blush abate. Wren swallowed hard. "Yes. Well."

When it became apparent he could say nothing further, Shrike bent to kiss him.

It began as most kisses had between them since Wren's retrieval from beneath the ice. This time, however, as Wren opened his mouth beneath Shrike's, Shrike obliged him by deepening the kiss.

And withdrew all-too-soon.

Wren opened his eyes to find Shrike striding away from the nest and toward the hollow stump. He relaxed somewhat at seeing Shrike only meant to wash up and return rather than leave him wanting forever. It certainly didn't lessen his growing interest to watch Shrike strip off his tunic, shirt, and hose, and lather and rinse the strapping sinews of his arms. Soon he returned to slip beneath the bedclothes and straddle Wren with another kiss.

Unbecoming sounds escaped Wren's throat with every caress. He trembled at Shrike's touch as if it were the first time they'd lain together like this. His cock leapt the moment Shrike's fist closed 'round it. He moaned into his beloved's mouth beneath his kiss.

And then, with a single stroke of Shrike's hand, a fortnight's worth of denied desire rose up within him, burst forth, overflowed, and with an arched back and a strangled cry, he shamed himself across Shrike's brawny chest.

Shrike released him. Wren fell back against the pillows, Shrike's arm still twined 'round his shoulders, and the blurred form of his beloved loomed overhead with the noble brow knit in concern.

"Are you all right?" Shrike asked.

Wren nodded, too embarrassed to speak. After all his pleading, all his begging, this was all he had to show for it. Less than a minute gone and a fortnight's worth of unspent seed now bespoilt Shrike's chest. A pitiful performance by any standard.

Yet Shrike didn't look half so disappointed as Wren felt. He bent to kiss him again—a long and languid kiss, drawing Wren out of his confused and humiliated thoughts—and when he withdrew, it was to murmur against Wren's lips, "Again?"

"Yes," Wren whispered, a hiss of desperation. "Yes, yes, please, yes—"

Shrike obliged him with another kiss. It lingered on his lips even as Shrike's mouth moved on, nipping down his jaw towards his ear and bestowing such whispers as made Wren shiver in delight. The bruises that bloomed along his collar and throat in the wake of Shrike's descent held a delicious ache.

Then, with all the speed and fluidity of quicksilver, he caught Wren by the wrist and brought his knuckles to his lips for a chaste chivalrous kiss. What followed proved far less chaste, as he turned the inside of Wren's wrist toward his mouth. His kisses teased the soft and sensitive skin therein whilst he traced the icy blue veins with his tongue and nipped along them-ever-so-gently.

His other hand, meanwhile, slipped further down to trail up the inside of Wren's thigh.

Wren wished to get his hands on Shrike as well. With one wrist deliciously trapped in Shrike's hold, however, and the rest of him weak as spider's-skein, he could hardly do more than entangle his free hand in Shrike's flowing silver-shot locks and drag him down for another proper kiss. This done, he fumbled lower, until at last—more through Shrike's understanding what he wished and manoeuvring himself to make it possible than by any success of his own feeble efforts—he laid his fingertips upon the familiar curving heft of Shrike's cock. To hold it again proved as much an aphrodisiac as the ample attentions Shrike paid to his flesh, until, by the time the gentle touch on the inside of his thigh arose to grasp his no longer over-sensitive prick, it fell upon something that had grown almost to half-mast.

Which was more than enough for Shrike to work with.

A few strokes sufficed to send Wren's hips rolling into Shrike's hand. Wren served him the same in turn, savouring the heat of the velvet-sheathed rod rigid in his palm.

But then Shrike slipped out of his grasp altogether, withdrawing and descending, kissing his way down Wren's chest and ghosting over the bandages swathing his waist until, at last, his mouth reached the half-mast cock and let it slip between his lips.

Wren's head fell back against the pillows. He arched his back with a gasp as Shrike's tongue paid particular tribute to the slit at his tip, then slipped beneath the fore-skin to encircle the ridge before trailing down the vein on its underside. His prick pulsed in the soft wet heat as Shrike hollowed his cheeks and swallowed him down. Another moment or two of this sufficed to bring him to a full stand. It felt still better than Wren remembered, and yet he wanted something more.

So he let his hand fall from Shrike's silver-shot locks to graze his jaw and tilt his chin up until his dark gaze met Wren's own. Shrike appeared curious at the interruption but by no means put off.

Wren swallowed hard, yet his voice remained hoarse as he begged, "Come here."

Shrike required no further bidding. In an instant, with the same quicksilver grace that marked him out as fae, he crawled up to loom over Wren and bent to bless his lips with another kiss. His hips aligned with Wren's own. His hand dipped down between them and brought their cocks together in his strong grasp.

Wren moaned into Shrike's mouth as his shaft slid against his lover's. Their twin blades crossed, entangled, withdrew, and clashed again, an erotic duel made all the more delightful by the clever manipulation of Shrike's fingers. His own nails carved furrows into Shrike's scarred back. To feel his cock alongside the one he loved so well together in the tight sheath of his beloved's fist sent Wren to the brink of ecstasy. Another thrust of his hips in rhythm with the stroke of Shrike's arm and the ravenous kiss that devoured both in turn sufficed to thrust him over the precipice. For the second time in a single hour he spilled his seed. At the same moment Shrike's cock pulsed against his own and his lover's ragged groan reverberated through his own ribs. The surging torrent, wave after wave, cascaded over Shrike's fingers, the mingled foam of two storm-tossed seas.

Whatever happened immediately afterward, Wren knew very little of. When he returned to his senses, safe and warm in their shared nest, he lolled his head to behold Shrike lying beside him, caught in the midst of withdrawing his own fingers from his mouth as he sucked the seed from them. If Wren had his full vitality, he thought the sight might have very well set his prick to a third stand.

As matters stood, however, he retained enough strength to catch Shrike's wrist and bestow a kiss on those very seed-stained fingers to taste himself and Shrike on his own tongue.

Shrike's low rumbling laugh ended as his mouth met Wren's, and this, the first of untold soft, languid, undemanding kisses, soothed him down into dreaming bliss.

* * *

SHRIKE'S HEART brimmed to bursting with joy.

To have his Wren in his embrace again. To hear his gasps and moans of delight and desire. To feel him writhe in pleasure rather than pain. To take him in hand, to taste him, to cross his sword with his own. To draw him up alongside him to the soaring heights of ecstasy—twice, for that matter, which struck a note of pride in his heart despite the extraordinary circumstances.

To lay with his Wren had always brought Shrike joy. But particularly now, when he could feel Wren's vitality returning, his beloved so frail and fragile yet fighting to regain his strength with a tenacity few fae could claim. There was beauty in that beyond the sharp features, dark eyes, and bespeckled lips.

And as Wren returned to a sleep more blissful than many he'd had over the past fortnight, Shrike held him in his arms, safe and sound at last.

* * *

A MUFFLED thumping roused Wren from slumber.

He raised his head from where it'd rested against Shrike's shoulder and peered blearily around the cottage, searching for the source of the noise. Nothing within seemed to make a noise. But outside, at one of the round windows limned by the soft light of early dawn, perched the furred body, feathered wings, and antlered head of a wulpertinger. At first glance it appeared like a particularly lumpy snow-drift, thanks to its silvery white fur and plumage, with the antlers like two dead branches stuck through it. As Wren squinted, however, the wulpertinger blinked its dark eyes and stomped its hind feet to create another thump.

Shrike, meanwhile, arose from the nest and went to the window to answer the creature's summons.

Wren fell back against the pillows and waited for his return. His aching wound gave a dull throb, but nothing worse.

A chill draught insinuated its way through the cottage as Shrike opened the window. The wulpertinger fluttered inside to perch on the slate in front of the hearth. Shrike shut the window and followed it. He fiddled with something amidst its fur for a moment before returning to the nest. There he sat on the edge beside Wren and handed him an envelope.

Wren recognised the curiously angular handwriting of the address at once as that of his pupil, Hull. He broke the seal and read apace.

To His Lordship *the Holly King of Blackthorn,*

Greetings and glad tidings. I write to inform you Mr Grigsby and myself continue to get on splendidly. His mignonette grows apace and he is quite pleased at its progress. He has also received word from Miss Fairfield in Canada that her marriage to Mr Daniel Durst has taken place and they've set up their household in Port Hawksbury, which news I'm sure will bring you as much delight as it has done Mr Grigsby.

The only blot in Mr Grigsby's happiness is that he has not heard from you in some weeks and consequently begins to worry. I hope with your reply I can assure him you are quite well. He's expressed several times his hope that you will visit again soon.

Your obedient servant,

Mr Hull.

. . .

WREN HAD RATHER a lot to consider. He knew Hull's report of Mr Grigsby's concerns must prove an astounding understatement. On an average day these all-too-common concerns had invariably been misplaced. Now, however, not only must he crush Mr Grigsby's hopes of any visit in the near future but also do so without letting slip the why, because the truth of the matter would doubtless send the poor old gentleman into an apoplectic fit of anxiety. Nevermind that Wren felt himself out of danger and had confirmation from Everilda that such was the case.

Furthermore, while Mr Grigsby knew the full truth of Hull's fae nature, he had only the barest hint of Wren and Shrike's. Hull had confessed he'd let slip that Shrike was fae after Mr Grigsby had asked him direct. Wren didn't begrudge him it. Mr Grigsby deserved the truth. Wren only asked that Hull let Wren tell Mr Grigsby the whole of it himself.

Trouble was, he hadn't exactly got around to that in the months since.

Which meant a letter to Mr Grigsby announcing that he'd gone on a Wild Hunt for an ethereal beast and fallen into a lake of eternal ice and been bit by a ferocious monster the true nature of which he did not yet understand, but it was fine because his own position as the Holly King of Blackthorn afforded him certain powers which made him more able to survive hypothermia than most gentlemen might expect, and also the Ambassador of the Court of Spindles had an apothecary brother who provided a potion of eternal sleep at the most critical moment, and their previous alliance with the Court of Bells and Candles granted them access to a chirurgeon experienced in treating mortal patients... would all prove a bit much for the poor old gentleman to take in at once.

Still, he must reply with something, and so he asked Shrike to bring his writing desk so he might make an attempt.

The end result, after several hours and as many or more cups of tea later, was two letters. The first, to Hull, informed him of the entire long and complicated story, concluding with the instruction that Mr Grigsby was not to hear a word of it. The second, to Mr Grigsby, explained amidst profuse apologies that his work for Mr Butcher had taken up all his time of late, but as Wren had got through the worst of it, he would write to Mr Grigsby with greater frequency from now on, though Mr Grigsby must not expect him to visit Staple Inn until, at the earliest, late spring.

The wulpertinger, meanwhile, had stretched itself out lengthwise before the fire and happily accepted Shrike's offering of dried sloe berries. Wren felt a touch sorry for sending it back out into the cold to deliver his replies. Still, it made no complaint as Shrike slid the sealed missives into the little leather satchel strapped across its back between its wings. It hopped over to the door. Shrike opened it.

And there stood Everilda upon the threshold with her hand upraised to knock.

"Oh," she said mildly, blinking down at the wulpertinger. "Beg pardon."

The wulpertinger seemed to take no offense. It wriggled its coal-black nose and hopped around her to get out into the snow-drifts just beyond. She entered in its wake, and Shrike shut the door behind her.

"How are you feeling, my lord?" she asked Wren.

They'd run through an almost identical script every morning since Wren had first awoken after his icy plunge. His answer had altered subtly as the days ran on into weeks. Today, he could reply with honesty, "Rather well, I think. Just an ache."

This seemed to satisfy her. With little more than a brisk nod, she directed him onto the work-bench. His pulse and temperature likewise met with her approval. She clipped through the stitches of the bandage and let the soiled linen fall away. Wren set his jaw as she poked and prodded—gently, of course, but poking and prodding nonetheless—at the wound. While he no longer depended entirely on Shrike's support to hold himself upright, he still very much appreciated the strong arm entwined with his own and the hand that clasped his in turn.

"I believe," Everilda said softly, as if half to herself, "the wound has closed."

Wren perked up. He didn't quite dare believe that phrase meant what he thought it might. Yet as he glanced to Shrike, he found his own hopes reflected in his dark eyes.

The sharp stench of vinegar warned Wren of Everilda's intentions. As she poured it over a clout and began dabbing at his wound, however, he felt no sting. Just a dull ache deeper within.

"You might try bathing yourself as before," she said, observing the flesh she'd cleansed. "An' it so please you."

The prospect of a proper bath at last pleased Wren very much.

"You'll only need a bandage for bracing afterwards," she went on. Then she turned to Shrike. "You've watched me dress his wound these past weeks, have you not?"

"Aye," Shrike answered warily.

"And you've dressed your own wounds before?" At his nod, she further asked, "Splinted any broken bones?"

"Aye," Shrike said again with still more hesitation. Wren knew not why. Every scar Shrike's skin bore represented a wound he'd treated on his own, doctoring himself up for centuries before Wren ever entered his life. But Shrike did always seem to underestimate his own talents.

A faint smile flickered at the corner of her mouth. "Then I think you can well manage a bracing bandage after a bath."

Shrike didn't appear entirely convinced.

But Everilda simply smiled, packed up her instruments, and told the kings of Blackthorn that she would return in the evening if they didn't require her before. With that, she left the cottage.

Shrike helped Wren down off the work-bench to sit in its chair whilst he ran the copper tap. The steam arising from the hollow basin proved a welcome sight to Wren, who remained bare save for his night-shirt draped across his lap, and who'd begun to feel a chill draught in the wake of Everilda's departure. He'd longed for the decadent pleasure of a proper soak throughout his convalescence.

At last, Shrike returned to guide him to the bath. Rather than take Wren by the hand or arm, however, he slipped his arms beneath his knees and shoulders to gather him up altogether in his embrace and carry him bodily to the hollow stump. Wren's heart skipped a beat for reasons beyond his infirmity.

A sigh of sheer relief escaped Wren as he stepped into the water and slipped beneath the warm waves up to his shoulders—a well-appreciated contrast against his last memory of icy submersion. While Shrike had taken very good care of him in the daily stand-up wash, he'd missed the delicious pleasure of a proper soak. The heat alone did wonders for the ache in his side.

With Wren safely stowed in the hollow, Shrike stepped back to strip off his own shirt. Wren lolled his head along the rim of the stump to watch magnificent brawn rippling beneath dashing scars across Shrike's bare chest and stomach—admirable scenery indeed, and a landscape he'd rendered many times over in his gyrdel-book, yet never oft enough, it seemed.

And now those muscular arms dipped into the water up to the shoulder to bathe Wren.

The scent of lavender and honey arose alongside the steam as Shrike worked up a lather against Wren's skin. The smooth glide of familiar fingertips gently rubbing against his body granted long-awaited relief to his sore flesh. A firm reassuring grip took hold of each of his limbs in turn, and Wren felt more than content to follow where they bid as Shrike scrubbed him down. While Everilda had never manhandled Wren by any means, still there remained a certain tenderness to Shrike's ministrations which hers had lacked.

At Shrike's murmured instruction, Wren slipped forward and tipped his head back to dip his hair into the bath. His locks swirled around his face as Shrike worked his hands through them. He let his eyes fall shut with another sigh, more ragged and drawn out than the first, but no less appreciative. The waterfall flow from the pitcher in Shrike's skilled hands seemed to wash away all his cares alongside the grime.

Wren could feel perfectly content, he thought, if only Shrike would join him.

* * *

SHRIKE WAS glad of the opportunity to treat Wren's flesh with all the tender care and devotion it deserved. It balmed his heart's-wound to be able to do something with his own two hands towards healing his beloved.

To feel knotted muscles relax beneath his fingertips, to hear the soft sighs of relief escaping those bespeckled lips, to see the pained furrows in his brow smoothed away and a gentle smile grace his perfect mouth.

Yet after his Wren's beloved body was soaked and scrubbed and washed clean as fresh-fallen snow, Shrike's sense of pride became a pang as he helped Wren step out of the bath.

And the bright crimson brand of the wound that'd only just begun to scar appeared all-the-more undeniable against his pale skin.

Only when Shrike beheld a shiver ripple across Wren's flesh did he realise he'd lost himself in staring. He hastened to snatch up a linen towel and wrap it 'round Wren's body. The shivers ceased as Shrike patted him dry. Wren leaned against him as he hobbled to the workbench and looked back to Shrike to lift him up onto it. This Shrike did with ease.

But it was with considerably less ease that he beheld again the wretched wound as Wren unwrapped the towel from his waist and draped it over the tops of his thighs.

As Everilda had said, Shrike had dressed his own injuries countless times throughout the centuries. Yet all his own injuries combined felt like mere scrapes and bruises compared to the thought of his Wren's singular wound. He couldn't look away from it now if he were to wrap the bracing linen 'round Wren's waist. And now that he was forced to look he found he couldn't look away. The mute horror of it compelled his gaze.

Then Wren's hand arose to gesture toward it. Shrike forced himself to look up and meet Wren's eyes.

Wren gave him a wry self-deprecating smile. "Seems I'm well on my way to catching you up."

Shrike furrowed his brow in confusion.

"The scars," Wren elaborated. "One to your many. Though mine is rather larger than most of yours, so perhaps it ought to count for more?"

His lilting tone bespoke a jest. Yet to hear him speak of it so lightly left Shrike feeling still more disturbed. Before Shrike could think of anything to say, much less say it, something of his churning torment must have shown in his features, for Wren's face fell to match it.

"You don't like it," said Wren.

"What?" Shrike said before he'd quite understood him.

Wren's expression grew still more pained. "The look of it."

"No," Shrike hastened to explain; he couldn't bear the sight of Wren's heartbreak. "It isn't that."

Wren didn't look comforted. "Then what?"

Shrike hesitated. His hand arose and traced the shape of the wound in the air above it. "Because of this… I almost lost you."

It took considerable force of will to thrust the words out past his teeth. He couldn't speak on it without thinking of it, and he couldn't think of it without drowning in the wretched memory—Wren's scream as the beast bit him, the blood freezing against his broken flesh, his shivers and broken moans of agony, his sunken eyes and hollowed cheeks—then further back, to Rochester, with another monster holding him up by the throat, and how he'd collapsed insensible for what must only have been moments but which felt like eons of anxiety as Shrike waited for his wheezing breaths to bring him back to consciousness, for his eyes to open and focus on some fixed point rather than wandering along the edge of oblivion, the cracked pain of his voice when at last he spoke, and how Shrike's heart had wrenched itself in twain for the sorrow at the evident suffering in his creaking words and the sheer relief at hearing his beloved speak again—and further back still, to his first failure, when he'd left Larkin alone and defenceless and returned too late to find him broken and gone forever.

A hand caressed his cheek.

Shrike jerked his head up. It'd fallen again, his gaze ever-returning to the haunting lodestone of Wren's wound. But now, as he met those soft dark eyes, he saw something bittersweet in their fond depths.

"How many times have I almost lost you?" Wren asked.

Shrike furrowed his brow as he ran over the sums. "Once, by my reckoning. In my fight with the old Holly King. But your sigil kept me from danger."

Wren shook his head. While Shrike stood in silent confusion, Wren reached for his bared chest. His hesitant fingertips gently touched the star-burst puncture just below Shrike's collarbone and above his heart.

"Did I not nearly lose you here?" Wren asked.

Shrike said nothing. An errant arrow in the Wild Hunt had struck him there some centuries ago. Yet what Wren did now seemed to strike a surer blow to his heart.

Wren's hand descended to trace the long diagonal gash across Shrike's navel, beginning at the crest of his left hip-bone and ending beneath the floating rib on the opposing side.

"And here?" Wren asked.

Another tournament—one of many—had not ended in victory for Shrike. Still, he'd held his entrails in with one hand and kept his sword in the other as he staggered away from the field, alone, with no one but himself to tend him. Wren didn't need to know of it, so Shrike said nothing.

Wren moved his hand again, this time to ghost along the gash in Shrike's side from his duel with the Holly King. "And here?"

Shrike found his voice at last. "Your pentangle protected me."

Wren's mouth twisted with impatience. "And the others?"

"You didn't know me then," said Shrike, his discomfort with this conversation only growing.

"If you had found the pain of any one of these wounds too great and given up your will to live... I would still be clerking in Staple Inn." A bitter smile twisted Wren's mouth. "Just as dead as you, in spirit if not in body."

The thought of their never meeting didn't sit easily in Shrike's mind.

"But you survived," Wren continued, his smile growing more sincere. "And because you survived, we have each other."

For which Shrike felt very glad indeed. His Wren well-deserved someone to cherish and defend him. Shrike was honoured to take up the charge.

"I admire your scars," Wren said, the words rushing out of him with an air of confession. "They prove your strength and courage."

In vainer moments now and again, Shrike may have thought the same. To hear someone else say it, however, seemed to raise it up from mere vanity. And to hear that his beloved Wren thought so sent a pulse of warmth throughout Shrike's chest.

"Is this not the same?" Wren asked, gesturing to his own wound, a hint of desperation creeping into his voice. "Not of strength or courage, perhaps, but—may this not likewise become a mark of our victory?"

Until that moment it had never occurred to Shrike to think of it as anything other than a mark of his own failure. He'd failed to protect his beloved, and Wren had paid the price in pain.

Yet neither could Shrike bear the idea of Wren thinking he held his scar in scorn. And so he replied, resolving to believe it as he spoke it, "It may."

Wren's tentative smile of hopeful relief both broke and warmed Shrike's heart. He could answer it with nothing short of an embrace. Gentle and mindful of Wren's broken body, he enfolded him in his arms, and Wren slipped his own around Shrike in turn and upraised his face to meet his kiss.

Still, it relieved Shrike as much or moreso than his Wren to cover the wound with bracing swathes of linen.

* * *

"Is THERE something I might do beyond this?" Wren asked.

Almost another se'en-night had passed since the outer lips of his wound had closed. This circumstance had not altered the exercises Everilda gave him. He lay on the workbench with his knees drawn up, having just completed the third round of five repetitions, and while still winded, he felt rather less exhausted by them with each passing day.

Everilda blinked down at him. "Swimming would be best. Though that'll have to wait 'til summer, most like. Or springtime at the very least."

Wren felt as though he couldn't wait another hour, much less three months or more.

Shrike appeared thoughtful. "How far may he travel?"

Everilda looked at him curiously. "He oughtn't walk far. And I'd advise against the strain of keeping himself in the saddle."

Wren wished they wouldn't talk about him as if he weren't there.

"Perhaps a sleigh?" Shrike asked.

Everilda raised her brows. "Perhaps."

Wren shot Shrike an enquiring look.

But for the moment, it went unanswered.

* * *

No sooner had Everilda arrived to check on Wren the following morning than Shrike arose from their broken fast and made a peculiar declaration.

"I must go," he said, to Wren's bewilderment. "I'll return by nightfall."

Wren wondered what could drive Shrike from the cottage. He wondered still more at Shrike's not divulging it at once. Nevertheless he trusted that whatever reasons he held for his actions, they were doubtless important, and Shrike would tell him the whole when the proper moment arrived.

At present, he indulged in a parting kiss before he let Shrike go on his way.

Which left him alone in the cottage with Everilda.

He expected it might—nay, must—feel awkward. But as moments passed into minutes with Everilda focused upon her gyrdel-book and only the crackling of the hearth-fire breaking the silence, Wren found himself rather more comfortable with her presence than he'd felt before. Perhaps now that she knew his body outside and in and had answered his most damning questions, he could at last discard the final flimsy barrier of mortal propriety that lay between them.

Although it did discomfit him to think she knew almost all of him and he knew almost nothing of her.

Despite the laudanum weighing down the wheels of his mind, he tried to think on what he did know. She had come from the Court of Bells and Candles. She served as chirurgeon and bone-setter to Lady Aethelthryth. She appeared no older than himself—indeed, perhaps somewhat younger. She was mortal, yes, but had she come from a mortal realm? If so, which one, and when?

"Everilda," Wren said before his better sense could catch up to his curiosity.

She raised her head to regard him.

"You've travelled rather a winding road to come here, I should think," said Wren.

Her left brow approached her hairline. "As have you."

"How did you arrive in the fae realms? Forgive me," he added, as her right brow joined her left. "It's just—I've never met another mortal here."

She levelled a long considering look upon him. Then, to his surprise, she got up from her seat by the fire and settled onto the stool at his bedside.

"It was my duty to tend the abbey gardens after supper," she began. "One night, beneath the full moon, a creature appeared amidst the greenery. I mistook them for a cat at first, until I beheld how they walked on their hind legs and wore a little mouse-skin cloak to cover their wings. Veined glass," she added in response to Wren's bewildered look. "Like damselfly wings. They approached me—which was aston-ishment enough—and spoke. They told me the life of their prince hung in the balance and begged me to do all in my power to save her. My power, I thought, would not fill an egg-cup. Still, I had my herbal, my faith, and my years spent assisting chirurgy in the abbey, and I had taken vows to do all I could to aid those less fortunate. And so I followed the little fellow not out of the abbey, but further into the garden to a toadstool ring I'd never noticed before. I stepped through it and found myself in a forest. The creature led me through the winding paths to a palace growing out of the very trees—a realm of pure viridi-tas. There I met the Lady Aethelthryth, who lay dying of a curse laid on her by her foes. I tended her as best I could, never expecting to do more than ease her suffering. Yet, by miracle, she emerged victorious from the fight within her own flesh and offered me a boon of my own naming. The idea of performing a kind of chirurgy never done before, and for those who could not do for themselves, struck me. And so I asked if I might remain to heal the sick and wounded of her court, and not just assist them, but by doing so learn a different sort of anatomy and alchemy by which I might help still more. She agreed. There I have laboured ever since."

"Never leaving?" Wren asked.

"Oft leaving," she replied easily. "I journey throughout the realms to learn from others in my trade. But always I return."

"And... for how long have you done this?" Wren enquired with some hesitation.

She considered it for a moment, then replied, "It is *anno Domini* eighteen-hundred-and-forty-six, now, is it not?"

Wren nodded, half in confirmation of her enquiry and half in admiration of her aptitude for time-keeping.

"Then I have wandered and returned for some four centuries." She smiled. "And a little more."

Wren stared.

"And you?" she asked, startling him a great deal. "How did you come to the fae realms?"

"Oh." Wren hadn't considered himself interesting enough that she— or anyone else—would want to turn the question around on him. Furthermore, his journey contained rather more sordid detail. "Rather less exciting and less noble than your own history, I'm afraid. I clerked in a solicitor's office in Staple Inn. One day a gentleman in medieval garb arrived and declared I would assist him in defying his fate. And the rest... well." He shrugged. "I went along with it, I suppose."

She had fixed him with her studied gaze throughout his short recitation. "More similar than otherwise, it would seem. The fae came to seek your aid. And you answered their call."

Wren felt forced to concede her point. "The ways of the fae are somewhat more amenable than the ways of the mortal realm to men of my sort. I gained as much as the Oak King in the bargain. Likely more."

Her soft and knowing smile bespoke as well as words her complete understanding of that particular phrase—*men of my sort*. "So too do I find the ways of the fae are better suited to my pursuits."

The door-latch clattered open. Shrike stepped into the cottage. He knocked a great deal of snow off his boots as he hung up his cloak by the door.

"Did it go well?" Wren asked.

Shrike glanced up, startled. "What?"

Wren supposed his enquiry had come rather abrupt. "Whatever it was that took you out of the cottage. How did it go?"

"Oh." A sly and handsome grin overtook Shrike's features. "Very well indeed. I'll show you on the morrow."

* * *

WREN'S EXCITEMENT very nearly precluded sleep.

The confirmation that Shrike's secretive quest was a fun one rather than anything dire did a great deal to soothe his worries, which left only the delightful anticipation of knowing something wonderful awaited on the morrow.

And even without this, just the simple promise that he would get to venture out-of-doors for the first time in almost a month would have sufficed to keep him awake.

Still, even with his heart racing against his ribs, the brawny embrace of Shrike in his arms and his beloved's low steady breaths reverberating through his own chest eventually persuaded his mind and body alike to drift down, down, down into unconscious bliss.

He awoke to the scent of toasted cheese and the sight of dust-motes drifting gently through shafts of soft dawn sunlight. Shrike knelt before the fire cooking their breakfast. He'd left behind a pocket of warmth in the nest, which Wren curled up in with the bedclothes up to his nose whilst he watched him work.

Mere moments passed before some slight sound or faint flicker of movement alerted Shrike to his observer. He turned to regard Wren with a smile and a low rumbling good-morning.

Wren answered him in kind, though he remained on tenterhooks throughout the breaking of their fast.

Shrike seemed almost as eager to reveal the secret as Wren felt to learn it. A smile frolicked across his lips as he helped Wren dress to go out-of-doors—the first time in over a month Wren had bothered to don his waistcoat, much less his frock coat and boots. By the time they both had their scarves, gloves, mittens, and cloaks on, Wren thought the anticipation might well drive him to distraction. The cold draught through the cottage door as it opened felt refreshing as a summer's breeze on what little of his face remained exposed to the elements.

And just beyond the cottage door stood a sleigh.

Even as he realised he ought to have expected as much—after all, Shrike had asked after the very thing when enquiring of Everilda how an invalid might travel—Wren couldn't keep from gawking. The sleigh looked as though it'd grown out of the wood alongside the shoots and saplings of spring. Stout oak planks curved into a rounded body not unlike a curled ivy leaf, stained a deep shade of Kendall green with trim in the particular green-yellow shade of sunshine seen through the undersides of the forest canopy. Curled saplings formed its gleaming runners. It appeared not quite so large as the horse-drawn sleighs Wren had seen whilst in England. He supposed since Shrike had no horses, he'd sized it to suit his goats—or perhaps a stag.

"You made this?" Wren asked, his voice soft with astonishment.

Shrike looked abashed. "'Tis not much, but twill serve."

"I'll say!" Wren wondered how many years would pass before Shrike understood the worth of his own handiwork. "I think it's splendid."

A dashing hint of rosy hue appeared across Shrike's sharp cheek-bones as he graced Wren with the small-yet-handsome smile he loved so well.

"When did you build it?" Wren asked, recalling the weeks he'd spent cooped up in the cottage. He remembered Shrike as remaining by his side at all hours, though the first week or so he'd slept a great deal and supposed Shrike might have snuck out then to construct this marvel. Surely he couldn't have done it all yesterday in the few hours he'd been gone. He knew from watching Shrike weave withy over the summer months that wood had to be green or steamed—ideally both—to bend into the graceful, polished curves of the sleigh and its runners. No green wood grew in the dead of winter, and where Shrike might have steamed it in so short a time Wren knew not.

Wren had thought the question a simple one, but Shrike seemed to give it a great deal of consideration.

"A century and a half ago?" Shrike replied at last, much to Wren's surprise. "I needed something to bring home larger game and take greater quantities to and from the Moon Market."

Wren marvelled at the remarkable preservative powers of the fae realms—or perhaps the care Shrike took in his creations—for it looked as if it could've been built yesterday.

Shrike bundled him into the sleigh alongside some provisions. No more than required for a day's picnic, which gave Wren some hint as to the length of their journey. More linen than he expected, though, and what seemed like half the medicine chest besides. A fleece covered all, which Shrike then belted into place with leather straps, so Wren couldn't have fallen out of the sleigh if he'd tried.

Wren waited for Shrike to bring out the goats or summon a stag to draw the sleigh. Now that he thought of it, he'd never been quite sure whether the stag Shrike summoned to ride in the hunt was a different stag each time or the same one over and over again.

But rather than goat or stag, instead Shrike simply took up the reins, slung them over his shoulders, and began trudging forward through the snow, pulling the sleigh behind him.

"Wait!" Wren blurted.

Shrike ceased at once and whirled to regard him. "What's amiss?"

Wren hadn't meant to give him alarm. "Aren't I too heavy for you?"

Shrike stared at him. Then a slow and handsome smile crept up his cheek. "I mean no offense, but you weigh not even half so much as a dead bear."

Wren felt a blush blooming over his face beneath his scarf. "Oh."

A soft huff of laughter escaped Shrike. Then he turned, adjusted the reins on his shoulders, and strode on.

Shrike's strength alone oft proved ample fuel for Wren's admiration. To have that strength bent to his service inspired his ardour further still.

And with these very pleasant thoughts dancing through his mind, Wren leaned back into the sleigh and stared around at the world that had been denied him for so long.

Ice-sheathed barren broad-leaf branches and snow-covered evergreen needles drifted past him overhead. Icicles as long as swords caught the sunlight and scattered it brighter than any fine-cut diamond. Now and again a titmouse flitted between the trees. More often he heard the birds rather than saw them, their songs muffled by the snow yet resounding stark in the otherwise-silent wood. Wren wished he could sketch a fraction of what he saw. He resolved to bring his gyrdel-book and pencils along when they went out again. He hoped it would happen soon.

As they passed through a particular arch in the Grove of Gates, the scenery altered but subtly. They wandered through a different forest now, formed of more hills and dales and with a better-defined path, though no less wintry. At least, not until they came around a particular bend, and Wren noted how the snow drifts grew smaller and smaller, thinning into a mere icy sheen over the ground, until they vanished in patches where greenery began to peep through, and then, on the broad side of something too small for a proper hill yet too big for a mere mound, disappeared altogether, leaving only verdant moss and ferns in its wake.

Here Shrike halted.

Wren gazed around in bemused wonder. He saw nothing of note beyond the mossy hillside. He doubted Shrike had brought him all this way just for that—unless he thought Wren needed to see something green after so many days cooped up indoors, in which case Wren quite agreed. It was certainly a beautiful sight to behold.

Shrike dropt the reins and turned to unbuckle the belts securing Wren to the sleigh.

"Where are we?" Wren asked.

"One of the Realms of Hidden Folk," Shrike replied.

Wren hadn't realised there were multiple.

"They've granted us the use of this place," Shrike continued. "On the condition that we return to join them the following Mabon. You don't mind, do you?" he added, a furrow of concern appearing between his brows.

Wren smiled. "Not in the least."

Shrike returned his smile and drew him upright. Then he slung their basket of provisions over one shoulder and took Wren's arm. He stepped forward as if he meant to climb the hill. Wren's gut gave a twinge at this; he didn't know if he felt quite up to climbing.

But instead of up the side of the hill, Shrike's steps brought them through it.

Wren blinked. He half-expected another mead hall—though it would be quite unlike Shrike to spring a throng on him. But instead of a fae crowd revelling beneath walls of skin, he found a stone cavern as grand in scope as any cathedral, its ribbed walls worn smooth with time.

And in its centre a bubbling spring with steam rising off the water.

For the second time in the same morning, Wren lost himself staring. The water, more than a pond and flowing from a source he couldn't perceive, appeared in a crystalline aquamarine shade, so clear he could see the bottom of its pool. It swept in currents that had evidently carved out this hollow in the earth over centuries, creating gentle curves along its smooth stone shore. The splashing echoed throughout the cavern, reverberating against itself in a quiet yet all-encompassing sound that soothed Wren's nerves—interrupted only by the slight shifting noise of Shrike setting down their provisions basket behind him and laying out the fleece beside it.

Shrike glanced up with a shy smile as Wren turned to face him. "I thought we might have a swim, as Everilda suggested."

Wren laughed. "We might, indeed!"

Shrike's smile broadened into a grin.

With Shrike's assistance, Wren shed his garments. The air within the cavern had already begun to feel a touch too warm with all his layers. Even laid bare, he hardly felt a hint of chill. It seemed the spring had banished winter. The loss of the bracing bandage gave his stomach the same lurch as it always did, though less so now that Everilda's exercises had restored some of his strength.

And, if all went according to plan, a swim might restore him so he didn't need it at all.

Again with Shrike's aid, Wren lowered himself down to sit on the smooth stone edge and dipped into the water up to his calves. It felt as warm as his baths in the hollow stump at Blackthorn. Peering down, he saw the bottom of the pool did not drop away all at once—at least, not from where he sat—but rather the water or perhaps some fae influence of the hidden folk had carved the stone away by degrees to create a series of steps down into the deep. Further on, it did fall away into a depth Wren thought would close over his head if he ever dared venture so far.

And it was toward this depth that Shrike dove over Wren's head to plunge into the water with a tremendous splash.

Wren flinched with a gasp half-astonishment and half-delight. Shrike had oft performed such feats when they'd swum together over the past summer—particularly at a splendid waterfall which Wren hoped they might return to when the weather warmed again.

And now, like then, Shrike breached from the waves as if he himself were a geyser, throwing his head back to fling a thunderstorm's worth of water from his hair.

Wren had to admit he quite liked the sight.

Shrike gave his head another shake, not unlike a hound, or a wolf for that matter. Then he caught Wren's eye with a grin and swam to rejoin him in long swift strokes. He folded his arms up against the rim of the pool beside him. A gleaming glance from his dark eyes said as well as words, *Join me?*

Leaping and diving had never been Wren's specialty. Even a simple jump and plunge felt rather beyond his powers at the moment. Still, he dared to inch forward and slide down a single step into the pool. Warm water lapped against the tops of his thighs. He slid another step. The water swirled around his waist.

And there he halted.

His breath ceased. His heart climbed into his throat. He knew not why at first, even as his hands gripped the rim of the step with white knuckles. But as the scarred tooth-marks torn into his side perceived just a touch more heat than the rest of his skin, so too did he realise this felt all-too-much like the last time he'd plunged beneath the waves.

Within that instant, Shrike shoved off from the pool's edge and swam to twine his arm 'round him.

"Are you all right?" he asked. "Has something torn?"

"No," Wren said honestly, biting back the bitterness that threatened to seep into his words. It was nothing wrong with his body. Certainly nothing wrong with Shrike. Only his own cowardice come back to haunt him with visions of a sleek hunter darting from the darkness to drag him down.

A soft touch smoothed back the lock of hair that'd fallen across his forehead. Shrike, as always, soothing him with undemanding but no less constant affection. Wren forced himself to breath steadily in time with the waves lapping against the rim. This was a pool of perpetual warmth, he told himself, not a lake of eternal ice. As far as his eye could perceive, from one shore to the other, there were no shadows for beasts to hide in. He could see for himself there were no monsters here.

And besides, he had his Shrike beside him.

"If you would take my arm," Wren said at last with forced calm. "I think I might take another step down."

No sooner had he spoken than Shrike's far hand twined with his own. The other slipped around his waist to rest on his hip.

Wren took a deep breath and stepped in up to his breast-bone. From here the water supported most of his weight. It eased a great deal of the strain on his stomach that even the simple task of standing demanded. A sigh of relief escaped him despite his anxieties.

Shrike's thumb caressed his hip. "Perhaps I might hold you up if you float on your back...?"

The thought of turning his back on the water sent a bolt of fear through Wren's veins. The thought of Shrike holding him, however, alleviated his fear almost as soon as it struck, until it became a dull throb at the edge of his mind rather than burning throughout his brain. He nodded.

Another step brought him in up to his throat.

Just when Wren thought his courage must fail him, the arm around his waist shifted, and Shrike released his hand, resettling his grip with one arm across Wren's shoulders and the other against the backs of his thighs. Wren drew in a deep breath and allowed himself to fall backward. It wasn't the first time he'd fallen into Shrike's embrace. The descent was easier than ever, a fraction of a moment passing before the water buoyed him up and saw him drifting gently down into Shrike's arms.

And then he had Shrike smiling down at him, which was always a pleasant sight.

Wren reminded himself to breathe. He was warm and safe. Shrike had him. Even if there were a beast lurking in the water, Shrike would slay it before it ever approached him.

Still, he found he didn't like not seeing it for himself. He rolled over —a far easier feat in the water than in his sickbed—and endeavoured to swim. Shrike kept his arms under his chest and thighs at first. Then, when it became apparent Wren wouldn't sink, he let him slip from his grasp.

Wren struck out for the rim. It took him far more strokes than it ought, for he'd never been a strong swimmer even before his injury. Yet he made it all the same. He intended to catch his breath there and then set out again to swim back to Shrike, from one safe hold to another.

Only to turn and find Shrike already beside him.

Shrike served him an apologetic smile.

Wren supposed it wasn't hard for Shrike's naturally long strides to keep up with a swimming invalid, even when walking through water. And he could hardly blame Shrike for following him.

"Where does it drop off?" Wren gasped.

Shrike struck out for the appointed place and remained there as a guiding lighthouse for Wren to aim toward.

It didn't take many repetitions of Shrike to shore and back again to tire Wren. Then he simply sat on the steps and watched appreciatively as Shrike performed feats of aquatic agility. When at last they left the water, Wren felt twice as heavy as when he'd gone in. But the ache in his limbs wasn't the grinding throb of fever; rather the satisfying sensation that came after splitting firewood or swinging a scythe.

While Wren dried off, Shrike set out the picnic that Wren himself had almost forgotten. He devoured it with an appetite he hadn't realised he possessed until it touched his lips—the bread Shrike had baked just that morning before Wren had even awoken, slathered with lingonberry jam and butter from the Court of Hidden Folk. A comfortable silence descended on them as they ate. Wren's mind wandered as he chewed—which meant he had a question for Shrike when he finished swallowing.

"When will the Wild Hunt ride again?" Wren asked.

Shrike looked altogether bewildered at the suggestion.

Wren had no notion how Shrike knew when the Wild Hunt would meet. On some occasions—like the white hart hunt—he received a missive, usually from Nell. On others he seemed to learn it from the turning of a particular leaf or the rustling of a breeze or the way the clouds happened to drift across the moon. More often he seemed to know just on pure instinct.

"Likely soon," Shrike admitted with some hesitation. "Though I shall not join them."

"Well, not the very next one I suppose," said Wren. "But perhaps the one after or the one after that—whenever I'm well enough to join you."

Shrike stared at him in something that looked very much like disbelief. "You wish to rejoin the hunt?"

"I enjoy it," Wren insisted. "Perhaps not for the same reasons as you, but—it's exhilarating. And more sporting than a fox-hunt, certainly."

He'd hoped that last remark might provoke the hint of a smile in Shrike's sombre features. Instead they grew still more clouded with concern.

At length, Shrike replied, "I know not how to keep you safe."

His words emerged half-mumbled, as if to speak them louder would loose the full wellspring of helplessness behind them.

Wren ceased swimming and spun to stare at him in turn. "You have kept me safe."

Shrike's eyes dropt to the ragged burgundy scar in Wren's side, then flicked up to meet his gaze again. "Clearly not."

"You did," Wren insisted. "I fell through the ice because I ignored your advice and wandered away from the stag. It's my own folly. There was nothing further you could've done—unless you wanted to tie me to it?"

He'd meant it in jest, but Shrike looked as though he were seriously considering it.

"You rescued me," Wren hurried on. "You carried me home and

restored me to life. You've tended me for months whilst I regained my strength. I'm alive before you now *because* you kept me safe."

Shrike looked but half-convinced, if that.

A single stroke through the water brought Wren to him. Here the water was shallow enough for him to stand before his Shrike. He slipped his arms around his waist and drew him close, tilting his head up to meet his gaze.

"I'll be safe," Wren promised. "So long as I'm with you."

Uncertainty still showed behind Shrike's dark eyes. Yet he met Wren's glance with his own and held it. Then, returning his embrace, he bent to grant him a kiss. Wren smiled up at him as they broke it off, and after a moment's pause, Shrike returned it.

"Then..." Shrike said with unaccountable hesitation. "Would you want to accompany me when I go to slay the skull-crusher?"

Wren blinked up at him, glad for the invitation but stunned nonetheless. "You intend to hunt it?"

Shrike gave a solemn nod. "I've months yet to wait to satisfy my rage against the beast. My thirst for vengeance against Tolhurst was slaked within moments."

Wren stared at him. It hadn't occurred to him to think of Tolhurst's murder as an act of vengeance. He'd assumed Shrike had slid his misericord into the bastard's throat to prevent Tolhurst's shard of glass from finding its sheath in his own flesh. He swallowed hard. "You would have slain him for revenge, then? Not just in self-defence?"

Shrike furrowed his brow. "He raised his hand against you."

"And that is enough for you to kill him?" Wren knew he ought to feel horrified. Yet his pulse quickened for reasons far beyond dread or fear. That Shrike should value him so highly... and to realise, in his heart, that had he a fraction of Shrike's strength, he would do the same himself in turn.

Shrike held his gaze. "Your word alone would stay my hand."

Wren's heart skipped a beat as the words sang through his blood. Still, he had other concerns to hand. "Tolhurst was a man. The skull-crusher is a beast. Don't mistake me—I'd sleep far better if the thing were dead. But... ought we to hunt it?"

Shrike stared at him.

Wren coloured. "It's not as though it attacked me out of spite. It wanted to eat me because it needs to eat. It seems a little hypocritical for us to exact vengeance on it for doing what it must do to survive, doesn't it?"

Shrike gave him a long considering look before he spoke. "Once, in a springtime long ago, I spent some days lying in wait for a stag where a stream fed into a pond. Many other creatures lived there, including a pair of ducks whose eggs had just hatched. From my covert I watched the ducklings take their first toddling steps from their nest towards the pond where their mother and father taught them to swim. Then a winged shadow swept over the water."

Wren tensed.

"I knew it at once for a hawk," Shrike continued. "The ducks did as well, for they quickly began to herd their children back to the nest. But the ducklings were small and awkward, and it didn't seem likely they'd all make it to safety before the hawk swooped. The hawk didn't prey on them out of malice; it needed to sate its hunger, as all creatures do, and a duckling is an easier meal than most."

Wren still didn't like where this story was headed but nodded all the same.

"The hawk descended," Shrike went on. "Its talons narrowly missed one of the ducklings. The ducks caterwauled, but this did nothing to dissuade the hawk from making another dive."

Wren braced himself for nature's brutality.

"Then," said Shrike, "the trees burst with a shrieking cacophony. Finches, buntings, warblers, larks, fig-birds, grosbeaks, robins, nuthatches, sparrows, swallows, swifts, martins, bee-eaters, starlings... even wrens," he added, with a sidelong glance. "Every songbird in the forest, it seemed, flocked forth at once, and all flew straight for the hawk. The hawk, which I don't think had ever feared anything besides perhaps an owl, was pelted on all sides by scores of tiny beaks and perching claws. They drove it out of the sky down to the ground. Hawks mislike landing flat; they won't do it unless they've no other choice, and this one had none. And there it sat, stunned, flinching as screaming songbirds kept swooping at it. Only when the ducks had got back safe to their nest did the songbirds let up. Still the hawk waited a while longer before it felt safe enough to take flight again, and then it wheeled off far from the pond and did not return within my time there."

Wren could do naught but stare.

"The hawk did only what was in its nature, true enough," Shrike continued. "But so did the songbirds in seeking vengeance for every one of their number ever hunted by the hawk. And while the beast beneath the ice may only be doing what is in its nature by hunting to eat, I am likewise merely doing what is in my nature by defending my own heart."

Wren's own heart warmed alongside his beloved's words. Still he couldn't keep from adding, "And revenging it, as well."

Shrike gave a half-shrug and a half-smile to match it.

* * *

THE MORNING of Ostara dawned resplendent.

Wren still felt a twinge of guilt for his long convalescence preventing Shrike from taking on any mask commissions. Yet in the last fortnight or so—with Wren no longer quite so helpless as before, and indeed strong enough to look after himself if Shrike would let him, his wound closed and the work-bench no longer required for chirurgy—Shrike had found the hours required to create masks for them both.

Wren's mask resembled his namesake, with a sharp pointed beak over the nose and intricately tooled pale feathers speckled with dark dye. He'd laughed to see it, remarking how it resembled his own freckles, which brought a handsome blush to Shrike's high cheekbones. For his own mask, Shrike had crafted a simple domino from black leather, adding only a long, curved raptor beak.

Thus disguised, they ventured forth arm-in-arm through the Grove of Gates to the appointed glade.

At least a hundred masked fae had already gathered. Most turned to regard Shrike and Wren as they passed through the crowd. Whispers sprung up in their wake. Wren supposed those who knew of his fate in the white hart hunt had spread the tale far and wide. He wondered if any of the fae had expected the mortal Holly King to survive his wounds at all, much less attend Ostara.

Unlike last year, Shrike and Wren did not wander throughout the whole of the glade. Instead, Shrike led Wren to an outcrop of broad, flat stones covered over with moss and framed by a patch of forget-me-nots. Shrike laid his own cloak over the rocks and gently guided Wren down to lounge upon it. No sooner had Shrike himself sat than he insinuated his form beside Wren's until Wren sat almost in his lap with his own head supported by Shrike's collar.

Satisfied at last, Shrike reached out and plucked up a handful of forget-me-nots and began twining them through his fingers. Wren, already well-familiar with his habit of idle fiddling, left him to it and took out his pencil and gyrdel-book to do some fiddling of his own.

Remaining in one place in no way limited their view of the crowd. On the contrary, it gave the wandering fae a fixed point to approach if they wanted to glimpse the Oak King and his mortal consort, neither of whom had been seen abroad since the white hart hunt. While Wren didn't necessarily enjoy being gawked at, he found the mask eased a great deal of self-conscious feeling.

And while the fae came to look at him, he looked upon them in turn and recorded them in his gyrdel-book sketches besides—as he'd wished he'd done with all the marvellous masks he'd seen last year. With so many visitors to their queer corner of the glade, Wren began to feel like a king holding court for the first and only time since his coronation.

Thus Shrike and Wren passed an idle hour in companionable silence and contemplative crowd-watching, broken only by the familiar cry of—

"Oi, Butcher!"

Wren glanced up at the sound of Nell's voice. To his surprise, he beheld not just Nell approaching (in a black domino mask rather like Shrike's, only without a beak and made from papier-mâché rather than leather), but beside her a figure whose white mask obscured all their face save the eyes, and yet whom Wren had the unmistakable impression must be Everilda. Perhaps the hair gave her away, or her garb. Or perhaps it was merely that she walked almost arm-in-arm with Nell.

Everilda had left Blackthorn a fortnight hence, accompanied by Nell. They went to Fathomseek so Everilda might consult with the ambassador's apothecary brother.

"If you require me," Everilda had said as they parted, "send a starling."

Nell had said nothing but had worn a knowing smile. She wore a similar smile now as she halted before Shrike and Wren.

"Good morning," Wren said, which seemed the most appropriate thing to say.

Everilda returned the greeting in kind, the sound of her voice removing all question as to her identity, as well as her adding, "How are you feeling?"

"Very well, thank you," Wren told her truthfully.

She accepted this with a brisk nod.

Nell, meanwhile, insinuated her arm around Everilda's waist, which Everilda didn't seem to mind.

"Take care, Lofthouse!" Nell called out with a cavalier wave as she led Everilda away. Or perhaps Everilda led her. Wren couldn't quite tell which.

Their second pair of visitors arrived a few moments later. Wren recognised Drude from halfway across the field; his bright scarlet coat and horns jutting up far above the general throng defied any disguise, much less the admittedly striking bronze mask he wore, complete with engraved beard. His companion, not much shorter than him, appeared likewise singular, but Wren didn't believe his own eyes until both crimson incubus and Payne's grey huldrekall halted right in front of him.

"Hull?" said Wren, the incredulous syllable falling from his tongue before he could think better of it.

A grin split Hull's blue-black beard. His wicker mask covered just the top half of his face, leaving everything below the nose exposed. "You've found me out, my lord. We find you well, I hope?"

Wren supposed he ought to get used to the now-customary enquiry into his health. He gave the honest reply. "Far better than I was. And yourselves?"

"Very well indeed! I left Mr Grigsby in Dr Hitchingham's capable hands," Hull said before Wren could ask, adding, "Not that he's ill! Merely that I think he's better off in good company. I would have brought him, except…" He glanced over the meadow. "It seemed a bit much to spring on the poor fellow all at once."

Wren quite agreed. "Do give him our best wishes when you return to London."

Hull swore he would do so.

Drude, meanwhile, had entered into conversation with Shrike. Both spoke too low for Wren to make out their words. It ended in smiles and clasped forearms, after which both Drude and Hull withdrew.

Wren turned to Shrike to ask him what Drude had said. However, he found himself distracted by Shrike's hands, which held not the tattered remnants of forget-me-nots but rather a crown woven of them.

Shrike raised the crown with a smile. Wren caught his impish glance and lowered his head. Shrike laid the forget-me-nots on his brow.

"It's not the solstice yet," Wren reminded him.

Shrike kissed him regardless.

The music wafting across the glade subtly changed its tune. Fae began to gather at the roots of the enormous gnarled tree looming in the centre of the field.

Shrike shot Wren an enquiring glance.

Wren nodded.

Shrike stood and drew Wren up beside him. Arm-in-arm, they strolled toward the winding thread of fae encircling the ancient beech. Wren glimpsed the ambassador almost vanishing around its trunk; he'd acquired another plague doctor's mask of someone else's make and waved with great enthusiasm upon spotting Wren in turn. Nell and Everilda stood hand-in-hand further down the line with nymphs on either side. Hull appeared between a delicate faun and a broad-bearded fellow who could've passed for Pan, horns and all.

Wren wondered who would take up his left hand with Shrike jealously guarding his right. He didn't have to wonder long, for soon a familiar crimson figure loomed on his left.

Drude bowed not so low as to put Wren in any danger from his horns. "If I may?"

Wren accepted his proffered hand with a smile. He noted how, over his head, Shrike and Drude exchanged a knowing glance and affirming nod. No doubt they had coordinated this earlier to ensure Wren had a strong arm to lean into on either side. Part of him felt he ought to consider this a slight against his masculine pride. The part of him which very much enjoyed having a strong man on either side of him drowned it out.

Shrike bent low to murmur into Wren's ear. "If you need to break away…"

Wren smiled up at him. "You'll know."

Fiddle, hornpipe, and tambourine struck up the fae hymn. The grapevine dance began. Shrike and Drude half-carried Wren through it —he felt almost as if he flew rather than stepped and twirled along. The thread of fae wove together, ever-winding tighter 'round the sacred tree. The beating of the tambourine came faster and faster, until, just when Wren thought he might have to drop out of the dance if he wished to keep his breath, the song ceased with joyous fanfare.

Other dancers broke apart. Drude and Shrike, however, retained their shared grip on Wren. Only after Wren reassured them he could stand under his own power did Drude drop his hand, but not before giving it an affectionate clasp. Shrike, meanwhile, relinquished his hold on Wren only as it became apparent he would need both hands to make the votive offering.

While Wren felt well enough to dance, he still couldn't stretch over-far, nor had he grown any taller since last Ostara. As such, he could only tie his mask to the lowest-hanging twig before them.

But it did not hang alone, for no sooner had he stepped back than Shrike bent to tie his own mask beside it, the leather cord winding through Wren's own and rendering them inseparable on their shared branch.

And no sooner had Wren shot a knowing glance up at Shrike than Shrike bent again to grant him a most welcome kiss.

THE BALLAD OF DANIEL DURST

Port Hawkesbury, Canada
May 15th, 1846

"*E*xpectin' company, Mr Durst?"
Daniel's head shot up from where he'd bent it over the ledger laid out on his desk.

The office boy, Thomas, had leant just far enough into the doorframe to make his enquiry. His shrill and strident voice had shattered the gentle atmosphere of small repetitive sounds—the scratch of pen-nibs against paper, the rustling of turning pages, the occasional footsteps or muffled coughs that served as a reminder of the otherwise-silent human presence—that hung over the shipping firm. Despite this sudden interruption, none of the other clerks seemed to have taken any notice of him yet, for which Daniel gave silent thanks. Despite being, technically, a city, often Port Hawkesbury reminded Daniel of Rochester —in that small-town way where everyone seemed to have their nose perpetually in everyone else's business.

Daniel, meanwhile, kept his countenance free from any sign of the alarm which had begun ringing in his chest. His voice remained dull and disinterested as he replied, "Why do you ask?"

"Two gen'lemen just disembarked from Liverpool and keep askin' folks where to find you," said Thomas.

This answer did nothing to assuage Daniel's increasing concern. He turned a page in his ledger and dipped his pen whilst his mind whirled.

It couldn't be Tolhurst searching for him, though that had been his first fearful assumption. Mr Grigsby had written him some months back to inform him of that monster's demise. Perhaps it might be Felix, the prodigal son returned at last. But Thomas had mentioned two gentlemen, and Daniel knew not who would accompany Felix in search of his vanished betrothed. Furthermore, Felix had no idea of Daniel's true identity—unless he had encountered Lofthouse in his wayward travels and Lofthouse had divulged Daniel's secret. Although Daniel realised as he recalled the existence of Lofthouse, it might just be that Lofthouse had accompanied Mr Grigsby across the Atlantic to see how Daniel got on. A spike of anger struck Daniel's heart at the thought of Lofthouse breaking his promise to secrecy, but if Mr Grigsby had come to see him and asked after him by a description which resembled a copy clerk in a shipping firm rather than a runaway heiress, it would seem to indicate that Mr Grigsby had taken the shocking revelation rather better than Daniel had expected, and the thought of his guardian's approval did warm Daniel's heart despite himself.

"Did they give their names?" Daniel said without looking up from the columns of figures.

Thomas shrugged. "Not in my earshot."

Useless, Daniel thought. Aloud, he said, "Did you notice anything particular in their appearance?"

Thomas snorted. "Certainly did!"

Daniel waited with no small amount of impatience for him to elaborate.

"One fellow's taller than a lamp-post," Thomas went on, his words carrying a tinge of admiration. "With a massive furred cloak and big leather boots and a cap with a feather in it, all in black."

Daniel blinked. "A furrier, you mean."

"No!" Thomas scoffed. "He's wilder than that. Like Robin Hood or something."

Daniel didn't wish to waste any time debating the relative wildness of furriers and highwaymen. At any rate, the description matched no one he'd known in England. "And the other?"

Thomas twisted up his face. "Dull. Like a clerk."

Said to a roomful of clerks. A smile twitched at the corner of Daniel's mouth. Still, he did know one clerk in particular, and so he asked, "Chestnut hair? Freckles?"

Thomas blinked in astonishment. "Yeah."

There was half the mystery solved, then. Lofthouse had arrived in Canada. For what purpose, Daniel knew not. Still, he realised as he considered the matter, he would have to catch Lofthouse up on his cover story before he spoke to many more townsfolk.

Daniel had not attained his present position through entirely honest means. He and Sukie had arrived in town hardly six months ago. With Daniel not yet in possession of his entire fortune, they had only the remainder of their profits from selling his hair and pawning what delicate articles he had no use for. They'd gone first to visit Sukie's Aunt Molly, who worked as a cook in the household of a ship's captain and who didn't take kindly to the notion of her maiden niece sharing a cross-Atlantic cabin with a gentleman. (The announcement that Daniel had asked Sukie to marry him calmed her ire somewhat, but she didn't smile upon Daniel until the wedding actually took place some weeks later.) There Sukie remained whilst Daniel trod all over town looking for work.

While Mrs Bailiwick's Academy had given Daniel an education, it had not given him a gentlemen's education, which left a few gaps in his instruction he must leap over if he wished to find employment. He had stopped in at every sort of office he encountered as he wandered the unfamiliar streets—for, if nothing else, he had splendid penmanship and a head for figures. The banks, post office, and solicitors weren't taking on any new hires. The shipping firms proved more promising, and one in particular, Swift & Allen, had an office manager who let him take their clerking exam on the spot. The exam itself felt at least somewhat intuitive, and despite his nerves Daniel kept his hand from trembling. His audacity paid off, for no sooner had the manager, Mr Peakes, reviewed his exam than he offered Daniel the position starting the very next day.

However, though Daniel had passed the exam honestly enough and had worked still more honestly ever since, he had got his foot in the door by claiming to have clerked previously in the Staple Inn law office of Mr Ephraim Grigsby, Esq., under the senior clerk, Mr Lofthouse. Which meant Lofthouse's sudden arrival in Port Hawkesbury made things rather awkward.

So Daniel, as casually as possible, plucked up a scrap of scratch-paper from the discard pile and dashed off a quick note to his wife.

Dear Mrs Durst,

I beg you will forgive the short notice, but Mr Lofthouse has arrived in town today with an unknown companion. I intend to invite them both to await me at our house for dinner.

Your ever-devoted,

Mr Durst.

This he folded, sealed, and handed off to Thomas to deliver, with a ha'penny for his troubles.

Daniel had taken rooms for himself and Sukie at a lodging-house when they first arrived in Port Hawkesbury. But this had been a temporary measure. After he attained his clerking position, they began their hunt through the newspaper advertisements for a proper house. Then, when they'd married at last, Daniel wrote again to Mr Grigsby to inform him of the happy occasion—or rather, a version of it, wherein "Miss Flora Fairfield" married a Mr Daniel Durst—and request the remainder of his inheritance be wired to Mrs Daniel Durst. Mr Grigsby, ever-dutiful, followed through within a few short weeks. With his rightful fortune in hand, Daniel acquired the charming little house Sukie had selected; a cottage, almost, some distance from the amenities of town, but all the more beloved for the privacy said distance afforded.

Daniel had developed a distinct desire for privacy whilst at Mrs Bailiwick's Academy. As the wealthiest pupil there, he'd had the especial privilege of an upstairs bedroom all to himself from the age of fourteen. He found it a welcome relief from the ceaseless chatter of his fellow pupils and a shelter from the notice of the all-too-attentive music master. And all the moreso as his body chose that particular year to betray him. It became suddenly very important for him to dress and undress in private, for while he looked no different from his fellow pupils, he felt very different indeed and preferred no one besides himself gaze upon the parts of him which felt most at odds with his soul. Nor did he need anyone else commenting on his habit of throwing a sheet over the stand-mirror before he performed his morning ablutions.

When the lunch hour finally arrived, Daniel did not avail himself of the hand-pie baked and packed for him that morning by his devoted wife. Instead, he abandoned his luncheon to go out wandering the streets in search of Lofthouse and his queer companion. The description of Lofthouse didn't get him very far when questioning passers-by. The description of his unknown cohort, however, as provided by Thomas, proved far more useful. It brought Daniel in short order to the stationer's shop, where he beheld the oddity for himself.

The stranger was almost exactly as the boy had described—much to Daniel's surprise. He'd assumed the lad had exaggerated. But indeed, he found himself confronted with the vision of a tall gentleman in dark garb of the medieval sort, with a feather in his peaked cap and leather boots folded down just above his knees and an enormous billowing furred coat all in black. He wore his hair unfashionably long in a queue at the back of his neck. Daniel could discern little of what the stranger might think from the severe cast of his long face as he examined reams of tinted paper and plucked up a particular bottle of red ink for closer inspection.

The gentleman speaking to the clerk behind the counter, however, proved far more familiar.

Daniel recognized Lofthouse at a glance. An inch or so shorter than Daniel himself, with chestnut hair and a face spattered with freckles. He'd dressed in an unassuming black frock-coat—the exact match for the grey one Daniel himself wore now, for Lofthouse had donated it under Daniel's pretense of assisting indigent sailors. It wasn't the only item of Lofthouse's that Daniel had acquired under less-than-above-board circumstances. Denied Latin at school, Daniel had thrown himself into French and Italian and, in just the last year, had taken the opportunity of stealing a dusty Latin grammar from Lofthouse's garret to teach himself. When Lofthouse had asked after "missing papers," Daniel had initially thought the theft had been caught out. He still wondered if he ought to return the book by post or if he ought merely to send what money the book was worth along with a note of apology and hope it hadn't any sentimental value. He'd taken it on impulse; its discovery amongst Lofthouse's novels rather a surprise and the feelings the sight of it invoked no less surprising—covetous thoughts of the education Lofthouse and gentlemen like him had received, jealousy seething as the dust told how far Lofthouse had taken that education for granted, until the bitterest dregs of Daniel's heart told him to take it, just take it, Lofthouse would never miss it, and he himself had far greater need of it, and he'd snatched it up and stuffed it into the voluminous pocket of his despised skirt.

Then, of course, Lofthouse had caught up to Daniel and Sukie in their escape, but rather than drag them back to Mr Grigsby and Tolhurst, he'd sworn to keep their secrets and wished them well on their journey. Which cast rather a guilty pall on Daniel's own behaviour towards the man.

After a few moments of waiting, when it became clear the conversation between Lofthouse and the clerk would not abate, Daniel cleared his throat.

"Good morning, Mr Lofthouse," he said.

The hem of the black frock-coat arose as Lofthouse whirled to face him. Mild irritation at the interruption vanished into astonished delight breaking over his freckled features. To Daniel's surprise, he stepped forward with hand outstretched and a genuine smile. "Mr Durst! Splendid to see you again."

Daniel shook his hand with a grip he'd practised often in the months since leaving Mrs Bailiwick's Academy; firm grasp, two pumps, drop and withdraw. Lofthouse seemed impressed with it. But before he could say anything further, Daniel had to cut him off.

"I cannot thank you enough," Daniel said with careful emphasis, "for the recommendation you gave me after I left Mr Grigsby's employ."

Whatever shock Lofthouse felt at this blatant lie, he limited his expression of it to a single blink. Then he replied, "Of course. You did very well for us. The least I could do, really."

Daniel let out a breath he hadn't realised he'd held.

"May I introduce my associate?" Lofthouse continued. "Mr Butcher. Butcher," he added with a glance over Daniel's shoulder, "this is Mr Durst."

Daniel turned to find the medieval highwayman had crept up beside him in total silence. He flinched, then scolded himself for it, and struck out his hand. Butcher matched his firm grip and gave him a small yet sincere-seeming smile besides.

"May we offer our congratulations as well," Lofthouse went on. "Mr Grigsby gave me the glad tidings of your nuptials—after a fashion," Lofthouse added, much to Daniel's relief.

"Thank you," said Daniel. "I regret I cannot tarry long; I must return to the office."

Lofthouse gave him a look of far greater sympathy than Daniel thought the statement warranted.

"However," Daniel continued, "my wife and I would be honoured if you would join us this evening at our house for dinner."

Lofthouse and Butcher exchanged a glance. Daniel thought he saw the faint flickering shadow of fond indulgence at the corner of Butcher's mouth.

"We'd be delighted," Lofthouse replied, with what seemed a genuine smile.

* * *

DANIEL's own interest in women became apparent to him shortly after his arrival at Mrs Bailiwick's Academy. It grew from a fixed fascination with the elder girls to some small flirtations with those his own age around the time when his own body began to betray him. His fellow pupils reciprocated his interest, and he proved rather popular amongst them, for he had, if he were to flatter himself, a certain handsome quality which no amount of frills or flounces could ever quite disguise.

But of all the girls there—many beautiful and talented, most very interested in him—none sparked his notice quite like the arrival of one particular maid in his sixteenth year.

She was of a like age to himself, as he soon discovered. Unlike him, however, her eyes shone a deep amber to match her ebony locks, and the rosebud lips which annoyed him in his own face attracted his admiration in hers. And, unlike his fellow pupils, he had to steal his moments of admiration, for she didn't sit beside him in drawing or French, or carry his hand or waist in dancing. Whilst he might offer to hold the pincushion of a young lady engaged in embroidery, he knew not how to make himself known to a maid who must keep herself unheard and unseen, lest she lose her place.

Still, he observed her whenever she crept into a room to start tidying-up just as the young ladies left it. More than a few times he glimpsed her in the halls slipping in or out of the servants' stair. His attic bedroom, attained in his fourteenth year, put him rather nearer to the servants' quarters than the pupils' dormitory. Yet her work forced her to keep such miserable hours that she had vanished altogether either before he awoke or well after he fell asleep.

But, on the occasion of one particular afternoon tea, he'd had his chance.

Most of the young ladies ignored the maids, having been brought up to believe staff beneath their notice and expecting only to communicate with those who ranked so high as housekeepers or cooks. Daniel, however, caught the new maid's eye as she brought in the tea-tray. He leapt up to accept it from her—after all, according to Mrs Bailiwick, he would have to conduct his future husband's tea service, so why not take charge in the academy as practise? Audacity and confidence shielded him from reproof of teacher and pupil alike.

And, as the maid relinquished the service into his hands, his fingertips brushed against hers.

She glanced up at him, startled.

He gave her his most becoming smile, a bundle of nerves behind it, his heart in his throat.

A heart which flew with joy when she shot him a small, sweet, sincere smile in return.

Then the full weight of the tray bore upon his arms, for she had let go of it altogether and vanished again as though she'd never been.

Daniel retained his composure as he set down the tray and dispensed tea to his classmates. He waited until after he saw them all served, then turned to his headmistress.

"Pray tell, Mrs Bailiwick," Daniel asked her whilst the girls distracted themselves with tea-cakes. "What is the new maid's name?"

Mrs Bailiwick blinked at him. "I believe she's called Sukie. Why do you ask?"

Sukie. The name resounded sweet as birdsong in Daniel's thoughts. So sweet that he quite forgot to answer Mrs Bailiwick's enquiry. But Miss Sophronia Wilkinson happened to drop her teacup into its saucer with a splash at that very moment. Daniel gave silent thanks for her accidental distraction of the headmistress and amused himself for the remainder of the afternoon with thoughts of brushing out soft ebony tresses whilst staring into deep amber eyes.

The sweet birdsong kept echoing through his mind all night and on into the morning, when, just before Italian lessons, he glimpsed a black-and-white figure scurrying away down the upstairs hall.

He thanked Providence he wandered the hall alone at that moment and called out in a voice of forced calm, "Miss Sukie, is it not?"

Her steps halted. For a moment, she hesitated with her back still to him, and he feared he'd overstepped. Or, heaven forefend, received her name wrong from Mrs Bailiwick.

Then she turned, and the glance from her amber eyes stole all power of speech from him. She ducked her head and curtsied, saying as she arose again, "Yes, Miss Fairfield?"

The honourific gave him the same twinge of discomfort as it always did, though the voice that spoke it sounded far softer and more sweet than usual. He brushed it aside and approached her until hardly a yard remained between them. She watched him careful all the while.

"I'd like to welcome you to our academy," he said.

She dropt her head again and murmured her thanks.

"My chambers are upstairs," he continued. "Just beneath the attic. Not very far from your own, I believe."

She glanced at him curiously.

"And," he added, "if you aren't too preoccupied with your own engagements, I wonder if you might join me in my chambers this evening after dinner. That is, if you've the inclination?"

Having made his offer and half-expecting a refusal, his heart only began to beat again when she, with a small and secretive smile, accepted.

Dinner seemed to last a century. He could hardly manage more than a few mouthfuls, until he reminded himself that much of it had likely come from Sukie's handiwork, and a respect for this allowed him to consume a more respectable portion despite his fluttering stomach.

Then he bid his fellow pupils good-night and climbed the flights to his bedroom with his heart pounding at his ribcage as if it could break free.

He arrived and found no one within. Which was reasonable, he reminded himself. Sukie had a lot to do washing up after twenty-three young women, their instructors, their headmistress, and Daniel. He couldn't expect her to arrive upstairs until at least another hour had passed. Two, most likely.

And so he lit a candle, opened a book, and settled in to wait.

He knew not what book. His eyes wouldn't rest on the page long enough to absorb the words. With every half-imagined floorboard creak they flicked to the door, which Daniel had left open the barest crack. The mantle-clock over the empty fireplace ticked. The candle burned down.

Then, just when Daniel had abandoned all hope of ever seeing Sukie this night, a true footstep creaked in the hallway outside.

Daniel's heart leapt into his throat. He whirled toward the door. It swung inward with another long, low creak.

And Sukie stepped over the threshold.

She paused just afterward, taking in the room with wide dark eyes, and let out a low whistle.

Daniel, who had balanced on the brink of considering his private chamber a gilded cage, now found his opinion beginning to reverse as he beheld how it seemed to astonish and delight Sukie. He stood from his desk and offered her the choice of seat; his chair or his bed.

Without any hesitation she sat on the corner of his bed as casual and comfortable as if it were her own.

Daniel, after some small dithering on his part between what was prudent and what he truly wanted, sat down beside her.

And immediately realised he knew not what to say.

The nerves which had knotted his stomach and fingers alike now tied his tongue and forced it still.

But just when he felt on the verge of panic, staring into Sukie's beautiful dark eyes, she smiled and parted her perfect rosebud lips.

"Do you read novels?" she asked.

Daniel confessed to this vice, which seemed to please her. She spoke of her favourites (mostly penny dreadfuls) and enquired after his (mostly chivalric romances) and grinned the most charming grin he'd ever beheld when he offered to let her borrow his books. Then the conversation turned to the academy and how she liked it and what she thought of its inhabitants, and from there Daniel learnt a great deal more than what he thought he knew about his fellow pupils. Whilst his tongue remained fettered, hers flew free as any bird. And indeed, her voice sounded sweeter than birdsong to his ears. He could listen to her chatter about anything for days on end. She spoke with a spirited air that quite belied her meek and mild comportment in the household below.

They whispered for hours, until the candle became a guttering stub in its tin holder and Sukie began to interrupt herself with yawns.

"Forgive me," she said, stretching her arms wide.

"Perhaps we ought to part ways," Daniel said—against the wishes of his own heart, which would have bid her stay and sleep beside him. "At least, until tomorrow eve."

Sukie quite agreed and stood to go, smiling through another yawn. "Goodnight, Miss Fairfield."

"You don't have to call me that," Daniel blurted.

Sukie blinked at him. "What ought I to call you instead?"

Daniel hesitated. He did not then know quite what he wished to be called. It felt foolish beyond words to ask after his true heart's desire. But after a moment, he settled on the answer. "Just Fairfield."

After all, Felix's friends at Eton called him simply, "Knoll."

Sukie gave him a considering look. Only when a slight smile tugged at the corner of her beautiful mouth, just enough to dimple her left cheek, did Daniel dare draw breath again.

"Very well, Fairfield," said Sukie.

DANIEL FINISHED out the remainder of the work-day with his head in a whirl. He gave thanks that the moving of figures from one column to another didn't require him to be particularly mindful. Still, his nerves increased as the sun crept ever closer to the western horizon, and when the clock struck the closing hour at last, he felt a curious mixture of nervous relief. He had to force himself to walk rather than run home. The sight of his cottage, its front windows shining a merry glow of candle-flame out into the street, proved a balm for his heart. He passed through the garden gate, up the flagstone path, and lifted the familiar latch of the door to the unfamiliar sound of gentlemen's voices within.

Sukie and he had never entertained guests before in their humble home. Daniel had a dim idea of how the thing ought to be done. He'd never attended a dinner party in his life, being too young to accompany his parents before they died, and life in Mrs Bailiwick's Academy being as much or more sequestered than any cloistered abbey. Still, in the months leading up to his escape, he had acquired second-hand copies of

217

etiquette guides—one for gentlemen and one for ladies—which offered some hints on how to conduct himself and how the thing itself ought to be conducted. However, some time had passed since last he read those particular pages, and he hadn't the opportunity to review them in the hours between his invitation and the dinner itself, the books in question stuck at home whilst he remained stuck in office.

Still, as he opened the door into his own warm and familiar front hall, his surroundings suffused him with renewed confidence. He tossed his hat and overcoat lightly onto their hooks and proceeded with a surer step into his wife's parlour.

The joyful chime of Sukie's laughter greeted him as he stepped over the threshold. She sat in her chair, the armless twin of Daniel's own, by the fire. Butcher and Lofthouse occupied the sofa opposite, side by side and rather closer to each other than the spacious furniture required. Both bore smiles to match Sukie's, though Lofthouse's changed to a mildly startled aspect as he turned to behold Daniel in the doorway.

"Mr Durst," Sukie said, raising her hand so he might clasp it. "Mr Butcher was just telling me of the goats kept on his estate and what scrapes they find themselves in. Dinner is ready," she added. "All covered and waiting."

"Not long, I hope?" said Daniel.

She smiled and assured him they hadn't waited for more than a few minutes before his arrival.

"Then," said Daniel, turning to his guests and speaking with far more confidence than he felt, "if you would join us for dinner, gentlemen?"

The cottage had no formal dining room. Still, its kitchen table had room enough for four chairs around it, and neither Lofthouse nor Butcher looked askance at its offerings. Daniel had learnt how to carve a roast from books—his guide to gentlemen's etiquette, as well as Sukie's cook-book—and distant childhood memories of his own father presiding over the dinner table. He had not yet found the opportunity to test his skill in company. He kept his hands steady whilst he carved, and if Lofthouse or Butcher noted anything amiss, they gave no hint of it in look or speech but merely accepted their plates with smiles and thanks as Daniel passed them down.

Sukie likewise smiled at him, which was more than Daniel felt he deserved after ambushing her dinner plans with two more mouths to feed and barely a few hours' notice. He knew better than most gentlemen how much work that entailed. Not just through what house-keeping arts Mrs Bailiwick had taught him in anticipation of his marriage to Felix, but also through Sukie herself instructing him in all she knew of cookery, which proved a fair bit. She could not, she had informed him, make him even half so good a cook as her Aunt Molly. But she could teach him enough to make him useful.

The dinner itself went on well, Daniel thought. Butcher main-tained his stoic silence yet did not seem displeased with the fare or the company. Lofthouse proved a little more talkative, if a touch nervous and consequently awkward. He complimented Sukie's cookery as well as her decoration of the house. Her bashful smile made Daniel's heart bloom with affection all over again. He couldn't resist reaching for her hand under the table. She gave him an affec-tionate clasp in reply.

At the meal's conclusion, Daniel drew the gentlemen into the parlour again so Sukie might clear the table in private. She rejoined them shortly. No sooner had she reappeared than Lofthouse reached into the leather satchel he'd left by the sofa and withdrew two jars.

"A housewarming gift," he explained, handing one off to Daniel and the other to Sukie. "Honey and sloe preserves from Mr Butcher's estate."

One mystery solved, then, Daniel concluded. Mr Butcher was a gentleman farmer. Though, given his garb, still a rather eccentric one. The golden honey and dark purple sloe looked delicious regardless. He gave his sincere thanks.

"And," Lofthouse added with some hesitance, "there is another matter as well."

Daniel's hackles arose. He forced himself to reply with an even tone. "What matter might that be?"

"Have you heard tell," Lofthouse asked gently, "of Tolhurst's passing?"

"I have," Daniel admitted—much to Lofthouse's evident relief. "Mr Grigsby wrote to inform me. Can't say as I'm sorry for it."

A wan smile flickered across Lofthouse's lips as he replied, to Daniel's surprise, "Nor I."

Butcher's face proved more difficult to read, but the grim line of his mouth seemed to imply he felt likewise.

"There is, I think, a small inheritance due to you," Lofthouse added, dipping his hand into his waistcoat pocket.

A frost of icy dread crept over Daniel's heart. If Tolhurst had left him anything, he would as soon have had him take it to his grave.

These feelings were not dispelled when Lofthouse withdrew a delicate golden chain. He knew, even before the charm dangling from it turned to face him, what it was.

There, with the chain drawn between Lofthouse's fingers and the back of it braced against his knuckles, lay the beloathed miniature.

And a hundred horrid memories came flooding back with it.

Tolhurst had commissioned the wretched thing. For Felix, of course. A gift for his nephew's birthday, celebrating his impending nuptials with a beautiful bride. He'd already fulfilled his part in the portrait by paying the artist. Yet he insisted on attending every session of the painting process as a *chaperon* when a maid or even another pupil would have sufficed. And though he didn't need to study Daniel's features for the painting, still he stared with even more intensity than the artist himself. It was remarkable, really, Daniel had thought as he gazed off out the window over the artist's shoulder and studiously ignored Tolhurst lurking in the corner of his eye, how a man could stare so and yet never once see the truth staring back at him.

The same went for the artist. The end result appeared hardly worth the excruciating process. It showed an even worse reflection of Daniel's true self than any mirror. His strong jaw and hard gaze had transformed into a simpering, slope-shouldered, wide-eyed creature he couldn't recognise as human, much less as himself.

Of course Tolhurst had loved it. Pride rang through his voice as he showed it off to Daniel. The caress of his fingertips around its minuscule gilded frame made Daniel's skin crawl. Daniel had wished he'd had a knife to hand in that moment, as if he could carve away from his own flesh the traces of Tolhurst's touch on the miniature.

In the end, it hadn't required a knife. He could change himself from caterpillar to moth by shedding his old raiments for garb that fit who he truly was. His old name vanished the moment his real name first fell from his own lips. When he looked in the mirror now he couldn't perceive a trace of the form the world had forced him to assume for so long.

And yet here it was again. The empty shell of someone who never was, a pallid husk lurching forth from the grave to reach its icy fingers toward his soul.

He didn't expect Lofthouse to understand. After all, how many living men could claim to be haunted by their own ghost?

"I had thought," Lofthouse explained, oblivious to Daniel's turmoil, "that if anyone had a right to it, it was yourself."

"Keep it," Daniel said, his words clipped.

Lofthouse balked. Evidently Daniel's sharp tone took him by surprise. He turned first to Butcher, then to Sukie, and back to Daniel. He cleared his throat. "If you're certain…"

Daniel forced a smile. "Might make things awkward with the wife to keep a miniature of another woman around."

A snort of laughter escaped Lofthouse. He attempted to cover it up with a cough. "Yes—well—quite right."

And to Daniel's infinite relief, he slipped the miniature back into his pocket.

"How long will you remain in town?" Daniel asked, as much to change the subject as to know the answer.

Lofthouse shared another glance with Butcher. "Mr Butcher's ventures may detain us for some time."

Nothing in Butcher's aspect gave any hint as to what those ventures might be, and the man himself said not a syllable.

"Perhaps," Lofthouse continued, "long enough me to perform some small service in honour of your nuptials."

Daniel's eyebrows took flight.

"A wedding portrait," Lofthouse hastily added. "Or a pair of portraits, if you prefer, to hang side-by-side."

This cleared up a great deal of the mystery but still left Daniel in the dark on a few points. "You are acquainted with an artist?"

Lofthouse blinked. "No, I—well," he blurted with yet another glance at Butcher. Then he dipped a hand into his jacket. "Here—perhaps I had better show you."

And so saying, he withdrew a palm-sized book in a leather shroud from his inner jacket pocket, opened it, and held it up for Daniel's inspection.

A remarkable pen-and-ink sketch of sloe blossoms met Daniel's gaze. Before he could take the book from Lofthouse's hands, however, the page turned, this time to a drawing of goats leaping across a stream. More glimpses into the natural world followed—songbirds, squirrels, flowers, rabbits—along with a few architectural sketches of tumbled-down castles and sundry other ruins.

"You've done these yourself?" Daniel asked.

"Yes," Lofthouse admitted, turning another page.

Daniel was on the verge of pointing out how, while this was all admittedly impressive work for one he'd known only as a solicitor's clerk, a wedding portrait required one to draw human figures rather than plants, animals, or architecture. But the pages Lofthouse turned to now showed human figures—lounging beneath berry-bushes, dancing through meadows, crouching in tree-forks, or simply leaning against a convenient pile of stones to stare back into the viewer's eyes.

Or rather, not-quite-human figures. For as Daniel peered closer he saw Lofthouse had replaced some figures' feet with hooves, added horns or antlers to particular brows, affixed damselfly or moth's-wings to certain shoulders, and subtly (or not-so-subtly) pointed the ears of every single character depicted. They were rendered in a startlingly realistic style considering they must have come whole cloth from Lofthouse's imagination.

Only one sketch appeared altogether normal. A particular portrait of a man with a long twice-broken beak of a nose and hawkish brows above his dark eyes, with rivers of ink-black hair shot through with streaks of silver. A drawing of Butcher, and a particularly flattering one at that, which cast his severe features into something more tender than otherwise.

Daniel had but a glimpse of this before Lofthouse snapped the book shut and tucked it away into his jacket again. A glance at his face showed a faint rosy hue beneath his copious freckles. Butcher, meanwhile, still looked as stoic as stone.

Lofthouse cleared his throat. "While it might not have been my profession these past few years, I've put in some practise at it. And," he added, "if you would consent, I would like to put what little talent I possess into your service."

Daniel hadn't considered the prospect of a wedding portrait. Indeed, some days he could hardly believe he was lucky enough to be married at all, much less living openly as himself with the most wonderful woman in all the world. He glanced to Sukie to see what she thought of it. She appeared more intrigued than otherwise. He returned to Lofthouse.

"I think," Lofthouse ventured, "you deserve a better likeness than what others have previously painted."

A bark of laughter escaped Daniel. He recovered himself enough to reply that he quite agreed.

A short conversation sufficed to arrange the particulars. Lofthouse would return with his art kit on Saturday, after Daniel arrived home from his half-day at the office, and come back again on Sunday afternoon, and so on for as many weeks as it took to complete the portrait. Lofthouse seemed confident it wouldn't take terribly long. Butcher seemed not to mind that this adventure would deprive him of his clerk's services for hours on end. Daniel shook hands on the bargain with both of them and they took their leave, with Sukie bidding them come for dinner again when their calendars permitted.

"I think," she said when the door had shut upon their guests and both Lofthouse and Butcher had vanished down the lane into the evening, "that went off rather well, don't you?"

Daniel agreed and told her so with a kiss.

* * *

THE NIGHTLY CONVERSATIONS betwixt Sukie and Daniel in the attic of Mrs Bailiwick's Academy continued for some weeks.

And throughout those weeks, Daniel agonised over when, if ever, he ought to kiss her.

Touch had come easily. Far easier than he'd expected. It began on a night like any other since their evening visits first ensued, when, in the midst of one of the yawns that signalled an end to their conversation for the day and thus gave Daniel an otherwise unaccountable pang, Sukie had reached up not just to pluck her black-and-white cap from her head but also to unpin her hair. The severe bun tumbled down over her shoulders in carefree waves. The sight made Daniel's heart skip a beat.

"Oh!" said Sukie when she recovered from her yawn and caught his wide-eyed stare. "Forgive me, I didn't mean… that is, I didn't think…"

Daniel felt she had nothing to apologise for in letting her hair down. But rather than say so, or anything else sensible for that matter, he instead kept up a reverent silence as his hand reached out of its own accord to take a particular curling lock between his fingertips.

Sukie stared at him.

"Pardon!" he blurted, yanking his arm back to himself as if burned.

Yet while her astonishment remained, she didn't appear in the least bit upset or angry with him as she replied, "I don't mind."

Daniel could hardly believe his good fortune. Slowly, hesitantly, his fingers faintly trembling, he reached out again and idly brushed his fingertips through her hair.

She closed her eyes with a soft sigh that washed over Daniel's heart.

While he misliked washing or brushing out his own hair—the length of it annoyed him, and the time it took to tend it annoyed him further still, until it required almost more willpower than he possessed to resist hacking it all off—he found when it came to the walnut locks on Sukie's tender head, he delighted in taking the utmost care. He could spend many happy hours combing it out for her, weaving his fingers through it to work out the knots without causing her the least pain, until it shone with a glossy glow. And she, against all odds, seemed to enjoy letting him do so.

After such an intimacy as this, it seemed silly to go on denying each other the small comfort of touch, and so Daniel felt emboldened when next they sat together, cross-legged with their knees almost meeting, to lay his hand on the floor-boards between them, palm-up, at her mercy.

And she, to his infinite delight, deigned to grace his palm with her own.

They held hands throughout that night's conversation. And the following night. And the night after that.

Another subsequent night, whilst they held hands and whispered of nothing and everything, Sukie reached up to her own shoulder and winced.

Daniel was on the alert in an instant. "Are you all right?"

She shrugged. "Just an ache. Gone by morning. Or I hope so, at least."

Small wonder she ached, given all the hauling and scrubbing she did in a given day throughout the whole academy. Still, Daniel wondered a great deal at his own boldness as he raised his hand to her shoulder and asked, "May I?"

She blinked at him in something like confusion but nodded all the same.

Daniel rearranged himself to sit beside and behind her. Then, with his breath held and his heart hammering at his ribcage as though it would burst free, he laid his hands upon her shoulders and began to knead.

Her head fell forward with a groan of relief.

Slowly and steadily he worked the knots from her muscles with his soft hands—shamefully soft, when contrasted against her honest and hard-earned callouses. It became another part of their night-time ritual. And there were nights when, stretched out across his bed and under the ministrations of his fingers, she would fall asleep altogether. Then he dared not disturb her but dressed himself for bed as quiet as possible and laid down beside her, careful not to let his form touch hers, though the bare inch between them hardly seemed to suffice in either direction, neither near nor far enough for his liking.

Yet no matter how oft they touched, it always felt—to Daniel, at least —like the moment their fingertips had first brushed against each other at afternoon tea. Terrifying. Exhilarating. And, somehow, as natural as a rosebud unfurling into full bloom.

He didn't dare to imagine how a kiss might feel. Still, the thought of it burned in his mind throughout the day, flaring forth at odd moments of idleness to consume him in day-dreams far beyond anything that had ever preoccupied him before.

And then, one evening, Sukie arrived with a barely-repressed smirk on her face and something held behind her back.

No sooner had Daniel shut the door after her than she held out to him a package wrapped brown paper and twine. He accepted it with some bewilderment. Unwrapping it revealed a battered but no less beautiful copy of Scott's *The Monastery*.

"I thought you might like it," she said, beaming. "I know you haven't the opportunity to procure them yourself, and if I may be so bold, I noticed Mr Knoll's gifts don't come very often, and when they do they don't seem to suit you. If you asked him for a novel he might well return with a string of pearls—and not the penny dreadful, neither. So I supposed it was up to me to supply the lack."

He laughed and thanked her, though words felt hardly sufficient to express all he felt at this marvelous escape from the dull day-to-day of the academy.

Sukie bit her lip (which made Daniel's heart perform acrobatics) and asked if she might have something in return for her gift.

"Oh—of course, yes," said Daniel. He supposed the price of an entire novel, even second-hand, must prove trying on a maid's salary. "How much—?"

"A kiss," Sukie blurted.

Daniel blinked. Surely he'd misheard her.

A primrose tint came into Sukie's beautiful face. "That is—I rather thought—if you don't mind—but if you do mind, it's all right by me, I only—"

Daniel leapt forth and kissed her.

Soft lips met his own. Their touch thrilled his whole being, exceeding all expectation. She gasped against his mouth and threw her arms around his shoulders. The warmth of her embrace suffused his very bones. He found himself entwined with her in turn, his hands settling onto the soft curves beneath her uniform. A thud resounded through the attic as the book fell to the floorboards all-but-forgotten.

Kissing likewise became another vital part of their evening routine.

Despite this, or in some way because of it, Daniel still held the most crucial fibre of himself apart from her. Quite aside from and yet alongside with her arrival he began to understand certain truths of his own soul. The further his body transformed in a wildly different direction, the more sure he felt in what he was and what he ought to be.

Yet how could he possibly tell anyone that the heart of a man beat beneath his breast? And expect to be believed?

Even if Sukie were to believe him, it might still dash all they held to pieces. Perhaps she only loved him as a lady, and her affection would wither when she knew him for a gentleman. He could bear the scorn of all the world—the scorn of God himself—but if she spurned him, he knew not where to turn.

He contemplated this one particular evening whilst he waited for her arrival. So deeply did he think on it that he didn't hear her footstep in the hallway beyond his door. The creak of its opening made him flinch. Sukie noticed.

"You look grave as saints, Fairfield!" she observed with wide eyes. "Whatever's the matter?"

Daniel swallowed hard. He couldn't bear to lie to her any longer. "There's something I must tell you."

Sukie shut the door in silence and joined him in sitting on the bed. He wanted to take her hand, as always, but tonight he lacked the courage, having used it all up in forcing speech from his clenched throat. He couldn't even look her in the eye as he began. But begin he must. And so he cast his gaze to the rafters, took a deep shuddering breath, and spoke.

"I am a gentleman," he said.

Four words he had oft spoken in his own mind but never yet breathed aloud. He knew not how Sukie took them; he couldn't bear the sight of her face just now. So instead he continued. How his body resembled that of his fellow pupils, but his soul was quite another thing altogether. How trapped he felt both in his own flesh and in the role thrust upon him by Mrs Bailiwick and Mr Grigsby and his long-dead parents who'd promised him as an inheritance to another boy scarce older than himself before either of them could even talk. How his blood had boiled over with envy when Felix's voice broke and his bones stretched beyond the bonds Daniel himself might never escape. How to hear folk call him "Miss" Fairfield sounded like coals raked over his soul and how "Mrs Knoll" sounded even worse. His voice grew raw and hoarse with the telling, until at last, his heart torn from his chest and its secrets spattered all across the room, he fell silent. The silence grew. His eyes felt drawn toward Sukie, as ever, and at last he ceased to resist their natural gravity.

She stared at him with her beautiful dark eyes flown wide.

"I am a gentleman," he repeated, the words no less strident for the rasping quality of his voice.

She continued to stare at him. Then that impish smile he'd loved so well tugged at her lips.

His heart sank. After all this, she thought him jesting.

"Is that all?" she said.

Daniel balked. "All?"

She cast her laughing eyes upon him; he realised she smiled not with mockery, but with relief. "I thought you meant to tell me you were going away or something else horrible!"

The potent mixture of astonishment and relief in the wake of having braced himself for dread unrealised left him quite unable to speak or do anything but gaze at her.

"What ought I to call you?" she asked. "Aside from Fairfield, I mean. That's only your surname. You've a given name as well, haven't you?"

Given from himself, to himself, indeed. He steeled his nerve and replied, "Daniel."

"Daniel," she echoed, with bright eyes and lips parted in wonder.

It was the first time he'd heard anyone besides himself call him by his real name, and the sound of it made his heart soar. It flew higher still as she leaned in to kiss him. She left her palm against his cheek as she withdrew to fondly gaze at him from those dark and beautiful eyes.

"My darling Daniel," she said and smiled in a reflection of his own joy.

* * *

NEITHER HIDE nor hair of Lofthouse or Butcher appeared in town throughout the rest of the week. Daniel supposed their business, whatever it was, kept them tucked away.

Saturday morning passed in a flurry of figures. The noontime bell jolted Daniel from a suspended reverie, half-anxiety and half-eagerness, not unlike what he'd felt before he'd hosted dinner. His prior experience as an artist's model had not produced fond memories.

However, he reminded himself (not for the first time) as he walked home, this particular portrait did not spring from Tolhurst's commission. Nor would it come from Tolhurst's own hand. Tolhurst was dead. And perhaps this particular adventure would replace malcontented remembrances with something brighter and better to look back on.

He arrived home to find Sukie in the parlour. She sat mending in her wedding gown. It had originally been Daniel's—the cornflower-blue poplin. Daniel had never liked the look of it on himself. Sukie had surprised him by picking it out for her own when they'd gone through his ill-fitting wardrobe selecting which items to keep and which to sell off to fund their journey. But the moment he saw it on her, he realised its beauty. She'd looked resplendent in it on their wedding day. She looked resplendent even now. He could do no less than approach her domestic throne and bend to kiss her.

She smiled up at him when he pulled away. He sat down in his armchair beside her and accepted her gift of his own shirt, needle, thread, and a button to re-attach to it. They mended together in companionable silence until the ringing door-bell roused them.

Daniel opened the front door to find Lofthouse standing with both hands clenched around the strap of the leather satchel slung across his shoulder.

"Not too early, I hope?" Lofthouse asked with a nervous smile.

Daniel assured him he'd arrived just in time and ushered him into the parlour.

Sukie set her mending aside and arose to accept their guest's handclasp.

"Will this do?" she asked, a little shyly, as she plucked at the skirt of her gown.

Lofthouse blinked. "Very well, I think. Splendid colour."

Sukie's beaming smile washed over Daniel's heart and banished any nerves he might have fostered there.

"Now, then," Lofthouse continued, glancing over the room. "May I rearrange a few articles? And—how would you prefer to pose?"

Daniel hadn't the foggiest. "What would you suggest?"

"The traditional composition has the lady seated whilst the gentleman stands behind," Lofthouse explained. "Though, if I may be honest, the best posture is one which you may find comfortable keeping for hours at a time. Perhaps," he added, his eyes alighting on their matched chairs, "seated side-by-side?"

Daniel glanced to Sukie. She nodded. He returned his gaze to Lofthouse and gave his assent.

With Daniel's assistance, Lofthouse moved the two chairs into the centre of the room, where they caught the best light from the south-facing window. Sukie grabbed a third chair from the kitchen so Lofthouse needn't stand whilst he worked. Sukie sat in her chair, and Daniel took his rightful place in his own beside her. On impulse, he reached out to her, and she laid her hand in his palm.

"Will this do, Mr Lofthouse?" Sukie asked.

Lofthouse glanced over their pose. "Quite well, I should think."

And in the time it took him to say so, he had sketch-book and pencil in hand and had already begun to draw. Not, Daniel noted, in his little leather-shrouded book, but a rather larger one that he propped up on a board on his lap, which all but hid him from view. For some moments the only sound in the cottage was the tick of the clock on the mantle and the scratching of pencil across paper.

Prior to the start of the portrait, Daniel had mostly concerned himself with how he might feel about being stared at for artistic purposes once again.

It did not occur to him to wonder how it might feel to have another man stare at his wife.

Yet, as he sat with her hand-and-hand and confronted the sight of the artist before them, he found his mind returning down old avenues, and the gnawing concern grew within him. If, heaven forefend, he saw Lofthouse looked at Sukie as Tolhurst had once looked at him—well, he did not think he could be held responsible for what he would do to the man.

But the stirrings of outrage proved short-lived as Daniel stared hard into the clerk's face. Lofthouse's gaze didn't strike him as judgmental, as Daniel had assumed it might. Nor did it appear indifferent, as the prior portraitist's had. Nor, to Daniel's great relief, did it in any way resemble the covetous burning looks Tolhurst had once cast upon him.

Rather, Daniel found Lofthouse's glances up from his sketch-book had an enquiring air. Studious and practical, the looks of a man endeavouring to puzzle out the scene before him, revolving the matter in his mind. When his eyes fell upon Sukie, they held nothing approaching ardour; aesthetic appreciation, at most.

"Ought we to keep silent, Mr Lofthouse?" Sukie enquired suddenly.

"What?" said Lofthouse, jerking his head up sharp. "Oh—no, it's quite all right to speak. I'm not working on your faces just yet. Only blocking in the pose and composition. See," he added, evidently in response to Daniel and Sukie's twin confusion, and turned his sketch-book around to show what he'd done thus far.

It appeared as almost entirely vague shapes. In them Daniel recognized their own parlour, after a fashion, as if seen through fogged glass. So too did he see himself and his wife in the pair of figures, with the half-erased remains of the boxes and circles that had built them still visible beneath the stronger strokes bringing them into a more human shape. Their brightness, illuminated by the southern window, contrasted against the dark hearth behind them, which formed a sort of frame to anchor the whole image. All told, rather familiar to Daniel, who'd been taught to draw a little himself, albeit in a young ladies' academy.

The important thing was that Sukie looked delighted by it.

"Pray tell, Mr Lofthouse," she asked, "is this your usual method?"

"After a fashion," Lofthouse admitted, turning the sketch back toward himself and resuming his drawing. "I've not done a wedding portrait before, strictly speaking, but most of my drawings begin this way, yes. Pencil sketch to compose it, then watercolour sketches to sort out the colours and lighting, and then on to the oils. I might do the oils elsewhere," he added with an apologetic glance. "The fumes are unsavoury indoors, and I prefer to paint with them out in a garden or some other sort of place with a breeze."

Daniel found no quarrel with this method.

"And is this the sort of work you do for Mr Butcher?" she pressed.

Lofthouse dropt his pencil.

Daniel suppressed a laugh, though he had to let slip a smile. He'd had the same questions himself.

Lofthouse bent over to retrieve his lost instrument in a manner that reminded Daniel more than a little of Mr Grigsby. He cleared his throat and resumed sketching. "When Mr Butcher wants such a thing done, yes, he asks me to do it. More often I manage his estate."

"The sloe berries and the honeybees and such?" Sukie offered, her coy half-smile adding a dimple to her cheek as she exchanged a glance with Daniel.

Lofthouse confirmed this was so, adding that he assisted in the management of goats and hens as well. "And the keeping of game."

Daniel understood him to mean he oversaw the game-keeper and the other labourers who attended such matters. "You are his steward, then."

Lofthouse looked quite relieved to have someone else speak the title. "Exactly so, yes."

Whilst Lofthouse might be the sort of man to struggle in speech, and Daniel himself felt rather too nervous for much talk, Sukie remained both clever and curious and thus both inclined and able to keep up a light and merry string of conversation between the three of them. Thus she coaxed Lofthouse to divulge small details of his life after leaving Mr Grigsby's employ—how he far preferred the countryside to the smog of London and how Butcher encouraged his pursuit of fine arts. She kept it up all through the afternoon, until the sunlight faded into sunset and Lofthouse packed up his kit and bid them good-night. He couldn't stay, despite their invitation, as he was previously engaged to meet his employer for dinner, though he would see them again on the morrow.

What the deuce could bring an English gentleman farmer and his steward to Canada on undisclosed business, however, Daniel couldn't begin to fathom.

* * *

FELIX HAD VANISHED the previous spring.

Daniel felt half-glad of it despite himself. No longer need he dread the scene that would ensue in breaking off the engagement. Not that he thought Felix bore him any particular affection, but several of his fellow pupils would doubtless prove inconsolable, for they'd invested far more of their own emotion in the romance of Daniel's engagement than either he or his *fiancé* could possibly feel toward each other.

However, as Daniel had told Lofthouse when the clerk had arrived to make queer enquiries, a betrothal did a great deal to discourage other would-be suitors.

Daniel had considered breaking off the engagement before. When Felix's majority began to draw near and the wretched wedding seemed imminent, Daniel had visited Mr Grigsby to make certain enquiries. The results of these enquiries seemed promising—until Daniel had returned to Mrs Bailiwick's Academy and found Tolhurst far too attentive. He could imagine how much bolder Tolhurst might become if his nephew didn't stand between them. And so Daniel decided to remain engaged to Felix as long as possible to ward off Tolhurst's advances. Ideally, long enough to set up his own modest household in the countryside with Sukie. After all, a young heiress couldn't live without a lady's maid.

But then Felix had vanished.

And Tolhurst grew too bold by far.

It began in May. A certain spring entered Tolhurst's step for reasons then unknown. Daniel noted a satisfied smile, like that of the cat who stole the cream, perpetually playing about Tolhurst's thin lips in idle moments.

Daniel noted also how, whilst teaching the piano-forte, Tolhurst, who had never stood as far away as Daniel would've preferred, now hovered directly behind him, near enough for Daniel to feel the rank heat of him through the back of his gown, almost near enough for them to touch. Their hands did touch, Tolhurst laying his over Daniel's to direct his fingers on the keys when before mere verbal instruction and visual demonstration had sufficed. Daniel felt compelled to scrub his hands thoroughly after each lesson.

This would all have been bad enough, but Tolhurst wasn't sated with tormenting Daniel in music alone. He began attending dinner at the academy every night—much to Mrs Bailiwick's delight, who took it as a compliment to her housekeeping. She didn't notice, or chose not to notice, how Tolhurst ate but half his portion and spent the bulk of the meal stealing glances at Daniel with that smug little smile on his wretched mouth. Daniel returned not a one, but this did nothing to deter Tolhurst's attentions.

Other lessons, too, became haunted by a certain hulking presence in the door-frame. Italian, French, and embroidery, none of any possible interest to Tolhurst, nevertheless drew him like a moth to a flame, and his towering shadow lurked over all, with his blazing blue eyes ever-fixed on Daniel. Daniel pretended very hard not to notice. This did nothing to dissuade Tolhurst.

Drawing lesson typically provided Daniel a welcome relief from the stuffy confines of an academy no better than a convent. Yet he began to feel watched even out in the garden. Glancing all 'round for the source of this creeping sensation over his skin, he happened to track the flight of a swallow out of the hedge and wheeling up towards the eaves in the academy roof.

And there in the attic window stood the looming shadow of Tolhurst.

Daniel stared back in mute horror. Then he forced his gaze down to his sketchbook and did not raise it again for the remainder of the afternoon. Bad enough to be watched. Worse still to know how near to his own bedroom Tolhurst must venture in order to reach that vantage point.

All this continued throughout the month of May. At first Daniel didn't understand what had changed to embolden Tolhurst.

Then came the interview.

On the first of June, Tolhurst asked Mrs Bailiwick if he might have a word in private with Daniel. Mrs Bailiwick, who adored Tolhurst for reasons Daniel couldn't begin to fathom, of course agreed. Tolhurst asked Daniel to join him in the music room. Daniel, who bore no desire to go behind closed doors with his beloathed music master and without a chaperon, demurred, and suggested they meet out-of-doors in the garden. If worse came to worst, he supposed, a shout in the midst of Rochester's quiet streets would summon rapid aid. Or he could try climbing over the hedge himself, his hampering skirts be damned.

No sooner had Tolhurst led him out to the garden than Daniel knew he'd made the right decision in insisting the interview be held out-of-doors. Tolhurst had the impudence to offer Daniel his arm. Daniel pretended he didn't notice the gesture.

Then Tolhurst offered Daniel a seat on the stone bench. Daniel, having no wish to endure Tolhurst looming over him, declined.

And so Tolhurst stood beside him—again, near enough for Daniel to feel the rank heat coming off his bulk in waves—and began to whisper terrible things.

He had surmised for some time, so he said, how Daniel seemed somewhat less-than-eager at the prospect of marrying Felix. (Daniel felt rather surprised Tolhurst had gleaned even that much of his true feelings, as he remained so blind to every other one of Daniel's truths.) If so, Tolhurst believed he had found a solution to that particular predicament. Would Daniel like to hear it?

Daniel said nothing.

Tolhurst spoke on anyway. He proclaimed, at first, a stalwart filial affection. Then, seeing Daniel unmoved, he grew more passionate in his speech. He stepped nearer as he declared his delight in all the feminine features Daniel despised in his betrayer body. He brought his lips almost near enough to touch Daniel's ear as he told of his descent into madness and obsession—not his words, but unmistakably his meaning—over a figment of his imagination that he deluded himself into believing existed in the young man before him. Worse than his words were the pauses between them, when his ragged breath echoed in Daniel's ear like that of some rutting beast given the power of language to abuse.

And then, to Daniel's outrage, Tolhurst had the absolute gall to seize Daniel's hand in his own and bend to kiss it.

It took all Daniel's strength of will to refrain from bringing up a sharp knee to smash Tolhurst's nose.

But as Tolhurst ducked out of his line of sight, Daniel espied a familiar figure coming around the garden hedge. Lofthouse, of all people, emerged from the greenery. Moreover, he appeared appropriately horrified at the sight before him.

Never before had Daniel felt so happy to see his guardian's clerk. Happier still to hear him interrupt Tolhurst's impertinent display and, furthermore, demand (however politely) to speak to Daniel alone. A hideous weight lifted from Daniel's chest as Tolhurst banished himself back into the academy.

The resulting interview with Lofthouse proved far more pleasant, though still troubling. It wasn't just Daniel who hadn't heard from Felix since the beginning of May. And this, combined with Tolhurst's sudden increase in overbearance, led Daniel to conclusions that made his stomach twist. He revolved the matter in his mind well after Lofthouse took his leave. And by the time Sukie had joined him in the attic that evening, he'd come to a decision.

"I'm running away," said Daniel.

A thousand thoughts flew across Sukie's beautiful face in an instant. Then she smoothed her furrowed brow and set her trembling chin to reply, in a voice not of a lover but of a girl in service, "I see."

Her evident assumption that he would leave her behind broke Daniel's heart. Yet still he feared her answer as he asked, "Will you come with me?"

The dull look in her eyes vanished with a gleam. "Yes."

Daniel's tongue stumbled in his mouth. He'd already prepared his case, laid out in his mind how he would explain his plan to her and what place she might have in it, how he would attempt to retain his dignity even as he begged her to leave behind all she knew for a future with him. And she'd needed to hear none of it.

So instead, he kissed her.

* * *

LOFTHOUSE RETURNED to Daniel and Sukie's cottage at noon on Sunday, just as promised. He explained, in his own nervous and apologetic way, that he didn't require them to pose together again, for he intended to make close-up pencil sketches of their individual faces, to better capture their likeness in the final painting. As such, he need detain only one of them at a time.

Daniel volunteered to sit first. He pulled his chair into the best light from the southern window, just as they'd done yesterday. Unlike yesterday, Lofthouse drew the kitchen chair up very near to him—within a yard or so. Daniel braced himself for whatever awkwardness must assuredly ensue. It helped a great deal when Lofthouse brought out his sketchbook and set its board up between them as a barrier. Though, given he drew Daniel's face, their eyes must by necessity still meet now and again.

Sukie, meanwhile, took up her mending on the sofa. Likewise she took up the threads of conversation from where they'd left off the previous day. She enquired what Lofthouse thought of Port Hawkesbury and indulged him with her own opinion of its charms and virtues.

Lofthouse confessed he likewise found Port Hawkesbury refreshing and added, "I've seen a great many remarkable birds."

Daniel blinked. Lofthouse coloured.

"What sort of birds?" Sukie asked. Daniel could hear the smile in her voice.

Lofthouse dropt his gaze to his sketchbook again as he replied, "There was a pileated woodpecker just this morning. And a black-and-yellow warbler. And a blue jay—have you seen? You must have—delightfully vibrant, positively cerulean in parts."

"We've seen blue jays," Sukie confirmed, still audibly smiling. "And woodpeckers, though I don't know if they're pileated."

"The ones with red caps and black-and-white bodies," Lofthouse explained. The hunch in his shoulders relaxed just a hair. "I only know the name because my mother had a book that illustrated the North American birds. It's been something of a treat to come and see them for myself after all these years. You must have seen the robins as well?" he added, bringing his head up at last.

"Yes!" Sukie chimed in. "About twice as big as those in England, I'd wager. Did you see any puffins?"

"Puffins?" Lofthouse flicked his gaze away from studying Daniel's face to meet her eye with a bewildered glance.

"Fat funny little fellows," Sukie explained. "In black-and-white suits with bright blunt beaks. We saw them on both sides of our boat crossing."

Lofthouse blinked. "Oh. No, I haven't had the chance, I'm afraid. But I should very much like to."

Daniel wondered to himself how Lofthouse could've avoided seeing them on his own Atlantic crossing. The fat funny little fellows, as Sukie called them, had flocked all over the rocky coasts of Britain and Canada both. For that matter, Lofthouse hadn't mentioned any other seabirds in his list. Perhaps they weren't colourful enough to attract his notice—puffins aside.

Lofthouse cleared this throat. "Mr Butcher has espied several water-fowl in his own excursions. Loons, harlequin ducks, green-winged teal, red-breasted merganser..."

All freshwater birds, Daniel noted.

"What sort of excursions bring Mr Butcher to so many ducks?" Sukie asked.

Lofthouse glanced up as if the question had startled him, though Daniel couldn't see how. After a moment's hesitation, Lofthouse replied, "He hunts."

There was half the mystery solved, then. Butcher could hardly do worse than the Canadian wilderness for catching wild and hitherto unseen game. A single pair of elk antlers would suffice to make conversation for decades if brought back to England and hung up in his study.

"There," said Lofthouse, jerking Daniel out of his private musings. "What do you think?"

He turned his board around as he spoke, and Daniel found himself confronted with his own face.

Daniel realised a half-second afterward how hard he had braced himself for an unpleasant result. His mind remained stuck on the miniature and the dozen-odd portrait sketches his classmates had done of him for drawing practise at Mrs Bailiwick's Academy. Only within the last year had any looking-glass deigned to show his true self in his reflection. He hardly expected the art of drawing had caught it up.

Yet as he gazed upon what Lofthouse had wrought, he discovered something more like his true reflection than otherwise. A gentleman stared back at him. A young gentleman, yes, but one with smooth sharp cheeks, strong jaw, and a confident gaze which leant a brightness to the slight smile at the corners of the mouth. Something rather like what he saw in the looking-glass as he shaved each morning. A touch grander, perhaps.

"Good," Daniel said when the silence stretched a half-second too long and he realised his opinion was still wanted. "Very good."

A fleeting bashful smile crossed Lofthouse's freckled face. "Splendid. Now, if Mrs Durst would be so kind…?"

Daniel graciously arose so his wife might sit. As she took his place, so he took hers. She had left her mending basket behind beside her chair. Without thinking, he reached down to bring it up into his own lap.

Then he paused.

He had, in bending sideways, happened to catch a glimpse of Lofthouse again. Lofthouse, busy with arranging sketchbook and subject both, didn't appear to have noticed him in turn, but no matter. This glimpse nonetheless served to remind him how he and his wife did not now sit alone in their parlour. And while Daniel and Sukie shared household duties between them, including mending, he remained acutely aware that most gentlemen did not.

Perhaps Sukie sensed something of his discomfort, for she happened to turn toward the window at that very moment and in so doing met his gaze. She held it for a moment before returning to face the stranger in their midst.

"Who does your mending, Mr Lofthouse?" Sukie asked. "A laundress?"

The enquiry appeared to unnerve Lofthouse far more than Daniel thought warranted.

"I do my own mending," Lofthouse admitted after an uncomfortable silence.

"Do you, indeed?" said Sukie, mild as a lamb. "Your future bride will appreciate that, I'm sure."

Another uncomfortable silence descended, unbroken even by the scratching of pencil against paper. At length, Lofthouse replied, "I suppose she will."

He spoke, Daniel noted, in a very similar sort of tone to what Daniel had himself used whenever his fellow pupils would chatter about their future husbands and enquire after Daniel's own *fiancé* in particular.

Something tapped at the window. Daniel glanced over to find a songbird on the windowsill. It bore grey and white feathers with black wing-tips and tail, and a black mask over its eyes.

"Oh, Mr Lofthouse!" Sukie cried, her voice nevertheless soft lest she startle it. "What sort of bird is that?"

Lofthouse stared at the window for a long moment. Finally he said, "It is, I believe, a shrike."

The bird tapped at the window-glass again. Then, with a queer little leap, it flew up into the air and veered off out of sight altogether.

Lofthouse resumed drawing. Sukie returned the conversation to the subject of birds. Daniel picked up the mending, feeling rather foolish for avoiding it in the first place. After all, Lofthouse knew full well Daniel's education and background. It could hardly astonish him to see Daniel sewing. Particularly when, by his own confession, Lofthouse—a

240

gentleman whom society had always perceived as a gentleman—did his own mending.

And whilst Daniel mended, his mind wandered.

He didn't precisely know what made a gentleman handsome in the eyes of a lady. But from what he'd observed, he didn't think Lofthouse's face half-bad. Certainly not repulsive. There seemed nothing in it that a lady might object to, unless she had a particular loathing for freckles. His behaviour and comportment likewise appeared perfectly unobjectionable. A bit awkward, perhaps, but that needn't hobble a gentleman of good character and good credit, as Lofthouse was, by Daniel's own assessment. His treatment of Sukie and Daniel had proved kind, at least. Kinder than Daniel would expect of most gentlemen, should they ever learn his secret. Which would suggest, on Lofthouse's part, a sort of sympathy towards not just ladies but likewise those whom society mistook for ladies. All told, Daniel thought Lofthouse might have a bride whenever he wished.

If he were inclined toward a bride at all.

* * *

IN THE WEEKS following Sukie agreeing to run away with him, Daniel began practising dressing as his true self in the privacy of their attic sanctuary. He'd acquired his first few pieces earlier by writing to Mr Grigsby under pretense of assisting the Society of Friends of Needful Seamen. What he could not procure from his guardian's cast-offs, Sukie acquired for him at Rag Fair, including a splendid pair of boots which shone far beyond their years after she'd got done polishing them.

Daniel, meanwhile, set about turning one of his whalebone corsets into something actually useful. It took a great deal of stitching, un-stitching, and re-stitching, and he very nearly lost an eye as one of the bones snapped back at him when he tried to cut it to size, but in the end he had something that would make his chest as flat as that of other gentlemen. Not that he'd had terrible much up there to begin with. Still, it was rather more than he'd have preferred. The tight binding around his ribs felt like freedom compared to corseting his waist.

With the whole kit assembled at last, one evening, he dressed himself as he ought to have been for the past nineteen years.

He began just after dinner, before Sukie finished with her duties and came up from the kitchen. He didn't like having a witness to his body. He found he misliked it less when Sukie saw him, but on this particular occasion, he wanted to know himself alone.

Each individual article had staggered him as they'd arrived piece-meal over the past fortnight. Now, with smalls, shirt, stockings, trousers, waistcoat, frock coat, and necktie all laid out on his bed before him, a queer sort of euphoria blocked up his chest and head and threatened to overwhelm him. And yet there also came a grim sort of satisfaction, of self-righteous vindication, at finally attaining the costume for the role he was born to play.

Every piece as he donned it sent a thrill shivering over his skin. And when he finally found the courage to tear away the sheet covering the long looking-glass stand in the corner of his room, what he beheld in its reflection made all his suffering worthwhile.

For the first time in all his life, he saw his true self.

There stood a youth with a strong jaw and ice-blue eyes brimming with confidence. There stood everything Tolhurst and Felix and Mrs Bailiwick and all the rest of the world refused to see within him. There stood the gentleman imprisoned in his heart, set free at last.

He'd kept his hair pinned up. Now, he found if he held his head at the correct angle to the glass, he could almost imagine what he would look like when he finally had it cut like other gentlemen. The top hat, when he left off staring at himself long enough to snatch it up, hid his hair from view altogether, rendering the transformation complete. The top hat had proved one of Sukie's most difficult finds and had cost a pretty penny in the end, but to see it now, Daniel knew it'd proved its worth.

Vindication flew through his veins with a tingling burn. He could stare at himself all evening. He could stare at himself 'til dawn. He could stare at himself for the next fortnight and never feel satisfied. He might never leave off, and Mrs Bailiwick would find him a withered corpse still smiling at the mirror, a modern-day Narcissus.

The door creaked opened. Daniel's heart shot into his throat. He whirled.

Sukie stood on the threshold. And to see his joy reflected in her face warmed his heart thrice-over.

"Goodness!" she said softly as she shut the door behind her. "Aren't you a beau?"

For that, he could do no less than kiss her.

Yet as they parted, he couldn't keep from asking, "Do I look like a gentleman?"

"You always do," she replied—which was sweet, if not exactly helpful. Then she added, "But yes, in this garb even a dullard would know you for the gentleman you are."

Shaving proved a particular predicament. Daniel knew the tools required—razor, brush, soap, and strop—but didn't know how to employ them without slitting his own throat. Still, Daniel felt determined to make the attempt, and so when next Sukie went into London to gather surreptitious supplies for their escape, he added razor, brush, soap, and strop to her list. She returned that evening with a bundle of the promised goods and a beaming smile besides.

"I went to a barber's," she said by way of explanation as Daniel, bewildered, watched her set it all out on his wash-stand. "And I told him my cousin had an accident in the mill what left him unable to do for himself and asked him if he'd be so kind as to show me how a man ought to be shaved, or at least let me sit and watch while he went about his work so I might learn through observation, promising as I'd be very quiet and not at all a bother. It took some doing but I finally convinced him to let me stay, and I saw him shave a half-dozen fellows at least. And by the end of it he liked me well enough to give me a special demonstration on a particular sailor who'd just come off a merchant vessel and was in sore need of a trim. So this is how you begin," she said, plying the brush in the soap dish to whip up a great deal of foam.

She handed the loaded brush off to him. Under her instruction, he brushed a white beard of lather onto his face. Then she showed him how to hold the razor by laying its blade against his throat. His heart beat rather faster at that, but not in fear. His fingers entwined with hers along the ivory handle. With slow swipes and careful strokes, they scraped away the lather together. By the end, she withdrew entirely, and he alone revealed his fresh new face to himself in the looking-glass.

Though he bore no beard before he'd begun, still he fancied he saw a difference in his reflection. The blade had scraped something away after all. No longer did the soft downy face of a child look back at him, but rather the smooth sleek cheeks and jaw of a gentleman.

He didn't get out of it entirely without nicks. These he passed off as mere blemishes, daring without words for anyone, fellow pupil or otherwise, to comment upon them. None did, though Tolhurst looked somewhat baffled, as if he had detected some difference in Daniel's countenance but couldn't quite define it. It would be rather ironical, Daniel thought, for this of all things to finally prove his truth to Tolhurst. But Tolhurst said nothing aloud, and his obsession with Daniel faded not a whit.

"Where are we going?" Sukie asked the following evening.

Daniel blinked. "Anywhere, I suppose."

Sukie screwed her mouth up to one side of her face. "I don't think we'll get very far wandering off at random."

Daniel conceded they would probably not succeed in that venture. "Far enough that Tolhurst won't bother following."

Privately, he didn't know if such a place existed, but the horror felt too enormous to voice.

Sukie bit her lip. "My aunt's settled in Canada."

Daniel shot her a startled glance.

"There'd be a whole ocean between us and him," she continued. "And we'd already have a relation there. Unless you think it's too far?"

"Not at all," Daniel replied. "I'm only surprised you're willing to go so far away from all you know."

She gave him a look that said as well as words she thought him rather dull for that. "The one I know best is coming with me. So really I'm not going very far at all."

Daniel knew no better reward for her cleverness than a kiss.

"We ought to travel as cousins," Daniel said when they parted. "I don't think we could pass for siblings. But cousins may likewise keep company together regardless of their sex without attracting any undue notice."

Sukie agreed.

Daniel wondered if he imagined the hesitance in her voice—a hesitance he himself had felt when he'd concocted the plan. And one he felt again when his heart bid him make another bold addition to an already wild scheme.

"When we arrive in Port Hawkesbury," he said, beginning by looking away from her, then forcing himself to meet her all-too-beautiful gaze, "will you marry me?"

Sukie stared at him. "What?"

"In Canada," Daniel explained, forcing his voice to remain steady. "I should like to live as husband and wife. With you."

After all, they already behaved in all regards as husband and wife in the attic of the academy. For three years they had opened their hearts to each other every night. And for the past year or so, beneath the cover of darkness and bedclothes, Sukie had been to Daniel what Mrs Bailiwick claimed Daniel ought to have been to Felix.

(And what an informative afternoon that had been, when Mrs Bailiwick called Daniel into her private parlour and told him exactly what would be expected of him as Felix's bride. If he hadn't already known he'd no wish to wed Felix or any other man, that interview would have fixed his preference in his mind. As matters stood, it enlightened a great deal of his own feelings towards Sukie, and when next they met in his boudoir, he found her eager to experiment in how best he might fulfill the role which felt most natural to him.)

At present, Sukie continued to stare at him.

Silence was as good as a refusal. Daniel endeavoured to buck up beneath the blow. "Forgive me, I—"

"Yes," Sukie blurted.

Daniel choked on his own apologetic speech. "What?"

"Yes," she repeated, and kissed him, parting just long enough to say again, "Yes," as she cradled his face in her hands, and then another whispered, "Yes," as she bore him down onto the bed.

Some moments afterward, Daniel lay with her curled against his side and her head nestled in the hollow of his collarbone, staring up into the shadowed eaves with his heart still soaring. She would marry him. She would make him her devoted husband. She would willingly, gladly, ecstatically become his wife. And yet something nagged at him.

"I cannot give you children," he confessed into the darkness.

Sukie shrugged, a gesture he felt rather than saw. "There are more than enough waifs in the world to fill our cradles, should we want them."

* * *

THE WATERCOLOUR SKETCH went off largely without incident. Daniel and Sukie sat together as they had for the initial composition. He recalled well the sight of watercolour pans from his own drawing lessons. His old set was still kicking around somewhere in his steamer trunk; he wondered if he ought to bring it out to try his hand at it again.

Lofthouse appeared to paint with more vigour and enjoyment than the art master at the academy. And when the sunshine streaming through the southern window turned from afternoon gold to evening crimson and he turned his sketch-board around to show his subjects what he'd wrought, Daniel found the result far more pleasing than any technical still-life ever produced under the academy's roof. The black-and-white sketches had caught their likeness. The warmth of colour seemed to bring them to life. Sukie clapped her hands in delight and redoubled Daniel's own.

With a shy but no less pleased smile, Lofthouse packed up his kit and bid them adieu, promising to return with the finished painting, "Soon."

A fortnight passed with neither hide nor hair of Lofthouse or Butcher seen in town. This Daniel knew not just from what he himself had witnessed—or rather, failed to witness—but from the gossip Sukie gathered from her Aunt Molly. If anyone in Port Hawkesbury had glimpsed a Gothic highwayman or his modest companion, none mentioned it. Nor, Aunt Molly added, had the staff of the lodging-houses found any of their guests matching the distinct description. This despite Lofthouse stating his intention to paint the final version of the wedding portrait out-of-doors.

Indeed, it seemed no one had seen Lofthouse or Butcher in town since Daniel and Sukie had invited them to dinner.

Daniel wondered at this, but likewise wondered at himself for never once bothering to ask Lofthouse himself where he stayed in town.

"Perhaps they made camp in the woods," Sukie suggested when Daniel wondered aloud one evening.

"Perhaps," Daniel conceded. "Lofthouse didn't look like a fellow roughing it in the wilderness, though."

Sukie shrugged.

While their guests didn't appear in town, there nevertheless appeared a visitor in their garden. Several mornings just after dawn when Daniel left the cottage to walk to the office, he noticed one of those queer little black-masked grey birds flitting alongside him. A shrike, Lofthouse had called it. And Daniel had a dim recollection of seeing one before back in the garden of Mrs Bailiwick's Academy—just a hair over a year ago now. Curious to find such birds on both sides of the Atlantic. Daniel supposed birds could fly wheresoever they pleased. Yet it wasn't just this curiosity that nagged at him.

One particular evening, he returned to find yet another shrike perched on the gate trellis awaiting him.

Or perhaps the very same shrike.

The notion was absurd. Yet as Daniel paused with one hand on the gate to stare at the diminutive creature, and it cocked its head at him in return, he couldn't shake the suspicion that he'd seen not just this sort of bird but this exact individual specimen before.

"I know you, don't I," he said—even as he knew talking to a wild bird was behaviour fit for Bedlam.

The shrike blinked at him and cocked its head again at the opposite angle.

The idea of a bird listening and responding to his words ought to have unsettled him. Instead he felt queerly comforted. And besides, he told himself, more likely the creature was just confused from being squawked at by a giant featherless, flightless thing.

"I drew you once," Daniel continued. The more he spoke to it, the more soothed he felt. He knew not why. "Whatever are you doing here?"

The bird blinked at him again. It made a little sideways hop across the trellis. There it preened itself before locking eyes with him once more.

Daniel supposed shrikes were not quite enough like parrots to speak for themselves. He tipped his hat, smiling at his own folly as he did so. "Well—good evening to you, sir."

And to his astonishment, the bird bowed as if in reply.

Daniel hardly had time to do more than widen his eyes before it flicked out its wings and took flight, veering off to vanish in the evening's shadows. He stood staring after it for some time before he went into the house. Sukie met him in the front hall.

"Do you recall seeing shrikes in England?" he asked her after he'd kissed her.

She blinked at him in a manner not unlike the bird. "Not particularly. I saw plenty of finches, swallows, and sparrows."

Daniel supposed these were all good birds in their own way. "Have you seen any by the house here?"

"Oh, yes," said Sukie. "Since Mr Lofthouse pointed them out it seems I see them every day. There must be a flock roosting nearby."

"You see more than one at a time, then?"

Sukie furrowed her brow in thought. "No... Now that you mention it, there's only ever just the one."

Daniel knew not how he ought to feel about that.

"Do you mislike it?" Sukie asked, studying his face.

"I don't think so," Daniel replied.

That was good enough for Sukie, who smiled and entwined her arm with his to bring him into the kitchen for dinner.

The shrike sightings did not abate throughout the fortnight.

"Is Mr Butcher married?" Daniel wondered aloud to his wife on a Saturday afternoon.

She blinked at him. "You'd stand a better chance of knowing than I."

They stood together in the kitchen. Daniel peeled and chopped vegetable matter whilst Sukie beat a dough into submission. He couldn't blame her confusion at his bringing the matter up now. It'd been more than a fortnight since anyone had seen the gentleman. And yet, whenever Daniel wasn't thinking of Sukie or the novels they read together or figures in a ledger or shrikes, he found his mind wandering again and again down the familiar path of what the deuce Butcher and Lofthouse got up to.

From what little Daniel had observed of him, Lofthouse seemed very much inclined toward the company of his fellow bachelors. He had begun in the employment of Mr Grigsby—who'd never married, despite being a nice enough fellow, and of a rather advanced age—and had moved on to Butcher, an eccentric. Though perhaps Butcher had married after all. It would account for him bringing his steward along on his travels instead of leaving him behind to manage the estate. Perhaps Butcher had left matters in his wife's hands instead. Daniel still thought that a rather backwards way of doing business. He said all this aloud to Sukie, who listened with increasingly raised brows.

"Why does it trouble you so?" Sukie asked.

"He knows all my own history," said Daniel. "Yet I know nothing of his."

"Not all, surely."

"Well, no. But more than most gentlemen." Daniel furrowed his brow down at the pile of potato peelings he'd produced whilst making his argument. "And I think he may likewise live an unconventional existence."

He continued to explain his reasoning. If there existed such a thing as a lady who preferred the companionship of another lady over any gentleman—as Daniel felt assured there must, from the whirlwind romances he'd witnessed between his fellow pupils at the academy—then he supposed there must exist after all a sort of gentleman who preferred the companionship of another gentleman over any lady.

Sukie didn't look nearly so shocked at this train of thought as Daniel might have otherwise supposed.

"And I think," Daniel concluded, "that Lofthouse may be one such gentleman, and Butcher another."

"Of course," said Sukie.

Daniel glanced up sharp from his half-chopped onion. "Of course?"

"They do remind me a great deal of my uncles," Sukie said, mild as anything.

Daniel blinked at her. "What?"

"Uncle Jack and Uncle Jem—though Jem isn't a blood relation," she added. "They've a fishing boat out of Yarmouth. Thick as thieves for as long as I've known 'em, which is all my life."

Daniel, his mind in a whirl, blurted, "Why didn't you say anything?"

Sukie raised her brows. "About my uncles?"

"No—about Lofthouse and Butcher."

"Well, y'know," Sukie replied with a shrug. "Glass houses and all that."

"Yes—but you might have said something to *me*," Daniel pointed out.

Sukie blinked at him. "Thought you knew. You're usually rather clever."

Daniel didn't agree with her assessment of his intelligence at that particular moment but laughed and kissed her, nonetheless.

Just then, the ringing gate-bell interrupted them.

Sukie shared a glance with him that sufficed to send him on his way. First to the sink to rinse the vegetable residue from his hands, then to the front hall to shrug on his frock coat and answer the door.

Lofthouse stood on the threshold. Butcher stood beside him in all his Gothic glory. Between them they carried a board some four feet broad and almost as tall, draped in buckram.

"Do forgive our arriving unannounced," said Lofthouse. "May we come in?"

Daniel stepped aside to let them pass and ushered them into the parlour. At his urging they propped their burden up on the sofa. Sukie joined them from the kitchen.

"Oh, Mr Lofthouse!" she said, clapping her hands. "Is this...?"

"It is," Lofthouse replied. His eyes danced in a way Daniel had never seen before. He laid a hand on the corner of the buckram. "Shall I? Or would you prefer to reveal it yourself?"

Daniel shook his head and made an encouraging gesture towards the artwork that even now he could scarce believe existed. "By all means."

Lofthouse and Butcher exchanged a glance. Together, in a singular swift and fluid movement, they whisked the buckram off the board.

And there before Daniel's eyes lay bare his own wedding day.

His eye fell first upon Sukie. In life she appeared ever-beautiful to his eye, even (or especially) with streaks of flour through her mahogany hair and smudges across her brow. He'd always despised his blue poplin on himself, but to see it on her, and how she beamed with happiness to wear it, rendered the whole more beautiful still. How well he recalled on their wedding day the way the gown's colour brought out the blush in her smiling cheeks and the rosy tint of her perfect lips. And now, rendered through Lofthouse's brush-strokes, her form seemed to glow with radiant joy, the brightness of hue exceeded only by the evident bliss captured in her resplendent face.

When he could tear his gaze away from the perfect portrait of his wife—which took some doing—he forced himself, with no small amount of trepidation, to look upon his own image.

What he saw there left him thunderstruck.

Never before had he recognised even a fraction of himself in any artistic representation. Only within the past year had he coaxed the looking-glass into reflecting his soul.

And now, in Lofthouse's painting, he saw his soul again.

A gentleman sat before him. A young gentleman, and yet, confidence beyond evident years shone in the blue eyes and the set of the strong jaw (Daniel's favourite feature of his face and one of the few he didn't despise). The grey frock coat fit the figure as if moulded for him alone, and not acquired under questionable means from another's wardrobe. With his shoulders drawn back, his spine straight, his head held high, and his thighs set apart with all the command of a king, he looked every inch who he was. Even the carefree wave of the golden curls appeared more like a crown beneath Lofthouse's brush. His strong hand clasped Sukie's, and the slight smile that played about his lips bespoke a joy beyond all possible expression.

"Butcher made the frame," Lofthouse added just as Daniel's eyes fell upon it. An oaken frame, carved in the shape of its own leaves and acorns, surrounded all.

Sukie praised it at once and thanked him effusively for his contribution. Daniel thought he beheld a faint rosy tint in the otherwise stoic features as Butcher bowed and murmured that they were quite welcome.

Daniel returned to the painting. Lofthouse hadn't attended that blessed day—few had, with Aunt Molly as their only guest and the vicar as their only witness. And yet he had captured all the joy of it.

Their relationship hadn't met with quite so much approval as they might have wished for. Aunt Molly, no doubt wary of unfulfilled promises from gentlemen to parlour maids, had strong opinions about their decision to share a cabin on their Atlantic crossing. The assurance from Daniel that they were engaged met with poorly-disguised disbelief on her part. Likewise she had fretted over whether or not they were rather too young to marry at all. (No one, Daniel noted, had considered it at all odd for him to wed at nineteen when they'd supposed him a young lady rather than a young gentleman.) However, when the day itself finally arrived—not a minute too soon, by Daniel's reckoning—Aunt Molly had shed a steady stream of joyful tears from the moment they entered the church and on after Daniel carried Sukie over the threshold of their cottage out of her sight.

The kiss Daniel gave his Sukie at the altar was perhaps not so modest as Aunt Molly might have wished. It expressed all the exhilaration he felt to bind himself to his beloved for all eternity, to protect and cherish her to the end of his days and beyond. Words he'd dreaded throughout his engagement to Felix, and after his escape had hardly dared to ever hope he might hear, echoed again in his ears with newfound bliss. "I now pronounce you man and wife."

The painting blurred. Daniel blinked hard and tilted his face up to the ceiling beams. A gentle hand entwined with his own.

"Where shall we hang it?" Sukie asked.

Were it not for Lofthouse and Butcher standing before them, Daniel could've kissed her. Trust her wisdom to know when to give him a task that would draw him out of the labyrinth of his mind. Over the mantle, they decided, and then Daniel had to fetch hammer, wire, and nail, and, with Butcher and Lofthouse, raise the painting against the wall whilst

Sukie directed them how to straighten it out. Then came the hammer-blows and the tying-up and when at last they all stood back to admire it again, Daniel could do so with clear eyes.

Sukie broke off admiring it long enough to ask Lofthouse and Butcher, "You'll stay for dinner, won't you?"

Lofthouse hesitated. "We wouldn't want to impose…"

"It's no imposition whatsoever," Daniel declared.

Lofthouse glanced up at Butcher. Butcher gave him a small encouraging smile in return.

"Very well," Lofthouse replied with a shy smile of his own. "Will you let us help prepare it, at least?"

Daniel blinked. Butcher appeared in no way surprised.

And Sukie simply beamed, twined her arm through Daniel's, and bid them all follow her into the kitchen.

ABOUT THE AUTHOR

Sebastian Nothwell writes queer romance. When he is not writing, he is counting down the minutes until he is permitted to return to writing.

He is absolutely not a ghost and definitely did not die in 1895.

If you enjoyed this book, you may also enjoy the following by the same author:

Mr Warren's Profession (*Aubrey & Lindsey*, book one)

Throw His Heart Over (*Aubrey & Lindsey*, book two)

The Haunting of Heatherhurst Hall

Hold Fast

Oak King Holly King

CPSIA information can be obtained
at www.ICGtesting.com
Printed in the USA
BVHW082317211222
654816BV00004B/83